STARGLASS

ALSO BY PHOEBE NORTH

Starbreak

Stardawn (an eBook original)

STARGLASS

PHOEBE NORTH

SIMON & SCHUSTER BFYR

NEW YORK • LONDON • TORONTO • SYDNEY • NEW DELHI

SIMON & SCHUSTER BFYR

An imprint of Simon & Schuster Children's Publishing Division
1230 Avenue of the Americas, New York, New York 10020

For information about special discounts for bulk purchases, please contact Simon & Schuster Special Sales at 1-866-506-1949 or business@simonandschuster.com.
The Simon & Schuster Speakers Bureau can bring authors to your live event. For more information or to book an event, contact the Simon & Schuster Speakers Bureau at 1-866-248-3049 or visit our website at www.simonspeakers.com.
Also available in a SIMON & SCHUSTER BFYR hardcover edition
Book and cover design by Lucy Ruth Cummins
Cover photo-illustration copyright © 2014 by Aaron Goodman
The text for this book is set in Bembo Standard.
Manufactured in the United States of America
First SIMON & SCHUSTER BFYR paperback edition July 2014
2 4 6 8 10 9 7 5 3 1
The Library of Congress has cataloged the hardcover edition as follows:
North, Phoebe.
Starglass / Phoebe North. —1st ed.
p. cm.
Summary: For all of her sixteen years, Terra has lived on a city within a spaceship
that left Earth five hundred years ago seeking refuge, but as they finally approach the chosen planet,
she is drawn into a secret rebellion that could change the fate of her people.
ISBN 978-1-4424-5953-3 (hardcover)
ISBN 978-1-4424 -5954-0 (pbk)
ISBN 978-1-4424-5955-7 (eBook)
[1. Science fiction. 2. Interplanetary voyages—Fiction. 3. Insurgency—Fiction.
4. Jews—Fiction. 5. Fathers and daughters—Fiction.] I. Title.
PZ7.N8153St 2013
[Fic]—dc23
2012021171

For Susan Garatino, my fifth-grade language arts teacher,

who told me I could write as many stories as I wanted

as long as I dedicated my first book to her.

My darling daughter,

Know that I never would have left the earth if it hadn't already been doomed.

They told us that we had five years before the asteroid came. There was no way to deflect it—no way to shield our world. First panic set in, then the riots. They burned buildings down, packed government offices full of bombs. You could walk through the city streets and think the roads were made of broken glass. These were the end times.

At first I was preoccupied. Annie, my lover of thirteen years, was dying. Cancer. And so I ignored the clamoring and the frantic hysteria. I cared for her, bathed her, and spooned her soup until she could no longer eat.

A few days before she went—only hours before she lost all words— she put her fragile hand on my hand.

"Find a way to live on," she said. "I can't bear dying if you're going to die too."

I loved my home. I loved the way the sky, red with pollution, shivered between the skyscrapers before a storm. I loved the sidewalks, marked with the handprints of people long dead, and I loved how the pavement felt beneath my feet. I loved the feeling of anticipation as I waited in the dark subway station, leaning into the tunnel to watch for the lights.

You'll never know these wonders. And you'll never know the way it feels to lie in a field of grass late at night and smell the clover and look up at the sky, wondering at how small you are. Wondering what other worlds are out there.

You'll know different constellations. And you won't be tethered to a dying rock. Instead you'll be up here, among the stars.

Because when Annie left, I went down to the colonization office and signed myself up. The little harried man in the rumpled suit at the front desk said that I was too late. That the rosters were nearly full. He said that my expertise and genetic profile would have to be exceptional for me to be granted passage, said my application was little more than a technicality.

But then he drew blood and had me spit into a tube. Unlike Annie, there was no cancer in my family. No alcoholism. No epilepsy. No stroke. Not even eczema. The little man came back, a clipboard in his hands, and his eyes grew wide.

He told me that I would be placed on the Asherah—506 passengers, and me among them, and we would leave for Epsilon Eridani in one week's time.

And so I prepared to say good-bye.

PART ONE

JOURNEY

1

On the day of my mother's funeral, we all wore white. My father said that dressing ourselves in the stiff, pale cloth would be a mitzvah. I ran the word over my tongue as I straightened a starched new shirt against my shoulders. I was twelve when she died, and Rebbe Davison had told us about mitzvot only a few days before—how every good deed we did for the other citizens of the ship would benefit us, too. He said that doing well in school was a mitzvah, but also other things. Like watching babies get born in the hatchery or paying tribute at funerals. When he said that, he looked across the classroom at me with a watery gleam in his eyes.

That's when I knew that Momma was really dying.

In the hours after the fieldworkers took away her body, Ronen locked himself in his room, like he always did back then. That left me with my father. He didn't cry. He wore a thin smile as he pulled off his dark work clothes and tugged the ivory shirt down over his head. I watched him while I held my kitten, Pepper, to my chest. It wasn't until the cat pulled away and tumbled to the floor that I lost it.

"Pepper! Pepper, come back!" I said, drawing in a hiccuping breath as he scampered out my parents' open bedroom door. Then I brought my hands to my cheeks. Back then I cried easily, at the slightest offense. Knowing I was crying only made my grief cut deeper.

My father turned to me, the stays on his shirt still undone.

"Terra," he said, putting a hand against my shoulder and squeezing. My answer was an uncontrollable bray, an animal noise. I let it out. I was naive—I thought that maybe my abba would draw me into his arms, comfort me like Momma would have done. But he only held me at arm's length, watching me steadily.

"Terra, pull yourself together. You're soaking your blouse."

That's when I knew that he wasn't Momma. Momma was gone. I brought my hands up to my face, veiling it, as if I could hide behind my fingers from the truth.

After a moment, between my own panted breaths, I heard him sigh. Then I heard his footsteps sound on the metal floor as he drew away from me.

"Go to your room," he said. "Compose yourself. I'll get you when it's time to go."

I pulled myself up on weak legs. My steps down the hall were as plodding as my heart. When I reached my bedroom door, I launched myself over the threshold and thrust my body down into my waiting bed. Pepper followed me, his paws padding against the dust-softened ground. He let out a curious sound. I ignored him, my hands clutched around my belly, my face pressed against my soggy sheets.

Usually it was Abba's job to ring the clock tower bells. But that day, the day my mother died, the Council gave the job to someone else. As we marched through the fields of white-clad people, I couldn't help but wonder who it was who pulled those splintered ropes. Perhaps my father knew, but his jaw was squared as he gazed into the distance. I knew that he didn't want to be bothered, so I held my tongue and didn't ask any questions.

I walked between them, Abba on my one side, his hands balled into fists, and my older brother on the other. Ronen slouched his way up the grassy atrium fields. That was the year he turned sixteen and shot up half a head in a matter of months. His legs were nearly as long as my father's by then, and though he seemed to be taking his time, I had to scramble to keep up.

The bell tolled and tolled beneath a sky of stars and honeycombed glass. Underneath the drone of sound I heard words—murmured condolences from the other pale-clothed mourners.

By then we'd learned in school about Earth, about the settlements that had held thousands and thousands of people. They called them "cities." I couldn't imagine it. Our population was never more than a thousand, and so the crowd of people—a few hundred, at least—felt claustrophobic. But I wasn't surprised by the throng of citizens that gathered in the shadow of the clock tower. Momma had been tall, lovely, with a smile as bright as the dome lights at noon. She'd made friends wherever she went. As a baker, working at a flour-dusted shop in the commerce district, she had encountered dozens of people daily.

Everyone wore white. On a normal night we'd be dressed in murky shades of brown and gray, the only flashes of color the rank cords the adults wore on the shoulders of their uniforms. But there were no braided lengths of rope on our mourning clothes. Rebbe Davison said that rank didn't matter when we grieved.

"Terra! Terra!" A voice cut through the crowd. My best friend Rachel's lips were lifted in a grim smile, showing a line of straight teeth. She was the kind of person who couldn't stop herself from smiling even at the worst times, especially in those days before she started saving most of her smiles for boys.

I moved my slippers through the muddy grass, afraid she might apologize, offer empty words like all the others had done. But she only reached out and took my hand in hers. As we walked across the field together, she looped her pinkie finger around mine. We neared the clock tower and the grave dug deep below it; her hand offered a small, familiar comfort.

When we reached the grave, she pulled away. She gave my fingers one final squeeze, but she had to go join her family, and I had to join mine. I watched her leave. At twelve she was already willowy and lean, and her dark skin seemed to glow against her dress in a way that reminded me of freshly turned soil. I knew that in comparison I was little more than a shadow, faded and pale, my complexion sallow and my dirty-blond locks stringy from tears.

This is why I was surprised when I turned and saw a pair of black eyes settle on me. Silvan Rafferty was watching me. He was my age, in my class. The doctor's son. His lips were parted, full and soft. I hadn't told anyone yet, but I knew those lips. Only a few days before, Silvan had followed me home after school.

That afternoon he'd called out to me across the paths that spiraled through the dome. At first I blushed and walked faster, sure he was only teasing. But then he broke into a jog, his leather-soled shoes striking the pavement hard. When he neared me, he reached out like he meant to take my hand.

"I heard your mother is sick," he said. "My father told me. I'm sorry."

I wouldn't let his fingers grace mine. Abba had always said that good girls didn't hold boys' hands until they were older and ready to marry. I didn't want to give Silvan the wrong idea. We'd never even spoken before that day.

"It's all right," I told him, fighting the strange desire to comfort him. His eyelashes trembled. He looked so *sad*. I didn't want to be pitied. So I did the only thing I could think of—I stood up on my tiptoes and pressed my mouth to his.

It was a quick kiss, closed-mouthed, but I could smell the sharp scent of his breath. He tasted like strong tea and animal musk. He leaned in . . . then I pulled away.

"I have to go," I said, trying to ignore the heat that spread over my ears and face. "They're waiting for me at the hospital."

As I walked I didn't look back. I thought of the things Abba had always told me about being good, about not giving boys the wrong idea. Over the dinner table Momma scolded him. *Don't be so old-fashioned, Arran,* she always said. Perhaps she was right. Even Rebbe Davison said that there was nothing wrong with going with boys, once they'd had their bar mitzvahs. And Silvan was nearly thirteen. Still, Abba insisted he knew better. He'd *been* a boy, after all. And standing there, still and stupid and blushing at my mother's funeral as Silvan's eyes pressed into me, I wondered if he was right. This was no time for flirting. It was time to do my duty, to be an obedient daughter.

Abba and Ronen stood at the head of the crowd. I drew in a breath as I pushed through the crush of bodies. My mother waited in the black earth, her body wrapped in cloth. I told myself it wasn't her, that all those stories about how the dead wandered the atrium dome on lonely nights were just kids' stuff. Momma was gone, and this was only flesh. But I couldn't deny the familiar shape of her—her long thin figure—underneath the cotton wrappings.

My throat tightened. I squeezed myself between Abba and Ronen, doing my best to resist taking either of their hands.

It's a mitzvah, I told myself. *To be brave. To be strong. To stand alone.* And then I cast my gaze up to my father to see if he noticed how hard I worked to keep my trembling mouth still. But his eyes were just fixed forward.

The sound of gossip crested beneath the bell's final toll. I watched as the crowd parted, making way for the captain's guard. The square-shouldered soldiers were dressed in funeral whites, ceremonial knives dark and glinting against pale cloth. As they marched, their boots drummed like rain against the grass.

In their wake Captain Wolff appeared. Everyone pressed two fingers to their hearts in salute. But my own fingers hesitated at my side.

I knew that I was supposed to believe that Captain Wolff was brave, noble, and strong. She'd instituted the search for capable shuttle pilots, lowered the sugar rations to make room for more nutritious crops, and raised the number of guards to almost fifty in order to better keep peace among the citizens. Her leadership skills and self-sacrifice were going to lead us straight to Zehava's surface. It was treason to think otherwise.

But she frightened me. She always had. Whether staring back at me from the pages of my schoolbooks or making speeches to a crowd, her sharp, hawkish features and her long, white-streaked hair always moved a shiver down my spine. Perhaps it was the scar across her face, a gnarled line that ran from her left cheekbone to her chin. They said it was from an accident when she was small—she'd saved a boy who'd gotten caught up in a wheat thresher in the fields. That noble act had been the first thing she'd ever done for the good of the ship, and the scar, a memento of her bravery.

But I always thought it made her look creepy.

As she turned toward us I focused on her eyes—drops of pitch-black ink. Her gaze willed me to do what I had to do. I pressed my fingers to my heart.

"Honored citizens. I come to you on behalf of the High Council to lead you in your mourning duties," she began. I noted how she spoke of *our* mourning duties, not her own. Her words always excluded her from the rest of us. "Today you bid farewell to your cherished sister, Alyana Fineberg, spouse of Arran Fineberg, mother of Ronen and little Terra."

My jaw tightened. I was twelve, but I no longer thought of myself as a child.

"Alyana was a baker, but her loving smile warmed your spirits just as much as her work warmed your bellies. She was, indeed, a true Asherati."

Captain Wolff paused as she surveyed the people spread out across the field before her. It looked like she expected someone to disagree. My eyes darted out to the citizens gathered in the pasture.

Most of the mourners were solemn as they waited for Captain Wolff to go on. But to my surprise a few men and women wore faces as pale as their clothing. Their eyes were wide. Their lips trembled. They were afraid of Captain Wolff.

At least I wasn't the only one.

No one spoke. Satisfied with our silence, Captain Wolff lifted her hands through the air. "Now let us sing the kaddish," she said, and began to croon. Her old voice warbled.

Numb, I sang along, moving through the verses by rote. "On our hallowed ship or on Zehava," I sang, hardly feeling the words. "May there come abundant peace, grace, loving kindness, compassion. . . ."

A few verses later it was all done. Captain Wolff was the first to step forward. She bent low and took a fistful of black dirt in her delicate hand. Against the spotless cloth that waited, she cast it down. Then, wiping her palm on a rag that one of her guard members provided, she turned and was gone.

We all watched her disappear. At the far edges of the field, sheep bleated. Finally, at last, Rachel came forward, her family trailing after—her curvy, beautiful mother; her handsome father; her younger brother tottering behind. Rachel pressed her lips into a thin smile. Then she bent down and tossed another fistful of dirt into the grave. Three more handfuls followed. Then dozens more.

Every family stepped forward together to throw their own dirt down over my mother's body. Each family had a mother, a father, a daughter, a son. When it was at last our turn, I couldn't help but notice how only three clumps of dirt were cast down. For the first time I realized how we were different. Broken. I stood there for a long time, waiting for the fourth handful of dirt to fall, until Ronen touched my shoulder and told me it was time to go.

That night they invaded our quarters. I'd never seen our home so full of people before. Busy and crowded, it felt completely alien. Pepper seemed to agree with me. He ducked behind the bath basin, crouched down beneath the tangle of pipes, and refused to come out.

I couldn't hide. It was my job to take the kugels and pies and tuck them away into our icebox. But I decided that I didn't have to be nice about it. I pushed out my lower lip, sulked and stomped. I knew my father's eyes were on me as I snatched a tray of salted meats from Giveret Schneider's hands. But Abba wasn't the one who had to rearrange all the shelves in the icebox to make room.

I wanted them all to leave us alone, but they wouldn't. They mingled and joked and then grew silent again, as if they suddenly remembered why they were there. I glared at them from my place in the corner. I watched as Abba's family crowded around him, ignoring me. It had been years since we'd seen them last, not since Grandpa Fineberg had twisted Ronen's arm as a punishment for feeding their dog table scraps. Momma had refused to visit them after that, but now that she was gone, they had no reason to stay away.

Ronen sat on the stairwell, making out with Hannah Meyer. Since they'd turned sixteen, she'd been hanging around more and more. Her parents had come too, and though they weren't wearing their gold-threaded cords, you could tell that they were Council members. It was the way her father held himself, posture stiff and proud. Abba saw it too. When they came in, he practically fell over himself trying to shake the man's hand. Momma would have laughed at that. I could almost hear her voice in my ears.

Arran, you're such a suck-up.

But there was one visitor he ignored. Mar Jacobi, the librarian. He was a small, copper-skinned man, serious-looking, and he wandered in through the front door holding a tin in his hand and looking lost.

"I'll take that," I said, scrambling up from my chair when I realized no one else would. The corners of his eyes went all crinkly. He bowed his head.

"Thank you, Terra," he said. I tensed at his words. Before that day, we'd only ever spoken at the library's checkout counter. And even then our words had been polite—perfunctory. "Hello," and "This is when they're due," and all of that. But now he held out the tin for me. "I brought you macaroons. Chocolate. Alyana told me they were your favorite."

"I didn't realize you knew Momma," I said, taking the tin from him. The metal box had been recycled many times, rust ringing the edges. The glue seemed hardly strong enough to hold the label down. I tugged on one of the loose ends of the paper, lifting wary eyes to the librarian. His smile was small, strained.

"I certainly did."

But it didn't make sense. He didn't fit into our tiny galley, packed with familiar mourners. He floated around alone while Momma's bakery coworkers drank all the wine they'd brought for Abba, and while Rachel came in and sat with me, holding my hand and gossiping about the other girls from school. Mar Jacobi stood there with a plate in his hands, stirring the food around and not eating anything. And then, when people began to leave, yawning their apologies once again, the librarian stayed, sitting across from us at our galley table.

"I don't know why they keep saying they're sorry," I said to him at last, eager to plug up the silence that had begun to fill our home. "It's not like it's their fault Momma died."

The librarian lifted the corners of his mouth, quietly amused. But Abba didn't find it funny.

"Terra," he said. "It's time for you to go up to bed."

"Ronen gets to stay up!"

My brother had slipped out with Hannah, his arm draped over her shoulders. But Abba wasn't hearing any of it. He only shook his head. "Your brother is sixteen, a man. He can stay up as late as he wants. You're still a child."

Mar Jacobi's eyebrows were knitted up, but he didn't argue with Abba. I pushed my chair away from the table, huffing.

"Momma would let me . . . ," I started. Hearing my father's silence answer me, I winced.

"Sorry," I muttered. My father's hard gaze softened. Still, he urged me toward the stairwell with a tilt of his chin.

"Bed, Terra," he said.

I pulled myself up the stairs. When I reached the dark second story, I stopped, my hand curled around the banister. It felt like I had broken some sort of sacred rule, reminding Abba that Momma was gone.

Gone, I said to myself. *Gone.* And then I began to wonder whether she felt anything now that she was dead. Maybe she just stared into the empty darkness of the atrium, a darkness not so different from the one that waited for me in my windowless bedroom.

I shuddered at the thought of it—an endless black so dark that sometimes you couldn't even tell if your eyes were open or closed. Meanwhile the warm light of our galley flooded the metal wall along the stairwell. I couldn't bring myself to face the darkness. I sat down at the top of the stairs, holding my head in my hands. Pepper crept out of the bathroom to curl up at my side. I tucked my hand against his soft belly, listening to the men talk.

"She's a good girl," Mar Jacobi said. I sat forward at the words, desperate to hear what they were saying about me. "There's much of her mother in her."

My dad let out a snort of disagreement. "Alyana wasn't so good."

"No?"

"No, not good. Kind. But you knew that." Another pause. When my father's voice came again, it was garbled. He wasn't crying. But he was closer than I'd ever heard him. "She was mine."

"I'm so sorry, Arran."

My father kept talking as if the librarian hadn't said a word. "All these years of mitzvot, all these years of working up in that clock tower alone, doing my duty. I'm a good man, Benjamin. But what has it brought me?"

"You'll reach Zehava. Only four more years. Then we'll be rid of this ship."

"I'll be alone." My father's tone wasn't wistful or sad. He said it like it was a simple fact, like there would be no arguing with him. I knew that tone all too well, even at twelve. "Alone, Benjamin. Alone."

"You have your children. Your daughter. Your son."

Another snort. "Ronen's all but ready to declare his intentions to the cartographer girl. He won't be living with me for more than a season. If it weren't for Terra, I'd . . ."

"Arran." There was a warning in Mar Jacobi's voice. "You'll take care of your daughter until she's grown. You'll do your duty so that she can join you on Zehava. It's what our forefathers wanted. What *Alyana* wanted. It's why you're here."

Chair legs squealed against the scuffed metal floor. I tensed, afraid that my father was coming close. But his voice went to the far end of the galley instead.

"A burden," my father said. "That's what she is. Trouble. Like her mother."

My stomach lurched. I bent forward, pressing my face to my knees, and squeezed my eyes shut. I could see stars against my eyelids, but they didn't distract me from the pain that I felt.

I heard the slosh of liquid then as my father spilled wine into a cup. There was a long pause, then a crash as he slammed his tumbler back down on the countertop. He filled it again.

When he spoke at last, his voice had hardened. "Leave me, librarian," he said. "Leave me to my grief."

I didn't wait to hear Mar Jacobi's reply. I knew that my father would soon come stomping up the stairs. He was going to slam his bedroom door, blocking out the world. And I didn't intend to get in his way. I knew what would happen if he found me here, still awake. There would be yelling, and lots of it.

So I picked up Pepper, clutched him to my chest, and retreated to my room. When I stepped inside, I pressed the door closed behind me. I stood there for a moment, still as stone, waiting to hear my heart beat out its rhythm in the dark, a reminder, however small, that on the night my mother died, I still lived.

leaned my weight against a maple bough and watched as the ceiling panels overhead went dark.

I was on the second deck. Up on the main deck, beneath the dome's glass ceiling, I would have been able to see the stars as the artificial lights dimmed. But here, between the forests and the grain storage, there were no stars. The squares of sky were turning purple and would soon go utterly black. I'd have to stumble blindly through the forests to make my way to the lift and then home. That was all right with me, though. I'd never been afraid of the dark.

I sat with one leg on either side of a knotty branch, balancing my sketchbook between my knees. I had to make quick work with my pencils to capture what stretched out before me, the shape of the branches that crowded the second-deck walkways and the vines that shadowed the path. Below, people hurried along on their way home from the labs. They wore white coats that glowed in the twilight. They were scientists—specialists like my father, wearing blue cords on their shoulders and grim expressions. I knew I had little time to spare.

Momma had given me the pencils years ago. I hadn't cared much for them at first, but lately they'd become a comfort. On nights that were too dark and too awful, I'd draw, letting my mind go blank and my hands do the thinking for me. Usually it soothed me. But not on this night.

I penciled in another tree, crosshatching the shadows that now grew short in the twilight. As I cocked my head to the side, considering the way the branches bent in the wind, I tried not to think about what was waiting for me in the morning. My job assignment. My real life. The end of school and free time to spend whittling down my evenings in the forest. I was nearly sixteen, and it was time to be serious, as my father always reminded me. At the thought of his deep voice, I clutched my pencil harder, overlaying violet in dark strokes across the top of the page.

Perhaps I'd gripped the pencil a little *too* hard. It snapped in two in my fist, and I watched as the pointed end fell through the branches. With a sigh I tucked the other half behind my ear and then began the long climb down. I gripped the boughs in my hand, swinging my weight. It felt awkward, but then I always felt awkward lately, all knees and elbows since I'd had my last growth spurt. Abba hadn't been happy about that. Such a waste of gelt to buy me clothes I'd surely outgrow *again*.

The pencil was nestled in a crook in a lower branch. I crouched low, steadying my back against the trunk. That's when something in the gnarled bark caught my eye.

Words. Words carved in deep and then healed over. That alone wasn't unusual—what tree in the atrium *didn't* bear the initials of some young couple who had declared their love hundreds of years before? But these words were different. There wasn't any heart looping around them. No arrow sliced through either. They were a little hard to make out in the fading daylight, but I ran my fingers over the rough bark, reading them with my fingertips.

Liberty on Earth. Liberty on Zehava.

I frowned. We were only months away from reaching the winter planet. The Council had been preparing us in their usual, regimented way. This year they'd said there would be more specialists among the graduating class. More biologists to wake burden beasts from cold storage. More cartographers, like my sister-in-law, Hannah, who would draw maps and find us a suitable place to live. More shuttle pilots too, to rouse the rusty vehicles that waited in the shuttle bay. The other girls whispered that it didn't matter what the results were on our aptitude exams. It didn't matter if we studied, or flirted with the counselors. The Council would make good use of us in preparation for landing, whether we liked it or not.

Liberty.

I heard loping footsteps on the path below. At the sound—heavy, uneven—I stiffened. I knew those footsteps. I'd grown up with them echoing on our stairwell and thundering in the bedroom down the hall. I scrambled for an overhead branch and then settled into the shadows cast by the budding leaves. Maybe if I sat back, with my sketchbook clutched to my chest and my breath shallow, he wouldn't notice me.

I watched as my father's bald head passed below my feet. He'd stopped just under my tree, one thick hand resting against the bark.

Walk on. Walk on, I thought. The pubs were still open in the commerce district. He had every reason to continue on his journey home, every reason to head for the lift. *Just keep going.*

I squeezed my eyes shut, unable to look. That's when I felt his hand close around the heel of my boot.

I was tall—the tallest girl in my class. But my father was still taller than me, bigger and stronger. His arms were lean and strong from years of ringing bells. He moved up through the branches like it was nothing, gripping my calf and pulling it hard. I knew that I should have just climbed down, keeping my chin against my chest and my gaze contritely away. But anger rushed through my body. It overwhelmed my good sense, like it always did.

"Terra, get down!"

"Leave me alone!"

He balanced on the branch now, his eyes level with mine. They were clear and brown, sober. And they fixed on my sketchbook.

"This again?" he asked, tearing it from my arms. "I told you not to waste your time with this."

He cast it at the forest floor below. It drifted down like a handful of autumn leaves. The colors scattered in the twilight.

This was why I never drew at home.

I scrambled down after it, plucking it out of the mud. The pages were rumpled. One or two drawings of flowers had gone soggy in the rainwater. But it wasn't *too* bad. Still, my father gazed at me, a victorious smile smoothing his lips. He was *so* self-satisfied. It made me want to scream at him. My temper was a white-hot ball, sticky in my chest.

"Is everything all right here?"

We turned. A guard had stopped on the path, all dressed up in her woolen uniform blacks. The red rank cord stood out on her shoulder, twisted with Council gold. Her hand rested on the hilt of her blade as if to warn us.

My father came to stand beside me. He put his hand on my shoulder, giving it a clean thump. It was meant to be a friendly gesture. He was telling the guard that everything was normal, that *we* were normal. But I stayed frozen, my gaze blank. I couldn't even make myself force a smile.

"Everything is fine," my father said. "My daughter, Terra, receives her vocation tomorrow. She was worried about her assignment. Weren't you?"

"Worried" wasn't the right word. When it came to my assignment, I was resigned to whatever fate the Council doled out. But I spat the word out anyway. "Yes," I said.

The guard's eyes, small and close set, narrowed on me. "Every job is useful if we're to achieve *tikkun olam*."

"That's what I told her," my father lied. I cast my gaze down. My cheeks burned with anger. I could feel how happy this conversation made my father—how noble he was feeling, how righteous. He loved any opportunity to spout Council rhetoric. He thought it made him a good citizen, no matter how many nights he lost to the bottle.

"You'd better move along," the guard finally said. "I'm sure your girl needs her rest for tomorrow."

"Of course," my father agreed. He gave me a little shove forward.

I took small, shuffling steps. Not because I was afraid, but because I knew it would bother my father. And he wouldn't be able to say a word under the guard's watchful eye.

"Terra?" she called, her voice slicing through the cooling evening. I looked up over my shoulder. Her hands were balled into fists at her sides inside her leather gloves.

"Mazel tov," she said. I didn't answer at first. But then my father flicked his finger against my ear.

"Say 'thank you,'" he growled. I rubbed at my earlobe, trying to smother the pain.

"Thanks," I said at last.

That night, as Pepper hungrily looped around my ankles, I sat at the galley table and watched my father pace.

"If only I could get you to do something *useful* with yourself," he chided, his hands clamped tight behind his back. The harsh overhead lights reflected against his bald head. My father had lost his hair early, one of the few genetic flaws the doctors didn't bother to breed out of us before we were conceived. It made him look much older than he was. Or maybe he had just gotten old lately, what with the hours he worked, and the wine he drank, and the number of nights he stayed up yelling at me. "They're always looking for volunteers at the granaries."

I scowled. I had no desire to spend my nights shucking corn just so that the Council could be impressed by what a good citizen I was. Abba leaned his hands against the table, staring down at the splayed-open pages of my sketchbook.

"Have you told anyone about this rubbish?" he demanded, paging through it. His movements were brusque. I watched the pages bend beneath the force of his fingers, nearly tearing from the spine. I wanted to dart my own hands out, to grab my book and hold it to my chest. But I knew that it would only cause me more problems.

"No," I said, and hoped he didn't sense my lie. In truth, it had been only a month before that I'd sat with a trio of counselors in a windowless schoolroom. They'd stared me down as I'd stammered through my rehearsed monologue. I had repeated all the things that my father said were important to people like them. About how I'd do my duty, work hard at any job, find a good husband, be a wonderful mother. I went on and on. The only sign they gave that they were even listening was the way that one woman's mouth twitched when I finally mumbled myself into silence.

She leaned forward. "Now, Terra," she said. "That's all very nice. But please tell us what you'd really like to do."

My heart thundered in my throat. I glanced down at the school-bag that sat open by my feet. Then I bent over and pulled out my sketchbook. I held my breath as I passed it to her.

They all leaned in, their expressions blank as they leafed through the pages.

Hardly anyone knew about my drawings. My father always told me it was a waste of time. Art was a luxury. It did nothing for our lives on the ship. It wouldn't help us once we reached Zehava. I was doing nothing for *tikkun olam*. And sure enough, my first efforts were terrible, the pencil all smeared, then erased, then heavily layered in again. But over time I'd gotten better. The lines were looser now, more expressive. I'd learned to block in broad shapes first before squeezing in the details. Now when I sketched out the crocuses that poked their heads up through the snowy ground, or the vines that twined through the oak trees beneath the dome, the final outcome actually looked close to what I'd intended. But the counselors didn't seem to notice my improvement. They stared straight down at my drawings, their mouths tight.

"Thank you," the woman had said at last, and handed the book back to me.

"No," I said again to my father now as he stared me down. "No, I haven't shown anyone."

"Good," he said, and shoved the book at me. "Keep it that way. I won't have anyone thinking that my own daughter doesn't know how to be a good Asherati."

For what felt like the longest moment, I didn't move. Part of me wanted to argue with my father. After all, art wasn't *totally* useless. There was even a portrait gallery in the ship's fore, where oil paintings of all the high-ranking families sat beneath dusty velvet curtains. But I knew it was no use. He'd already gone to the cupboard to uncork an old, cloudy bottle of wine. I grabbed my sketchbook, tucked it under my arm, and rose from the table.

At the bottom of the stairs, I stopped, turning toward him. "Will you be coming to the ceremony tomorrow?" I asked, not even sure what I wanted the answer to be. My father squared his shoulders.

"Of course," he said. "It's my duty."

I trudged up the stairs.

Lately all of my dreams embarrassed me. They'd start out normal enough. I'd be in school, or walking through the atrium, or killing time while Rachel shopped in the commerce district. All of a sudden Silvan Rafferty would appear, speaking in low tones. His breath, hot and wet, fogged the cool spring air. He'd press my body to the nearest wall, slipping his tongue into my mouth. I drew him to me—the very thing my father had told me never to do. Then I woke up, my heart beating wildly. In the endless dark of my room, I was terrified that someone would somehow know what I'd been dreaming about.

Years ago, before Momma was even sick, I could count on her to wake me up in the morning. Her knock was only a little rattle of sound, knuckles on the wooden door. It was just enough to get me out of bed. Of course, I couldn't count on my father like that. I would have bought an alarm clock, but when I asked Abba for the gelt, he scoffed.

"What, and have the shop owners think I can't be bothered to get my own daughter to school in the morning?"

He *couldn't* be bothered, but I wasn't going to argue with him. Still, I'd hoped that the day I received my vocation would be different. Maybe he would wake me early. Maybe we would eat breakfast at the galley table and then walk to the ceremony together like a normal family might. I'd made the mistake of getting my hopes up, and so when I woke in the darkness, breathing hard as Pepper walked back and forth across my chest, I couldn't help but feel disappointed.

I grimaced and swatted the cat away. Then, stumbling to my feet, I remembered what day it was.

"You should have woken me sooner!" I scolded the cat. I began to dress, shoving my feet down into the cracked leather of my boots, pulling my favorite moth-eaten sweater over my head. I ran my hands over my long, rumpled hair—as if it made a difference. But it would have to do.

Downstairs the galley was already empty. Dirty dishes were spread out across the counter, collecting flies. The jar that my father had filled up with wine the night before had dried out. The glass was dark as a jewel. I scraped some leftover meat into a dish for Pepper, then threw my sketchbook into my schoolbag and went on my way.

From the outside you wouldn't have known the mess inside our house. Our pale curtains were drawn in the windows. The flowers, which had only just started to bloom in the early spring, were the same purple saxifrage and arctic eyebright that blossomed in every yard. Abba liked to keep up appearances, at least right up to the front door. Our home blended right in with the long row of town houses that filled our district, where specialists hung up white cotton curtains to conceal their supposedly orderly lives.

I entered the commerce district. The streets had already begun to flood with workers, and they shouted sales from the curb as they lifted their storefront shutters. But I had no gelt to buy anything, and no time, either. I ducked into the atrium, passing through the muddy fields and under the shadow of the clock tower. The bright clock face read five past nine. I wondered if my father was still up in the belfry, drinking behind his desk, or if he'd taken off for the captain's stateroom already.

I heard his voice in my head. *Portrait artist isn't even a specialist position. It would be a step down for us. You would be doing nothing for your people, your ship. . . .* As I crossed the pastures, then passed the school where I'd spent every day for the last ten years of my life, my father's words thundered in my ears.

Do your duty, Terra. I won't have you disappoint your mother's memory.

What a joke. If Momma knew what I was like these days—a knotty-haired truant, always blushing and tongue-tied—she'd be disappointed for sure.

Sometimes I was glad she hadn't lived to see what I'd become.

3

My classmates waited for me near the lift at the fore of the ship. They loitered around the paved pavilion, looking bored in their formal wear. Rebbe Davison had squatted against one of the stone curbs. He was young for a teacher—at six we'd been his first class of students—and had dressed smartly in a dark linen suit. The white thread on his shoulder stood out in stark contrast. I felt a twinge of guilt as I saw him lift himself up from the ground, mud on the hems of his pants and the seat of his trousers.

"Terra Fineberg," he said, but not sternly—I don't think he had it in him to be stern. "We've been waiting for you."

"Sorry," I said, shoving my heavy hair from my face as I hustled to stand beside Rachel. "I overslept and—"

Rebbe Davison waved his hand, cutting off my excuse. To be fair, he'd heard plenty of my excuses over the past decade. If he'd had his fill of them, I couldn't entirely blame him. He looked out across the class, quietly taking a head count.

"That's everyone, kids," he said, and went to the lift to press his hand against the panel. My classmates began filing in, in scattered clumps of twos and threes.

Rachel and I lingered near the rear of the crowd. She turned to me, looking me up and down. Her gaze was pointed. I tugged on the hem of my sweater, trying to conceal the fact that I was wearing the same rumpled cotton shirt and pants that I'd slept in. She looked great, of course, in a tweed skirt, gray blouse, and dark red stockings. Her clothes were clean and new, like they always were.

"Late on Vocation Day?" she said at last, cracking a slight smile. "That's bad even for you!"

My shoulders tightened. "Well," I said, trying my best to look like I didn't care what she thought. "It's not like it really matters to *me* what assignment I get."

Rachel rolled her eyes. She'd spent the past year fretting over her future job. She wanted to work in one of the shops in the commerce district, channeling her fashion sense into something that would gain the approval of her own merchant parents. And she wanted me to work with her. I'd done nothing to disabuse her of this notion.

"Sure you don't," she said.

"Move it along, girls," came a firm, clear voice from behind us. We turned—Rachel opened her mouth to offer a sarcastic word in return. But her expression softened when she saw who had spoken. It was Silvan Rafferty, and a smile curled up one corner of his lips. I felt my heart stutter in my chest, but his dark-lashed eyes were firmly on Rachel.

All we'd ever shared was that one kiss. But just the season before, he'd turned sweet on my friend. They walked through the atrium together, just like the older couples, holding hands and making out in beds of dry leaves. She was smitten, and so I never told her what had happened between me and the doctor's son just before Momma died.

I pretended I didn't care. But Silvan had grown handsome, well muscled and tall. His amber skin was smooth. Shining black curls tumbled down his shoulders. A smirk was always lifting his lips, as if he were secretly laughing at his own private joke. He grinned at us now.

"We're not 'girls,' Silvan," Rachel said as we stepped into the crowded lift. Silvan stood between us. I could feel the heat of his arm right through his shirt. "We're practically women."

"You look like a bunch of silly girls to me," Silvan replied. Rachel darted her tongue out at him and then exploded in a fit of giggles. He whispered something to her. I couldn't hear his words—only the heavy murmur of his lips against her ear.

My face burned. I turned away, watching through the glass walls as the pastures disappeared beneath us as we flew up into the bow of the ship.

The captain's stateroom was at the bow of the ship, far from the atrium and the shops and the busy traffic of the day. Despite the name, Captain Wolff didn't live there. Her family occupied a house in the ship's stern, surrounded by other Council members. This was meant to illustrate how she stood on equal ground with other Asherati. But of course, no other citizen had a personal guard standing watch over his front door.

The suite was reserved for ceremonial purposes—vocation ceremonies, retirement parties, things like that. Rachel had told me how some couples were married there, but only if their families were in good standing with the captain. I'd never been invited to such a wedding.

I'd visited the stateroom only once, at our school convocation when I was six. I remembered how dark it was and how the ceiling was made of glass, but my memories didn't do it justice.

For one thing, everything was clean. Most of the ship felt ancient, rickety, and dusty. We had a few computer terminals in school, but the old tech was mostly too important to waste on ordinary citizens. There were rumors that the Council families had their own terminals, though most of us were stuck with books and paper. But in the hall that led to the captain's stateroom, little blinking lights and computer screens were set into the walls. Everything felt strangely new. No expense had been spared.

We filtered in. The ceiling panels here weren't lit to simulate daylight. It was midmorning, but the sky above was star splattered. Hazy illumination spilled out of sconces in the wall. The black marble floors beneath our feet seemed to shine as much as the dark space above.

Our families were waiting for us. Rachel spotted hers and gave a wave of her slender hand to her mother, who waved back from her seat in the crowd. But when I found my father, he only turned away—muttering something under his breath to Ronen.

My brother had brought Hannah with him, of course. We never saw Ronen alone anymore, not since their wedding four years before. They moved together like a freakish two-headed lamb, her hand firmly glued to his arm. But she was the only one who smiled at me, waving. I forced myself to wave back. In truth, I felt bad for her—married to someone like my brother. But at least the marriage had been good for *him*. A gold thread was laced through the brown cord on his shoulder, marking him as a Council member now. It was only honorary. I don't think he'd ever been to a meeting. But it made our father happy.

Beyond our seated families, at the far end of the room, a pair of metal doors gasped open. The captain's guard stepped through, resplendent in their pitch-black uniforms, brass buttons gleaming against wool. I recognized the woman who led the pack. It was the guard from the night before. She carried a woven basket in her arms, weighted heavily by sealed rolls of paper.

Captain Wolff followed on their boot heels. Her uniform matched theirs—all black and brass. But where they wore bloodred braids on their shoulders, the cord on hers was violet, threaded with gold. Supervisory staff and a Council member, too. She was the only one to wear those colors.

At the center of the room sat a podium, ready and waiting. Captain Wolff marched right up to it, smiling. But the way the scar twisted her lip made it look more like a grimace. She rested her hand on the hilt of her ceremonial knife as she spoke.

"Dear children," she said, leaning hungrily forward, "and honored citizens. Remember that today is not simply the day that your sons and daughters earn their vocations, taking the last step toward becoming full citizens in the eyes of our society. No, indeed today is the day we all see our last class of children begin to ascend to adulthood within the confines of our ship." Captain Wolff pointed a knobby finger straight toward us. I was too close to the front for my liking. I squirmed, letting my hair veil my face.

"*You*, children, represent the pinnacle of our journey. You are the reason our ancestors departed from Earth so many years ago. As we begin the next step of our voyage, your loyalty is of the utmost importance. It is the work you'll do that will cement our meager colony's future on our new home. You are the foundation of everything that will follow. Through each mitzvah you perform, the dutiful execution of your work assignments, and the fulfillment of your marriage contracts, each of you will bring us closer and closer to repairing humanity's uncertain future."

She was staring at us. Everyone was—an audience of steady, piercing gazes, and my father's eyes among them, most piercing of all. I could practically feel the weight of his expectations bearing down on me from above.

"And now . . ." She paused, folding her hands in front of her. "It's time to give you what you've been waiting for. Aleksandra, the scrolls?"

The woman beside her stepped forward, hefting the basket in her arms. I saw now that each scroll was made of white paper, the smooth kind that cost a fortune. Each was tied with a ribbon and sealed with a bubble of wax. Some of the ribbons were brown and green. Those would go to the laborers—fieldworkers, shepherds, granary assistants, carpenters. I saw scattered silver ribbons, for merchants, and a dozen curling blue ribbons for specialists, too. I leaned forward, searching for a flash of bright color. But I didn't see any tied with the yellow bow of an artisan.

The woman came to stand by the captain's side, holding the basket by its handles. Captain Wolff hesitated for a moment; then her lips parted into some semblance of a smile.

"You know," she said to the audience, her cold eyes sparkling and sharp, "I was so proud on the day when my daughter received her own assignment as a guard member. I knew she would serve our ship well—always dutiful, always obedient. She works so that we may all achieve *tikkun olam*. As I'm sure your children will."

There was an appreciative rumble of voices in the crowd. I glanced between Captain Wolff and Aleksandra. If it hadn't been for the scar, I would have noted the family resemblance more readily. They had the same hawk nose, the same sharp features. The look was almost pretty on the younger woman. I wondered if Captain Wolff had been pretty once too, before the thresher did its work.

She looked only scary now—scarier as she reached in and lifted the first scroll. We all sucked in our breath as she read off the name that was sewn into the brown ribbon—

"Jamen Dowd. Granary worker."

—and exhaled when we realized that we weren't the one being summoned to the podium. We watched as Jamen marched forward, his hands balled at his hips. Once he'd been a soft, silly boy, but the years since his bar mitzvah had hardened him. When Captain Wolff stopped him before he could stamp off, a frown creased his wide mouth. Still, she took his hand and gave it a stout shake.

"Congratulations, Jamen," she said.

Jamen lowered his unkempt eyebrows and stalked off.

Granary worker will fit him, I said to myself. *Wouldn't want him to have to talk to anybody.* I scolded myself for the thought. Every assignment was important, no matter what my father always said. That's what we'd learned in school.

But it was hard to be happy for Deklan Levitt, a rail-thin, weasel-faced boy who was told that he would be a plowman. Or happy for the families who would be assisted with deliveries down in the hatchery by Ada Wyeth, a notorious bully who always wore a vicious scowl.

But then Rachel's name was called, and it was announced that she'd gotten the shop job she'd been hoping for. Her parents lifted their fists in the air, pumping them victoriously. My heart twisted in my chest. Sometimes it was hard to be friends with someone who always got whatever she wanted.

I tried to steady my smile as Captain Wolff moved on to the next name and Rachel slid into the line beside me.

"Koen Maxwell," Captain Wolff said, holding a blue-ribboned scroll. Her inky eyes searched out a gangly chestnut-haired boy who was known for being good at math and not much else. She added, "Clock keeper."

I bit the insides of my cheeks in surprise, keeping my smile tight. That was my father's title. I'd no idea that he'd requested a *talmid*. Out in the audience Abba's expression was flat, unreadable.

But even my father glanced up at what transpired next. Captain Wolff reached into the basket and pulled out a scroll tied with a purple ribbon.

"Silvan Rafferty," she said, and then added, in a tickled tone, "captain."

Rebbe Davison, who had spent most of the ceremony nodding his silent approval from a chair in front, dropped his jaw.

"You're retiring?"

His words cut through the confused murmurs of the crowd. Captain Wolff glowered at our teacher. Her lips drew back a touch, showing teeth.

"This is Silvan's moment," she warned. And then she looked at her new *talmid*, taking in his tall, muscular figure and proud jaw. She reached forward, gripping his hand in one hand, touching his shoulder with the other.

"Congratulations, Silvan," she said. I couldn't be sure, but I thought I saw tears dot her eyelashes. The boy just gave a small, bored nod. There was no gratitude in the gesture, as if he'd been expecting this all along. When he strolled over to where the rest of us stood, clutching the only purple-ribboned scroll in the whole basket in one proud fist, we all turned to stare. He was blushing faintly, red along the bridge of his nose and the tops of his ears, but that was the only indication he gave that he knew we were gawking at him.

Beside me, Rachel looked like she'd just swallowed glass.

"Silvan?" she whispered, and her hand groped out for mine. "Captain?"

I knew what she was imagining. It was a possibility grander than she'd ever considered: Rachel, the captain's wife.

I began to picture it. Beautiful Rachel, her coarse curls pulled up, revealing her long, slender neck and the dark skin of her throat above a harvest-gold wedding dress. Silvan would wear his navy-blue uniform. Maybe they'd be married here, beneath the star-dotted sky, the way that the Council members' children so often were.

My best friend, married to the captain. That would make her a Council member.

A lump began to rise in my throat. I could see it so clearly—the two of them kissing on their wedding day. Would I even be invited? Rachel might want me there, but I couldn't be sure. Why would Silvan want the scrubby daughter of the clock keeper at his wedding? I was certain he didn't remember that day in the dome. It had been so long ago and hadn't meant anything, anyway. We were just kids. The thoughts swirled in my mind. I wasn't listening to Captain Wolff's long, droning list of names.

Rachel tugged at my hand.

"What?" I asked. My voice cut through silence. A few of my classmates tittered. When Rachel spoke, it was through laughter too.

"Terra! That's you!"

"Oh!" I felt my cheeks grow hot. Everyone had turned to me, watching and waiting. I took clumsy steps toward the podium. *I don't even know what she said!* I thought in a panic as I took the rolled paper in one hand and barely touched the captain's fingers with the other. I noted the color of the bow. *A blue thread. Blue. So much for art. A specialist position . . .*

"Congratulations," the captain said. Her tone was droll as she snatched her hand away from mine. I guess I'd held on a moment too long. She wiped my sweat off her hand by pressing her fingers to her wool-wrapped hip. I watched, frozen at first. Then I hurried to slip in again beside Rachel. At the front of the room, the captain continued to call my classmates to her. But I tuned her out again, scrambling to peel away the seal with my nail.

I scanned the lines of black calligraphy. The date was at the top. My name was inked below it. Then there was the captain's name, and her title, and a long line of words—*On this sacred day* and so on and so forth. I skimmed to the bottom of the page.

I couldn't help but spit out the word that I found there.

"Botanist?"

It tasted bad on my tongue. Before I could turn to Rachel, to whisper to her of my confusion, I heard a sibilant *shhh* of air rise up from the audience. I looked out across the jumble of smiling faces, searching for the source of the sound—until my eyes fixed on a familiar glower.

My father glared at me across the sea of heads. His jaw was set firmly, his lips pursed. I felt the searing burn of blood rise up across my cheeks and throat. Blushing furiously, I crumpled the paper into a ball in my fist.

"Stand up straight," my father commanded before turning to Hannah's father.

The ceremony was over. I held a plate of pickles and chopped liver out in front of me as if they could shield me from the horrors of small talk. My classmates all seemed to move easily through the crowd, laughing and chattering with one another. Even Rachel had drifted away, flirting with Silvan in the corner, leaving me here with my family—and sinking fast.

"We thought we'd all go down to the hatchery," Hannah said. I could feel her pointed gaze upon me. "And visit your niece."

The thought of being around all those wires and bio-conduits made my stomach flip-flop. "No, really, thank you," I muttered in a low tone. "I promised Rachel's parents I'd eat with them."

"The Federmans are merchants," my father said, pursing his lips as though the idea tasted bad. Beside him, my brother cast his eyes to the floor. He wasn't much better than a merchant—only a carpenter. But the gold thread in his cord meant that we pretended he wasn't. "But the Meyers are Council members. And you're a specialist now, Terra. You shouldn't—"

"I *promised*," I said again, my words hotter this time. I could feel how Hannah's family stared at me, waiting to see if I'd crack. I decided that I would spare them that. I shoved my plate into Ronen's hands and turned on the heels of my boots. "I'm out of here."

"Terra!" my father called as I went to grab my bag from the coatroom. "Terra, come back here!"

But I ignored him, leaning my hands against the heavy doors, hustling down the long hall toward the lift. Who did he think he was, anyway? Rachel was my *friend*, my oldest friend. I slammed my palm hard against the lift's lock, waiting in the dim light for the doors to come shuddering open.

Footsteps sounded down at the far end of the hall.

"If you're here to lecture me . . . ," I began, turning. But my words puttered out when I saw that it was not Abba who hustled toward me. It was Benjamin Jacobi, of all people. The librarian.

"Mar Jacobi," I said. My words sounded thin, annoyed. I suppose that I was. "What are you doing here? Don't you already have a *talmid*?" I thought he did, at least. A redheaded boy. He'd been in Ronen's class.

"I always attend on Vocation Day. It's a mitzvah, you know." His dark eyes sparkled like he was making a joke. But I didn't get it.

"I know," was all I said.

And then there was a burp of awkward silence. Mar Jacobi reached over, pressing his hand to the lift panel—as though I hadn't just done so myself. "Do you mind if I join you on your trip down? I hate all of this chitchat. I'm really very eager to get out of here."

I couldn't help but smile at that. I let out a breath I hadn't even realized I was holding. "Oh!" I said. "I hate it too."

"I suspected you might," Mar Jacobi said as the door at long last dinged open. He held it open for me. "You've always been *remarkably* like your mother."

Momma! I felt a stab of emotion. She'd seemed so composed, so charming. Nothing at all like me. We stepped into the huge lift. Our voices echoed against the walls.

"She hated small talk too?" I asked. Mar Jacobi let out a chuckle.

"Oh, yes," he said. "Of course, you would have never known it at first. But she used to say that you can't really get to know a person until you've broken bread with them."

"You must have known her pretty well," I said, less a question than a statement. I remembered him there, of course, on the night of her funeral.

"Alyana was . . ." He stumbled over his words and was able to recover only after swallowing hard. "A dear friend of mine."

I wasn't sure what to say. I nodded.

"She would be so proud. I'm sure you'll be able to do great things as a botanist," he offered at last. I gave my shoulders a shrug, clutching my bag in front of me like my life depended on it. I hadn't given any thought to my new vocation. I wasn't sure what a botanist even *did*.

"How, planting flowers?"

"Perhaps." He gave a grin. His teeth were yellow and crooked. When I didn't smile back, he added: "I think you'll be truly working toward *tikkun olam*. Are you familiar with the term?"

I let out a snort. "It's all Abba— I mean, it's all my father ever talks about."

"Duty always was important to Arran," Mar Jacobi said. He leaned back on his heels, staring up at the lights set into the ceiling. "But you know, Terra, there are many ways to do your duty, to work toward carving out a place in the universe for humanity."

"Are there?" I glanced down at the polished floor. There was something hungry about his voice, like he'd been waiting for this conversation for a long time. I didn't like the intensity behind it. It made my cheeks warm.

"Well," he said, "when our ancestors left Earth, they thought they were saving mankind. The Council will tell you that the way to fulfill that mission is to do your duty, to work hard and marry and raise happy children and obey the captain."

Behind him the door dinged open, revealing a fury of green, tangled space. A rush of air wafted in, perfumed by the clover from the pastures and the wildflowers from the forests below. Neither of us moved.

"Yes," I said sourly, "I know. They taught us that in school. How we have to do mitzvot for the good of the ship or it'll fall out of space or something."

Mar Jacobi's eyebrow ticked up. He was looking at me closely now, the pupils in his brown eyes shrinking down to pinpricks. "I used to talk about *tikkun olam* with your mother. She always thought there were other ways. Alyana said we needed to protect our liberties, too. Otherwise mankind was never worth saving."

"What do you mean, 'our liberties'?"

Mar Jacobi stepped aside, offering the open door to me. After a moment I stepped through. "I'd be happy to discuss it with you sometime. If you'll stop by the library, I could give you some books to read. I'm sure it would do your mother proud to know that you're considering what's truly necessary to work *tikkun olam*."

My lips tightening into a frown, I trudged past him. "All right," I said. But I felt uneasy as I walked out into the dome.

The librarian only waved a hand at me. "Mazel tov, Terra," he offered. I saw him press his hand to the button, and then I watched as the door slid shut again.

"Thanks," I mumbled in return. But a thin birdsong was the only thing that answered.

I found a mossy incline spread out between a pair of trees. The artificial daylight was feeble, spotty; the ground muddy from the latest rain. Everything seemed cool and brown. But near my feet there was a flash of purple: a crocus head pushing up between the gravel. As I fumbled for my pencils, I gave the flower a wistful smile.

A spring flower, I thought. *But it won't last long. Spring will be short this year.*

I turned to a blank page near the back of my book and ran my hand over its bumpy surface. When I first started drawing, I tried to draw people: Ronen and Rachel, my father. Momma. But in the dim light of my room, their faces looked all wrong—the eyes uneven, the mouths too wide. So I'd given up on that. It was only away from home, in this solitary space, that I had begun to look—really look—at the flowers and branches in front of me. Now my hands and my pencils confidently sketched the right shapes. I found my mind clearing, my heartbeat growing steady again. There was only color. Violet with yellow undertones. A touch of green where the petals picked up the shade of the moss around it. And I found myself happy, or something close to it.

I drew the crocus—how the petals folded in on themselves like the pleats of a purple dress. The way the green stem was thin and delicate and stately, like a woman's slender neck.

I worked until it was too dark in the forest to draw anymore. In the distance the clock bells rang out. I pulled myself to my feet, tucking my pencils back into my bag. In the fading daylight I squinted at the image of the flower one last time. There it was, preserved for all time inside my book. I smiled, touching the crosshatched shadows with my index finger. Then I closed the cover and stumbled back toward the lift.

Dinner at Rachel's was always an improvement over dinner at home. Though her quarters were the same shape as ours, they were different inside, warm and comfortable, decorated with paintings of fruit and lit with glass-shaded lamps. Her parents chatted amicably as they cooked together. Rachel and I poured drinks and set down plates. Even her little brother helped, laying out the tarnished silverware, chanting, "The spoon and knife is husband and wife." He didn't even complain about it. I don't think Ronen had ever helped with dinner without whining.

It was nice, really. It let me forget about the weird run-in with the librarian, if only for an hour or two.

Before we ate, Rachel's mom took down a pair of electric lights from her cupboard and set them in the center of the table. It was something that was done once a week in her household. Her mother was so grave about it, serious. When we were little, Rachel had asked me if my mother did the same thing. I'd only frowned, given my head a shake. Momma hadn't done *anything* like that. Rachel said that it was something that the women in her family had always done.

"Will you join us, Terra?" her mother asked now. "My mother always said it was a mitzvah for a woman to welcome in the end of the week." I glanced over at Rachel's father, who hovered over the kitchen counter, smiling. Rachel's brother watched us too. Everyone was waiting for me.

"Sure," I said, the heat spreading over my cheeks. I watched as her mother flicked the switch on the bottom of the lights.

"Blessed is the universe," her mother said, veiling her face with her hands. Rachel did the same, lifting her long fingers to her face. So I did too, even though I had no idea why. "And the commandment to kindle the light in the darkness."

We dropped our fingers, watching the bulbs flicker. Their yellow light danced across the dinner table.

"Well, now that that's done with," her father said, smacking his hands together. "Let's eat."

· · ·

But by the end of dinner, Mar Jacobi's words were weighing heavy on me again. *Alyana said we need to protect our liberties.* I gnawed at the dried fruit that was our dessert, thinking about his words. I hadn't realized how quiet I'd become, until Rachel slipped her hand in mine under the table, squeezing my pinkie finger tight.

"I don't think we'll be having any tea, Mother," she said, standing and pulling me along. "We have a *lot* to talk about."

She gave me a wink as she dragged me up the stairwell. But when she shut her door behind her, she turned on me.

"What's with you?" she demanded. And then, before I could answer, she broke into a grin. "Is this about a boy? Do you *like* someone?"

"What? A boy? No." I fell against her bed. The sheets were pulled taut, tucked neatly under the mattress. Rachel made her bed every morning. I *never* did. "It's about the librarian."

"The librarian?" In the dim circle of light cast by her bedside lamp, Rachel wrinkled her nose. "You . . . you *like* Mar Jacobi?"

"No! He stopped me in the lift after the vocation ceremony. He said he has books for me."

"That's so weird. You know, he always kind of creeped me out. Every time I go in there, he's all, 'What books would it please you to read today, Ms. Federman?' Like he thinks we're chums."

"Lies," I teased. "You don't *read*, Rachel."

She threw one of her pillows at me. I caught it easily. Then I froze, looking down at the tiny floral print sewn into the pillowcase.

"He said he knew Momma."

"So? Who doesn't know everyone else on this ship?"

"Plenty of people," I said. Plenty of people who weren't Rachel, that is. A frown was playing on her features, just below the surface of her smiling eyes. "It just seemed strange," I said at last.

"I think that's just how he is," she said. "You're being paranoid."

"Really?" I finally passed the pillow to her. She took it, tucking it behind her head.

"Really," she said, in a tone that told me there would be no more talking about it. Then she sat up straight. "Besides, we have more important things to talk about."

"Such as?"

"Our new jobs, silly. Botanist! That was a surprise."

I groaned, hiding my face in the crook of my arm. But Rachel didn't want to hear it.

"It's not so bad! A specialist position. Your dad will be happy."

I bit down on the inside of my cheek, thinking about it. "Maybe. You should have seen him after Ronen got his assignment. It was bad enough that Momma had a service job. I think he'd just about *die* if both of his kids did."

Something hardened inside Rachel. I realized too late how I'd misspoken. A merchant was ranked *lower* than a service worker. "He must have known it was a possibility. It's not like everyone can be a specialist."

"Of course! And it's not like everyone *should*," I assured her. But my words didn't help. It was like a door had closed inside her and I was standing on the other side. "You know it's my dad's issue, not mine."

"Oh, I *know* that!" She forced a high, weird laugh. "I guess I just hoped we'd get a chance to work together. Despite what your father thought."

"*I* always hoped—" And then I stopped, pressing my mouth shut. I'd never told Rachel about my plans to become an artist. After the way it had gone with the counselors, I wasn't sure I wanted to.

"Hoped what?"

"I thought maybe I could be an artisan. A portrait artist," I finally concluded. Rachel's eyebrows lifted.

"A portrait artist? Since when did you care about art?"

"I care!"

But Rachel just gave a sort of vague shake of her head. "Terra, I've never known you to care about *anything*."

Her words sank into me like a stone. I guess I shouldn't have been mad. It was true, wasn't it? I spent most of my time rolling my eyes at other people's passions, not talking about my own. But still, a small spark of defensiveness lit up inside me. I found myself rising to my feet. My hands bumbled blindly through my bag, shoving aside the torn papers and notebooks until I found my sketchbook, the old familiar pages rough and curled. I thrust it at her. My heart sounded in my ears. But as she thumbed through it, something changed. Rachel's mouth fell gently open.

"Oh, *Terra!*" she breathed. "These are . . . well, they're not perfect. But they're *good.*"

I felt the heat rise to my face. "Um," was all I managed to say.

But Rachel hardly noticed my stammered answer. Instead the corner of her mouth edged up, revealing a dimple. "But you know, Terra, if you didn't want to be a botanist, maybe you should have drawn something besides trees."

Rachel's dark eyes seemed to dance as she watched me.

"I *couldn't* draw anything else," I protested. "Abba hated how I wasted all my time drawing. I had to go outside where he wouldn't catch me. . . ."

"And draw flowers and plants and vines," she said. I sighed, clutching the book to my chest.

"I guess it's my fault, then." I tried to sound lighthearted about the whole thing, but I'm not sure Rachel bought it. She knew me too well for that. "I showed the counselors my sketchbook. They must have thought I was saying I wanted to work with plants."

"There are worse things that could happen."

"Like what?" I demanded. "I don't know the first thing about *botany*."

"Oh, I don't know. They could have made you work in a *shop*."

The heat returned, this time spreading over my neck and ears. "I'm—I'm sorry, Rachel," I stammered.

But Rachel only let out a laugh. "I was only kidding!" she said. I studied her face. From the crinkles around her eyes, I could tell that the laughter was genuine. So I laughed too.

"I'll miss you, you know," she said to me.

"What do you mean? I'll be around."

But Rachel looked at me meaningfully, and I knew it was the truth. Our lives were about to change. I wouldn't sit with her in school every day, whispering, sharing laughter.

I reached out my hand, offering it to her. She took my pinkie in hers. That was our secret signal, the one we had always made to each other when we'd sat side by side in school. When something funny happened, or strange, or sad, we always reached down and linked pinkies. It was our way of saying, *I'm here and I see it too.* It was something we'd done since we were small, and though perhaps we should have long since outgrown it, we hadn't, not yet. I savored the warm, familiar pressure of her hand.

"I'll miss you too," I said at last, and meant it.

4

When I got home that night, a lumpy package was waiting for me on our doorstep. I prodded it with the toe of my boot. It bore the seal of the High Council—gold wax with a circular imprint that I think was *supposed* to be a pomegranate—and my name in neat calligraphy. I hefted it into my arms and dumped it on the galley table, tearing away the brown paper as Pepper circled my ankles and whined.

The package was filled with unbleached cloth—rough linen that wasn't quite funerary white but still depressed me. I lifted the first length of it and held the long lab coat against me. I might be tall, but the sleeves still trailed over my arms. I wondered who it had belonged to before they'd given it to me. Clearly, it was recycled. It definitely hadn't been cut to my measurements, and the pale color would do my equally pale complexion few favors.

But it was definitely mine. My name was even stitched onto the breast in blue thread. *Terra Fineberg*, it read, *Specialist*. I ran my fingers over the embroidery. Then I reached out and touched the rank cord on the shoulder. The braid was the color of bluebells, just like the one on my father's coat. But the braided threads were much newer, not dingy and dirt darkened like his. I touched it tentatively, slipping my finger into the loop at the top.

This means something, I told myself. *This means you're a citizen, almost an adult.* But I didn't feel it. In fact, I didn't feel much of anything. With a grimace I thrust the coat down at the table and went to the icebox to fetch Pepper his dinner.

I scraped the leftover meat and bonemeal into his bowl, then watched for a moment as he pawed at it before diving in. As he licked the bowl clean, I went to the sink, where the tower of crusty dishes had been waiting since the night before. I switched the sink on. The pipes clattered and rang before a murky stream of brown water trickled out. I pulled up my sleeves and went to work, scrubbing the old dented pots and nicked china, letting the rhythm of the water wash over me.

I didn't hear my father come in. His footsteps were lost beneath the steady drone of tap water and my own tuneless whistling. But I heard the windows rattle when he slammed the door shut, and I jumped, splashing water over the floor. I waited for him to say something about his visit to the hatchery, to comment on how big his granddaughter was growing and what a wonderful father Ronen would be. But he didn't. He only went to one of our cupboards, uncorked a cloudy bottle of wine, and took a long draw from it. As he passed, I got a nice whiff of him—that sour smell of alcohol and sweat. Drunk already.

"You're wasting the water," he said, reaching past me to turn it off. I held my hands tight at the edge of the sink, not wanting to let his skin brush mine. On nights like these I never knew if I could trust him. His broad, age-spotted fingers had backhanded me one too many times.

"Sorry," I murmured. He gave a grunted response, then crossed the galley and collapsed at the table. For a moment he just sat there, shoulders slumped, turning the bottle in his hands. But then he spotted the pile of flaxen cloth.

"What's this?"

I put the last dish on the rack, fumbled through the greasy water for the drain stopper, then turned, bracing myself.

"My uniforms," I said.

He put the bottle down on the table. His fingers skidded across its splintered surface, finally grasping one of the coats by the sleeve and pulling it toward him.

"Specialist," he said, flatly at first. But then his hand alighted on the cord, and I saw something unfamiliar dance across his mouth. A smile.

"Terra," he said. He rose to his feet, still clutching the coat in his hands. Then he crossed the galley and crushed me in a hug. I didn't know what to do with my hands. I held them high between our bodies, shielding myself even as my face was pressed against the brass buttons of his coat.

"Mazel tov, Daughter," he said, rocking me. "Your momma would be so proud." I started to let my eyes close, to lean into his embrace. He was still my father. I could smell the remnants of the clock tower under the rank stench of wine and body odor. He still smelled like the dust in the rafters and the cedar of the wide floorboards.

Finally he pulled away, holding me at arm's length. His face wrinkled in a grin.

"You've done well," he said. I shrugged at that—it's not like I'd *done* anything. "A specialist, like your old man."

It was true. Abba did more than just ring the clock bells. He was an advisor to the meteorologists and doctors too. It was his job to help the people of our ship get used to the changes we'd inevitably face when we arrived on Zehava. Longer winters. Longer days. I knew he was proud of his job, of the ratty old blue cord threaded into his double-breasted coat.

"Thanks," I said. But I couldn't stand the intensity of his gaze. I turned to the empty sink, starting to wipe it clean with an old dish-rag, glad to have something—anything—to distract me from his stare. Meanwhile Abba folded my uniform for me, holding the arms against him like they were another body. Then he gently set it down.

"Botany," he said. Then he repeated it, more darkly this time. He reached for the bottle again. I saw his Adam's apple bob as he swallowed. "Botany. You'll be working with Mara Stone, you know."

"Will I?" I asked carefully. I'd never heard of her before, didn't understand the shadow that had fallen over Abba's words.

"Be careful," he said finally, smearing his lips against the back of his hand. "I've worked hard to see that you grow up right. I won't see it ruined by *that woman.*"

I didn't know what to say. So I gave a timid nod. My father sank down into his seat, glowering at the wine bottle like it had insulted him. But he didn't say anything.

"Um," I said at last, groping for some words to fill the silence. One side of his lip lifted in a sneer of acknowledgment. I went on:

"I was wondering why you requested a *talmid*. I mean, it's great, but I'm just . . . It surprised me. And I was wondering why. You requested him, that is."

My father lifted the bottle again, but it was empty. He let it thud down on the table as he let out a long sigh.

"Because I'm tired," he said.

Then he rose and trudged up the stairs. His footfalls were heavy. I stayed still for a moment. Both Pepper and I kept our ears cocked toward the stairwell.

Finally it came—the sound of his bedroom door thundering shut.

When I had finished putting the dishes away, I carried the lab coats up to my room. I threw the lot of them into the corner and didn't even bother to scold Pepper as he settled into the pile of soft cloth.

Even with the light off, within the confines of my narrow bed, I couldn't ignore them. They seemed to glow up from the darkness, taunting me. I turned over to face the wall. My mind raced. Maybe I should have reached for my sketchbook, my pencils, poured out all my worries across the rough pages. But instead I just stared at the wall, my eyes wide and my body stiff.

I couldn't help but feel that, somehow, this was all Momma's fault. If she hadn't died, maybe I wouldn't have taken to spending so much time in the atrium alone, looking at trees and sketching the splayed fingers of oak leaves in red and green. When I was little, it had been *our* place—she would take me walking every night after supper. Girl time, she said. Of course, those walks stopped when she first got sick, a few weeks after I turned twelve.

At first her illness seemed to be nothing out of the ordinary. Nearly every winter a rash of flu ran through the ship, and it was almost impossible to stay healthy when we all shared the same air. But Momma *stayed* sick long after the rest of us went back to school and work. *I just feel a little queasy*, she said, *a bit under the weather.* It wasn't until the end of the season that we finally convinced her to go to the hospital.

In the waiting room I tried to ignore the fact that it was Doctor Rafferty and not one of the normal medics who tended to my mother. The blue cord on his shoulder was threaded with gold. Council member. Ronen noticed it too.

"Why would she need the head doctor for the flu?" he demanded, jostling my father's arm. "If it's viral, she should be better already!"

But our father didn't answer. He didn't have to. Doctor Rafferty had appeared at the door, his olive features drawn.

"There's a mass on her liver," he said. "It's . . . very unusual. I've read about this but never seen it. 'Cancer' is what it was once called. Uncontrolled cell growth. It seems to have already reached her lymphatic system."

Doctor Rafferty's expression was wrong. His lower lip twitched. There was something in his eyes, something I couldn't quite pinpoint. But my father and Ronen accepted the diagnosis without question, so I told myself I must have been crazy—told myself there was no time to worry about Doctor Rafferty. There was only Momma, dying.

A few weeks later she was gone, and high spring came stumbling back. And there was no one left to walk with me.

That night I dreamed of her.

We were walking through the atrium together, down the twisted paths. It was summer, a season I hadn't seen since I was a little kid. Dragonflies, their long bodies gleaming like ancient amethysts, swarmed the dome. As I followed my mother over the overgrown brick, I swatted insects from my face. But it didn't do any good. Between the tangle of vines and the fury of wings, I lost my mother down a fork in the path.

"Momma?" I called. I crossed a wooden footbridge where flashes of green caught my eye from over the rail. Turtles milled through the water below. Everything was too bright, too hot. It made me dizzy.

Then I heard movement in the jungle. I stalked forward, squinting through the heat.

"Momma?" I pushed the branches aside.

There, standing in the jungle, was my mother. She smiled at me, reaching out a hand. I pressed forward.

But then she turned, and I saw that she wasn't alone. A boy stood just behind her. But his face was obscured by a veil of Spanish moss that spilled off one of the tree branches above.

I couldn't make out his features, but this much I knew: He was tall, taller than Momma. Taller than me. The flowers all turned their faces to him, like they couldn't wait to soak up his warmth. In turn his thin body bent unnaturally toward me as I stepped close. It was like he had no spine, no bones, like he was just a reed bending in the breeze.

I woke in the pitch dark of my bedroom, my heart doing a wild dance in my chest.

5

The next morning I hustled across the ship, pushing my sleeves up over my hands and listening to the clock bells strike out the quarter hour. It wasn't entirely my fault that I was late, of course. The labs were practically a world away from the grimy port district where we lived. To reach them I had to make my way through the commerce district, then the fields, then the pastures, then cross the narrow foot-bridge between the library and school. The concrete buildings that housed the labs rose up out of the ground near the far wall of the ship.

I made my way through the winding hallways, smiling nervously to the other specialists as I passed. They hardly noticed me as they rushed by, white coats streaming. When I finally reached the door to the botanical lab, I hesitated.

Truth be told, when I pressed my hand to the panel by the door, I hoped, for just a moment, that the door would stay shut.

No such luck. It slid away, revealing metal floors and walls. Everything would have been gleaming if it weren't for the junk everywhere. Metal shelves reached up to the ceilings, but the books had begun to topple off them. Waterlogged papers spilled like leaves off a row of steel tables. And there were plants everywhere. Vines curled out of pots of soil and from planters overhead. Little trays of seedlings were stacked along the floor. Open bags of fertilizer steamed heat into the cool air.

The lab smelled like disinfectant, soil, and heady pollen. I wrinkled my nose.

"Hello?" I called as the door slid closed behind me. I walked carefully, doing my best not to trample any of the books that were set open on the floor. For a moment there was no answer. But then I heard movement near the rear of the lab. A woman hovered over one of the desks, behind a massive monitor. The computer terminal looked like it wasn't often used. The keyboard was strewn with papers.

The woman was sharp eyed, with gray-threaded hair cropped

close to her head, and a hook-shaped nose. And she was tiny—much shorter than I was, and slender, too, though her coat fit much better than mine. It had been taken in at the waist and sleeves, tailored to her. I watched as she squinted down into the long tube of a microscope, her expression a sort of grimaced wink. She didn't acknowledge me standing there, waiting.

"Um, Rebbe Stone?" I said, clearing my throat. "I can come back later if you want."

She waved a hand at me, but her gaze didn't move from the microscope. "Don't call me 'Rebbe'! The Council might think they can make me teach you, but they can't force me to be as formal as all that."

I chewed my lip. "You didn't request me?"

"Bah," Mara said. "'Request.' They've been trying to strong-arm me into retiring for years. They think you'll be my deathblow. Sit down!"

The only chair was behind her, and it was piled high with books. So I crouched in place between a stack of field guides and a prickly needled bush.

"On Earth there was a country called Iceland," she began. She had a craggy, sort of froggish voice. It matched her nose. "Of course you haven't heard of it. Their chief cultivars were potatoes, kale, cabbage. Hardy grasses. That sort of rubbish thing, and limited to the warmer lowlands. But with geothermally heated hothouses, they could add almost anything to their diet. Tomatoes for vitamin C. Grapes for wine. Small scale, mostly, but still. They've been an excellent model for us." She finally looked up at me, one eye still squinted.

"Only problem is, for the last year, blight has been hitting our hothouse fruit trees. And Zehavan fruit salad's going to be exceedingly bland if all we have is crab apples and figs. You know, when they told me they were sending me a girl, I was worried you'd be an addlebrained fool. But I'm glad to see they didn't send me one of the pretty ones."

I blanched. I'd long known that I was no Rachel—my frame was gawky, and my fair hair hung in a frizzy curtain down my shoulders— but I wasn't used to people saying it so plainly. The woman scowled.

"Oh, don't *worry* about it. You're fine. It's better off, anyway. You'll be doing all sorts of digging around for me. Wouldn't want you to be afraid to get your hands dirty."

I didn't say anything. The woman looked amused. She offered me her hand.

"I'm Mara Stone."

Her knobby fingers were cold. "I know," I said. "My father told me . . ." Then I trailed off. I wasn't sure if it was a good idea to share what my father had said.

"Terrible things, I'm sure." Mara turned to her microscope. "Terra, isn't it? It's an interesting name, considering. Do you know what it means?"

"No," I said, and then added: "Considering what?"

"Considering your new vocation. 'Terra' was another name for Earth. But also for the stuff on it. The land, the soil."

"Oh," I replied, not really sure what to say to that. "It's a family name. My mother named me after some ancestor."

"Your mother, yes." With those words something about Mara's expression changed. Her hard mouth didn't exactly soften, but her frown sort of crumbled away. "You know, I'm sorry about that. Well, not *sorry*. I didn't do it, you know. But sorry enough. The founders tried to safeguard us against that. But they couldn't anticipate every eventuality."

I was used to people apologizing for my mother's death, but I wasn't used to *this*. "It's okay," I said at last. And then we just stood there, staring at each other for a minute, the terrible silence stretching out.

"What do you know about plants?" she finally demanded. I opened my mouth, letting it form a helpless O.

"I know the names of some flowers," I offered. "My mother taught me. Daffodils and cyclamens and—"

"Ha!" Mara said. "Lot of good daffodils'll do us. Here."

She strode over to the desk in the corner, where a heavy volume waited in a nest of papers. It was open, the pages yellow from water that had drained from the planters above. She fanned through it. There were illustrations of plants on every page, each one lavishly illustrated in shades of brown and green. I wanted to reach out and run my fingers over the images. But there was no time.

"I'll take you into one of the greenhouses. You'll find each of the marked plants and bring me a cutting." She fished a pair of rusted shears out of her deep pocket. I took them from her and then glanced down at the book. Even looking at it sideways, I could see that almost a third of the pages were marked, the corners folded over.

"All of them?" I asked, doubt seeping into my voice. Mara showed me her teeth. It didn't look so much like she was smiling as it did that she was hungry.

"Yes," she said. "All of them."

She led me to one of the adjacent greenhouses, where, beneath the condensation-dusted canopy, a jungle of green seemed to have exploded. A few workers milled about, tending the plants. But they didn't even look up at us. It was like they were somewhere else entirely. Mara and I stood on the central path, where we listened to the steady alternating sound of the sprinklers coming on in different parts of the room. The air here was muggy. I began to regret the heavy sweater I'd put on that morning between my undershirt and lab coat.

Mara gestured to a few of the plants. "Cycads. Gnetophytes.

Bryophytes. Pteridophytes," she said, like that was supposed to help me. Maybe it was. Other than a few pea plants, none of them were marked. I stumbled over her last word, sounding out the syllables: "Pter-i-do-phytes?"

"Ferns."

Mara wrested the shears from my hand, knelt down in front of some sort of scrubby bush, and showed me how to clip a branch off. She dropped the gnarled thing into my palm. "Start with that," she said. Without another word she clomped down the path, leaving me there alone.

I turned to the first dog-eared page.

"*Gnetum gnemon,*" I mumbled to myself. "'A midsized tree. Evergreen. Emerald leaves, with fruitlike st-strobilus.'" I tried to commit the image of the red, clustered nuts and green-fingered branches to memory and hustled off through the tangled mass of plants at the greenhouse's center.

It took hours. By nineteen o'clock—a few hours after the other workers had departed, smiling apologetically at me—my sweater was soaked with sweat, my trousers caked with mud. I wandered in circles through the overgrown paths. When I finally dragged myself into the lab, I felt dizzy, waterlogged, and exhausted. But Mara didn't say a word when I set the book on the desk in front of her. I watched as she typed something into her computer, carefully ignoring me.

"Well?" she said at last. I gestured to the book. She spun the volume around and opened it, eyebrows ticked up in annoyance.

"Good . . . good . . . no, this isn't right. Neither is this one. This is *M. intermedia*, not *M. struthiopteris.*"

Mara pulled my clippings out, tossing them down at her desk. She scattered them over the mess of papers. Then she hefted the book in one hand and passed it to me. I extended a hesitant hand, taking it from her.

"I'll do better tomorrow . . . ," I said, my voice trembling; I almost instantly regretted how weak I sounded.

"What you'll do is go back out there and find them." *Mara's* voice was firm.

"But the time . . ."

She didn't say anything. Instead she just stared me down, flaring her nostrils.

I pressed my lips together, trying to stop my chin from trembling. Then I shuffled down the hall.

Two hours later I was finally finished—each clipping carefully pressed between the rumpled pages. My back ached from crouching low all day in the bushes; my eyes felt heavy and watery. There was a long rake of scratches across my arm from where the thorns of one plant had dug in. I dragged my muddy boots against walkway floors, so tired that I could hardly lift my feet.

But I straightened a little when the door opened and I found the once-bright lab dark. At the rear of the room, I found a torn scrap of paper taped to the dim computer monitor. I held it up to the light that spilled in from the corridor.

Couldn't wait any longer.

it read in thin, jagged script.

Will see you tomorrow.
Promptly at nine.

I clutched the heavy book in both hands, feeling rage swell my rib cage and crest in my throat. For a moment I considered slamming the field guide down against the desk, letting the legs shake, sending her papers and her precious slides flying.

But I didn't. I only stood there for a moment, breathing, shivering. My anger faded from a prickly mass of light within me to a dull, tired gray lump. I tossed the book down on Mara Stone's desk and headed home.

There were two ways I could have walked home that night: I could have cut across the pastures, then through the commerce district. It was probably the way I should have gone—the most direct route and the safest.

But it was late and I was tired. I knew the streets would be crowded with shoppers at this late hour—I'd see people I knew there, who would try to prod me into small talk about my new job.

So I went the other way, past the greenhouses and labs and down the lift, then across the second deck of the ship. There forests edged the fields of purple and yellow. The overgrown dirt paths were practically empty now except for the crickets that called to one another, their song echoing beneath the ceiling.

At the edge of a field, a scuffed wall rose up out of the soil. A single door was cut into it, and it formed an imposing rectangle of black. Inside were the engine rooms and the long corridors that looped around the now-silent machines. The dark hallways led to the large central lift, which went straight up into the districts. This section of the ship wasn't off-limits, not exactly, but it was the type of place you didn't venture off to alone except on a dare. For one thing, our parents always warned us that the engine rooms might be dangerous, all those skinny pathways suspended above the ship's inner works. For another, the engine rooms were spooky. They seemed like the kind of place where you might stumble across a ghost—if you believed in ghosts.

But I didn't. I was almost sixteen. Soon I'd be earning a wage, finding a husband, living on my own. I had no reason to be afraid of the hollow, echoing corridors. So I stepped through the narrow doorway.

When I was little, I'd been scared of the dark. I wasn't anymore. Still, these hallways were so *quiet.* The only thing that I heard was my footsteps.

Momma told me once about her great-grandmother who remembered the days when the main engine still ran. She'd hear the vibrations all the time, even at night, humming through the thin walls of her quarters.

But now we only coasted to our destination. They'd shut the main engine off ages ago, when Great-Great-Grandma was still a girl. Someday soon they'd activate the reverse thrusters, stopping us completely. But that was months away. Now everything was quiet, and there were no workers left littering these rooms. Just me and my noisy boots, shedding mud against the hollow floor. Alone, or so I thought.

Until I heard a scream.

It came from the far end of the corridor. The lights here were dim, and they flickered, bathing whole sections of the hall yellow, then black. It looked like I was alone, but there was a scramble of movement in the distance, then a shout.

"Grab him! Don't let him get away!"

I don't know what made me run *toward* the distant voices, but I

did, turning a corner and making my way down the narrowing corridors. At last I reached the end of the hall, then spilled down a step into a wide-open space. I barely managed to catch myself with my hands. Beneath my weight the metal grate swayed. I could see massive tubes spiraling down into the darkness through the gaps in the metal. They hugged the frozen engine tight, holding it aloft. There was the sound of wings fluttering from one end of the darkness to another. Apparently, bats had taken up residence there.

"What was that?" A woman's voice pulled me out of myself. I pushed my hands against the grate, scrambling to my feet.

"Nothing!" A second voice—a man's—answered. "It's nothing! Hold him down!"

The rail that bordered the walkway was thin and precarious, lit only by a series of amber lights. I took hesitant steps, following the curving pathway around the massive central column. And then I stopped, peering forward.

In the flickering light stood Aleksandra Wolff. Her wool-clad shoulders faced me. She held her hand against the hilt of her knife like a silent threat, watching as two of her comrades wrestled a man to the floor.

I crept forward. Past Aleksandra and the scuffling trio, there was another pair of men in the shadows—another guard who held a man against the ground. Long red locks hung in the citizen's face. I noted the white cord on his shoulder. Academic class. A flash of recognition lit my mind. It was the librarian's *talmid*. Vin or Van or something.

That's when I realized who his companion was. Benjamin Jacobi. The librarian, who'd spoken to me about my mother in kind tones only the day before.

He was on his knees. One of the guards held the blade of a knife against the soft underside of his jaw.

"The names! Give them to me!" the man on his left shouted.

But it was Mar Jacobi's student who answered.

"Leave him alone!"

I watched as he struggled toward his teacher, stepping into the feeble light. He was hardly even an adult. Though his compact body was covered in lean muscle, there was a curve of adolescent softness to his features.

"Get back, Hofstadter!" Aleksandra snarled. "This isn't your business!"

And then I heard Mar Jacobi's voice. It was soft, gentle. "Van, it's all right."

The boy gave an uncertain nod. But then his gaze ambled up through the dark. His eyes were green, and they seemed to glow even in the dim light. He'd seen me watching in the shadows. He mouthed words to me, forming the syllables silently with his trembling lips: "Run. Now."

Before I could obey, I heard Mar Jacobi's gentle voice rise up one last time.

"Liberty on Earth," he said. I saw the guard's blade glint as it lifted. "Liberty on Zehava!"

The knife came down.

Red. Blood.

I did my best to ignore the strange gargle of sound that followed me as I raced down the twisting hallway. When I reached the lift, I jammed my hand against the panel over and over again. But before the door could shudder open, I heard Van Hofstadter's voice barrel toward me through the silent corridors.

"Ben!" he sobbed. "Benjamin!"

I was still shaking when I stumbled through the front door of my house. The sound of Van's anguished cries kept echoing through my head. I didn't even see my father sitting stone-still at the table, waiting for me.

"Terra. You're late."

I jumped, nearly dropping my bag on Pepper. There was my father, hands flat on the tabletop, a series of covered dishes laid out before him. And he wasn't alone. Koen Maxwell sat across from him, his brown eyes wide. He seemed afraid to speak or even breathe. I knew that feeling.

"I know." I shook my head. "Something happened—"

"I don't *care* what happened. I made supper for you so we could eat like a family for once. I expect you to come home at a reasonable time."

I was doing my best to keep my cool, but I could hear the emotion cresting in my voice already. "Mara kept me late, and then I came home through the engine rooms and—"

"Don't *talk* to me about Mara Stone. And the engine rooms are no place for a girl to go off walking alone!" He slammed the flat of his hand against the table. The dishes shook. Koen's eyes got even bigger. I wondered if he regretted his vocation. But that wasn't my problem.

"I'm not a *girl!* I'm fifteen years old—"

"I don't care, Terra!" He pushed up from the table. As his chair came crashing to the floor behind him, Pepper darted up the stairs. My father towered over me. He was still so much taller than I was. "So long as you live in *my* quarters, what I say goes, and I *won't* have you roaming the ship like some hooligan!"

As if he didn't roam the ship alone *all the time!*

"Abba—" I clamped my hands over my mouth. The syllables had squeaked out like a baby's cry. Beneath my fingers my face burned with shame. My gaze shifted to Koen, who was staring down at the tabletop, pretending he was somewhere else.

My father didn't notice my embarrassment. He was still caught up in our argument. "Don't 'Abba' me! I *won't* have you roaming the ship like some worthless little slut!"

I'd heard those words before, of course. They always hit me just as hard as any blow. Between my clamped-down fingers I let out a small noise. A cry. I fought it. I didn't want to cry in front of Koen. I didn't want to let him see the way things were in our house.

So I took off running for the stairs and locked my bedroom door behind me.

I stood there for a moment, trembling. I wasn't sure if I was angry, or hurt, or terrified, or all of those things; the only thing I knew for sure was that my heart was thrumming furiously in my throat. At last I threw myself face-first into my blankets. The bed was unmade, still rumpled from the morning. My father had given up trying to get me to straighten my sheets in the morning years ago. That used to be our old battle—my messy room, my twisted blankets. Momma had been my defender.

"What's it matter what her room looks like in the morning," she asked, "so long as she gets to school on time?"

Now there was no one to defend me. Just like there had been no one to defend Benjamin Jacobi.

And now they're both dead, I thought, weeping into my pillowcase.

6

Another dream.

I was in the atrium again. I stood in a grove of pines, dressed in my plain cotton nightgown. The perfume of the air was sharp, the ground soft with needles as I padded across it. Barefoot. I should have been cold. The spring was too new for me to go around without boots on. But I didn't shiver or tremble. The air felt hot against my face.

"Terra!"

I traced the line of trees to the ceiling lights. It was Silvan's clear tenor, and it came from the treetops. I gazed up into the branches that were splayed out above me like long-fingered hands.

He gazed down between the boughs. He was wearing dark wool—the same uniform coat that Captain Wolff wore, purple and gold gleaming on his shoulder. The brass buttons were unfastened, and the front hung open. But he'd forgotten his boots. Instead he was barefoot too. I could see the pink soles of his feet, clean against the scrubby branches.

He smiled at me, then gestured for me to join him. I fixed my hands to the branches and began to shimmy up. The world bucked and swayed beneath me. But the higher I climbed, the higher the tree seemed to grow. And Silvan wasn't getting any closer.

"Wait!" I called. "Where are you going?"

"To Zehava!" he shouted, his voice laced with laughter. I paused for a moment, looking up. It wasn't right. We were on the second level of the atrium. I shouldn't have been able to see the dome here or space beyond it. But there it was, gleaming black and pinpricked with light.

"Do you see that?" I asked Silvan. Suddenly he sat beside me on my branch. I felt him there, his presence. A wave of warmth began to crest within me. But somehow I knew not to turn and look at him.

Because he'd changed. He put his three smooth, soft fingers against my cheek, and I felt how weird they were, unmarred by the ridges of fingerprints.

Who are you? he said. He didn't speak through words. I couldn't hear his voice at all. But I *felt* him, reaching out to me through the darkness.

Bashert, I thought back. Bashert. Bashert. Bashert. *Your heart's twin. Your destiny.*

But when I answered him, he recoiled from me. Surprised or shocked. I don't know. I felt it again, a hollow echo, as if he hadn't heard me at all.

Who are you? You're not supposed to be here.

I turned, but when I did, he was gone, the uncountable stars my only companions.

"Terra?"

I woke with a gasp. My room was black, lit only by the sliver of light that fell through the open door. But then my eyes adjusted, and I saw my brother's broad-shouldered silhouette against the door frame.

"Ronen," I mumbled, pulling myself up. "What are you doing here? What time is it?"

"Five thirty in the morning. You need to get up." His voice was grave. I peeled off my covers. The cold of morning hit me.

I slid from bed, fumbling for the lights. When they came on, I had to blink away the brightness. But Ronen didn't seem to notice the sudden glare. His mouth was an almost invisible line.

"There's been an accident. Benjamin Jacobi was found dead last night."

I froze in place, my feet glued to the cold metal floor. Ronen must have seen the blood drain from my face. "His *talmid* found him in the library," he offered. "Underneath a stack of books. Seems he went for one on the top shelf and the whole bookcase toppled on him."

"Is that what they're saying?" I blurted.

"What do you mean?" he asked. Lines settled in on his forehead, underneath the line of his thinning hair. That frown made him look very much like my father.

"Nothing," I said. "Never mind."

"We have to hurry, Terra," he said. "They're doing the funeral before work hours today."

I squinted into the darkness. We always held funerals soon after death so that the body would have no time to decompose. But it was *so* early.

"What if I don't want to go?" I asked, but the set of his lips, so like Abba's, silenced me.

"Abba said you have to. It's a mitzvah. He's gone to ring the bells. He asked me and Hannah to walk you to the field."

"I can walk by myself," I said, giving my head a firm shake. But Ronen only shrugged.

"Abba said we should take you."

I was nearly old enough to earn a wage—old enough, almost, to be wed. But our father *still* didn't trust me to walk from the districts out to the pastures under the cover of night. And I knew there would be no fighting with Ronen about it. He always lived just enough within our father's rules to avoid scrutiny. After Momma died, they even stopped bickering, like her death had drafted a peace between them.

But not between *us*. There was never any friendship between my brother and me.

"Fine," I said, gritting my teeth. I reached into the bottom of my dresser for my funerary clothes—an old set I'd inherited from Momma, but they would have to do—and huffed off toward the bathroom to change.

Another funeral, another white-wrapped body lowered into the ground. I stood at the back with Rachel, chewing my nails.

We went together to the edge of the grave, knelt in the dirt, and threw handfuls of black soil down. When I rose up from the grass, a pair of bright green eyes caught mine. Van Hofstadter. He was standing at the other end of the unmarked grave, holding a child in his arms. It must have been his son—red hair curled up from his neck, a shock of color in the dim predawn light. But even though Van clutched the little boy to his chest and even though his wife leaned against him, his attention was fixed on me.

Those eyes flared a wild warning.

"Are you okay?" Rachel asked, leaning close. She went to grab my hand, but I didn't want to let her see how mine was shaking. I pretended not to notice, wiping my palm against my trousers.

"Last night," I said, "I saw him, with Mar Jacobi, on the way home from work."

"Oh, that's so *sad*," she replied. "That must have been right before he died, right?"

I turned to look at her. Her eyes were large and shining. Everything was so *simple* for Rachel—black and white.

"Must have been," I said quickly as I started off across the field.

After the funeral Rachel asked me to go with her to Mar Jacobi's quarters to pay our respects.

Normally, it wouldn't have even been a question. No matter how many times my father had tried to force me to become a proper, respectful daughter, I just wasn't that kind of person. I was bored at weddings, at parties, at harvest celebrations. At school I sighed and doodled in the margins of my notebooks. And funerals were even worse. Everyone always stared at me sidelong, waiting for some morsel of wisdom to spill from the mouth of the girl whose mother had died.

But this funeral was different. I had business to attend to.

As soon as we stepped through the door, Rachel rushed forward, kissing the wet cheeks of Giveret Jacobi. Rachel shoved a small box of homemade cookies into the woman's hands. I don't know when she'd had time to bake. The sun had just barely begun to rise.

But the curtains were drawn tight, bathing the corners of their quarters in inky black. Even the mirrors were covered, holey sheets thrown over them. Mar Jacobi's children sat on low stools. Their round faces were blank, as stiff as concrete statues. I saw his daughter, a fawn-haired child who picked at the embroidery on her woven cushion. I suddenly felt like the metal floor was sinking beneath me, like the entire ship had tipped right out of space. Of course, that was impossible. I crouched down beside her.

"I'm sorry," I offered, shrugging as I said it.

"Why?" she asked. Then she looked at me, her gaze piercing. Her eyes were pale gray, nothing like her father's. "*You* didn't kill him."

"That's right," I said after a moment, swallowing the lump in my throat. It was almost funny. I had said those words myself many, many times before.

I didn't find what I was looking for in the Jacobis' dark, crowded quarters. I thought he would be there—Van Hofstadter, the librarian's copper-haired student. But there was no sign of him with the other men, who shared raunchy stories of Benjamin's younger days. And he didn't stand beside the old ladies who clucked their tongues over losing such a fine citizen so young. Finally Rachel leaned forward, squeezing my hand.

"I have to go," she said. Her mouth formed an apologetic smile. "I need to get ready for work, you know?"

I *did* know. I had work to attend to too. But for some reason I couldn't bring myself to take off for the labs, not yet. Not with so many questions weighing heavy on my heart.

"I'll see you soon," I told her.

After she left, I went outside and sat down on the Jacobis' front steps to watch dawn light up the districts. Someone's rooster had started crowing. Sparrows were waking to life in the barely budded trees that lined the starboard streets. The birds didn't know any better, that the sky overhead was false, that we'd carried them so, so far away from home.

"Terra Fineberg."

I hadn't even realized how my gaze had strayed to the yellowing ceiling panels, until Van's voice called out to me. I swiveled my head toward the sound. He stood right at the end of the Jacobis' front walk, looking like a ghost in his mourning clothes. His long hair veiled his face, but I could see that he'd been crying. His eyes were sunken and ringed with red.

"You didn't even know Benjamin," he said. A note of accusation rang in his voice. I stumbled to my feet, fixing my hand against the metal railing, whose surface flaked off paint beneath my palm.

"I knew him," I protested, rushing down the steps. "We spoke the other day on the lift. He wanted me to come see him in the library."

Van pressed his lips together. "He wasn't supposed to do that. You're just a child."

"I'm not a child!" But my words were whined. I think we both knew how false they were.

"You're not sixteen yet, *Talmid* Fineberg." And then he added, in case I had any doubts: "And you didn't see anything last night in the engine rooms."

Now my cheeks burned. I lifted my chin, looking squarely at Van. He wasn't very tall, though his shoulders were broad, imposing beneath white cloth. "I *did* see," I whispered, as much to myself as to Van. "I know I did."

"I don't know what you're talking about." He started taking wide steps toward the door.

I waited until his hand closed around the doorknob to say it. Standing tall, I threw my tangled hair over my shoulders.

"Liberty on Earth."

He froze, his fingers tense against the door. But he didn't turn or speak.

"Liberty on Zehava. I *heard*, Van. I heard him say it. Treason. Those words are treason. They taught us in school that—"

"Shh!" Van gave a hiss. His eyes were narrowed down to slivers, jaded flints like broken glass. But then the clock tower bells rang out nine o'clock. At the sound, low and droning, Van's stiff posture began to soften. He started to shake his head.

"Van? Terra?"

We both turned. Standing on the street behind me was Koen Maxwell. His pale cheeks were ruddy, his shaggy hair disheveled. He'd already changed out of his mourning garb, dressing himself in the familiar wool and corduroy of the clock keeper. The heavy coat fit him poorly. His long, pale wrists showed beneath the cuffs.

"Koen. Shouldn't you be at work?" I squinted at him, wondering what that broad smile was doing lighting up his face.

"Shouldn't you?" he asked, letting out a small, awkward laugh. I stared at him. This was no time for laughter.

"Yeah," I said. "I suppose I should."

Van's fingers were still curled around the doorknob, but it seemed he couldn't make his feet move forward. Finally his eyes darted up at me, sharp and hard.

"Remember what I said, Terra. You're a child. You didn't see anything."

With that, he threw the door open and slammed it behind him. Koen watched him leave.

"I wonder what that was about," he said. I looked at him, at his rumpled hair and his jangly smile. He had the sort of kind, open features that made you want to tell him all your secrets. It was a dangerous sort of face.

"I have no idea," I said, and hustled down the empty street.

7

My second day at work was hardly any better than my first. Mara kept me running through the greenhouses, snipping branches, pressing them between the pages of the field guide. I kept turning down the wrong corridor. Before I knew it, I stood lost in a hothouse full of fruit trees, or an enclosed field of purple grains. After only a few hours sweat poured down my face in little rivers. Thorns had worked their way into the weave of my lab coat. That morning, after the dreams, and the funeral, and my visit to the Jacobis' home, I was exhausted, too, and it felt like my head was wrapped in cotton gauze. When I stopped inside the lab before lunch, offering Mara the heavy tome, I almost didn't notice how she looked at me—her close-set eyes narrowed, as if she'd been chewing over some idea.

"Did you know him?" she asked, tossing the book onto her desk without looking at it. It fell with a heavy thud.

"Know who?"

"Jacobi. You know." She waved her hand at me. "The dead guy."

Her thin lips curled, showing her pale gums. Her pointed jaw was tight. I wondered if this might be a test, sent by Van Hofstadter himself. But I knew that was a ridiculous idea—what use would Mara have for someone like Van? She hardly had any patience for me.

"No, not really." It wasn't a lie, of course, so I shrugged and shoved my hands down into the pockets of my coat. Mara studied me.

"Good," she said at last. "Good. You're young, Terra. There's no telling the kinds of wind that might sweep you up."

"What do you mean?"

"Jacobi and his ilk. Rabble-rousers, all of them. Convinced the golden light of justice shines right down on their empty heads." Mara snorted laughter. Deep inside my pockets I dug my fingernails into my palms, trying to stop myself from remembering the impassioned words that had spilled, quick as blood, from Mar Jacobi's mouth.

"Don't worry," I said, though my throat and lips felt dry, my tongue huge and awkward in my mouth. "I've never been much of a joiner."

"Good!" Mara said, and she gave my shoulder a hearty thump. I swayed on my feet from the force of it. "A woman after my own heart."

I was surprised to come home that night to find our quarters bright and busy, clouded by the perfume of frying onions and garlic and spice. Hannah stood behind the stove, stirring something into a pan of hot oil. And my brother was at the galley table peeling pale carrots.

"Terra!" Hannah said, smiling wide at my arrival as I hung up my bag by the door. Pepper didn't run to greet me like he usually did, begging for food as though he might starve to death at any moment. Apparently, his belly was already full—he'd curled up to sleep at the end of the table.

"What are you guys doing here?" I asked. I peeled off my mud-stained lab coat and draped it over one of the chairs, watching my brother as he sliced a long, gnarled root in two.

I'd intended my words for Ronen, but he didn't even look up at me. Instead Hannah gave a happy hum and answered for both of them.

"We thought we'd come by and make you two dinner. Thought

you might need it, after what happened this morning."

My mind drifted to the memory of Mar Jacobi's body swaddled tightly in white cloth. As if I could forget it for even a moment. "Oh," I said. "That."

Hannah looked at me meaningfully. Then she brought over a bowl of ground lamb and set it before me.

"No one eats free in my kitchen," she said with a wink.

This isn't your kitchen, I thought. But I went and washed my hands anyway.

I worked bread crumbs into the raw meat, mashing it all together with my hands. The rhythm of work felt almost soothing. For a moment I could believe that Momma was still alive, that she, instead of Hannah, stood at the counter kneading bread. But the tenuous peace was soon broken.

"How do you like your job so far?" Hannah asked.

I grunted, letting my hands fall still in the bowl of meat. "I don't know," I said. "How do you like *your* job?"

My brother stopped chopping carrots. "Terra!" he said, but Hannah just let out a laugh.

"Oh, it's no big deal, Ro. It's not like you loved your vocation when you were fifteen."

"You didn't?" I frowned, but he only stared down at the cutting board. Hannah sauntered over to him and scraped the cut carrots into a dented metal bowl. She let her fingers alight on his shoulder, then gave her eyelashes a flutter.

"Of course not. Your brother whined about it for months. It wasn't until he started earning his wages that he seemed to see any use in it."

Ronen's shoulders lifted, tense. I watched as he squirmed under my gaze. I had never heard him complain about his job, but we hardly ever spoke back then. Not that we spoke much now, either.

"What about you?" I asked, turning to look at Hannah. She was stirring the carrots into the pan, her full lips pursed and thoughtful.

"What about me?"

"Do you love your job? Did the Council find you your *true calling* and all of that?" I regretted my words almost as soon as I said them. Hannah's *father* was a Council member. I should have known better than to disparage his judgment. But she didn't seem to care. She just shrugged.

"At first I hated it. Cartography, you know? What kind of job is that? I wanted to design clothes, like that rubbish uniform they gave you." She nodded toward the long lab coat that hung from the chair. "But after a while I came to like my work. I'll be one of the first humans to set foot on Zehava. That has to be worth something, right?"

"Sure," I said softly. "I guess."

"Don't worry, Terra," Hannah said, walking over. She took the bowl of ground lamb out from under my hands, leaving my greasy fingers frozen over the table. "You'll come to like your job. It's not easy for any of us at first."

I was about to protest that it wasn't true—that so far as I knew, Rachel had fallen into her new job duties just fine. And what about Silvan Rafferty? Surely taking on Captain Wolff's mantle was no struggle for *him*. But before I could, our front door burst open again, and my father came clattering through.

His steps were clumsy, hard against the metal floor. He'd been drinking. But he wasn't alone. Koen Maxwell stepped past him, setting a steadying hand on Abba's arm.

"Easy, there," Koen said. And then he lifted his soulful brown eyes, smiling at us. "Hello!"

I rushed over to the sink to wash my hands again, rubbing the sliver of tallowy soap between my palms. We all watched, silent for a moment, as Abba stumbled forward. He surveyed the scene.

"What's all this about?" he growled.

Ronen and I exchanged a look, our eyebrows lifting in a wordless agreement. We'd keep out of Abba's way, as we always did when he got like this. But Hannah didn't know Abba like we did.

"Arran," she said. "Come, sit. I'm making stuffed cabbage. Your favorite, isn't it?"

My father grumbled something incomprehensible. He looked up

at Koen, who stood by the door with his hands in his pockets. "You, boy. Get me my wine."

Koen shrugged helplessly. "I don't know where it is," he said.

I rolled my eyes. "I'll get it."

I crouched down beside the icebox to fetch Abba's wine out of its hiding place. I tipped it into one of our glass tumblers, handing it off to my father.

"We had a hard day," Koen offered. "We received some bad news from the Council."

"Oh?" Hannah tilted her head to one side. Her black curls spilled against her collarbone. Then the frying pan gave a hiss, and she scraped her spatula hastily over it. My father drank down a mouthful of wine.

"Winter," Abba grunted. "They're moving us back to winter soon."

We all went quiet at that.

"That can't be right," my brother protested. "Spring's only just started."

My father stared down into his sour wine, half gone already. He didn't answer, but then, he didn't have to. Hannah answered for him.

"Spring as we know it won't exist on Zehava," she said. "It's too cold. The Council must want—"

"—to get us used to winter." My father finished her sentence for her. Then he wiped his mouth against the hairy back of his hand. It left a purple stain there.

"When I was a boy," he said, "they still gave us a few weeks of summer. They let us camp out in the atrium."

None of us spoke—not even Hannah. She stood still over the stove, smoke drifting up into her face.

"Now no spring?" my father asked. And when he spoke again, his voice broke. "Who the hell wants to live on a planet without any spring?"

"No!" I said, slamming my fist against the counter. On the table Pepper jumped. The force behind my words surprised even me. "No, it's not right."

"Terra," my father said, a dark warning in his voice. But I didn't hear it. I slammed my fist against the counter again.

"It's not *right!*" I said. I thought of Momma's flowers, of the walks we'd taken through the dome on spring nights. I thought of the artificial sunlight and how it warmed our faces even as the nights turned to dusk. I thought of never feeling that again. "Why do they get to decide? It's not right!"

"Enough!" Abba roared. He drained the tumbler in one gulp, then slammed it down against the table. He ambled to his feet, stumbling toward me. "I won't listen to treasonous words under my roof!"

"But you said—" I began to protest, backing up until my spine pressed against the metal wall. I heard Ronen say my name in a low tone. He was warning me away from Abba, warning me about what waited for me if I continued down this path.

He didn't have to. I knew the dangers. Before my father could lift a hand to me, I shoved past him. Then I shouldered by Koen, too, groping for the door handle.

"I'm out of here," I said. "Enjoy your cabbage."

I slammed the front door shut behind me.

I tumbled past our front gate, my footsteps brisk against the cobblestone. The twilight air was chilly. I crossed my arms tight over my chest to keep the wind away. Maybe my father had already turned the dials up in the clock tower's control room, moving us toward autumn before we even knew what was happening. I wondered what the birds would do once the frost came in. They'd only just begun to lace their nests with downy feathers. Would their eggs hatch in the winter? Or would the baby birds freeze to death inside their brittle shells? I wondered if the Council even cared.

Liberty on Earth.

The words rang out in my mind. I wondered if this was what Mar Jacobi had died for—for spring and baby birds and the right to live our lives the way we wanted. In school we'd learned about the different forms of government. Democracies. Parliamentary republics. Military juntas. The names stuck out in my mind, but I could hardly recall what they meant. Something about voting, maybe. I'd memorized the definitions only long enough to pass our tests, then I'd quickly forgotten them.

Liberty on Zehava.

I knew the Council was meant to rule long past landing. After all, they'd been the ones to keep our little ship afloat these five hundred years, hadn't they? Rebbe Davison always said you didn't change horses midstream. Silvan and his cronies, Council sons all, had shared a hearty laugh. But I hadn't understood. What would a horse be doing underwater?

"Terra, wait up!"

I'd reached the end of our street by then. In the circle of light cast down from the corner streetlamp, I stopped and turned. Koen was rushing toward me, his dark hair tossing in the wind. It felt lately like wherever I went, there he was, following me like a lanky shadow.

"What do you want, Koen?" I asked. He came to stand breathlessly beside me. His cheeks were pink, though I couldn't tell whether it was from the cold or because of how fast he'd been running. Or maybe he always looked like that—red cheeked and sheepish.

"I wanted to see if you were okay," he said. I shoved my hair behind my ear so that I could better see his face—his strong jaw, his narrow nose, his pale skin, scattered with freckles.

"Sure," I said. "I'm fine. Happens all the time. It's nothing new."

He smiled at me like I'd cracked a joke, but I hadn't meant it to be funny. I turned toward the darkening street. The lights were coming on in the town houses, and they cast mottled yellow squares down from the curtained windows.

"I don't know why you keep coming home with him," I said. "It's not like it worked out so well the first time."

Koen chuckled. "I come because your father asks me." He waited a beat. His smile didn't falter, not a centimeter. "I come because it beats going home."

"Oh?" I asked, and turned my face up to him. Behind his grin I now saw the shadow of something else. But I couldn't quite read it.

"Your dad is nothing compared to my parents. They're at it all the time. It's like I might as well be invisible."

"Better invisible than a target," I said. Koen only shook his head.

"You might think that, but I don't."

Koen was a full head taller than I was, almost as tall as Abba. But he was slender and gawky. He had big hands, big feet, a big, smiling mouth. I thought about the night before—about Mar Jacobi's death and the way he'd cried out as he'd collapsed on the floor. I had the sudden urge to tell Koen about all of it, to let the weight of the secret spill from my lips. But I didn't know how.

"Koen," I said at last, dropping my voice to a murmur, "do you ever think about 'liberty'?"

Koen's coltish eyes darted left, then right before returning to me. "No," he said, in a tone that I didn't quite believe. "I don't think about that. All I think about is how I wish I could be normal."

I dropped my gaze. My throat tightened, full of tears. I didn't know why I ever tried to tell anybody anything. It was better to just keep it all locked inside, a secret.

"Oh," I said.

I felt pressure across my back. Koen had rested his broad hand against my shoulder.

"I don't know about you," he said gently, turning me toward home, "but I'm starving. That stuffed cabbage sure would hit the spot right now."

I forced a feeble smile to my lips. "Sure, Koen," I said as we walked together. "Sounds great."

Over the weeks that followed I tried to forget what had happened in the engine rooms—tried to wipe away the memory of a man's throat and how it had torn open like paper, and how I had seen, and how I had done nothing. If Van wanted me to be quiet, then I would. But the dark days sent my mind into a tailspin. Autumn set in, and there were hardly any green leaves to turn gold. Instead half-budded flowers browned and froze without blooming, and most of the fields that stretched out beneath the atrium dome lay fallow, with nothing to harvest. It was an autumn of root vegetables and pickled things and lots and lots of cabbage, and even though we all complained about it, there was nothing to be done. This early winter was, of course, for our own good, for the good of the *Asherah* and her passengers.

Personally, I thought I deserved it. The frost. The meager meals. Hunger and cold were easy—sensations I could grapple with, so much simpler than guilt.

The mornings were frigid. I piled on layer after layer every morning before work. Long, holey undershorts, torn stockings, tall socks. That autumn I began to outgrow most of my old sweaters, so I went into my father's room one day when he was working late and filched all of Momma's cold-weather clothes. I hated to do it, but I wouldn't begin to collect my wages until I turned sixteen, and I knew that it would be an argument if I asked. They all smelled like her, that strange mixture of soap and dusty flour, still, after all these years, and for that I almost couldn't stand to wear them—covering her smell with my smell, washing the last trace of her away. My father must have noticed that I had replaced my old threadbare clothing with her better stuff, but the only acknowledgment was a long, blank look one morning at breakfast.

We spoke less and less. After dark my father disappeared to the pubs or into his room with a glass and a bottle. I avoided home as best I could. Every night, I took off for the dome. I stayed there until it was too dark to see, filling my sketchbook with rough images of the flowers that occupied my daylight hours. It was better outside, even in the cold. Because within the gray walls of our quarters, silence had become a constant companion. It sat beside us at breakfast and laid itself down between me and Pepper late at night.

But not when Koen was around. He stopped by for supper at least once a week, filling the empty chasm of our lives with his broadlipped smile, his awkward laughter, his questions for my father, his jokes for me. Abba was a different person when Koen was there. He sat straighter and spoke in a tone that was almost mild. He rarely angered, and when he did, it was only ever at me and quick to pass. But I did my best to give him few reasons to be mad. Usually, I just listened while he and Koen discussed their duties.

They talked about how to turn the seasons and how to transition us into the coming frost. The way they talked about it made it sound more like an art than a science. Like how a painter layers one color over another so that the depth contained in all that pigment can show through. I said that once over supper, blurted the words between bites of boiled potatoes. My father watched me for a moment, then calmly set down his fork.

"It's nothing so soft as an art," he said. I was surprised, too, by how *patient* he sounded. Like my old dad was back and ready to teach me all about being a proper Asherati. "We're forcing our bodies—your body too, Terra—into new patterns. Why do you think we take these pills every day with supper?" He gestured to the little white dish of capsules that sat on the edge of his plate. "You wouldn't sleep otherwise. Humans weren't made for twenty-seven-hour days, for forty-six-week years, with three seasons. Everything must be factored in. It's no art." He paused, eying me for a moment. "I'd think as Mara Stone's *talmid* you'd know that. What's that woman teaching you, anyway?"

It wasn't a question I was meant to answer. He laughed at me, taking a hearty gulp of wine. But inside I recoiled. What had I learned from Mara so far, on all those days when she shipped me off to the greenhouses to keep me out of her hair? The names of plants, sure—I could identify a clipping of almost anything in the main greenhouse. But otherwise she hardly spoke to me, giving me only terse commands.

"Oh, I don't know that it's not an art," Koen interjected. He was blushing fiercely, bright red mottling his throat and ears. But his wide gaze was sharp, challenging my father. I braced myself. It was the kind of thoughtless comment that always led to an argument for me—but my father tilted his bald head toward Koen, listening.

"W-with all due respect, sir," he began, stammering at first, though his words grew firmer as he went on, "I think Terra was speaking metaphorically. And I think she meant it as a compliment. She's not so far off, anyway, right? Like good art, our work is the sort that looks effortless if you don't know any better. It's part of the background of everyone's lives. It doesn't call attention to itself. To most of them I'm sure we're nothing more than bell ringers. And frankly, I wouldn't have it any other way. Let them think less of us. If our work went around announcing itself, it would mean that we'd done something *wrong*."

My father gave a sort of grunt of agreement. He stared down at his meal. I could feel the grin spread across my face.

"Thank you," I mouthed soundlessly to Koen. His brown eyes shone.

Those days, no matter how cold the evenings got, I always took the long way home from the labs. Part of me could almost feel the engine rooms calling out to me—the dark, warm hallways that spiraled up, straight to home. But I knew now that the warmth was deceptive, a simple trick. The open sky of the dome was much safer. There, lit blue in the dimming light, the last of the fieldworkers wrestled with their plows, stopped, raised their hands to me in greeting. Once I would have resented that intrusion on my own peace and quiet. Now I was desperate for a friendly face. I smiled and waved.

Still, I moved fast through the pastures. The frigid air numbed my ears even through the curtain of my hair. I couldn't feel my nose. *But at least I'm alive*, I told myself, grimacing. Thoughts of Mar Jacobi always slipped into my mind at the strangest times.

Over the half-bare branches that dotted the fields, the clock bells rang out. I wondered what Abba was teaching Koen and felt a jealous wave at the thought. Mara hardly spoke to me, much less invited me for dinner.

I didn't have to wonder for long. Koen's voice called out to me over the soundless wind.

"Terra!"

I stopped, turned. As I saw the pale-faced boy who rushed toward me, I found myself smiling. Koen's grin was almost obscenely broad over the knot of his scarf.

"Koen," I said. "Hey."

"Walking home?" he asked. "Mind some company?"

I shrugged. I didn't mind. In fact, I felt a small, happy thrill at the thought of walking beside him, arm to arm. I was glad that our faces were both already red from cold. I didn't want to embarrass myself.

"Not ringing the bells tonight?" I asked, groping for something to talk about as we started through the scrubby grass. The last of the chimes was just ringing out. Nineteen tolls for nineteen o'clock.

"Nah. I promised my parents I'd be home in time for dinner. You know, 'as long as you're under my roof'—that sort of thing." Koen flashed his teeth at me. But I found myself frowning.

"Must be nice," I mumbled, "that they care."

Koen looked at me sidelong. "Terra," he said, "your father cares."

I let out a small white breath of laughter.

"Cares about me. Right. You see the way that he is."

But Koen just gave his head a shake, tousling his shaggy hair.

"He talks about you all the time. I know he's hard on you, but at least he *sees* you. My parents want me home tonight only because they're having friends over for dinner. They act so damned *perfect* when strangers are around, but it's an act. All they care about is how much they hate each other. I don't know why they don't just get divorced. I mean, I know it's rare, and they'd have no one but old widows to marry. But it's better to be alone than to be miserable all the time."

I thought about my parents, about how they were before Momma got sick. When I was little, she giggled and blushed at him over dinner. He'd spin her around the room when she was cooking, and bring home flowers for her when he knew she was working late. And then I thought about the sounds I sometimes heard down the hall at night, and blushed.

"My father loved my mother. He said she was his *bashert*." There were stories on the ship, stories of marriages so perfect that it was like being wedded to your second soul. That's what my father always said he lost. His other half. "Maybe that's the problem. He hasn't been the same since she died. I mean, he's always been strict. All about duty, about doing your job and *tikkun olam* and all of that. But he used to be nice sometimes. . . . He didn't used to be like this."

I felt a lump rising in my throat. I swallowed hard, cast my eyes down at the dark ground in front of us.

"Terra . . ." I was surprised to feel his hand touch my hand. He pried my cold-numbed fingers straight, slipping his palm against mine. "It's okay. It'll be okay."

It was the first time I'd held a boy's hand. I looked down at his fingers. They were narrow and long, prettier than mine. My nails were caked with dirt. His were clean and trimmed short. When I stopped in the path, his eyes were big with concern.

I saw something in those eyes. Not just flecks of gold, reflecting the growing starlight. I saw how he was open to me—how he wanted me to be happy, how he wanted me to be safe. I found the words tumbling from my lips before I could even stop them.

"I saw them kill Mar Jacobi. It wasn't an accident. The captain's guard. They killed him. They slit his throat. Down in the engine rooms. They—"

"Terra!" Koen pulled his hand from mine as though ashamed. I didn't know why. There was no one here but sheep, and even they slept, hunkered down in their woolen winter coats. Koen gave his head a shake. When he spoke again, his voice was ragged.

"I wish you hadn't told me that."

He could have balled his hand into a fist and punched me in the gut. That would have hurt me less.

"I thought . . . ," I began. But the words petered out. I didn't know *what* I'd thought. Koen watched me for a moment, his brows knitted up. At last his expression softened.

"Oh, Terra," he said. "It's all right."

To my surprise he pulled me to him in a sudden embrace. He was much taller than me. My face was smashed into the itchy front of his heavy jacket. But it felt *good* to lean on him like that, to feel his heart beating through his clothes, to feel his arms around me.

"It'll be okay," he said again. "As long as you tell no one else, we'll be safe."

I found myself nodding. Desperately, frantically nodding. This was what I'd wanted, wasn't it? To trust Koen. To let him keep me safe.

Finally, satisfied, he let me go. His expression was different now— not open, like it once had been, but murky, inscrutable.

"I should go," he said, his words coming out in almost a whisper. "My parents."

"Sure," I said. I stuffed my hands down into my pockets. I didn't know what to say or how to look. So I just forced a smile. "I'll see you later, Koen."

He only gave a small nod, then rushed out ahead of me, disappearing into the dark.

8

Soon the first frost came. On that cold morning I rose early, bundling myself beneath layers and layers of clothes. When I arrived at the lab, I found Mara already buried in her work. She chewed on the inside of her cheek and muttered about cellular damage, while peering through the microscope.

I headed for the bookshelf, ready to grab one of the field guides and head out again. But her cool gaze snapped up at me.

"Hold on, *talmid.*"

I turned, my hand lingering on the spine of the book.

"I'm meeting with the captain today," she said. Then she reached into one of her pockets and pulled out a scrap of paper. I took it hesitantly—it was stained with soil and bore her cramped, tiny handwriting. Three titles, each one written in Old American. They'd taught us how to read it in school. Most of the students struggled—the letters had shifted in five hundred years; the vowels had changed, creating the language we now called Asheran. But I'd always been good with dead languages. I read the titles easily: *Joy of Cooking. The Essential New York Times Cookbook. Charcuterie and French Pork Cookery.*

"I don't understand," I said. "Cookbooks? What's this have to do with botany?"

"It has to do with keeping you out of my hair while I meet with Wolff."

"Oh," I said. I stared down at Mara's cramped handwriting as if I could divine some sort of answer from her scratchy print. "What . . . what are you meeting with her about?"

"One of the probes we sent out to Zehava was due to return yesterday. We should be getting soil samples. Atmospheric readings. Five hundred years of building theoretical models of the plants we might sow on that damned planet. It won't be until we get those probe results that our *real* work can begin." She paused, bemused. "And I don't have time to deal with a *talmid* scuttling about under my feet."

"Don't worry," I mumbled. "I'd rather not be around for it. Captain Wolff gives me the creeps." I grimaced, regretting my treasonous words the moment they passed my lips. But Mara only let out a bark of laughter.

"Good. Never trust politicians. They don't understand the work we do and don't want to. They twist science to their own ends. If you learn anything from me, I want it to be that."

"But, Mara," I said, smiling faintly. "I don't understand. Cookbooks?"

"Use your brain, girl," she said. "Figure it out for yourself. Now off with you. Go." She shooed me toward the door.

The library's spicy perfume of book glue and leather covers greeted me. It was a familiar smell—the scent of all of those hours spent reading by light filtered through stained glass. The tall, colorful windows depicted scenes from our history: the asteroid's approach, the boarding of the *Asherah*, the signing of our contract. From the cracked blue-green globe of Earth, the atrium light came spilling through.

Mara's list of titles clutched against my palm, I approached the checkout desk. Van Hofstadter was right where I expected him to be, clacking away at the computer terminal. But when I saw he wasn't alone, the blood drained from my fingers.

Koen was there too, his arms crossed over his chest, loose laughter playing at his lips. I couldn't believe it. They were whispering to each other like old friends. But as I stepped close, both boys fell silent.

Koen's expression changed, flattening. I felt a stab of something, a sour feeling in my chest that I couldn't quite name.

"Hey," I said to him. Though I'd lowered my voice to library levels, he *must* have heard me. But Koen only cast his dark eyes toward the ground beneath his feet. He pawed his neck with his hand.

"Can I help you?" Van asked. When I glanced over to Koen, he looked away, so I passed Van the list of books. My fingers trembled, but we both ignored it.

"I need these."

"You can't take the originals out of here." Van spoke to me like we were strangers, like we'd never spoken before. Like this was only business. "You have to read them in the library."

"I know!" I said, too loud, then scowled. I lowered my voice. "That's fine."

Van's mouth tightened, little lines forming around his lips. Without another word he disappeared into the closed stacks behind him.

The silence was unbearable. It seemed to ring out, cutting right through my body. Koen's long neck was turned away from me; his unruly bangs shadowed his face. I thought of all those suppers with my father—thought of the way his arms had felt around me only a few days before.

"Did I do something wrong?" Worry mounted in my voice. Koen winced, his features contorting as though in pain.

"I'm trying to help you," he said. "I just wanted to take care of—"

He cut off midsentence, his head snapping up. Van had returned, a stack of books in his arms. I stared down at the counter as Van began to enter the call numbers into the computer terminal.

"My name is Terra Fineberg," I said, my tone hazy. "And my cNumber is—"

"I know who you are," Van said. His upper lip lifted like I was a piece of rancid meat. "You're Terra Fineberg. The girl who can't keep her mouth shut."

It was like he'd found a seam in my skin and torn it open with his fingernails; all my breath came out in one long hiss.

But then Koen spoke up. "Van! You promised."

Van glowered. But Koen wasn't looking at him. He was looking at me.

"Don't worry, Terra," he murmured. His voice almost broke. I'm sure if I spoke, mine would have too. "Van promised me that he wouldn't do anything. I told him you wouldn't tell anyone else, that you can be trusted. Right?"

My cheeks burned. My mind was filled with a cacophony of questions and not a single answer.

"I don't understand. Why can't we tell someone?" I demanded.

But when my gaze swept between the boys, I saw how closely both watched me. Van's eyes smoldered, silently threatening. When I spoke again, my words came out high and weird. "I won't tell anyone. There's nothing to tell anyway, right?"

I saw Koen crack a thin smile.

"See, Van?" he said. "I told you we could trust her."

The corner of Van's mouth twitched up. He pushed the books toward me across the counter. I grabbed for them.

"If you say so," he said. Then he turned away from me.

I gave Koen a small, brave smile. He solemnly looked back. Hefting the books in my arms, I started for the second floor, where the study desks waited. But their voices trailed after me as I made my way up the spiraling staircase.

"If she told you," Van was saying, "there's no telling who else knows."

I felt my grip on the books tighten until my knuckles turned white. He didn't trust me to keep a simple secret—and why should he? I was nothing but a weak little girl. A snitch.

Shaking my head at myself, I hurried up the stairs.

Over supper that night I watched as my father forked potatoes into his mouth and chewed slowly, the way that sheep in the atrium fields chewed the long grass. Pepper circled the legs of my chair, meowing incessantly, but we both ignored him. I waited for my father to speak.

When he didn't, I set my fork down at the edge of my plate and cleared my throat.

"I saw Koen today," I said, desperate to find any words with which to plug up the silence. "In the library."

He didn't look up. "What were you doing in the library?"

"Mara sent me to do some research."

My father took a long drink from one of the dented metal tumblers, set it down again, took another bite. I let out a sigh. Without Koen around, talking to Abba was like slogging through some sort of muddy field—I wanted to move forward, but the soles of my boots kept getting stuck.

My father finally paused in his chewing. "I gave him the day off. I suppose that Stone was trying to get you out of her hair as well? I saw her skulking around the captain's stateroom."

"That's right. She said you were getting probe results in today. From Zehava."

My father wiped the back of his broad hand against his lips. "That was the plan. Captain Wolff said that there's been some sort of delay in the probe's return. They're sending out a second one."

I stared at him, thinking about how Mara had said she'd been waiting for the results—waiting her whole career, from the sound of it. "That's strange," I said.

My father shrugged. "Who knows? Maybe there were storms on

Zehava. Maybe the original coordinates were incorrect. There's no telling."

I nodded uncertainly. My father narrowed his eyes at me.

"The library. I hope he wasn't schmoozing with that librarian again."

"Van Hofstadter?" I said faintly, fixing my hands to the edge of the table. But their grip felt uncertain; my palms had begun to sweat. "Why, what's wrong with him?"

My father didn't answer. He only picked up his fork again, then rapped the tines against the table—one time, two, three. The gesture was made all the more nerve-racking by the way the vein on his forehead bulged.

"There have been rumors," my father said. He spun his fork around, stabbing his overcooked potato with it.

"Rumors?" I asked. But my father only grunted through a mouthful of mushy tubers.

"I forget sometimes," he said at last.

I almost didn't dare to breathe. "Forget what?"

"That you're not your mother."

With that, my father put down his fork and rose on heavy feet. He crossed the galley and came to stand just behind me. Reaching down, he touched the blue cord on my uniform. His trembling hands moved slowly.

"If you're a good girl, Terra," he began. His voice sounded

strained, pinched. "If you stay out of trouble and do your duty, and if you're kind to Koen and treat him well, then I'm sure everything will be fine."

There was a long silence. A lump was rising in my throat. I didn't want to try to dislodge it. I thought doing that might break the spell.

"Koen's my student," my father went on. It was hard for me to hear his words over my thrumming heartbeat. "And you're my daughter. I care about you both, very much."

"I know," I lied, my voice a hollow rattle in my chest.

"You need to be careful of who you get mixed up with. Both of you."

"Okay."

He lifted his hands off my shoulders. One of my own hands darted up, rubbing the warm, clammy spot where his fingers had been.

"Good," my father said. Even though his plate was still half full, he started toward the stairwell. Then he paused at the bottom, grimacing. I couldn't be sure if he was talking to me or to himself.

"I won't lose you too," he said.

"Lose me?" I asked. But by the time my words moved past my throat, my father had disappeared upstairs, Pepper padding up into the darkness behind him.

The next morning Mara was a whirlwind of fury. I watched from the doorway as she stomped from one end of the lab to the other, pulling books from their shelves, then tossing them over her shoulder. They spun, then landed on the ground, splayed open. Her heavy boots trampled right through a tray of seedlings, but she didn't even seem to notice.

"Good morning?" I called as the door shivered shut behind me. Across the room the little woman let out a desperate laugh.

"I wouldn't call it *that!*"

Mara's forehead was a mess of wrinkles. She rubbed her hand over her brow as if her fingers could smooth them out.

"It's not you, Terra. The probe didn't come in yesterday. Or so the captain says."

"I know," I said. I hung back by the door, feeling more than a little afraid to come close. "My father told me. They're sending out another one. I'm sure it'll be okay."

She laughed again, but there was no humor there. "I'll bet you a million gelt that that one goes out and doesn't return either."

"They pay you well." I snorted. "But not that well."

I expected Mara to laugh. It had happened before—well, not *laughter.* Not quite. But I'd gotten her to smile at me once or twice. Now, nothing. Silence crackled between us.

"I don't have time for this, *talmid*," she said at last. She riffled through the papers on her desk. "Take a sick day. Go home. You're not wanted here."

I started to turn toward the sliding door. But I stopped halfway, peering over my shoulder at the botanist.

"Diet," I said, softly but clearly. I saw her angle her chin up at that, saw how she was listening. So I went on. "You had me read those cookbooks to demonstrate the variety of diet on Earth. It was nothing for them to have animal proteins in their recipes all the time. So obviously they weren't just slaughtering their goats and chickens when they were old, like we do. And sugar—I had to look that one up, but cane sugar was in everything. We use honey. Because the bees do a double duty, helping us pollinate, too. It saves us field space for protein-rich vegetables. They had all sorts of stuff I'd never even heard of. Food was abundant for them. They could just go to the market and get whatever they wanted, whether or not it was in season. And they had no idea."

Mara's back still faced me, but her shoulders sagged a little. Like my words were softening her resolve.

"It's like you were saying on my first day," I continued, "about the fruit salad. As our botanist, you do a lot more than figure out what trees they should be planting down in the atrium. It's diet and it's balance, and you have to think about climate and soil and oxygen and what kind of wildlife we need to help carry the seeds. And the funny thing is that people who are cooking—most people—don't even think about it. They don't even realize how our food has changed since we left Earth, except for complaining that they can't get anything besides potatoes down at the shops."

From behind I watched as Mara's shoulders shook. At first I had the terrifying thought that she might be *crying*. But then I heard her dry, hiccuped laughter.

"You'd think they were dying because I won't give them the iceberg lettuce their parents fed them," she said, finally turning to face me. "But what do they want from me? It's nutritionally worthless."

"I know," I said. And I did. I'd heard Mara grousing about it enough times to be more than familiar. Mara cracked the slightest smile.

"You know, we still have access to all those crops. None are lost. Not even sugarcane. We have thousands of seeds in cold storage, not to mention cell samples, DNA. Our ancestors worked hard to preserve as much life as they could. Even plant life."

"That's why you're so excited about the probe, isn't it?"

She let out a soft grunt of agreement. "We have some idea about the climate. We know it's a cold place, based on orbit and distance from Eps Eridani. But we don't know the details. Soil composition. Air quality. Once we find those out, we can engineer cultivars we can plant on Zehava's surface. It might be a chance to reinvigorate species that haven't been seen for *centuries*. Or to invent whole new crops— better crops. Crops that can feed us and sustain us better on our new home than they ever did back on Earth."

Talking like this, Mara seemed almost like a kid—not at all like the strange, brusque little woman I'd grown to know.

"I'll tell you what, Terra," she said, reaching her age-veined hands toward me. Hesitantly I placed my hands in hers. The gesture felt ill fitting, odd. "Come with me to the atrium. We'll walk around. See if there's anything this old fool can teach you about your vocation."

It was the first time she'd offered to teach me anything. At last I'd done something right. "Okay," I agreed, not even trying to hold back my smile in return.

In the silence we strolled along the lower paths, past the rivers and the fountains. What had once been a green, busy jungle had now given way to felled trees and scrubby bushes. Yellow grass swallowed the cobblestone. We walked down into the pastures. To my surprise, as we moved past a flock of scattered sheep, Mara let out a strange bleat of sound. She held her hand out to one. It ambled close, answering her.

"As a girl I wanted to be a shepherd," she declared, not looking me in the eye. I frowned at her. This was the first thing I'd ever learned about Mara's personal life.

"Always did like animals more than people," she said. Her fingers massaged the creature's black face. "They're easier to talk to. Easier to understand."

The sheep let out another belt of sound, then butted her head against Mara's hand. It was a massive ewe, body swaddled in yellow wool. But Mara petted it like it was a kitten, running her nails over its knobby head.

"I wanted to be an artist," I whispered. I hadn't thought my words through—and hadn't planned on sharing them either. I lifted my hand to my mouth, but it was too late. The words were already out, hanging there in the clammy air. But Mara only gave a laugh.

"I know," she said. She gave the creature's ear one last caress, then started out again across patchy fields. I followed. "The Council told me *all* about that little book of yours. I tried telling them that no fifteen-year-old would put together an amateur field guide, but I suppose they thought they were being clever, recommending you to me. They didn't want to listen."

Walking beside her, our hands almost touching, I felt a rash of heat go to my face. I couldn't help but wonder what they'd said about my drawings. "You knew? And you still chose me?"

Laughter flickered in Mara's eyes. We'd reached one of the pasture fences. She set her hand on the splintered wood. "Your scores were solid. Much better than any of your classmates. And your instructor said that you had . . . How did he put it? An unusual enthusiasm for any subject that interested you, at those rare times when he could get you interested. I thought we might make a good match. If you'll pardon the expression, I didn't want some little sheep who'd swallow anything I told her."

It embarrassed me to hear her say it, that we were alike in some ways. I couldn't bring myself to look at her. I think it embarrassed Mara, too.

"Anyway," she said, and thumped her hand against my shoulder. "What I'm saying is, I know you wanted to be an artist. I won't hold it against you."

And with that, she launched her small, wiry body right over the pasture fence and took off down the brick path that waited on the other side. I let out a burst of laughter, scrambled over the wooden rail, and followed.

We walked through the dimming light together, winding our way toward the labs. A few black-limbed trees still clung to their leaves, which throbbed like green-yellow hearts over our heads. Mara pointed out how skinny pines pushed their way up between the broad oak trunks.

"These were planted last year," she said, kneeling in the mud to touch one of the prickly branches to her palm. Then she turned to me. "Even though we arrive on Zehava in less than six months. Why?"

I chewed on my lip, scanning through my memories, through years of school lessons where I'd barely clung to consciousness.

"Um, we need oxygen until we establish orbit?" I offered at last. But even as I spoke, I suspected that my answer was the wrong one.

"Terra," she said, thinning her lips, "there's no guarantee that we'll be able to actually live on the surface of Zehava when we get there."

My frown deepened as she stood, dusting her hands against her trousers.

"What do you mean, there's no guarantee?" My voice wavered, betraying my emotions—fear, and a hot flash of anger, too.

But Mara ignored the frantic crescendo of my voice. "What are they teaching you kids in school these days? I told you. Almost everything we think we know about Zehava is based on conjecture—we can guess certain things about a planet based on how far it is from its sun, and the gravity it exerts on other bodies in its system, and how long the orbit is, and the rotation. But things like atmospheric composition? The presence of water? And whether it can support life? And more, life like ours?"

The hard look over her features finally softened. "You should know this. Our ancestors sent out many ships to many planets—because there was no guarantee we would make it and no guarantee that *any* of these places could support life."

"What happens if it can't?" I demanded. A thorny tangle of anger grew inside me. "What happens if we get to Zehava and can't even *live* there?"

Mara gave me a toothy grimace. "Well, then we detach the ship's dome. And land it. And remain within the glorious prison of the *Asherah*."

I searched for the ceiling between the broken boughs. I'd never thought of the *Asherah* as a prison before—in fact, I hardly ever thought about her at all. She was home, just like my family's quarters or my room. I paid her as much mind as I did my hands or my feet.

But I'd thought ahead plenty. In school, staring out the window at the atrium as Rebbe Davison droned on and on, I'd thought about life on Zehava. I thought about things I'd heard named only in songs or in books. Thunderstorms. The ocean. The desert, yellow and endless. And sky—*real* sky.

I'd thought about unknown continents. Sometimes I'd even doodled maps in the margins of my notebooks. I'd always known that someday some other world waited for me. Some better life.

Mara stared at me, letting her words sink in, and I thought of what my life might be like if that future were taken away. The anger inside me swelled. I wanted to bang my fists against the ceiling that glowed false twilight in the distance. I wanted to break out.

"The probe," I said, almost spitting the words. "The probe wasn't just supposed to tell you what kind of plants to make. It's supposed to tell us whether we can live on Zehava."

Mara reached out, fixing her wrinkled hand against my shoulder. And gave it a squeeze.

"Good," she said, her whispered voice rough, as coarse as the nettles that were tangled over the ground. "Good. Now you understand."

9

Our faces were mottled red from the cold, our lungs breathless from the day's walk. The unusually easy conversation of the day had given way to an equally easy but no less unusual silence. I rounded the corner of the long hallway that led to the lab, Mara following close on my heels. Then I stopped short.

"Dad?" I called. "Koen? What are you doing here?"

They stood together beside the door. Koen looked like a shadow of my father in his dark boots and skinny trousers, though his broad shoulders were slouched where my father's were squared. I felt my face flush. After the incident in the library, I wasn't quite sure how to act around him.

"Terra," my father said, pulling me out of myself. "You were supposed to meet me at the hatchery this afternoon. It's time."

I winced at the sound of my father's voice, tight with anger. I'd forgotten all about it. That explained why the domes were so empty that day—the workers must have departed to the hatchery to observe the birth of the final generation of ship-born Asherati. I looked to Mara, but she was busy jamming her fingers against the door panel. When I followed her inside, my father and Koen trailed after.

"Mara Stone," my father said, his words weighted with a familiar note of reproach. "Surely you'll let my daughter leave her duties early to see her brother's child's birth."

"You can come too, Mara," offered Koen. "After all, it is a mitzvah."

Mara, her back to us, had begun to take off her coat. But at Koen's words she froze. I saw a wince tighten her profile. She spun to face my father. The lift of her mouth was wicked. It reminded me of the sort of look an older sister might give a naughty little boy.

"You know," Mara began. I let out a silent breath—from her tone, and from experience, I knew a lecture was coming on. "There was a time when women carried children in their bodies like ewes bearing lambs. Squeezed them out between their own legs, even. But there's something wrong with human babies. Their skulls are much too big. Even in wealthy nations childbirth was always risky business. And it was much too risky for our intrepid founders to lose women of prime childbearing age when they could work like good little drones."

I buried my face in my palms. My cheeks were burning, searing hot against my hands. Through reddened ears I heard my father's response.

"I had no idea you were a student of animal husbandry too, Mara. Are you planning on getting a special dispensation for *that*, going to whelp a few pups yourself?"

Mara let out a snort. I peeked through my fingers at her, watching as she pulled her rusted shears from her coat pocket and pretended to prune one of her trees.

"Certainly not, Arran," she said. "I've had my babies, just like every other sow on this ship. One of each, a boy and a girl. Brilliant way to control population, isn't it? But I consider it my duty—all of ours, really, even if most of the ship's inhabitants distract themselves with mitzvah and *tikkun olam* and other hogwash—to be educated about our past. You know, that's where we get our 'bar mitzvah' for our boys." She paused long enough to wave her shears at Koen. "A week out of school, a little snip snip"—she sliced through the air with them—"and behold, men out of thirteen-year-olds! Wouldn't want them to go knocking up our precious workhorses, after all."

With that, she winked at me. I was dying inside, but Mara just let out a cackle of laughter.

"Thank you *so* much for your invitation, young clock keeper, but I'll be fine without paying a visit to the hatchery tonight. All that blood. It just turns my stomach. But . . ." She stopped short, studying my burning face. At last she forced her wicked smile to soften. "Oh, well, if you *must* go, Terra, be my guest. But please, no war stories tomorrow. I don't want to be up all night with nightmares."

"Thank you, Mara," I muttered, rushing to follow my father and his *talmid* from the lab. I couldn't bear to look at her, but Mara's high-pitched laughter echoed down the hall after us.

When I was eleven, Rebbe Davison brought us all to the hatchery to see "where life begins," a phrase that made everyone giggle, even the boys. Back then we all felt squeamish at the sight of the glistening eggs, dripping from the tubing like tomatoes on a vine. Their pinkish shells bulged with veins. The memory of the strange clumps of flesh had haunted my dreams for years.

But I'd visited a few times already in the year I turned sixteen, tagging after Ronen and Hannah to see the fishy, globe-eyed creature that would one day be my niece. I hadn't exactly become accustomed to the antiseptic smell or the sight of the babies, bumbling through the nutritive fluid, but it seemed important to *act* like I was. After all, only children were uncouth enough to blush when they stepped through the doors of the hatchery.

I did my best to keep my expression fixed ahead as I sat on one of the narrow sofas in the busy observation lounge, but it wasn't easy. Koen's hip pressed into mine, the lean line of his leg paralleling my own. Our shoulders nearly touched. Sitting beside him, I was acutely aware of his body. It didn't help matters any when he turned to me, smiling shyly.

"Mara is a very strange woman," he said. From beside the observation glass I heard my father let out a low chuckle. I just stared down at my hands. They looked awkward against my knees.

"She's different," I agreed. But when I spoke the words, they felt wrong, like a betrayal. So I added: "But I'm learning a lot from her about how the ship works. And what will happen at landing, and—"

"You shouldn't believe everything that Mara tells you." My father turned to face us. His expression was stony. "She thinks she's special. She thinks the rules don't apply to her."

Beside me, Koen's dark eyes flickered, revealing a faint glimmer of something I couldn't quite read. "What do you mean, sir?"

"Oh, like being a mother, for instance. She asked for *two* dispensations from Captain Wolff to delay having children before they finally forced her a few years ago. Said that her work was too important to deal with the 'inconvenience of motherhood.'" My father's nostrils flared at the thought. After all I'd learned about Mara, it didn't surprise me. But I knew how my father felt about those who put selfishness before *tikkun olam*.

Koen didn't speak for a moment. His thin lips were pressed flat, like he was turning something over in his mind. But I had no idea what.

"It's despicable," my father concluded.

I felt my heart squeeze out a labored beat. Mara hadn't made these last few weeks easy—I'd spent enough time hating her myself. But for some reason a bright flame of protectiveness flared up inside me. I attracted enough of my father's ire. I didn't want anyone else to catch it, not even Mara.

"She does her job well," I said, my words shaky but clear. "She really cares about the good of the colony, about doing all she can to ensure its success. Haven't you always said that that's a mitzvah?"

For a long time my father didn't answer. Silence grew between us, intercepted only by the sounds of the celebrations that raged across the observation deck, and the bustle of the hatchery beyond—the shouts of the workers, the cries of new children. I didn't look my father in the eye as he stared at me, but I didn't move, either. I couldn't speak or breathe. I didn't want to risk inciting his wrath even further.

That's when Koen slid his hand in against mine. His fingers were cool and dry against my clammy palm.

"Yes, sir," he agreed. "You *have* said that. Our work as specialists elevates us above ordinary workers. That would be true for Mara, too, wouldn't it?"

My father didn't answer. But he looked down at our interlocked hands. I saw a smirk, self-satisfied, lift his upper lip. Finally he looked toward the glass.

"It's beginning," was all he said. Hesitating only a moment, wiping my palm against my knee, I went to my father. His *talmid* followed, taking long, firm strides. There was a small crowd of people behind us—jovial workers, downing their wine rations together in celebration. But the three of us stood in solemn contrast. I saw our reflections in the glass: my father's muscular figure; Koen, lanky and lean; and me, between them, looking gaunt and pale. Then my father indicated something below with the angle of his chin, and my vision shifted.

The new parents milled beneath the eggs. You could tell which couples had been through this before. They knew what to do. They knelt under the eggs, slicing them open with shining surgical tools and letting the infants coast out in floods of pink-streaked fluid.

I found my brother in the sea of blue cotton scrubs. Ronen bumbled behind the doctors. He hovered over Hannah. When he finally took the surgical knife in hand, he dropped it, and Hannah had to stop him from fumbling around on the floor to find it.

Instead she snatched the new tool right out of the hatchery worker's fingers. Kneeling beneath the swollen egg, she sliced the artificial womb open in one brisk motion. Ronen hardly made it over in time to help her catch the slippery child in his arms. Beside me, my father let out a hiss of air at the sight. Ronen held their daughter as Hannah wiped the blood from her nose with a clean rag. I felt a quick flash of joy, strong enough to tighten my throat as they leaned their heads in to take their first look at their baby, a little girl so wrinkled, she looked like a shelled walnut.

Maybe Koen was touched too. Maybe that's why I felt the weight of his hand, sudden, heavy, against my lower back. A gesture didn't mean anything, I told myself. But I couldn't stop my spine from going stiff as I turned my attention to our reflections in the observation glass. Koen's eyes were wide, showing no hint of tenderness—but his hand made slow, firm circles on the small of my back. Goose bumps lifted over my arms.

Then Ronen and Hannah burst through the door, their scrubs splattered with blood, and Koen's hand fell like a deadweight. It left nothing but a gap of air at the back of my sweater. I pushed the memory of his palm from my mind. This was the time for me to do my duty as a sister: to embrace Ronen and to smile down at the little mewling girl in the tangle of blankets.

"We've named her Alyana," Ronen said as Hannah set the baby in my father's arms. My brother's tone was hushed, tear racked. "To help us remember."

I stared down at the baby. Up until this moment, I'd told myself I didn't care a whit about what Ronen and Hannah were doing with their lives. I'd never really thought about how my niece would be a little person. But she was, with dark hair pasted down to her perfectly round head, and minuscule fingernails tipping each of her ten tiny fingers. I watched her let out a yawn as she nestled in against my father's chest. Everyone laughed, and I found myself joining in. She was wrinkled and strange but somehow exquisitely formed—a whole, tiny human being.

But then I heard a murmur of sound. My father was speaking. Not to the child, not really. But to Momma.

"Alyana," he said. "Our time here is nearly done. We've waited so long to be free of this ship. So, so long."

He bent over and pressed a dry kiss to the baby's forehead. Then he handed her to my brother.

"You're a mensch, Ronen," he said, squeezing his shoulder. "Without this child I would have never achieved *tikkun olam*."

My father went to stand beside the glass, gazing through it solemnly. But I was the only one who watched him now. All other eyes were on Ronen, cradling the child. Hannah reached down and caressed her cheek. Then Hannah's parents spilled through the double doors, raising their voices in greeting.

"Mazel tov!" They rushed over, laughing. "Congratulations!"

They bent in to see her, cooing and speaking in gibberish. Hannah's face was streaked with happy tears. My brother turned to her and pressed kisses into her shining cheeks.

No one paid any attention to my father. He stared through the glass, holding his hands behind his back. As he murmured to himself, his breath fogged the pane. I was the only one who heard it, the only one who was listening.

"It's almost over, *bashert*. Almost . . ."

I felt a knot rise in my throat. I knew then in the pit of my belly that Ronen could cling to his new family all he wanted. It didn't change the rest of us. We were broken, damaged beyond repair.

But I didn't have much time to think about that. Because Koen leaned into me again, a gentle smile playing across his lips.

"It's amazing, isn't it?" he said. "If life works out like it should, she won't even remember this ship."

The baby's tiny hands curved into helpless fists. "It seems like a heavy burden for her to carry," I said at last. "All that hope poured into one tiny girl."

That's when Koen reached a hand out and drew me close, so that my shoulder was pressed to the warmth of his body. Close enough to smell him now. He was cedar and clean hair and the cool wind in the dome and something else, something I couldn't quite name.

"That's all right," he said softly. "She doesn't have to carry it alone."

· · ·

As I made my way through the streets that night, I watched the merchants pull down their shutters with gloved hands. Behind them store lights flickered off one by one. The sky went dim over the tops of the town houses, then black. Save for the streetlamps, the whole world was going dark.

Rachel's shop was on the last street in the commerce district. From this side of the glass, it looked warm and bright, with a whole line of colorfully dressed mannequins posing in the windows. I stepped through the door into the carpeted interior. A bell jangled overhead.

"We're closed," came a familiar voice from back near the dressing rooms. I stuffed my hands down into the pockets of my mud-stained work pants, moving forward between racks. It seemed almost wrong to be here looking like I did—so rumpled amid all this clean new linen.

"Are you now?" I called. There was a pause. Rachel's slender face and wild smile appeared from behind a row of jewel-toned frocks.

"Terra!" She let out a squeal, pushing through the rows of silk in her rush to greet me. The fabric rustled like leaves. "You came to visit!"

I leaned into her embrace, taking a long breath of the soapy, floral scent of her. Of course, these days the perfume of iron-rich soil followed me like a cloud. But she didn't seem to care what I smelled like. Rachel raked her long fingernails along my shoulder blades, then gave my arms a squeeze.

"What does that botanist have you *do* all day?" she asked, the space between her eyes crinkling. "You're all . . . muscle!"

I pulled away, shrugging. I'd noticed how my limbs had grown leaner, how my pants fit me looser even as my body had stretched, outgrowing them, but I'd been too tired to pay much attention to it.

"Digging around in the dirt," I said.

"I can tell," she said. Then she took my hand and pulled me across the store. We passed racks of wedding dresses in every conceivable shade of gold. They reminded me of the season that was fading just beyond the shop door. She led me to the ring of chairs that sat outside the dressing room. We both sat—she leaning forward in her seat, looking eager, and me on the chair's edge, precariously perched.

"So," I began. It had been so long since we'd last spoken that it felt difficult to find our old rhythm. "Ronen's child was hatched today."

"Oh, mazel tov! They had their girl first, didn't they?"

"They did."

Rachel gestured toward the rear of the store, where clothing for children hung from miniature hangers.

"Have Hannah come by, won't you? I'd love to help her pick out a few rompers."

I studied Rachel's face for a moment. She looked so happy, bright cheeked at the very thought of selecting a few items of baby clothes for my sister-in-law.

"You love your job, don't you?" I asked. She let out a laugh of agreement.

"It's so much fun to help people look their best. And I'm *good* at it. Sales are up more than forty percent from last year." She hesitated, biting down on her bottom lip. "I'm not supposed to let anyone know, but I've done so well that they've started to give me a commission. Less than what I'll be making when I turn sixteen, but some pocket gelt is nice, at least. Of course, a lot of it goes right back to the store."

I could tell. She was dressed richly—in a long dress the color of violets. It was sewn from thin cotton, with buttons up the long sleeves and a plunging neckline that showed the dark skin over her collarbone. It was all *very* stylish.

"You look great, Raych," I said, and meant it. "I'm sure Silvan just adores it."

"Oh," she said. *"Him."* She waved her hand at me, as if Silvan Rafferty were little more than a trifle. "Don't get me wrong. He's still gorgeous. And I'm still planning on, you know, asking for his hand. But we've just been so *busy* lately."

"Well," I began. My lips edged up into a cunning smile. "I'm sure you'll have plenty of time after you declare your intentions."

"Of course!" she said, blushing. "Only a few more weeks!"

My only response was a muffled groan. I'd almost forgotten our impending birthday. At sixteen we'd be eligible to marry, able to declare our intentions to any adult man, to consent if one asked us for our hand. Rachel always said that our *real* lives would finally start when we turned sixteen. . . . I wasn't entirely sure what she thought we'd been doing up till then. Not living, I guess.

"Terra!" Rachel chided. "You don't want to be an old unmatched biddy, do you? And to have the Council pick your partner?"

"No, of course not," I said, "but we *do* have two years. It's not as if we need to declare our intentions right away."

Rachel regarded me sternly. It was clear that she thought me half crazy. "Whatever you say. *I* can't wait until my life with my *bashert* begins."

The word stuck in my throat like a lump that kept me from swallowing. I couldn't move past it. *Bashert, bashert.*

"You really think you're fated to marry Silvan?"

"Oh . . ." Rachel looked down, away from me. "Maybe not *fated*. But my mother says that she and Daddy learned to be each other's true souls over time. I don't know. I know you think it's silly."

It was an old argument between us. Rachel believed in all of that destiny stuff; I never had. Not before, at least.

But I found myself lowering my voice. The memory of a smooth, printless hand ran through my mind. "No," I said gravely. "It's not silly. I—I sometimes hope . . ."

I clutched the sleeve of my coat with both hands, worrying the fabric. I didn't want to tell Rachel about my dreams. For one thing, they were almost too embarrassing to contemplate. I felt so naked in them. Like I was being split open, skinned alive.

For another, for so many years my dreams had been about Silvan. Silvan, who belonged to Rachel.

But, to my relief, she just put a soothing hand on top of mine.

"We all want to find someone special, Terra. You don't have to be embarrassed by it."

Of course, she didn't know that both of us dreamed about the same boy. I flattened my lips, forced a wistful smile. "No. I guess I don't. It just feels so strange to even *hope*."

"These hopes," Rachel began, "are they about any particular boy? Do you have someone in mind?"

"Well," I said, drawing out the syllable. I couldn't tell her the truth. So I talked about the next-best thing. Koen. Koen was easier to contemplate. "There *is* a boy, actually. Maybe. I think."

She looked almost hungry at the news. "Who?"

"My father's *talmid*," I said, feeling my face redden again. Rachel scrunched up her nose.

"Koen Maxwell? He's kind of awkward, don't you think?"

I thought about it—how Koen was always letting out loose bursts of laughter at exactly the wrong moment or how he pawed at his neck when my father asked him questions over the dinner table. But, to be honest, that was part of what I liked about him. He had a kind of nervous energy that was always spilling out, like he couldn't quite contain it.

"He is," I agreed. "But he's got those gorgeous brown eyes."

Rachel understood *that*. "And that *hair*," she agreed. "So are you going to do anything about it?"

I squinted, trying to envision it. But I couldn't. Every time the image of the two of us began to coalesce, it all evaporated again. "I don't know. Things feel strange with him. Tense."

"Oh, that's just who he is."

"Are you sure?"

"Absolutely." She set a reassuring hand on my knee, gave my kneecap a squeeze right through my muddy trousers. "You remember how he used to get when we had to give presentations in class, don't you? All red-faced and nervous. Glancing at the door like he was ready to bolt. I wouldn't take it personally so long as he's decent to you."

I thought of the little circles Koen's hand had made against my back, firm, insistent. And I found myself nodding. "Maybe you're right," I said.

Rachel flashed her teeth at me, straight and white as clean steel. "Of course I'm right, Terra," she said. "Trust me!"

Beneath the flickering streetlights Rachel locked the shop door. Then she wrapped her arms around me and enveloped me in a long embrace.

"It was good to see you," she said. "More, please?"

I let out a soft laugh. "Sure thing," I agreed, and gave her shoulders a squeeze. A moment later I watched as she headed off down the street. She stopped at the corner, gave a small wave, then hustled off through the night.

I should have hurried along too. It was getting late—the streets were long empty now, everyone at home with their families, as they should have been. But I wasn't sure what I would find if I headed home. No, that wasn't true. I knew exactly what I would find—my father, drunk and angry that I was home so late. I couldn't bear to face it, so I cinched my coat tight around me and headed out toward the dome.

It was too dark to draw—almost too dark to see anything at all. The wind shifted over the fallow fields, making the dry grass dance. I stumbled over the crumbled cobblestones and deep cracks that cleaved the concrete. A single owl called out, laughing at me. When I was a child, I'd been afraid of them. But then my father told me that they were here for a reason, just like I was. They were needed to control the population of field mice, who helped spread grain and nuts and berries, which we needed to feed the goats and sheep—which we needed to feed ourselves.

"Everything has its place," he told me. "Everything on the ship plays its part in *tikkun olam.*"

He'd believed it then. I think I had too. Now, as I bumbled through the darkness, I wasn't so sure. What part had Benjamin Jacobi played, or Momma? I couldn't see how their lives or deaths had done anyone any good.

In the darkness up ahead on the path, I saw a tall silhouette. A boy rested on a footbridge that bordered one of the fields. He leaned his weight against the metal rail. For a moment I thought it might be a specter—a ghost. He was dressed all in white, funeral colors. His long coat seemed to glow in the dark. I frowned at the sight, wondering who had died. But that wasn't possible—there was no way Abba would have let me miss a funeral. An affectation, then. But a strange one.

"You there!" he called out to me, shadowing his face with a hand. It was a rich tenor voice, the kind that made you want to listen. "Who is that?"

"Terra Fineberg," I called as I reached the end of the bridge. I could see who it was now; the black curls that graced his shoulders were unmistakable. As was the gold and purple cord on his shoulder, the only touch of color on his otherwise spotless outfit. Silvan.

"Terra," he said. I saw his teeth glint, bright in the night. And I tried to train back the instinctive smile that I felt forming too. "It's a cold evening for a walk."

"I don't mind the cold so much," I said. It was a lie; I hated the cold. But Silvan would be captain soon, due certain politeness. I didn't want to inconvenience him with my complaints. Then an echo of my father's words tumbled from my mouth. "Besides, it's our duty to get used to the cold weather, isn't it?"

"Mm-hmm," came Silvan's bored reply. I thought for a moment about what Mara had said, about how we might someday be stuck living in the dome if Zehava proved inhabitable. Surely if that were the case, then the Council would allow us our summers? I wondered if Silvan knew about that. But I didn't know how to ask.

"Have you been enjoying your work, *Talmid* Fineberg?" he said at last, after silence had begun to stretch out uncomfortably between us.

"Sure," I said, bristling at the formality of his speech. "You?"

He shrugged. I guess he was about as interested in this line of inquiry as I was.

"It's late. Shouldn't you be with your family? Not . . . alone?" I said, then winced. Who was I to ask such questions of a Council member? I expected him to rebuff me, but he didn't. He only scowled.

"Abba tried to tell me tonight that I'm to keep a guard member with me at all times. I'm not a child. I don't need a babysitter."

Silvan's eyes were hard, proud. If they hadn't been so heavily lashed, I might have been afraid of them.

"I can't imagine," I said. He snorted.

"No! Who can? After all, *your* family let you out tonight. *You* didn't have to ask permission."

I slid my hands down into my pockets, unsure of how to answer. In my household it wasn't a matter of rules. It was a matter of dark nights and drunk nights and navigating the space between them.

As he watched me, waiting for my answer, Silvan's expression changed. It was like a light flickered on in his mind, pale at first, then growing brighter. In our silence he stepped close. Soon he stood only an arm's length away. He smelled like strong tea and animal musk. I remembered that scent vividly, remembered the weight of his lips.

I remembered my dreams. And my jaw tightened. I told myself that Silvan wasn't *my bashert*. No, no, Silvan belonged to Rachel.

"Terra," he began. His tongue darted out, wetting his mouth. "You're a specialist."

"I am," I agreed, casting a self-conscious eye to the braid on his shoulder.

"Have you had any suitors yet?"

"Suitors?" I began uncertainly. "Silvan, we're not sixteen yet. You know that no one is allowed to declare their intentions."

"Oh, I don't mean all that pomp and circumstance." He gave his head a fierce shake. "I just wanted to know if any boys have *expressed interest* in you. Yet."

His eyes were so wide, they showed white at the edges. I didn't like their hunger or their intensity. So I stepped away from him, trying to ignore how my heart was suddenly sounding in my chest. *Had* anyone expressed interest? I thought of what Rachel had said. And I thought of Koen and his long, paper-dry hands.

"If you're asking if I have my eye on anyone," I said, lifting my chin. And maybe I didn't *feel* certain, but I did a good job of faking it. "Then the answer is yes. Yes, I do."

Silvan smiled politely. "I should have known," he said. "Mazel tov."

I was glad it was dark. My cheeks were burning hot. I shoved a strand of hair back behind my ear, hiding beneath the shadow of my hand. "I should go," I said, too embarrassed to thank him.

"Of course." The rising captain gave a stiff little bow, folding at the waist. "Be safe, *Talmid* Fineberg."

"Y-you too, Silvan," I stammered. And then I turned, rushing into the darkness.

nce, my thoughts of Koen had been half-formed, nebulous. But after I told Silvan my plans, Koen's image solidified. The idea of *liking* him became substantial. It had weight and volume, took up space. That space was shaped like him—tall and incredibly lean. Almost everyone on the ship was thin; our rations saw to that. But Koen was even thinner than most, the plane of his chest nearly concave, and I imagined resting my head against it to listen to the rhythm of his heart in the hollow of his rib cage. At night when I turned off my bedroom light, I thought about his hands, the big, knobby knuckles; I thought about the way his long fingers turned to narrow wrists, slender arms. I thought about the way he licked his lips, a quick little flick of pink tongue. I thought about the way his hair was always falling into his eyes, and how he'd brush it away before smiling at me, and the way I felt when he did.

I thought about other things too. I thought about kissing Koen. I thought about the way his breath might feel against my lips and wondered how I'd ever manage to close my eyes with his face, his beautiful face, so close to mine. I thought about how he was taller than me, how he'd have to scoop an arm down around my waist to pull me close. I thought about things I'd never tell anyone about. I thought about his hand on my lower back—and on other places too.

Bashert, bashert, I said to myself, as if chanting the word in my mind would make it true. The boy I dreamed about looked no more like Koen than he ever had. But that didn't stop me from telling myself that they were one and the same, that I would feel the same wild warmth when I pulled Koen's body against mine.

I did my best to keep my thoughts about Koen a secret, but I know that they showed. Even the mood at supper changed. It used to be that I sometimes spoke and even laughed along with Koen and Abba, but now I only listened. I withdrew, pulling into myself. I watched Koen with nervous bird eyes, flitting them up and then away.

When he looked at me, I'd just turn beet red. I could feel the burning heat over my face and throat and ears and even my chest beneath the itchy wool of my mother's sweater.

Seeing this, Father would give a hungry grin, like he'd done something wonderful. And Koen would watch him watching me, then look at me over the table. In those moments there seemed to be a tiny glimmer of a question beneath his lifted eyebrows. But if he'd hoped for any sort of connection, he'd hoped wrong. Koen would look at me and I'd just blush deeper, then force my gaze down to my plate.

It might seem like amid all of this—with Koen and his hands weighing so heavily on my mind—that I'd forgotten all about Mar Jacobi.

But I never forgot. That strange gargle of noise, his death rattle, stayed with me whenever I took the long way home from work. Every night, without fail, I remembered the way the knife had flashed in the light, and the sudden explosion of red, red blood.

Thinking of Koen didn't help matters any. Because every passing day that I distracted myself with thoughts of Koen's hands, of Koen's smile, my belly grew more twisted with guilt. I had seen the captain's guard kill the librarian—a kind man, a father, my mother's friend. And because I was afraid, I'd done nothing. Just pushed it further and further back in my mind.

But the truth was that I didn't know any other way to stay afloat. This was how I'd survived after Momma had died, keeping the pain and the guilt stuffed down inside me.

What was the weight of one more dead body?

We turned sixteen. The morning of our Birthing Day, I stayed in my bed for a long time, staring up at the shadows on the ceiling, ignoring Pepper's cries. I took quick stock of my body—fingers, check; rib cage, check; nose, and mouth, and jaw, still there too—and did my best to note any changes. I knew logically that I took up more space in bed and that my body weighted the mattress differently, bowing the material beneath my hips. But other than the strange heat that sometimes flared up from inside me, I felt the same. Unchanged.

"Terra!" My father called me from the bottom of the stairs. Pepper wanted me to get up too. He head-butted my shoulder and let out a rattling purr. So I pulled myself from bed and down our narrow staircase.

To my surprise, my father stood at the stove. The whole galley was perfumed by the scent of yeast and flour—it had to be challah, fresh-baked egg bread. It was Momma's smell, and it brought a lump to my throat. I gripped the banister.

"You're making breakfast?"

"You're sixteen," my dad said, as if that were an answer. "A grown-up.

I figured it was a special occasion." He stooped down to scratch Pepper behind the ears. He laughed, warm, genuine laughter. I made my way warily across the galley and sat down at the table.

My father brought over a scratched glass bowl shrouded with a damp cloth. I lifted it. Steam rose up the lumpy roll of knotted bread. It wasn't as pretty as what Momma used to make, but it was fresh and warm. I tore into it with both hands.

Meanwhile my father poured a cup of sludgy black liquid from our kettle, then another. He brought one over to me. It was potsum— an ersatz brew made of chicory root and bran.

"I don't drink coffee," I said. My father took a long draw from his own steaming mug, then smacked his lips.

"You don't now. But you will soon enough."

I peered down into my cup, eying the oily liquid. Then I took a tentative sip. It tasted like the charred bottom of a burnt piece of cake.

"That's terrible!" I said. My father only smiled.

"Eat your breakfast. I have a present waiting for you when you finish."

My father's expression was cryptic, closed. I had no idea how to read the faint lift of his lips. It had been so long since I'd seen my father happy. I was afraid that if I breathed wrong, the whole facade would fall apart.

· · ·

Abba's gift was a pair of boots. They were knee high, made out of leather the color of the honey candies we ate at harvest celebrations to ring in a sweet season. They were used, of course, with slight creases wrinkling the toe box and circling the heels. But they were beautiful, and they fit perfectly. I laced them up—Pepper, purring, rubbed his mouth against my hands as I did—and then I stood, looking down at them.

"I know that your old ones were falling apart," my father said. "They probably don't even fit you anymore."

He was right. Just the week before, my big toe had finally pushed a hole through the left one. I admired my new boots, how long and narrow my feet looked in them and how the leather had been polished to a high shine.

"Rachel helped pick them out," my father admitted, an apology in his voice. I couldn't bear to look up at him.

"They're . . . perfect," I said. But I kept my voice low. Part of me was afraid that if I showed too much enthusiasm, then the morning would shatter into a million pieces like a dream. But he looked so hopeful and happy that I couldn't quite help myself. I went to him and pressed a kiss to his cheek, making sure not to linger too long by his side in case his mood tumbled south.

"All right," he said at last, letting out a gruff, short laugh. "Best get to work. Wouldn't want you to invoke Stone's wrath."

· · ·

But things had gone better with Mara since the day Alyana was born. She let me stay in the lab now, so long as I didn't ask too many questions. For the past few weeks I'd watched as she'd worked her way through the blight problem, first identifying the affected plants, then isolating the mold that was causing the spots, then combing through the greenhouse to uproot them before they could spread the disease any farther.

As she did all this, she kept up a sort of running monologue. Sometimes it seemed like she was talking as much to herself as to me, but then she'd stop, stare at me, and quiz me on what she'd just said. Her expression in those moments was meticulous, her thin lips pursed as she waited for my reply—she was testing me, and we both knew it.

Luckily, I always got the answers right.

But our relationship wasn't exactly friendly. I knew that, too. So I wasn't surprised when I clomped into the lab in my brand-new boots and Mara didn't look up from her computer terminal.

I stood, waiting, my hands on my hips.

Mara lifted one of the slides toward the light. I watched as she squinted through the glass, searching for something. "I suppose you expect me to pay you now?"

I didn't answer her. After a moment she let out a heavy sigh. "I guess it can't be helped," she said, cracking a faint smile. "Now, come on. We have work to do."

After work that night I made supper: a hearty stew with carrots and turnips and the oxidized ends of what was left of our meat. My father was upstairs, hiding out in his bedroom, leaving me and Pepper to tend the stove. I bent over to place a slice of fatty meat in the cat's chipped porcelain bowl. And that's when I heard a knock at the door.

I turned in surprise. On nights without Koen we never had visitors, not this late. As I reached out to open the door, I heard Abba's footsteps sound eagerly on the stairwell.

"Is he here?" he shouted over the banister.

"Is who here?" I replied. But before my father could answer, I opened the door—and found Rachel.

Beneath her coat she wore a rose-red dress, just the color to bring out the golden undertones in her skin. But, despite her fine clothes, she was a mess. Tears streamed down her face, trailing over her jaw like a river. Snot sheened over her lips. Her ruby lipstick was smeared to her chin.

"T-T-Terra!" She hiccuped my name. I reached out for her hand, fixing my pinkie finger around hers. And then I pulled her inside and closed the door behind us.

"Abba?" I said, doing my best not to gawk at Rachel. We were sixteen now. We weren't supposed to go around sobbing like *babies*.

"It's Rachel. Can you get her a handkerchief?"

Disappointment twisted my father's face. He nodded wordlessly and made his way up the stairs.

"What's wrong?" I asked, pulling out one of our dining chairs. She sat, teetering on the edge.

My father returned then, and he handed her one of Momma's cloth hankies. Despite the way they'd conspired together on my Birthing Day gift, Abba had never really gotten along with Rachel. Thanks to everything I told her, she was afraid of him. She eyed my father. For once, he seemed to understand. He went and hovered over the bubbling stew, chattering at Pepper, doing his best to give us some illusion of privacy. Satisfied, Rachel finally dabbed at her eyes and began her story.

"I went to the Raffertys' quarters today after work."

Silvan. My stomach sank into my gut.

"I . . . I brought *flowers*. His favorite kind. White lilies. They cost me a fortune. The Raffertys were all sitting there at the supper table—his mother, his father. And *Captain Wolff*, of all people. I can't believe I humiliated myself in front of her. I should have . . . I shouldn't have done it!" I saw Rachel's lower lip curl, revealing her teeth. Before she could start bawling again, I reached out and grabbed her hand in mine. Her fingers were hot.

"I got down on one knee and I told Silvan that I would be honored to be his wife. That if he'd consent, then I was declaring my intent to marry. You know. All of that. They all just . . . just *stared* at me!"

I squeezed her fingers, which felt as clammy as dead flesh. She didn't squeeze back.

"Did Silvan say anything?" I asked. Rachel didn't answer, not right away.

"What did he say?" I prodded.

"He looked at his family. Like he didn't want them to hear. Then he took me outside. And he told me that . . . that I'm *beneath* him. Because of my job. Because of his! He said that once it might have been okay for him to court a merchant girl like me. But that now that he's to be captain, we have to be serious. I was serious, Terra!"

With that, my friend broke down again.

"Oh, Rachel," I said. Stormy emotions flooded my rib cage. Mostly guilt. I'd failed her. I should have seen the whole thing coming. I should have been there to protect her. But I'd been distracted.

I pulled my chair close to hers, drawing her in for a hug. Bowing her head against my neck, she collapsed into my arms. I didn't speak, didn't offer advice or even apologies. I just held her, the way I'd want to be held if I were in her position.

When we finally drew away from the embrace, I saw that my

father had set a trio of glasses down on the table. They were filled with cloudy, bloodred liquid.

"Wine," Rachel said, giving one final sniffle. "Mar Fineberg, you shouldn't . . ."

My father held up one hand as he took his glass in the other. "You girls are sixteen now. Old enough to drown your sorrows in a bottle or a cask, assuming you have the gelt or the rations. And we do. I've been saving this for tonight. I thought we'd have some after supper to celebrate, but it seems you need it now." He lifted the glass. We hadn't even taken ours from the table yet, but my father gave a grim smile and toasted the air.

"To adulthood," my father said. But the words sounded darker than he'd intended, especially after Rachel let out a wheezing breath. Still, he added the traditional toast: "To life, and to Zehava. *L'chaim!*"

"*L'chaim,*" Rachel parroted. I heard myself echo the words too, and we both lifted our glasses from the table, touched their edges, and drank.

The wine was old. That was just like my father, to share the stuff that had gone to vinegar. As I forced it down, wincing, another knock sounded at our door. This time it was a quick succession of knuckles against metal.

My father's head snapped up.

"I think you should get it, Terra," he said. No one else made a move. Even Pepper seemed to watch me closely, crouching low against the counter. I put down my glass, rose. My new boots suddenly felt like they were made of lead. Dragging the heavy soles, I went to the door and opened it.

It was Koen. Under the shadow of his unruly hair, his face was scrunched up against the cold. Pink mottled his cheeks and ears, though whether from embarrassment or the harsh wind, I couldn't be sure. His lips lifted, showing the crooked edge of his teeth.

"Can I come in?" he asked. His breath fogged the air. Behind me, Rachel was staring down at her hands, examining her fingernails like they were the most fascinating thing in the world.

That's when I realized what was happening. That's when I felt my blood drain from my head, when I heard the first labored *thud* of my heart in my ears.

"Um," I murmured, "sure." He stepped inside, flashing his gaze to my father and to Rachel, appraising the situation. Then he turned to me.

"Terra, if you'll have me . . ."

I knew those words. Tradition dictated that you couldn't hear or speak them until you turned sixteen. But I hadn't let myself think about it, not since I'd been a little girl. I was too gawky, too weird. This was something that happened to other girls. To Rachel. Not to me.

But Koen's eyes were open wide. In the galley light they picked up flecks of amber. "If you'll have me, then I would be honored if you'd consent to marry me."

I opened my mouth, drawing in a deep breath. Wasn't this what I'd wanted, what I'd told Silvan I wanted? I heard myself give my consent, but it was like someone else was speaking.

Behind Koen, in the shadows, I saw my father's head move up and down. He approved. Of course he did. He looked happy. So why did my own smile falter?

But then Koen stepped close, and my fears began to drain away. I could smell the cold night air rise off his body, fresh and sharp. He bent down and pressed his lips to mine. They were cool, chapped, and as dry as winter. I leaned in a little, entirely too aware of how we were being watched.

Maybe that's why Koen's lips didn't open to mine. Maybe he felt awkward too. His hands stayed frozen at his sides. My stomach twisted. *This is wrong*, I heard my body say. *This is all wrong.*

As if in response Koen pulled away. A small, tight smile played over his mouth. Then he stumbled out the open door and was gone.

I lifted the back of my hand to my lips. They throbbed like a bruise. Slowly I turned to face the galley table and the people sitting there. Rachel forced down a second mouthful of wine, tears welling up again. And my father grinned at me as if today, my Birthing Day, were the greatest day he'd ever known.

Daughter,

On my application forms they asked me to describe myself. Age, eth-nicity, country of national origin . . . religion. At the intake inter-view a smartly dressed woman tapped her finger against the words I'd scrawled.

"So you call yourself Jewish," she said.

I shrugged. "My mother was. But I'm not observant. Will that be a problem?"

"The Asherah is owned by the Post-terrestrial Jewish Preserva-tion Society."

"A religious group?" I asked, surprised. I'd heard that the ortho-dox of most religions had hunkered down to wait for their messiahs to come. The woman gave her head a shake.

"No. Secular Jews. Mostly American. A few Israelis. A few European Jews. Committed to the continuation of Jewish culture even after Earth—" She hesitated, unable to say it. But she didn't have to. I knew what she meant. She added, "There are other groups. Humanist ships. Nationalist groups. But they have waiting lists. We can't guarantee that you'll be given a spot. The Asherah is looking for passengers like you. They have a quota to reach

before liftoff. *Seventy percent of their passenger list must be of Jewish descent."*

"The Asherah *sounds fine," I said quickly, recalling the dimming light of Annie's eyes, the way she'd grabbed my hands, suddenly alive again, when she'd told me I had to live on. "Would have made my grandmother proud, I suppose. She could hardly ever get me to go to synagogue with her."*

The woman was not amused.

"The contract specifies that the governing council is committed to two missions: the first, to ensure the survival and unity of the passengers of the Asherah *at all costs. The second, the survival of Jewish traditions and culture even in the diaspora of space."*

At all costs. I hadn't thought it through, what those words meant. I clutched my hands between my knees, sat straight, looked resolute.

"Where do I sign up?" I said.

But I soon learned.

Tradition dictated that only men and women be married. Survival meant that all of us would. They matched me with your father. They checked our bloodlines, had us sign the marriage contract. The Council told us that our compatibility made us soul mates. He was my bashert, *my destiny.*

Hogwash.

Please don't be mistaken—I've come to have some affection for your father, an old man with soft laughter and kind, gray eyes. But at first our home was a silent one. Perhaps we were both grieving for what we left behind the day we boarded. Our families, our homes . . . our planet. We were strangers, and we had nothing to say to each other. I had never even loved a man before. But soon friendship blossomed between us like a timid flower, poking its head up through the soil. I called him the Professor, which had been his title back on Earth. He called me Mary Ann, a reference to an ancient TV show I'd never seen. It wasn't love, but it was fondness and friendship, and in those first long, dark nights in space, that was enough.

When the ship was five years out, we were told to procreate. On Earth I had known about the artificial wombs that were popular with younger, wealthier women, women who feared they would otherwise lose their figures. But then I felt certain that I would never use one, would never be a mother.

The Council made sure I knew how life on board was tenuously balanced, precarious. Every woman who chose not to be a mother and every man who turned his back on fatherhood would represent a job that would one day go undone and a precious bloodline that would one day die. You were our duty and more, our purpose. We would be parents because it would be so very wrong to be everything but. I did what they said. I became a good Asherati. After all, I'd agreed to *it—signed on the dotted line not once but twice, at boarding and on the day that I was wed.*

We made your brother first. I picked his name, one that fit with the growing tradition of the ship—the strong, masculine ending—but one that honored what I had lost, too. Anson. Because I wouldn't have known him if it hadn't been for Annie. Because he was, in a way, her son as well. Because no matter what the Council said, I knew that I'd met my bashert *years ago—and lost her.*

Four years later, before you were even born, your father named you. He pressed his gloved hand to your egg, saw the mass of cells, the flutter of a heartbeat moving within, and said one word: "Terra."

That's when I knew the truth about your father, how the seeds of discontent grew within him as they did me. He, too, was always looking back—over his shoulder to everything we had left behind, even when we both should have been looking forward.

PART TWO

ORBIT

PART TWO

11

Koen and I took to walking together. It was his idea—he said that it was how all the other couples spent their evenings. So we strolled through the districts, past the shops and by the grain and salt silos. We'd see our classmates, many of them paired now like we were. Koen would nod to the boys. I'd blush and look away; the other girls would do the same. That's how I knew that I was doing the right thing—the ordinary thing. Because I saw everyone else going for walks, red cheeked, exhilarated and a little embarrassed by the sudden onset of adulthood too.

So far we'd kissed only that once. Sometimes Koen would press his fingers into my palm and I'd feel their icy pressure and wait for the thrill of something, for that rush of lust that I was sure had been promised to me in my dreams. But it never *happened*. It was as if we were standing on the edge of a steep cliff ready to go tumbling over if only someone would give us a push. But neither of us was pushing. In fact, neither of us had budged.

One night I knocked on his door and straightened my shoulders, trying not to be unsettled at the sound of his dog's high-pitched yelps. By the time Koen's little sister, Stella, let me in, I managed to force a smile to my face. Standing in the doorway, I watched as he grabbed his knit hat and scarf. His parents' screams tumbled down from the second story.

It was so weird to stand in his quarters. His home looked just like ours, with the narrow entryway and the long metal table and the rickety electric stove in the galley. But it felt so *different*. Our house was blue gaps of silence punctured by the white light of the arguments my father and I had, while Koen's house was more like Rachel's, a constant busy jumble of color and life and sound.

He buttoned his coat, looking at me with a hint of a grim smile. "Come on," he said as he brushed by me. I followed him out. Then I heard him mutter something under his breath.

"Sorry about that."

"Why are you always apologizing for them?" As we started down the street, the knuckles of his fingers almost brushed mine. I wondered if it was intentional, but then he stuffed his fists into his pockets. Sighing, I did the same. "It's not as if my family is perfect."

"Yeah," said Koen, "but no matter how crazy your father is, I *respect* him."

I let out a snort at that. "I don't see why."

"Because he's good at his job. Because he truly believes in the ship's purpose, in *tikkun olam*. He's probably the best Asherati I've ever met."

I bit the insides of my cheeks. How could I respond to that? My father was a noble Asherati when it suited him, sure. But only then. In private he could be cutting and cruel, obsessed with rank and with keeping up appearances. Koen knew all of that, but he went on anyway. "Besides, you don't even know my parents."

"It's not like that makes a difference," I said. I couldn't bear to look at him as I spoke, timid, hesitant words. "They're going to be my family soon either way."

I stole a glance at him. But Koen seemed to be making a point not to look at me, instead gazing off into the distance. There the street narrowed into a cobbled path that ran between the cornfields. He didn't speak, just blew the warm air of his breath into his bare hands.

As we walked down the path, through the dead, towering cornstalks that bent like dusty bones toward us, I chewed my lip, peeling away the dry skin, tasting blood. If I were Rachel, I'd know what to say. I'd know how to prove myself, to prove that I was worthy of the things he'd asked of me—marriage, a partnership, his trust. Love. But what did I know about love? Only the strange moans of my parents down the hall when I was little, and the dreams I had at night, wrong dreams, embarrassing dreams, dreams where I lay down in the warm dirt and was naked except for the vines that crawled over me and the purple flowers that blossomed over my skin.

And so I did the only thing I could. I let my gloved hand dart out of my pocket and up and grab Koen's hat from his head. Then I took off running.

"Hey!" he called, and broke out in rough laughter. "Hey!"

I grinned, speeding forward down the brick path. Part of me kind of hated what I was doing—clutching his hat in my fist, blushing as Koen's footsteps pounded behind me. It seemed cute, sort of coy. Like something Rachel might do. But it was easy to run, much easier than it was to stand by Koen's side and take tiny, measured steps and feel like I might screw up at any moment. This felt different. Brave. I stepped into a gap in the rows of corn, kicking up loose soil with my boots as I did.

"Terra, where are you *going*?"

More of Koen's laughter came tumbling toward me, but I just pressed forward through the scratchy, bone-white leaves. Reaching the far end of the field, I spilled out onto another cracked-stone pathway. Soon I came to an overpass, a rusted metal bridge that seemed to rise up out of the soggy ground on iron girders. I went to the edge, touching the cold rail with my free hand. Below, the brambles seemed to form a tangled net. I looked over my shoulder—Koen had just reached the far end of the field, his hair a ruddy smudge amid all that yellow and gray—drew a breath, and launched myself over the side.

It was dramatic even for me. My boots hit the hard soil, and I pitched forward, just barely able to catch myself before I fell face-first in the dirt. The force of impact made my ears ring. But as I gazed up, I knew it was worth it. Koen stared at me over the rail, those brown eyes deep pools of surprise.

"Are you okay?" he called. I flashed my teeth at him to show that I was. Then I watched him do a quick calculation in his head. Between where he stood and the ground below, there was a gap of at least three meters. A look of fear crossed over his brow, so quick that I almost missed it.

"You shouldn't have looked!" I called, laughing.

"I'll come around," he said.

I waited there in the shadowed clearing. At first I stayed where I'd landed, crouched against the ground. But then a minute or two passed without any sign of Koen, and I started to get anxious again. I walked over to one of the girders that held up the overpass, pressing my spine against it. The metal was so cold that I could feel the bite of it straight through my coat. But I stood with my shoulders square against it anyway, resting my hand first on my hip, then in my pocket, shifting, suddenly hyperaware of what I looked like and trying desperately to look effortless anyway.

"Hey!"

I jumped, dropping Koen's hat on the ground.

"Shoot." I stooped over to pick it up. I tried to brush it clean, but the dirt seemed determined to cling to the nubby fibers. Koen came over and took it from me, pulling it down over his ears.

"Thanks," he said dryly.

He was standing close—so close that I could feel the warmth of his chest through my lifted gloves. His eyelids were down, showing only the smallest sliver of brown beneath his trembling lashes. I could see the slight line of fuzz along his jawline, could smell the sharp odor of his body, a familiar cedar scent that I couldn't quite place.

Then the clock tower bells rang out, deep and hollow, and I remembered: the floorboards beneath the bells. It was my father's smell, or another version of it. For a moment I was sure this was it— he was going to bend close and kiss me again, finally.

But instead he drew away, stuffing his hands into his pockets. He was blushing again, his skin so pink that it was almost purple. But he wouldn't look at me. "We should go," he said as he turned his shoulder to me, starting down the shadowed path. "It's late."

I let out a gasp of breath, one I hadn't even realized I was holding, and followed Koen through the darkening forest.

"What do you mean, he's hiding something from you?"

Rachel stood in the window of her store, holding a pair of straight pins between her lips and speaking out of one side of her mouth. As we talked, she pinned the pleats of a dress around the hips of an old wooden mannequin. She frowned as she spoke, though I think it was mostly because of the way the silky material kept sliding out of her grasp.

"I mean he's *hiding* something from me," I said, sitting down on the ledge beside her. "There's always this silence between us, this weird kind of . . . gap. Like we're never on the same page."

The corner of Rachel's mouth lifted. "And what page are you *supposed* to be on?"

I felt my cheeks heat. "Well, you know. We're intended. It wouldn't kill him to kiss me. Stop smiling like that! It's not like you weren't making out with Silvan Rafferty in the cornfields all last year."

My words were a misstep. Something twisted beneath the surface of Rachel's expression and nearly broke.

"Sorry."

She took a pin from her mouth and stabbed it into the fabric. "It's okay," she said, but I didn't believe her. "You're right. It's okay to want to kiss him."

"Not if he doesn't want to kiss me."

She smoothed the material straight with her palm. "I don't understand why he wouldn't want to. He asked for your hand, didn't he? I mean, I *saw* him kiss you that night."

"It wasn't a real kiss," I said, scrunching up my nose. "It was so fast. Like a kiss your brother might give you."

Rachel turned to me, frowning. I went on.

"Maybe he asked for my hand because of my job. Because I'll be making a lot of gelt. Even better once we get to the planet and Mara retires. Two specialists will earn a decent wage." I was speaking without thinking, and my words were beginning to tumble over themselves. If I'd stopped to consider it, I would have known how ridiculous my words were. What care did Koen, a specialist himself, have about gelt? But I just rambled on. "That would make sense. He's marrying me for my money. And he doesn't want to *kiss* me because I'm ugly, of course. But I really can't blame him."

Rachel stared at me.

"What?"

"Terra," she said; her voice was a little soft, and for a moment I worried she was still offended by what I'd said about Silvan. But then she said something that surprised me. "You're *not* ugly."

I let out a laugh. "It's okay. You don't have to be nice about it. I'm used to it. It's how things have always been. You're the pretty one that the boys like to kiss. I'm the . . . well, the other one. The smart one. Or whatever."

"Terra!"

"What?"

Rachel let out an exasperated sound. She hopped down from the window, then reached out and took both my hands in hers. She led me to the dressing rooms. Between the two half-open doors hung a mirror, gleaming in the dim track lighting. The last time I'd been here, I'd avoided looking at it. But now she shoved me in front of it.

"Look!" she said, laughing, though her laughter had an edge of disbelief that I didn't quite like. I glanced at my reflection. My usual self stared back. I shrugged at Rachel.

For a moment she looked me up and down. Then she gathered the fine strands of my hair in her fist and piled them up near the crown of my head.

"You always hide behind your hair," she said. "But this should help you see a bit." Lifting an eyebrow, I turned to the mirror.

My first thought was: *Momma.* But of course that was ridiculous. My mother's eyes had been a mossy green—mine were merely hazel.

Still, the shadow of her was there. Over the past few months my face had changed. My neck was longer, my jaw just a hint less square. My cheeks had filled out, and my lips, too. I'd grown into my nose. And there were other changes: beneath my holey cardigan and stained shirt and the fabric of my lab coat, I could see the slight swelling of my breasts, which I'd done my best to ignore these past few months, and how my hips had widened. I'd probably never be *curvy*, not like Rachel was—instead I was lean and brawny, strong. But I no longer had the stick-straight figure of a boy. I had, apparently, grown up.

"Oh," was all I said. And then I watched the woman in the mirror smile at herself. "When did that happen?"

"Don't ask me," Rachel said, dropping my hair down against my shoulders. Her mouth was twisted into a cockeyed smile. "You just showed up one day in my shop looking all womanly and stuff."

I angled my chin up, doing my best to look proud and, I don't know, regal. Like someone who knew she was pretty. But I couldn't hold up the illusion for long. I exhaled hard, my posture deflating.

"If I'm so good-looking," I said, turning to Rachel, "then why won't he *kiss* me?"

"I don't know. Maybe he's never been kissed before. Maybe he's shy. Maybe he's waiting for you to make your move." She grinned at me. "Maybe it's time you asked him."

·   ·   ·

It's not like we didn't have time enough to talk. Abba had been nudging us together for several weeks now. One night after supper my father pushed himself away from the table with both hands, giving a wink to Koen.

"I'd better get the dishes done," he said, and then added, entirely too loudly, "Why don't you go up to Terra's room? And don't mind me. I promise I'll give you kids your privacy."

Koen and I looked at each other, our complexions blazing bright red, both. It was weird, what my father was suggesting. Crass. I didn't know anyone who rutted around under their parents' roof. But what was I supposed to do, fight with him about it? I rose and made my way up the stairwell. I felt my father's satisfied gaze follow us up the stairs.

"I can't believe him. I'm so, so sorry," I said as I sat in my chair and cradled my head in my hands. I heard Koen's soft chuckle as he closed the door behind me.

"It's okay."

Of course it was. For Koen it seemed like everything was always okay, as long as I didn't look at him for too long or too intently. I dropped my hands, watching as he settled in on the thin throw rug. He held out his hand for Pepper, who was crouched inside the shadows of my desk. The cat sniffed at the air, then came trotting out.

"Attaboy," he said. "Good boy."

I watched as Koen's long fingers scratched the space between my cat's shoulder blades. I could almost feel the words on my tongue, pooling there, taking shape. But it was difficult to make my vocal cords move. When I finally *did* speak, I was surprised to find that my question had nothing to do with kissing—nothing to do with Rachel's suggestions to be direct.

"Did you always want to be a clock keeper, Koen?" I asked, then winced. Small talk—I was making small talk. With my *intended*.

"Actually, yeah." He gave a breathy laugh. "I was curious about that kind of stuff as a kid. Not the clock tower. I didn't care about that. But the seasons. And our sleep cycles. I thought that stuff was pretty interesting."

"Really?" I watched as Pepper climbed up into his lap, kneading his paws against Koen's trousers.

"Yeah. Do you remember our seventh year of school, when I always used to fall asleep in class?"

I cocked my head to the side. My memories of Koen were hazy. I sat near the middle, passing notes back and forth to Rachel. He must have been somewhere with his friends in the rows behind us. I knew he wasn't one of the mean boys, who'd thrown stuff at us and called us names. But other than that I couldn't remember him at all.

"Sure, I remember," I lied. Koen lifted an eyebrow but went on anyway.

"I decided to stop taking my pills. I just wanted to see what would happen, really. It was weird. No matter what the light looked like in the dome, it was like the day *inside* me was getting shorter and shorter. Eventually, I was conking out around nineteen o'clock every day, right in the middle of supper. My parents got freaked out. They thought something was wrong with me. They dragged me to the doctors, even though I kept trying to tell them that I'd just been palming my pills."

"So, like, the clock keeper's job was a lifelong dream. Or snooze."

Koen grinned. "You could say that. So what about you?"

I pulled idly at my sock. "Me?"

"Yeah. Why botany?"

"Mmm."

I rose, feeling Koen watch me as I walked by him. My sketchbook was waiting for me on my bed. I hadn't given up drawing, not entirely. But now every night before bed I pored over the pages, sketching plants, jotting notes. I did my best to capture everything that Mara taught me. Now every page was covered in names, labels, words in ancient languages. I passed it to Koen. He leafed through, laughing as Pepper rubbed his face against the spine. Meanwhile I braced myself, my hands gone cold. Would he belittle me like Abba always did?

But a smile just lit up his lips. "These are good," he said, paging through them slowly. "Yeah, really good. You're talented."

I felt the corners of my own mouth gently rise. "You really think so?"

"Yeah. I love your use of color here. It really looks like twilight in the dome." He swept his index finger over the blue I'd drawn against the treetops, and the faint line of gold that traced every skinny pine. I looked at him and felt a swell of pride. Koen was seeing what I'd seen. Koen *understood*.

"Thanks," I said, my cheeks warming. "Before we got our assignments, I thought I might have been an artist. But the Council had other ideas."

Koen scowled. "You know, it's such *dreck*."

It was like he had abruptly drained all the air out of the room. The atmosphere tasted different, somehow prickly. Koen cavalierly tossed the sketchbook down on top of my unmade bed. The pages splayed out like an open hand.

"What's dreck?" I asked cautiously.

"That they make you be a botanist when you wanted to be an artist. I mean, I would have chosen my vocation either way. But it's dreck that they chose it for you."

"It's not *so* bad," I said, my eyebrows knitting up. A few months ago I would have been right there with Koen, complaining about the injustice of it all. But since Mara had taken me on our walk through the dome, we'd fallen into a sort of tentative peace. I'd begun to look forward to my days in the lab. Sure, botany wasn't as much fun as drawing, but it wasn't all bad.

Koen sat straighter. There was something sharp about his expression, challenging. "You didn't *choose* it. They took away your choice."

"But I *like* my job. It's not perfect, but I'm learning a lot, and—"

"It's still not right. That they picked for you. Like they think you're some sort of *child*." Koen's face was all scrunched up.

"You're mad at me," I said, speaking the words very slowly.

"No." Koen's response came quickly, but I didn't believe it.

"You are. It's something I've done. Does this . . . does this have something to do with Mar Jacobi?" *Is this why you won't kiss me?* is what I wanted to ask. But I still couldn't find the words.

Across my dark bedroom, the cat still purring on his lap, Koen pinched the bridge of his nose. He didn't speak. I could hear my heart thundering in my chest.

"Come on," I said—not angrily but with worry. I stepped closer to him, holding out my hand. I don't know why. He wasn't Rachel. He wasn't there to link pinkies or reassure me. But maybe somewhere, in the back of my mind, I still hoped he would. "We're going to be *married*. You can tell me what I've done wrong."

"Nothing," he whispered. "You've done nothing wrong."

I dropped my hand against my thigh. I should have just accepted it—believed him, believed that it would all be okay. But I couldn't. I'd spent my whole childhood trying to tiptoe around my father, afraid to even breathe wrong. I didn't want to spend my marriage like that too.

"Liberty on Earth," I whispered, as if the words were an oath—as if they could somehow miraculously make Koen forgive me. I didn't expect him to answer, but then the strangest thing happened. I heard his voice come whispering back.

"What did you say?"

"Nothing," I said quickly. "I didn't say anything."

But his big brown eyes pressed into mine. We both knew the truth. He wrung his broad hands nervously, cracking the knuckles.

"Say it again," he pressed.

I licked my lips. When I spoke, the words were even softer than before. "Liberty on Earth."

"Liberty on Zehava," he said.

For a moment, an interminable moment, Koen didn't move. There was an animal sharpness about his gaze—his eyes were eager and alert.

"Tomorrow," he said at last. "Meet me outside the starboard bakery. The one between the delicatessen and the china shop."

"I know where you mean." Momma had worked there. I'd spent my baby years sitting in my high chair in the back, watching as she worked her hands into the dough.

The corner of Koen's mouth ticked up.

"Good," he said. With that, he stood, dislodging Pepper from his lap. The cat gave a meow of protest, but Koen ignored him. Instead he stepped close to the bed. He bent over and pressed a kiss into the part of my hair. I breathed in the cedar-struck perfume of him.

"Don't tell anyone," he murmured.

And then, before I could even open my eyes again, he was gone, leaving only a gap of cold in his absence.

The commerce district bustled after a long day's work. Children spilled over the cobblestones, hefting books in their arms. Across the street a gaggle of laughing women tumbled out from one of the pubs. The air that drifted from the shops was heavy with smells: the salt-preserved odor of fish, the sweet scent of overripe fruit, and the all-too-familiar perfume of freshly baked bread. My stomach gave a rumble. I ran the flat of my hand over my gut, hoping to quiet it. I wasn't here for food—couldn't let myself be lulled into thinking this was just another ordinary evening. After all, there was no telling when a member of the captain's guard might come swaggering down the street.

The shops didn't have names. But each one had its own insignia. Momma's bakery bore a blue star above it. Half of the paint had flaked off, revealing the concrete below. But I would have recognized those seven points anywhere.

Koen stood below it, waving his arms at me.

"Terra!" he called. His wide, giddy smile surprised me. So did the way he reached out, grabbing my hand in his.

"Hello, Koen," I said. I glanced down the street, hoping no one heard the way his voice rose above the crowd. But it was lost among the conversation and laughter. We looked like any other young couple, tending to their errands after a long day's work.

Without another word Koen turned toward the bakery. He shouldered the door open and dragged me in past the threshold. I'd avoided the flour-scattered place since Momma had passed. I preferred the port bakery. Even if their bread was never as soft, the store held fewer tender memories.

But Koen didn't give me time to absorb the familiar sight of the workers knotting bread into ropes. He dodged the crowd at the counter, ignoring how they shouted their orders to the counter girl. Instead he ducked inside a doorway at the rear of the shop. As I followed him I felt my hands tremble.

The corridor was dark, lit by a single flickering bulb.

"Where are we going?" I asked, my voice nothing more than a whisper. I'd put off my thoughts about Mar Jacobi for too long—I wanted to finally discover the secrets behind the words *Liberty on Earth*. But Koen didn't seem to notice my excitement. He just held my fingers limply in his calloused hand and pulled me forward.

"You'll see."

Our footsteps echoed across the tile ground. Then Koen shoved his weight against one final door, and we were out in the open air again. At long last he let my fingers go. I dropped my head back, gazing upward.

We were in a back alleyway. Brick surrounded us on all sides. At the intrusion a flock of birds had flown upward, dashing from one painted window to the next. I could see the ceiling panels over us, hanging only a few meters above the tops of the shop buildings. The only exit was up, then, or back the way we'd come—and the door had just slammed shut behind me.

At the back of the alley stood Van Hofstadter. He was slumped against the brick. He didn't even stand straight at the sight of us.

"Well, would you look at the lovebirds," he said dryly. Out of the corner of my eye, I saw Koen wince.

"You said I could bring her," he said.

"What was I supposed to say? She's an adult now, a full citizen. I can't stop you."

Koen leaned over, whispering to me. "You can become one of us only after you turn sixteen. Children aren't supposed to know about us."

"Us?" I said faintly, glancing between the boys.

"The Children of Abel," Koen said. And then he added, all in a rush: "Van told me that it's from a story. A very old story. Somewhere on Earth there was a garden. The first men were cast out of it, two brothers among them. One was a shepherd. Abel. The other worked the land. That was his brother, Cain. Abel did his duty, just as we've followed the rule of the Council. But Cain was greedy. He wanted the flocks for himself, so he murdered his brother. Struck him down in the fields."

I thought of Mar Jacobi, of how he'd fallen to the ground in a puddle of his own blood. I stuffed my hands down into my pockets.

"Be careful what you tell her," Van admonished Koen. "I don't trust her yet, and neither do our leaders. Benjamin might have had ideas about asking her to join up, but her father is no friend of Abel. There's no telling if she'll sell us out to the Council."

"'No friend of Abel,'" I echoed. "But my father believes in being a good citizen. It's practically all he ever talks about."

"There's more than one way to be a good citizen," Koen said, touching his hand to the back of his neck.

"Our leaders have demanded a tribute from you, Terra," Van said.

"Proof that you can be trusted. There's a book in your father's possession. We'd like you to take it."

"A book?" As far as I knew, Abba had never been much of a reader.

"It's a journal," Van said. "Very ancient. It belonged to one of the original passengers. It's long been significant to us."

"What would my father be doing with—"

Van lifted his hand. It cut through the cool air, clean and decisive. Slicing through my words. "That doesn't matter. Bring it to me, and we'll know that we can trust you."

I felt a wave of heat crest inside me. Of course I could be trusted. If I knew anything, it was how to keep silent—how to be invisible, how to be nobody. I looked at Van, my gaze hardening.

"Fine," I said hotly. "I'll get you your book."

I turned to leave, gesturing for Koen to follow. After giving Van a long, baleful look, he did. But as the heavy door swung on its hinges behind us, I heard Van's sharp tenor come calling for me.

"I'll believe it when I see it!" he said.

The door slammed shut behind me.

The next morning I opened my bedroom door a crack to let the cat out. Then I fell back into bed, the covers pulled up to my chin.

It wasn't unusual for my father to leave before I did. He had bells to ring, a *talmid* to teach. And I'd long preferred to skip breakfast, avoiding the clatter of dishes and my father's silence and his burning gaze. He always looked at me like he expected something. Sometimes over oatmeal he'd ask me strained questions about Mara Stone. I dodged them. For sixteen years he'd ignored my life, my interests— ignored *me*. I had no intention of making friends now just because I was about to move out of our dreary home.

That morning I listened to him rattle around in the galley. There was the slam of the cupboards, the crash of pans, and the sound of water rushing fast. From my dark bedroom I listened to it slosh over the floor.

At last came the slam of the front door. I rose and left my unmade bed behind. The space between my bedroom and my father's had never felt so huge before. I took a dozen silent steps, holding my breath.

As I stepped across the threshold of his room, I heard a rustle of sound behind me. I jumped, turning—but it was only Pepper, crouched at the top of the stairs with a catnip mouse held between his paws.

"Stupid cat," I muttered, shoving the door open with both hands.

The curtains in my father's bedroom were tightly closed, as usual. But he had left his bedside lamp on, and it bathed the room in warm light. The illumination spilled over his crisply made bed and down across the threadbare carpet. His room was the only one in our house kept clean. The sole sign of my father's chaos was the glass that sat encrusted with wine on the floor beside his bed, a line of ants circling the rim.

I moved quickly. First I ducked my head beneath the wide double bed that he'd once shared with my mother, but all that greeted me were cobwebs, cat toys, and dust. Then I went to the dressers, opening each one. I ran my hand along the dresser bottoms, beneath the reams of folded cotton. But the drawers held no books or secrets.

Finally I stood before my father's closet door. Down the hall my own closet vomited old toys and paper and clothing. But my father had hung up each uniform coat with care. I shoved the hangers aside, but only the wall greeted me.

Then my eyes strayed down.

There, between two pairs of leather boots, sat a wooden box. The top had a floral design carved into it. Once it held my mother's jewelry. Now the elaborate leaves and flowers and scrollwork were edged with dust. I fell to my knees before it and lifted the lid.

I found a tangle of necklace chains, the metal dark and in desperate need of a polish. And a pressed flower—what had once been a violet but whose delicate petals were now brown and brittle and nearly destroyed. I stared at the paper-thin leaves, wondering who had picked the blossom for my mother. A silly question. It must have been my father, of course. He was always bringing home flowers for her, their stems tied up with pretty bows. I set the flower down against the box's lid. That's when I saw something square, wrapped up in brown paper and twine.

I sat on my heels, holding it up in both hands. Momma's hand-writing was scrawled across the paper. She'd had a sloppy, jagged script—quite a bit like mine. I ran my index finger over the long-dried ink. It read:

Arran—

Great great (etc.) grandmother's journal. (private!!)

Please give to Terra before she leaves home, & know I always love you both.

—Alyana

He hadn't ever opened it—that much was clear. The twine was tied in a tangle of impossible-looking knots. Holding the volume out in both hands, I carried it to the bed and sat down. I was sup-posed to take this book and bring it to Van. The task had sounded easy enough. But I hadn't anticipated that the book would be Momma's or that she had meant it to be *mine*. What did I have of my mother? A small handful of memories? A few sweaters? Suddenly my hands woke to life. I tugged the twine downward, tore the paper aside. At long last I undressed the book. It looked ancient—cracked leather cover, and gold-edged pages, and gold letters stamped into the front. Old American. DAY JOURNAL, it said.

I leaned back against my father's bed, letting my hair fan out across the smooth blankets. Then I lifted the book and began to read.

At first it was difficult for me to decipher the handwriting. The writer, one of my long-dead ancestors, the matriarch of my bloodline, had written in nearly incomprehensible cursive. *Z*s that dropped below the line. *Q*s that looked like giant numeral twos. But eventually I got used to it. I don't know what I was looking for in those pages. No, that's not true. I knew, but I didn't want to admit it. I was looking for some shadow of my mother in that woman, an old woman who wrote daily letters to a daughter she had also named Terra.

I didn't find her. This woman was hard, bitter—nothing like my mother at all. She wrote all about her daily life on the ship, about how claustrophobic the light panels that lined the dome made her feel and how she didn't like the taste, mossy and stale, of the recycled water. These things meant nothing to me—after all, I'd drunk that water all my life. I'd never tasted what she called "the crisp tap water of New York City, the best water in the world," and I'd never experienced the wonders of getting sunburned after "sitting out all day under a hazy Manhattan Beach sky."

She hated the ship. She would lie down beside a man she didn't love, and her heart twisted and thundered in her chest. But she did it anyway. Over and over again she wrote about how someday, maybe, it would all be worth it—someday some descendant of hers, some distant great-great-great-great-grandchild, might have a chance to set her feet on a planet, a real planet, under a real, wide sky. And be free again. Spiritually. Emotionally. Physically.

Some of the things she wrote scared me.

> *The ship is governed by a group of wealthy men and women, chosen by virtue of their corporate ties on Earth. Families like the Raffertys— smug bastards, drunk with their own power. Who gave them the right to rule?*

and

> *I remember the day they took your brother away to be sterilized. Only thirteen years old. They told us to tell him that the "ceremony" would make him a man, that it was a mitzvah. . . . I may not be a good Jew myself, but it nauseates me, the way they've perverted religion.*

I read, and read, and read, tasting my own frantic heartbeat in my mouth. It wasn't until the clock bells rang out in the distance that I bolted upright. Ten chimes for ten o'clock. My hands shook as I smoothed down my hair, remembering Mara's lab and the duties that still waited for me. Ducking into the closet, I shut Momma's jewelry box and slid Abba's suits back into place. Then I gathered the crumpled paper and twine up, and held them close. Momma's words were on them. Her soft hands had touched this paper—this ink. I couldn't throw it away. So I tucked the book under my arm and carried it back to my room.

I folded the brown paper into a square the length and width of my palm and tucked it into my underwear drawer, buried at the back where no one ever looked. The journal went inside my bag. I dressed in a hurry, throwing my lab coat on and pushing a knit cap down over my untamed hair. Then I hustled downstairs. But as I made my way through the empty districts, I held my bag against my chest. I could almost feel the journal there, throbbing like a second heart.

After work I sat on a stone bench in front of the library. I watched children straggle along the path from the school toward the districts. Little girls walked along with their arms interlinked—young boys chased and jostled one another. I felt a sharp stab in my chest. Not for the first time, I wanted nothing more than to join them, to leave my bag with its heavy burden in the pricker bushes and go run and play until I felt dizzy and out of breath.

The iron doors finally swung open. Out stepped Van. He wore a smart sheepskin coat and heavy scarf. A leather satchel, weighted with books, was slung over one shoulder. In his gloved hands Van held an iron key. He locked the library doors with it.

"Hello, Terra," he said, hardly looking at me.

I rose to my feet. "I have the book!"

Van tipped his head.

"What book? I'm the librarian, girl. There are many books."

"The book," I said weakly. My hand settled on the flap of my bag. I could feel the shape of the journal there—the corners were sharp under my fingers. "The one you asked for."

"Come with me," Van said, and hurried away from the crowded pavilion.

I matched my strides to his. Together, not speaking, we made our way along the path that ran beside the pasture fence. It wasn't until we reached a narrow footbridge, shadowed with browning willow branches, that he turned to me.

"Stupid girl. What if someone heard you?"

"Sorry!" I said, my face warming. I lowered my voice to a whisper, though there was no one near except a few carrion crows that loitered in the branches overhead. "I got what you asked for. You know. The book."

"That was fast."

Van held out his hand.

I threw my bag open. But then I found myself staring down into the shadows. Amid the crumpled papers and the wrinkled pages of my sketchpad, I could see the journal's gilded pages. I ran my finger along them. The metal felt cool and smooth. I thought of Momma's note. *Give to Terra*, it had said. She had meant the book for *me*.

"Will I get it back?" I asked, still staring down. At first, Van scoffed.

"It doesn't belong to you. It belongs to all of us."

I looked at the librarian, and my voice took on a cold edge. "It was my mother's. And now it's *mine*."

Van's mouth stayed hard a moment. But then it fell open. He sighed.

"Fine," he said. "I can copy it, then return it to you."

He held his hand out to me again. I looked at his open, waiting palm.

"Liberty on Earth," I said to myself at last, hoping the words would help me to feel triumphant. I'm not sure it worked. I reached into my bag and then shoved the book at Van. I watched him throw it into his satchel with all his other books.

My eyes burning, I started down the path. But Van called out to me.

"Terra Fineberg!" he said. I stopped, but didn't turn. I couldn't stand to look at him. "The meeting's at twenty-three o'clock tonight. In the library."

Finally, finally, I'd done something right. A grin lifted the corners of my mouth. I turned to the librarian and touched two fingers to my heart in salute. He squinted in puzzlement, but touched his heart back in turn.

I hadn't realized how small my world had always felt, until the day when the Children of Abel invited me to join them. It was as if the dome walls had opened, leading me toward a brand-new place. As I hurried down the path toward home, I felt, for the first time, like I was walking toward something. Toward my future. Toward Zehava.

ow that the winter and long nights had begun in earnest, there was no artificial sun to pass through the library's stained glass windows. Instead the dusty chandeliers that hung from the rafters were on. Their feeble bulbs burned a slow, gloomy yellow, casting long shadows through the wood beams. I passed through the iron doors, nearly missing the figure in the shadows there. It was Van who slipped by me, hustling toward the door.

"They're up there," he said, gesturing toward the staircase as the key clanked in the lock.

Voices drifted down from the first landing, beside the ancient card catalog that stood gathering dust. Three strangers, men, who wore the brown, rough-hewn garb of fieldworkers, spoke in low tones. Green cords barely held on to the worn fabric of their coats. Among them stood Koen. My intended's gaze met mine, and he lifted his arm at the sight of me.

"Terra!" he called, grinning. "You came!"

Somewhere in the distance, acres and acres away in the center of the atrium's fields, bells struck the hour. The sound reached us even here. Van breezed by us and up the staircase.

"Follow me," he called.

The three men whispered among themselves as we trudged upward. There was something that felt dangerous about the way they all looked at one another—furtive, desperate, hungry, proud. My hands felt cold inside my lab coat pockets.

We made our way up and up and up the narrow steps. On the top floor a skinny walkway bordered the book-lined walls, shouldered by a once-polished railing that had gathered a fur of dust. The rafters hung low overhead. Koen had to bend his neck to make his way beneath them. At first all I could see was his back—dark corduroy over slumped shoulders—and the dim chasm of books and shelves below. But then we followed Van around a wide shelf of books and found ourselves on a balcony that looked out over the entire library.

A small crowd waited for us there, draped over leather-stuffed chairs and leaning their weight against the precarious railing. There weren't many citizens on the balcony that night—fifteen, perhaps twenty. Fewer than had been in my class at school. But there were a few familiar faces among them.

Sitting at a study desk, his hands folded in front of him, was Rebbe Davison. He smiled at me, then, swiftly, as if embarrassed, looked away. And there, stooped on a footstool, was Mar Schneider, our old neighbor who was always digging in his yard out front. His ancient eyes hardly seemed to notice me in the library's feeble light. I even spotted a few of our old classmates sitting wedged together on one of the overstuffed sofas. Deklan Levitt, the gruff fieldworker. And his intended, Laurel Selberlicht, pressed beside him. She'd been the best shuttle pilot in our class and was now training to ferry us to Zehava. And she caught my eye as I looked out across the balcony, lifted her hand, and waved.

Koen and I sat down beside each other on the dingy carpet. His grin was glinting and white.

"Meet the Children of Abel," he said.

Van pushed his way to the front of the crowd. He stood before the railing, his broad hands folded in front of him. The balcony was filled with whispers, hissed words. Koen leaned toward me again, his voice low.

"We're only a single cell of a greater movement," he said. "No cell knows who the other members are, except for the librarian. Van acts as a go-between, passing messages among all of us. Jacobi trained him for the job."

The memory of the guard's words echoed through my mind.

The names! Give them to me!

"Does the Council know he's been trained to do Jacobi's work?" I asked, leaning forward. Koen gave his head a sharp shake.

"Of course not. How would they?"

I thought of the way the knife's blade looked as it drew across Jacobi's throat. Then I glanced at Van. The skin of his own neck was very white under his ruddy stubble. He looked confident as he stood with his back against the railing, gazing out at us. I wouldn't have been so self-assured if I had information that the Council wanted.

The sound of Van's voice brought my consciousness slamming back into my body.

"What news do we have since our last meeting?" he asked. A woman who stood near the stairs shouted out to him, eager to have her voice heard.

"I've heard word that the Council destroyed the probes!" she said. "They're claiming they were lost, but there's been no evidence." There was a fevered rush of agreement. Van lifted up his hands for silence.

"Our leadership is well aware that the Council destroyed the first exploratory probes. We're working on a contingency plan should Wolff and her cohort follow through with the destruction or suppression of a second set of probe results."

A wave of grumbles worked its way through the balcony. After a moment it died down again. I saw Rebbe Davison raise his hand.

"How many times do I have to tell you that this isn't school, Mordecai?"

Laughter rippled all around him. At last Rebbe Davison stood, chuckling at himself. He held a heavy book.

"I've been researching the history of the ship's contracts. The powers currently held by the Council were not in the contract signed by the original passengers. They only specified the Council ruling from departure to landing. But that was changed in our grandparents' generation. Perverted by Wolff's predecessor, I presume."

Hearing my teacher speak so cavalierly of our leaders gave me an unexpected thrill. Goose bumps shivered their way down my arms. He opened up the book to a marked page and began to read.

"'Article 10.2, revision C. For the continued safety and assurances of the population of the *Asherah*, the captain's powers shall extend from the time of departure through landing and settlement of Epsilon Eridani S/2179 D, colloquially known as "Zehava," until he or she, in wisdom and with the full consent of the Council, deems it prudent to relinquish said powers. Upon relinquishment the Council shall establish a representative democracy in accordance with article 19.0 and the intentions of the original signers of this great contract.'"

"'Deems it prudent,'" Van said as Rebbe Davison slammed the book shut. Then Van repeated his sour words, louder this time. They echoed under the rafters, against the walls of books. "'Deems it prudent'! For how long will we live like children because the Council says they know what's best for us?"

All around me the men and women nodded, murmured words of assent. Mar Schneider even pumped his wrinkled old hand through the air. I felt something alien. My chest flooded with a wave of excitement. For the first time in my life, I wanted to nod, shout, pump my fist too.

"They picked our jobs for us! They choose where we live. And if we drag our feet too much, they'll even choose who we love."

"Yeah," Koen said. I studied his features. His broad mouth was open, the corners lifted in breathless excitement.

Liberty on Earth . . . The words rattled around my brain. I could feel them against my tongue like some sort of honey treat.

For the very first time I understood what they truly meant.

"It's even up to them if we live in the dome or walk free on Zehava," I said, but too low. At first I didn't think that anyone heard me over the jumble of agitated conversation. But Van's sharp ears practically pricked up at the sound of my voice. He turned toward me.

"Terra Fineberg," he said, smiling slyly. "What did you say?"

I felt my face flush. But I wasn't afraid of Van. I lifted my chin, looking squarely at him. "Mara Stone told me that if the Council decides we can't live on Zehava, then they'll pilot the dome to the surface and we'll continue to live inside it."

There was a sudden frenzy of dismayed conversation.

"That can't be!" cried Mar Schneider. Beside me, Koen's mouth fell open in disbelief. But from the sofa in the corner, Laurel spoke up.

"It's true," she said. "They've given each of the pilots a course in dome flight. It's the only possible answer. Why else would they destroy the probe results?"

Van stared. His lips were set firmly, taking it all in. "This is the first I've heard of it," he said. He sounded as if he couldn't quite believe that this news had passed him by. He beckoned us toward him. "Terra, Laurel, please come speak to me." Then he looked out to the rest of the crowd.

"That's all for tonight, folks." He touched two fingers to his heart. "Liberty on Earth."

A chorus of voices lifted toward him. I was surprised to find my own voice joining in. "Liberty on Zehava!"

After the meeting Koen and I waited on one of the sofas while Van spoke in hushed tones to Laurel Selberlicht. Most of the other citizens had left already, though Rebbe Davison continued to chatter on with a pair of men by the stairwell, the book of contracts tucked under his arm. I watched him for a long time. His hands flashed through the air in excitement, just like they had when he'd lectured us in school.

"I can't believe Rebbe Davison is part of all of this," I said. Koen sat forward, his hands folded beneath his chin.

"Hmm?"

"Rebbe Davison. You know, our teacher? Who taught us everything there is to know about being a good citizen?"

"Oh, yeah," Koen said, letting out a burst of awkward laughter. "I guess it *is* weird. Never thought of it before."

I frowned at him, following the line of his eyes. They were fixed on Van. The librarian had at long last dismissed Laurel, who touched her fingers to her heart before she hustled down the stairs. Now he collapsed in a nearby armchair. He didn't so much sit in the leather seat as sprawl, his limbs forming weird angles: one leg over the chair's arm, one muscular arm over the chair's back.

"So, Terra?" he called to me. "Is it true?"

I marched toward him, my chin angled up and firm. It felt good to know something that Van Hoftstadter didn't.

"That's what Mara Stone told me. If conditions on Zehava aren't favorable for our settlement—or if the Council says they're not—we're to stay within the dome."

"Hmm," Van said, the corner of his mouth twitching. "And we can believe Stone? She has made it abundantly clear she's not one of us."

"She's not one of *them*, either," I said. Out of the corner of my eye, I saw Koen rake his fingers awkwardly through his hair.

"Mar Fineberg *did* say not to trust her," Koen said.

"Well," Van said, at last sitting up straight, resting his elbows on his knees as he regarded me, "our leaders will appreciate this information."

"Who *are* the leaders of the Children of Abel, anyway?" I asked.

"That's a dangerous question to ask," Van said. He narrowed his eyes down to slivers.

I blanched. "Sorry," I said, turning toward the stairs to leave before Van noticed how pink my cheeks had become. But then I saw that Koen hadn't moved to follow.

"Are you coming?"

I watched as a faint blush blossomed across the bridge of his nose too.

"I need to talk to Van about something," he said.

"Suit yourself."

Koen squatted on the ground in front of Van, murmuring to him in low tones. I hustled toward the stairs. But Rebbe Davison stopped me before I could make my way down the spiraling staircase.

"Terra," he said. I felt an old familiar fondness in his gaze. This was my teacher—he'd watched me grow up, hadn't he? A smile lifted my lips.

"Hello, Rebbe Davison," I said. He let out a soft laugh.

"You're an adult now. Call me Mordecai."

"Mordecai," I repeated, though the name felt uncertain on my tongue.

"I'm so glad you're here with us," he said. Then he looked down at the book he clutched between his fingers. He pressed it into my hands. "Here, take this."

"A history of the ship's contracts?" I asked, wrinkling my nose as I flipped through it. The pages were as thin as an onion skin and nearly as translucent. Black, blurry text covered them.

"A bit dry," Rebbe Davison admitted with a reluctant smile. "But perhaps you'll find some inspiration in it."

Before I turned down the stairs, Rebbe Davison touched two fingers to his heart.

"Liberty on Earth," he said. I held the book to my chest.

"Liberty on Zehava," I said proudly back.

I stayed up late that night, Pepper dozing across my ankles. I balanced the heavy book of contracts over my head, leafing through the pages until all the blood drained from my arms. My hands went cold. My ears were filled with the steady, nearly silent buzz of my bedroom lights. Still, I read.

Every contract was longer than the one before it. Each new article was initialed by the hand of the ship's captain down through the ages. And every one expanded the powers of the Council. In school, history seemed like a straight line, running from the original passengers right down to us. Rebbe Davison had made it sound like there hadn't ever been a hiccup. He had always taught us that once we landed, life would continue, confined and regimented, as it always had.

I supposed that he never really believed it. Because it was right there, in the pages of that heavy book. The truth was written in the first version of the contract, and the second, and the third. Article 4.12. *The dissolution of the vocation system upon arrival on Epsilon Eridani S/2179 D, ensuring that our descendants, in full acknowledgment of their liberties, may explore for themselves the potential of their new home and their new lives.* Or Article 9.14. *The restoration of reproductive rights. So that our descendants may reclaim their full biological potential and multiply and bear children, or not, according to both their wishes and their needs.* The script was tiny and square, but clear.

Sometime near the start of the new day, I rose from my bed. Pepper gave a meow of protest, then stretched, exposing his white belly to me. I smiled at him through my exhaustion, but I didn't stop to lace my fingers through his silky fur. Instead I walked to my desk and sat down, opening my sketchbook to the first blank page.

"Who would I be if it weren't for the *Asherah*?" I wrote in jagged, loopy script. "Who did my ancestors want me to be?"

And then, with my inky pen, I sketched myself—my eyes, wide set with heavy lids; the slightly off-kilter line of my nose; my thin mouth; the long line of my neck. But I didn't know what to draw around me. What kind of world would I live on soon? I had no idea. For all I knew, it would be the same world. The sky above me would be shaded by the same dome, even if it was nestled beneath an alien sun.

With my pen I drew hashmarks. Jagged lines. Shadows all around me, impenetrable, inscrutable.

I streamed into the lab, hoping that Mara wouldn't notice my late arrival. No such luck. As soon as I dropped my bag beside my work desk, her voice called out to me.

"You're late, Fineberg," she said, hardly looking up from her work ledger. Mara's gaze was as chilly as the ice that now coated the dome rivers in thin sheets. I felt the determined line of my mouth soften.

"What would you like me to do today?" I finally asked.

She had me doing slide prep—slicing leaf samples down into translucent slivers and fixing them onto the tiny slips of glass. It was exacting work, and I couldn't steady my hand that morning. In fact, my mind raced, swarmed with words.

As I set out another tiny rectangle of glass, listening to the hum of the lights overhead, I thought about how our society had survived these five hundred years. By swallowing our lumps and doing what we were told. Even if it bored us—even if we hated it. I used my eyedropper to squeeze out a bead of fixative onto the slide. Then I lifted my blade again.

I wasn't looking at my hands or the leaf shredded to pieces beneath them. Perhaps that's why I sank the razor blade right down the side of my index finger.

Pain burned its way toward my bone. I let out a cry, doing my best to close the wound with the hem of my lab coat. But blood had already begun to gush out.

"Terra?" Mara called. In a moment she was beside me, her eyebrows lifted. Beneath her usual veneer of impatience, she was *actually* concerned. She pried my fingers away, revealing a thin cut that ran from the side of my knuckle to the tip of my index finger. "Put pressure on it. I'll get a bandage."

Mara wandered off to her desk. She seemed to be taking her time rummaging through it, whistling to herself. Finally she returned with a glass bottle of antiseptic and an adhesive bandage.

"Let's see," she urged, easing my hand away again. She splashed the antiseptic over it, and I drew in a sharp breath. But when I looked up, Mara was grinning.

"That wasn't so bad," she said as she wrapped it. I watched the blood pool beneath the surface of the bandage, congealing in a brownish, squished-down spot.

"Easy for you to say," I said. I could feel how Mara studied me.

"Terra," she said at last, "you're not your usually sunny self this morning." I glowered at her. But she was unperturbed. "You know, I heard there was a little gathering last night. In the library, hmm?"

I felt the blood drain from my hands. Even the cut seemed to throb a little less.

"How did you hear about that?"

Mara waved her hand through the air. "They invited me. They always do. I keep saying no, but they just never get the picture."

I didn't know what to say. But apparently Mara didn't expect me to say a thing. In a delicate tone she just rambled on.

"You need to understand," she said, "that historically there have been many rebellions. On Earth there were the peasant uprisings of France. The American revolts—three civil wars could be blamed on revolutionaries there, in fact. There were the Jacobite Risings. The Boxer Rebellion. The Indian Mutiny of 1857. So it's unsurprising that we've seen uprisings on the *Asherah*. One might say that such acts are a part of human nature. Like teenagers"—she made no effort to conceal the laughter that hid beneath her cool expression—"we all must eventually rise up against our parents."

I just stared at her, still holding my injured hand out in front of me.

"It's happened on the ship several times. The largest was the uprising that coincided with the deactivation of the ship's engines. That was . . . a dark time in the *Asherah*'s history. Without the sound of the ship's engines to drive them, many passengers felt lost. For the first time in their lives, they saw how empty their lives were. You know, before the uprising all marriages were chosen by the Council, as vocations are today."

"I know," I said. But I couldn't imagine it. At least Koen and I got along, mostly.

Even if he still wouldn't kiss me.

"Terra . . ." Mara spoke carefully.

"Yeah?"

She let out a deep sigh. "In the event that your tardiness this morning does indeed have something to do with the Children of Abel . . ." My ears pricked up at the name, but I did my best not to let it show. I only kept my mouth tight. "You should know that every single time they've approached me, I've turned them down."

"Oh." I was still being careful to look disinterested.

"They know of my feelings about child rearing and marriage. I can't imagine why anyone would be interested in such things, but you know how gossip travels through these halls."

I nodded.

"I always tell them that Mara Stone's never been much of a joiner. Movements are for people who can't move themselves, that's what I've always said."

She cocked her head to one side, looking at me for a long moment. It was the sort of scrutiny that would have normally made me blush—but I was too spent for that. "Really, I'd expect no different from you. You *are* my *talmid*, after all. *P. pungens*?"

I squinted at her. She held her palm out. "The *Picea pungens* sample, Terra. You know, *some* of us still have work to do."

I turned to one of the long boxes of finished slides that waited on my desk. As I ran my finger along the glass edge, I heard Mara make a strange noise—a rumble low in her throat, like she was trying to get it clear but couldn't.

"Funny thing," she said. It seemed she spoke more to herself than she did to me. "I can't remember the name of the woman who first asked me to join the Children of Abel. I do remember the smell of her, all yeasty. And there was flour on her shirt. I believe she was a baker. Yes, that's right. A baker. Now, what was her name? You know, it's been years since I last saw her. I wonder whatever became of her."

I swallowed hard, but it didn't do anything for the lump in my throat as I handed Mara her slide.

"Oh, well," she said, taking it from me. "I suppose it doesn't really matter now. Does it, Terra?" Though the words seemed casual, her gaze was piercing, pointed. Like she was sharing a secret with me.

That's when the pieces fell into place. The journal. Mar Jacobi. The bakery. Mara's words.

Momma was a Child of Abel. A rebel. Like me.

"No, it doesn't matter," I said quickly, and though my lips lifted in a giddy, exhausted smile, we both ignored it. "It doesn't matter at all."

14

A few nights later I came home to an empty house. I couldn't be sure where Abba had gone—out drinking or wandering the streets. But I was relieved to find our quarters silent and peaceful. I'd just begun fixing Pepper his dinner when a knock came at the door.

It was Koen. When I saw him standing in the doorway, his smile broad, I felt my heart swell in my chest.

"I have something for you," he said, and held the journal out to me. I snatched it from him, and hugged it to myself. Then I laughed a little. I must have looked foolish, clutching the leather book to me like it contained the spirit of my mother in its pages.

"Thank you," I said sheepishly. "Would you like to come in?"

My pulse raced as I said it. Now that we shared the rebellion between us, I wondered if Koen would finally take me in his arms, touching his lips to mine. He glanced into the dark galley behind me.

"Sure," he said.

We went up into my room together. Pepper soon appeared, wrapping himself around Koen's ankles. I waited in the doorway to see where Koen would sit. Maybe he would settle into the nest of tangled sheets on my bed. If he did, I would sit down beside him and press my leg against his. But, to my disappointment, he sat in my desk chair instead. I tried not to sigh as I sat on the end of my bed alone, drawing my knees up against my chest.

"So what *is* that?" he asked, pointing to the journal that he'd carried for me across the dome. My fingers caressed the smooth leather cover.

"Van didn't tell you?"

At this, Koen flushed lightly, scratching at the back of his neck. "Um, no. I didn't ask him."

"It belonged to one of my ancestors. She was one of the first passengers, but she wasn't like the signers we learned about in school. She was an agitator."

"Like us!" Koen exclaimed, his grin broadening. I couldn't help but smile back at him. I had liked the way it felt to chant along with the fieldworkers in the library, to touch my hands to my heart in salute and have it mean something for once.

"Yeah," I said. "She wouldn't have been happy to know that five hundred years down the line we still live under the Council's thumb."

"Can I see it?"

I passed it to him. He began to fan the pages, but then a scrap of paper that had been pressed between the cover and the first page fell out. It fluttered to the floor. Koen bent to pick it up.

"That's Van's handwriting," he said, frowning. He handed it back to me.

"'Terra,'" I read aloud, holding the scrap of paper between my middle finger and thumb, "'we need extract of common foxglove. Stone will have in herbarium. Bring to next meeting. Van.'"

I, too, frowned. "Did you know he was going to ask me for this?"

"No!" Koen said, and from the way that his eyes went wide enough to show the whites, I believed it. "What would they want with some plant?"

"I don't know," I said, biting my lip, "but I don't think I can help them. It's not like I've even seen the herbarium. Mara's the only one who goes in there." I'd seen the door at the rear of the lab but never even stepped past the threshold. And Mara wasn't eager to help the rebels. She'd made that much clear. So I crumpled the sheet into a ball and tossed it down to the floor. Pepper pounced after it, batting it as if it were one of his catnip mice. I smiled at the way the cat's tail furled and unfurled in slow waves. But then I saw that Koen wasn't smiling anymore.

"What?"

"You should do what they ask," he said. I was surprised to hear a note of fear in his voice, bright and clear. "From what Van tells me, they're not . . . they're not the kind of people you want to make mad."

On the floor Pepper took a running dive toward the paper and chased it underneath the bed.

"I've proved my worth to them. So why should I be afraid of people I can't even see?" I glanced at my intended. "Why should *you*?"

"You're not the only one who's had to do stuff for them." Koen raked his hand through his hair. "They asked me to watch your father, Terra. And report his activities back to them."

"My father? Really?" It was hard for me to imagine what sort of threat my drunken father might pose to the Children of Abel.

"I don't even know why. He never *does* anything. He mostly seems . . . kind of sad."

"My father is no friend of Abel," I said, an echo of Van's voice in my melancholy words.

"I guess he isn't. But he doesn't seem dangerous, either."

Silence stretched between us. Desperate to fill it, I slid down onto the floor and gathered Pepper in my hands. The cat leaned his body into mine, drawn to its warmth.

"I don't really understand how you got involved with them, Koen," I said softly. To my surprise, Koen set the journal on top of my desk. He came to sit beside me, his knee knocking mine. Pepper stretched slowly, then tiptoed over onto Koen's legs. I watched my intended run his fingers along the bony ridges of the cat's back.

"I used to always hang out in the library. Reading about the way the dome works. The changes of the seasons, all of that. Van started talking to me one day. We hit it off. He's just so passionate about everything. This was last year. I was worried that the Council would stick me with some job I didn't want. I don't know. Once I had my vocation, I thought things would change. That I'd lose interest in the whole thing. But I didn't, not after Van dragged me to a meeting. The way people talk there . . . it was so easy to get swept up in it."

I thought of the jumble of voices that had filled the library rafters, rattling the dust and the cobwebs from the corners. I thought of how I'd moved my fingers to my chest in salute without even a second thought. I'd felt proud to be part of something for once. Like it wasn't so bad that I was different—because there were other people here on the ship who felt as odd and ill fitting as I did. I could understand how someone could get caught up in that. But not Koen.

"I thought you wanted to be normal."

"I do," he said. "Of course I do. But . . ."

"But what?" I asked.

"But when it comes down to it, I don't think I ever will be."

I didn't know what to say. By then Pepper had settled in on Koen's lap. Koen's big hand rested between the cat's shoulder blades. His knuckles were bony, and blue veins lined his skinny wrists. Despite their size, they were fragile, delicate-looking hands. When I reached out and finally put my dirty, work-hard hand on top of his, our hands presented a strange contrast. Koen didn't turn his hand over, didn't take my fingers in his, squeezing them tight. But he also didn't draw his hand away.

"That's okay," I said gently. "I don't think I'll ever be normal either."

Two days later we entered the edge of the orbit of Eps Eridani, our new sun. The captain decreed it would be a feast day like the harvest, even though the weather was cold and the times were lean. We were excused from our duties and given extra rations, and the little kids all wore their best winter clothes—fur coats and velvet dresses and ribbons in their hair.

I didn't have anything nice of my own, only a green knit dress that had once been Momma's. It was too big, but I tried to look presentable, rolling the sleeves up around my elbows, knotting one of her old scarves around my narrow waist. It felt strange to be wearing something other than my lab coat and trousers—I almost didn't feel like *me*. But when Abba peered in and saw me staring at myself in my bedroom mirror, a smile lit up his weathered face.

It seemed I was becoming my mother in more ways than one.

The two of us went to Koen's quarters for an early supper. Koen's dad made an orange-colored curry and dry, flat loaves of bread that were so different from what we ate in our own household that it was hard to believe they were made from the same species of wheat. But I forced a smile as I chewed and washed it down with a big gulp of my rationed wine. Not that anyone was paying much attention to me anyway.

Koen's parents spent the whole meal fighting. I might have had the good manners to refrain from commenting on the food, but Koen's mother apparently didn't.

"I can't believe we wasted our protein rations on *this*," she said, tossing her napkin down over her nearly full plate. Koen's eyes widened in horror.

"Well, then *you* should have spent all morning in the galley!"

"Don't even start with me! You know I was busy with Stella!"

Koen's sister was dressed in layers of navy velvet. Her dark hair had been curled into spirals. As her parents argued, she looked somehow pleased, a wicked smile curling up the pretty bow of her mouth. Koen buried his face in his hands. I thought he might start crying, but instead he just stayed there like that, frozen through the rest of the meal.

The only gap in the Maxwells' argument came during dessert. After Koen's mother slammed a plate of steaming pie down in front of her husband, she spat, "There! *You* serve it!" and then collapsed in her chair again. Before her husband had a chance to respond, my father rapped the tines of his fork against his cup.

"I'd like to make a toast," he said.

Five pairs of eyes swiveled over to him. I think we'd all forgotten he was there. My father lifted himself solemnly to his feet. I watched as Koen's mom looked to her husband, shrugged. Reaching for our cups, we all stood.

"To my daughter," my father said. His voice was rough at the edges, a little sloppy. I wondered how much he'd had to drink that day even before this glass. "And to Koen, as they join our families together. To the promise of their lives ahead. To life, and to Zehava. *L'chaim.*"

Everyone clinked glasses. I only sucked in my cheeks. Then I felt my dad set his hand between my shoulder blades. I could feel the pressure of his wide fingers on my spine as he leaned in close.

"Your mother would be so proud of you," he said.

I gasped down the last mouthful of bitter white wine and said, *"L'chaim."*

We all gathered in the field beneath the clock tower. The grass was blue with frost and seemed to glitter with a thousand diamonds even in the evening's fading light. Everyone was bundled up in their heavy coats and hats and gloves. Though I'd layered myself as best I could, I could still feel the cold straight through my wool stockings. *This* was why I hated wearing dresses.

"You'll feel better when we get the heater going," Koen assured me, hefting the electric device.

"We could have sat with your family," I said, looking wistfully at the children who huddled around the heaters, warming their hands against the heating elements. We'd left his parents to bicker at the starboard edge of the field. Koen turned to me, one side of his mouth edging up.

"And we could have sat with *yours*," he replied. He was right—I hadn't given a second thought to dropping my father off with Ronen and Hannah and little Alyana not far from the clock tower. Abba had settled among them, his wrinkled face drawn and serious. I winced at the thought.

"Good point," I said. But the wind still cut through the weave of my dress. I clutched my hands around my shoulders, rubbing them for warmth. "Where are we going, anyway?"

"I told Van and his wife that we'd sit with them."

At that, I stopped where we stood. Koen glanced over at me, his tangled hair falling into his eyes.

"What?"

"Are you sure that's a good idea?" I asked, dropping my voice to nothing more than a murmur. "After all, you said that Van's not the sort of person you want to make angry, and I still haven't asked Mara about the foxglove, and—"

"Terra!" Koen reached out and took my hand in his. Even through his nubby mittens his fingers felt like ice. "I didn't mean *Van*. He's fine. I meant the people he reports to."

I thought about the way Van had looked at us in the alleyway, how his green-glass eyes had sliced into me.

"Are you sure?"

"Of course I'm sure. You're one of us now."

I felt a sudden flood of warmth from within. I found myself pulled across the field, my hand firmly in Koen's. We finally reached Van's little family. And I found myself smiling, too, despite my reservations. Van's wife, Nina, grinned up at me.

"Hello, Terra," she said. She was tugging a knit cap over her baby's red hair. They shared the same round cheeks, but little else.

Her black hair cascaded down her shoulders. "Joyous Orbit Day."

"Joyous Orbit Day," I returned. For a moment I hovered uncertainly over their little gathering. Koen put the heater down beside theirs and fiddled with the dials.

"Have a seat," Van said, gesturing with a pointed finger to the frozen ground. I bit the inside of my cheek, but then I pushed my worries away. I was a rebel now—one of them. I sat down beside Koen and let the heater's glowing coils blow hot breath over me. I showed a shy smile to Nina and Van. They squinted back at me as if my presence among their family was nothing of note.

"You found us," Van said, turning to Koen, who let out a laugh as he settled in beside me.

"Of course I did." He reached out his arms and gathered Van's son in them. It was clear they knew each other well. Koen began to sing "Tsen Brider," folding down the baby's fat fingers. The toddler did his best to sing along. He managed to pick up the rhythm of the song, even if his words came out in little more than an incomprehensible babble.

"We should be able to see Eps Eridani F at any minute now," Van said. Though he seemed to be speaking to all of us, it was Koen he was looking at, watching as the *talmid* cuddled the baby boy. But soon he glanced up. The dome lights began to flicker off. Overhead, through the honeycomb girders, we could see the sparkling expanse of space. Out of the corner of my eye, I saw Koen pass the baby back to Nina. But my gaze was firmly fixed to the glass above. I'd never seen a *planet* among all those stars before. I couldn't help but feel a small thrill at the thought of it.

"Hey," Nina said. A tremble underscored her voice, just fearful enough to pull me out of my excitement. "Look who it is."

She'd gestured to the other end of the field. A flock of dark-coated guards marched in a scattered line, stopping now and then around the huddled families. At first I couldn't imagine what was going on. Then Van's son lifted a pudgy finger and let out a little squeal.

"Capun! Capun!"

Sure enough, there was Captain Wolff, her long hair braided into a silver rope down her back. I watched as she stooped over to shake the hand of every citizen. She chatted easily with them. Still, an ominous silence descended on our strange, cobbled-together little family.

"Here she comes," Van muttered. We all watched as she drew near, flanked on either side by a guard.

"*Talmid* Fineberg." She spoke my name in a tone so sweet it was almost sickening. "The young botanist. Joyous Orbit Day." She took my hand and shook it much too hard for my liking.

"Joyous Orbit Day," I replied, shocked by her firm grip. I tried to avoid looking at her scar—focusing on her hairline, her chin, anywhere else. But before I could find a place to rest my eyes, she moved on to Koen.

"And *Talmid* Maxwell. How goes the clock keeping?"

"Uh," he stammered. "Fine."

Captain Wolff bent down to pinch little Corban's cheeks and to shake Nina's hand. My gaze strayed, catching a flash of white. It was Silvan Rafferty. He stood at the edge of her party, Aleksandra Wolff beside him. The guard tracked him as one might an animal with an inclination to bolt. But he hardly seemed to notice. In fact, he looked bored. Yet when he saw me staring at him, something behind his gaze warmed. He watched me for a long moment, his eyebrows nearly meeting, turning some new idea over in his mind.

My cheeks burned. I looked away. I felt no affection for him—not after what he'd done to Rachel.

"Good riddance," Nina said, exhaling hard as the captain's entourage finally moved on. At the edge of my vision, I saw Aleksandra nudge Silvan with the hilt of her blade. He waited just a moment longer before he turned and trudged away too. "I'm glad that's over."

"She didn't say hello to you," Koen noted. Van's lip curled in response.

"Good," he said, and then he added: "The murderous cow."

Nina rolled her eyes. Then she leaned back, resting her shoulders against Van's body. He drew her close. I watched as Corban snuggled into his mother's arms. They looked like the perfect family. Koen watched them too, frown lines deepening the edges of his mouth. Something clouded up beneath the surface of his expression, stormy and dark. He turned to me.

"Come here," he said, and when I only stared at him, he scooted forward along the frozen ground until he was right beside me. The outside of his lanky leg graced my thigh. I felt heat rise up across my face, and it sure wasn't from Koen's creaky old heater this time. He said it again—"Come *here*!"—and let out a rickety laugh as he pulled me against him.

My shoulders sank back against his chest. He was so skinny—I could feel his ribs beneath his sweater and coat. His body smelled like cedar and musk and dirt. I could feel Van and Nina watching us. I did my best not to look at them, focusing instead on the orange glow of our heater, looking at my own knees, and then up, at the dark dome and the freckling of stars above.

Koen leaned his chin into the place where my neck met my shoulder. *This is what you wanted*, I said to myself. My mind reached back to my dreams, where settling into someone's arms felt just as easy as settling into my bed at night. I ignored the little incongruities—the stuttered, frantic beat of my heart; the way that Koen's body felt, all knees and elbows, against mine. Here, in his arms, I should have been happier than I'd ever been before. So I closed my eyes and willed it to be true.

I felt his lips brush my earlobe. The little hairs on my arms all stood up.

"I'm so glad you're here with us," he said. I licked my lips, getting ready to echo his words back.

"I'm glad to be here t—"

But Nina cut me off. Her voice rose up over the rattle of the heaters.

"Oh!" she said, pointing. "There it is!"

We looked up. There, at the dome's edge, what looked like a new star crawled into view. It was different from the other stars—a bigger pinprick through the darkness of space, shining brightly. Unlike the others, it was green, the color of oxidized copper. Eps Eridani F. Our new neighbor. Applause spread slowly across the field. I should have clapped too. I was a part of something now. A part of Koen's life. A part of the Children of Abel. But for some reason my mind was stormy. I didn't clap; I only drew in a shuddered breath.

Later that night I came home to a dark house. I went from room to room turning on the lights, but it hardly did anything to beat back the darkness. I wanted to be out in the dome, under the sparkle of starlight and that new green speck of light. Of course, it wasn't Zehava—it was a gaseous body, no ground or breathable atmosphere. Still, it was the closest I'd ever been to a planet. Part of me wanted to lay myself down on the frozen ground beneath its light, to wait for my dreams to overtake and comfort me. But it was a crazy thought.

Almost as crazy as stealing plants for the rebellion. I stood frozen over the counter, thinking about it. I was one of them now, a Child of Abel. I needed to act, and soon. But I'd invented a million different reasons for Mara to take me down to the herbarium, and none seemed right when I was under the harsh lab lights. Mara would catch me. She would surely know. What if she turned me in to the Council? What if the guards came for me, just as they'd come for Mar Jacobi?

I remembered his strangled cry. My hands went cold at the memory. When the sound of a fist came, frantic, at the door, I nearly jumped straight out of my skin.

"Coming," I said, rushing over, throwing it open. It was Ronen. He held Alyana against him, cradling her tightly.

"Ronen, what are you doing here?"

My brother barreled past me. "I'm here to talk about Abba," he declared, and sat himself right down at our galley table.

"You don't live here anymore, you know," I said. I could see my brother's jaw flex.

"I know. That's why I knocked."

I sighed and fell into the chair at the far end of the table.

"So go ahead," I said. "Talk about Abba."

"Something happened today in the dome. It wasn't normal."

When was our father ever normal? I stared at Ronen. Jiggling his baby in his arms, he went on.

"The minute the planet came into view, he got up and started to storm off. He wouldn't stop when I called him, but Hannah chased him down. He lost it. Started screaming at her. I was worried he might hit her, the way he used to hit us."

Used to. I grimaced. It was all a distant memory for Ronen. But not for me. "So what'd he say?"

Ronen stopped jiggling. His eyes dropped to the table, tracing the knots in the wood. "He said that he doesn't want to go to Zehava without Mom. Hannah almost couldn't convince him to sit down with us."

I didn't answer at first. I couldn't think about Abba now. Not with the rebellion weighing so heavily on my mind. In the silence Alyana let out a ripple of tears. That was all I needed. I snapped.

"What do you want me to do, Ronen? Bring her back from the dead?"

My brother didn't respond right away. He was too busy hushing his daughter, his lips touching the baby hairs that curled like feathers from her head. When he spoke, it was in a whisper, as if he expected me to whisper too. "I'm concerned. I thought we should talk about it. That's what families do."

I let out a snort and rose from the table. My chair squeaked against the metal floor. "Don't you dare tell me about families. You couldn't wait to get out of here. First chance you got."

"I was sixteen," he said. "Hannah—"

I slammed my hand against the counter. It felt satisfying, echoing through our galley and reverberating all up and down my arm. "Hannah was nothing but a ticket out for you, and you know it. You're concerned now? He's been like this for years. And it's never bothered you before. No, no, not until he makes a scene in the dome. In front of everyone. *Embarrassing* you."

"That's not it."

"I've been living with this *alone* for four years now! And it's only now, when I'm about to *finally* get out of it, that you care? Thanks. Thanks for nothing."

Little Alyana cried and cried. But I turned away from them. Ronen didn't answer me, though I heard him suck in a breath. Like he was trying to hold his anger in. Maybe he really was one of us—an angry person, like my father.

But when Ronen finally spoke, he didn't sound angry at all. He only sounded sad. "Sorry, Terra," he said.

Then I heard his footsteps, and the front door close behind him, and I was alone again—all alone—in the empty silence of our quarters.

Ronen was right. Over the next several days Abba's mood grew even darker. He came home stinking of wine, grumbling his words. Sometimes he passed out in bed while twilight still rosied the dome ceiling. One night, after he'd skipped the supper I'd made to sleep alone upstairs, he barked my name from his bedroom. I stiffened, sure that he'd finally discovered that the paper-wrapped package had disappeared from Momma's jewelry box. But when I went to the door, I saw that his closet remained shut. He sat on the edge of the bed, his shoulders slumped.

"Terra," he said. I could hear the phlegm in his voice. His words seemed to burble up from it, sticky and hopeless. "Marry Koen. He's a good boy. A clock keeper. Just like your old man."

"I know," I said doubtfully, hanging back. "I've already given him my consent."

"Did you?" He swung his heavy head up toward me. His eyes were filmy, hazy, without understanding.

"Yes, Abba," I said, my words coming out in a whisper. "You were *there*."

"Huh," Abba said, chuckling to himself. "So I was."

He turned away from me and stared at the wall. I waited only a moment more before I rushed down the hall toward my room. After I closed the door behind me, shutting away the memory of my father's stiff posture, his gray face, I pulled out my sketchbook. I fumbled with my pencils, scribbling purple flowers across a rolling field. Each green stalk was meant to sag with violet bells. They were foxglove plants, or were supposed to be, at least. I'd looked them up in one of Mara's field guides. There hadn't been much information. Only a diagram. Long stalks. Lozenge leaves. Purple bells, spotted white inside. And the ancient name for them: *Digitalis purpurea*.

Soon I'd shaded nearly the entire page over with purple pigment. I looked down at the frenzy of color, at my hand, red where I'd clutched the pencil too tight. Then I thrust the pencil against the wall and buried my face in my pillow.

Koen kept me distracted.

Now when we walked through the dome after work, we spoke in hushed tones about the rebellion. Koen told me what he thought of liberty—how, when we reached the surface of our new home, he hoped to find the sort of happiness his parents never had. We no longer held hands. Koen's were too busy flitting through the air as he jabbered. And I didn't even try to kiss him. He was always too red-faced, breathless, and antsy for that.

"On the surface," he told me one night as we walked across the frost-blue pastures, "I'd like to have lots of kids. A whole gaggle of them. Because with the Council out of the way, we can have them make more than two down in the hatchery for us, right?"

"Right," I agreed. "But why?"

"Because it's too much pressure to have just one boy and one girl. I mean, look at your dad. He was so worried about whether you would be a specialist or not."

I blushed, stuffing my hands into my pockets. I'd told Koen almost everything about my father—and what I hadn't, Abba had covered for me.

"You really think it would help to have more than two?"

"Sure! It would spread that stuff around. And besides, I think I'd be good at it. Being a dad. I mean, Van's kid loves me."

I thought about the way that little Corban had beamed up at Koen, and I couldn't help but give a nod of agreement.

"He does," I said. I squinted, wondering whether Koen would have the same sort of relationship with our own children. But the thought felt somehow absurd. Even though we were supposed to have our first child within five years of marriage, I couldn't imagine motherhood, for the life of me.

"So," Koen said, "what do *you* want life to be like once the Children of Abel take over?"

He was talking too loudly again, and in such open air. I held a finger to my lips, shushing him. And then I shrugged. "I don't know. I just hope we get more of a say in the way things work."

"Like the job system?"

He was always harping on about that—about what a tragedy it was that I couldn't spend all of my time drawing.

"I told you. I don't mind Mara *that* much."

"Speaking of . . ." Koen stopped his progress across the field. His hands were suddenly still—his expression dire. I braced myself. I knew what was coming.

"Van says they can't move forward until they have the foxglove."

"Move forward with *what*?" I demanded, my eyes searching the ceiling panels overhead. They were just beginning to go dark, the first feeble stars shining through. But the blue onset of night did nothing to deter Koen.

"I don't *know*," he said. But his hands darted out. His icy fingers enveloped mine. "All I know is that they need you. *We* need you, Terra."

It wasn't quite what I wanted to hear. I wanted Koen to tell me that *he* needed me, that his heart wouldn't be sated until he pressed his lips to mine and pulled me down against the cold hard ground. But looking at his ruddy face and the determined expression that had tightened his mouth, I realized that this was as close as I was going to get.

"Okay, Koen," I said, and gave his cold hands a squeeze. "I'll try."

"Promise?" he asked.

"Promise," I agreed.

Koen threw an arm over my shoulders, drawing me close. Together, under the growing twilight, we moved across the frozen field.

My opportunity came only two weeks after we entered our new sun's orbit. Mara had spent all afternoon sowing cold-hardy seeds in plates I'd filled with agar. I suppose the work had finally begun to wear on her. She stifled a yawn against the back of her wrinkled hand.

"I need to get myself coffee," she announced, standing up. "Though I'm sure the *real* coffee we'll plant on Zehava will be a major improvement. Hardly any caffeine in our dandelion brew."

"There is no caffeine in dandelion brew," I said. Mara laughed and clapped me on the shoulder.

"Good! You're learning!" Without another word she turned out of the lab and was gone, and for the first time I was alone under the buzzing lights.

It took a moment for that fact to settle in. Mara's presence was a constant in the overcrowded lab, as expected as the tumbled seed trays and the worktables and the microscopes. Her absence left a strange gap of silence in her wake. I knew I had to take advantage now, before she returned and obliterated every chance I had to find the foxglove. I rose quickly and headed past Mara's desk to the steel door in the rear of the lab.

The door had a panel beside it, just like the ones that were used to lock each lab in the science complex. There was a chance that it wasn't calibrated to my touch—that the door would remain closed to me. In that case, I'd just have to return to my desk and my work. But I had to try. I pressed my hand against it, holding my breath as the light blinked to life beneath my fingers. To my relief, the door slid away, welcoming me in.

I stepped through. If the lab had been silent without Mara, then this space was practically airless. But it was a huge, echoing sort of airlessness—like the library, but sleeker. Rows and rows of white metal shelves spread out before me beneath dangling blue lights. As

I walked beneath the lights, I peered down the aisles. There had to be a thousand metal drawers, each labeled in tiny script and closed. It wasn't until I stumbled across a computer terminal at the far end of an aisle that I had any idea where I was going.

Common foxglove. *Digitalis purpurea.* I hunted for the correct keys, slowly pecking out the name. After a moment the display lit up. *Aisle D11, shelf 14, box C.* I hustled across the herbarium, my lab coat streaming behind me.

In the lab everything was always in disarray. But perhaps one of Mara's predecessors had labeled the shelves here. After all, the placards were yellowed with age, the paper curling. It would explain why the right shelf was so easy to find. Or maybe it was fate that pushed me down the correct aisle. I wondered if after this I'd finally be accepted by Van, by the Children of Abel. I ran my finger over the label, thinking of it. Then I pulled the drawer open.

White fog billowed out, a breath of cold that was icy enough that it burned my skin. I snatched my hands away. As the fog cleared I leaned in, looking down. The plants grew out of a layer of fortified agarose. Their gnarled roots twisted through the jelly. The leaves, jade green, shook as I pulled my hand away. The bells shook too. They weren't all the striking violet I'd expected. A few were pale purple or snowy white. They looked delicate, lovely. Like something Momma would have plucked to put in a vase on our galley table.

"Foxglove, eh?"

I jumped, slamming the drawer shut. There behind me stood Mara Stone, sipping at her coffee. She arched her eyebrow, studying me.

"I—" I began, fumbling for some excuse. But Mara lifted her hand, cutting me off. She stepped past me and opened the drawer again. Together we peered in.

"A pretty flower," she told me. "Useful, too. If it weren't, we'd have only seeds in the gene banks. Every couple of years the doctors ask us for a few new plants. They're useful medicine. Good for patients with heart problems. It's an antiarrhythmic agent."

"Is it?" I asked, staring down. My hands shook at my sides. I was sure that if I looked at Mara, then she would see my duplicity.

"Mm-hmm," she said. "Risky, though."

"Why?"

From the corner of my gaze I saw Mara look down the slope of her crooked nose at me. She fixed her hand against the drawer, slammed it shut.

"Because it's a poison. Difficult to regulate. Difficult to dose. Dead man's bells, they called it on Earth."

I stared at Mara, trying to keep my gaze even. But I couldn't. My mouth fell wordlessly open.

"Abdominal pain. Hallucinations. Tremors. Massive cardiac arrest, if you get enough of it. Not a pleasant way to go."

"Poison," I said, but the word echoed back too late. "Foxglove is a poison?"

Mara shook her head at me. Then she started down between the aisles, gesturing for me to follow. For a moment I stared at the closed drawer. The label's black letters seemed to burn themselves into my retinas. *Digitalis purpurea.* Poison. *Poison.*

As I went to join her, Mara clucked her tongue against the roof of her mouth. "Terra, dear," she said. "You have *so* much to learn."

That night I sat beside Koen again on the top floor of the library, surrounded by now-familiar faces. Van Hofstadter stood in front of the railing, lifting his hands high. He was orating right out of the copy of Momma's book.

"'I must trust that my sacrifices will bring my children's children closer to liberty,'" he declared, his strong voice practically shaking the cobwebs from the low rafters. "'I must trust that someday my descendants will set foot on the Goldilocks planet, the place the Council has dubbed Zehava, not as prisoners of these glass ceilings, not as slaves to the ruling Council, but as free men and women!'"

Murmurs of agreement rippled through the gathered crowd. I watched Rebbe Davison stroke his chin with his index finger, mulling over the words. I watched Deklan Levitt pound his hand against one of the study desks.

"Hear, hear!"

The mood among the Children of Abel was electric that night, far brighter than the lights that flickered from the chandeliers overhead. But this time I didn't feel the spark of passion inside me. At the end of it, when Van touched his hand to his heart and shouted out, "Liberty on Earth!" and the rest of them saluted and bellowed, "Liberty on Zehava!" I stayed silent, my hands pressed between my knees.

Koen didn't notice. As the other citizens began filing down the stairs, he rushed to greet Van. I watched him clap the librarian on the arm, complimenting his impassioned speech—a speech stolen from my ancestor's journal, of course. Van smiled easily. For a few fleeting moments they spoke to each other in low tones.

I sat in one of the overstuffed chairs, pulling a long thread of stuffing out of a crack in the leather. As Van and Koen came close, I pretended not to see them, instead focusing very, very closely on the ecru tuft of wool.

"Did you bring me the foxglove?" Van asked. I didn't want to lie, so I only shrugged. It was a sullen, babyish gesture, I knew, but it felt safe—familiar. That is, until Koen spoke up, his kind voice pained.

"Terra! You promised!" He looked sad. He wanted so badly for me to be one of them, for me to be like him.

"I couldn't get it," I said. "Mara caught me in the herbarium."

Van let out a throaty grumble. He lifted his hands, ready to chastise me. But I didn't want to hear it. I stood, swiftly pushing past him.

"Terra!" Koen called. I stopped at the top of the narrow stairwell, my hand lingering on the banister. But when I turned, I didn't look at Koen. Instead I looked Van Hofstadter directly in the eye.

"You didn't tell me foxglove was a *poison*."

"What did you think we wanted it for? Think the Children of Abel are going to start a community garden?" The corner of his full mouth ticked up. It was a self-satisfied sort of smile. "You're a botanist. I figured you would know."

"Well, I didn't. I'm not going to help you poison anyone."

Van stalked forward. His nostrils flared. "Do you think the Council deserves our mercy?" he demanded. "You saw what they did that night to Benjamin!"

I could almost still hear the librarian's final gurgle of breath, could almost see the wild-eyed look, animal and afraid, that had crossed his face as the dagger had slid across his throat.

"These are not nice people, Terra," Van said. And it was true. I remembered the sudden explosion of blood down Mar Jacobi's shirtfront and the way he'd fallen forward, collapsing on the metal grate.

"I can't," I said at last. "I would help you if I could, but I *can't*. Mara Stone will never let me get away with it."

"If our leaders find out that you've failed us . . . ," Van began.

But he didn't get to finish his sentence.

"Lay off her!"

Koen had shouldered his way between Van and me. He threw an arm over my back. I smelled sweat on him, cedar, the lanolin stink of his sweater. I could feel his heart pounding beneath my arm.

"If our leaders find out," he said, "they can deal with it."

"Koen," Van said, his forehead furrowing in confusion. But the young clock keeper just went on.

"Terra will be my wife soon. And if they trust me, they can trust her." High blossoms of color exploded cross Koen's cheeks. But he didn't look embarrassed. He looked proud.

"Are you sure?" Van asked. There was some deeper question hiding beneath his words, but I couldn't quite suss it out.

"Positive. Now come on, intended," Koen said, his voice a little too loud for the empty library. "Let's go."

We moved down the spiral staircase together. But tucked under his arm, I couldn't help but feel that I wasn't walking at all. Instead I flew over the creaky steps, my body suspended several feet above the floor. It wasn't until we stepped through the iron door and into the cold night of the evening that I touched ground again.

"Thank you!" I said to Koen, reaching out for his hands. It felt like the most natural gesture in the world, to hold his hands in mine. But his cold fingers stayed slack, like dead flesh against mine.

"Sure," he said. He pulled his hands away and shoved them down inside his pockets. They were balled into fists.

"I didn't expect you to speak up against Van like that."

"Oh." I watched Koen chew the peeling skin from his lower lip. At last he said, "Well, if I've learned anything from your father, it's that it's my duty now. You deserve to have someone looking out for you."

I wasn't sure what to say to that. I stood there, blushing. "Sure," I said. "But still—standing up to the Children of Abel."

Koen only shrugged.

We stood there for a moment under a glass sky splattered with stars. At last Koen stepped away.

"I should go. Work tomorrow. And all."

He didn't kiss me good-bye. He didn't even wait for my answer. Koen turned and hustled off, leaving me alone in the shadow of the huge, dark library.

I no longer dreamed about the atrium. Now, as the ship drew closer to Zehava, my dreams had changed, become stranger.

I'd be walking through a forest, but the shapes of the trees were all wrong. The bark seemed smooth, fleshy—and branches fanned out gently from the trunks. Indigo leaves stirred and moved overhead in what I assumed was wind. The *Asherah's* air circulated in only one direction, from starboard to port, over and over again. This wind was different—lively, capricious—and sometimes, for whole moments, it was still, too.

I was never alone.

At first I was sure that the boy who walked beside me was Koen. I wanted him to be. His strides matched my strides perfectly; sometimes he even laced his fingers in mine. I only ever saw him out of the corner of my eye, a shadow. But night after night I cobbled together a fuzzy image from those stolen side glances. Whoever he was, he was taller than Koen, much taller. And darker, too. Even in my dreams I could tell that he *smelled* different. Sweet, like flowers. And somehow green. His body beside mine had none of the animal musk of Koen's body.

Sometimes we stopped on the path. Around us the ground was soggy and dotted with white stuff. Snow. But there were still flowers on the branches. They turned toward us, watching. And I would hear a voice in my mind: *Who are you? I don't know you. You're not who I thought you would be.*

And then I would answer: Bashert. *I am your* bashert. *Your destiny. I know it. You must too.*

He fell silent at that.

In my dreams our bodies moved together in a way that felt completely natural, like it was what my body was made for. Like every moment I'd ever felt awkward or out of place or wrong didn't exist and never had. Sometimes the snow would be so cold against my skin that it nearly burned it. But then he would touch those pinpoints where my flesh had started to pink, and every sensation that wasn't *right* and *good* and *wonderful* would melt away. Soon the vines that masked the trees crawled down to cover us. They tangled round our limbs, binding us together. Our bodies were covered with flowers. Everything was a flurry of color and feeling and light.

In my dreams I was very, very happy.

I'd wake up with a lump in my throat, like I'd just been crying, or wanted to. Sometimes I turned to my pillow and *did* cry, hugging Pepper to my chest. I lost something in waking. I always did.

I just didn't know what.

One night Koen and I sat on a stone bridge that loomed above a river on the second deck of the dome. Our legs dangled above the burbling water. From above, it looked silver over the rocks. You almost couldn't see the artificial bottom that waited below, or the jets that pushed the stream fore to aft, circulating the water toward the districts in an infinite loop. I shouldn't have felt unsettled by the sight of it. This was what creeks looked like on the *Asherah*. But for some reason my belly clenched as I watched the salmon move through the stream. I wondered if rivers were different someplace else.

"Koen?" I asked. "Do you ever dream about Zehava?"

"Sure," he said, his hair whipped by the wind. "All the time. I can't wait to see what life will be like once we live there. You know, once we get rid of the Council." He turned his gaze down the river, watching as a pair of kids untangled their fishing line at the shore. It seemed cold to me for fishing—their bare ears were pink, their hands all wrapped up in their heavy mittens. But, determined, they spiked their bait on their hooks and cast the lines out into the water.

"No," I said. "I don't mean 'Do you *think* about Zehava?' Of course you do. We all do. I mean, do you *dream* about it?"

Koen stared at me, thinning his lips. "What do you mean?"

"Well, I have these dreams," I said, looking down at my dangling boots, at the untied laces that reached toward the current. "They're kind of weird. I'm always on Zehava in them. Every single night. It's always Zehava."

"What's it like there?"

I gave a shrug. "Wild. Weird. Hot."

Koen let out a snort. He fixed his hands against the railing, pulling himself to his feet. Then he stuck his hands into his pockets. "I've had dreams like that."

"You have?" I asked. The wind tangled our hair.

"Yeah. But I've never told anyone. It's kind of embarrassing."

I let out a sigh, relieved to share the burden. "I *know*."

"Terra," Koen began. A frown creased his eyebrows. "You know it doesn't mean anything, right? Whatever it is you dream about—it doesn't mean you can't be a good citizen, a good wife."

"Of course not, Koen," I said, frowning too. "Why would it?"

He smiled faintly. Then he offered me his hand. I took it gratefully, pulling myself to my feet. But as we walked beside each other, we both stared out ahead, our expressions as dark as the shadowed branches that twisted above.

We'd reached a comfortable stalemate, Koen and I. On some nights we'd lounge around my bedroom and whisper about the rebellion. I loved those nights, when his hands would make passionate gestures through the air. Sometimes I teased him, and he blushed, and we laughed together. Sweet, hopeful laughter, laughter that rippled like river water over stones. I felt real and whole and present, like a better version of myself. I wondered if this was what love might feel like.

Other nights didn't go so smoothly. We walked side by side in the dome, neither of us sure what to say to the other. I let my hair fall in front of my face, hoping it would shield me from his distant, empty stare. When he left me on my doorstep, he leaned forward—and only pressed a dry kiss to my cheek. I'd head inside our dark quarters with my stomach all twisted into knots.

I think we might have always stayed like that if it hadn't been for Abba. He was the one who always pushed us together, pressuring us to make good on our promise to each other. The first true step toward marriage was the reading of the bloodlines. Once it was confirmed that we shared no ancestors, then we would be able to set a wedding date and seal our match. One morning over breakfast Abba looked up from his coffee and over to me and told me that he'd made the appointment with the genealogist for us.

"That's supposed to be the bride's job," I protested. My father shrugged and pressed a napkin to his lips.

"I want to see to it that your marriage is secured, Terra. I want to make sure you're firmly promised to the boy."

"Koen," I said. "His name is Koen. I don't know why you're so worried about it." And I didn't. My father had never fretted over me before, not like this.

But he didn't answer. He only stared at me for a long time, his jaw clenched.

"Your appointment is tomorrow after work," he said at last.

The next morning, on the day when Koen and I were scheduled to have our bloodlines read, I woke up feeling jittery, ill rested. It was like I hadn't slept at all. As I dressed I paused to give Pepper a scratch behind the ear. It wasn't until a half-formed thought drifted through my head—*I wonder if Abba will mind if I take Pepper with me to my new quarters*—that I realized that it was actually happening, that I was *really* going to marry Koen.

With a pounding heart I made my way down the stairwell.

But I stopped halfway when the smell of charred oatmeal reached me. My eyes swept over our first floor, quickly appraising the situation: The sink was on, water streaming over a towering pile of dirty plates. There was a pot burning on the stove. All of the cupboards had been thrown open, revealing our banged-up pans and chipped dishes. And my father sat at the table, frozen, his head in his hands.

I hustled down, turned off the burners, the sink. I tried not to think of the wasted water. "Every cup of wasted gray water," my father had always lectured, "is another hour that some poor worker has to stay late at the plants. *Think* about your fellow citizen. About your duty!" I was never sure whether it was true or not, but he'd sounded serious about it at the time.

Now he let the water rush out of the faucet, let our rations burn to the bottom of the pot, all the while sitting with his hands covering his face.

"Are you okay?" I asked, standing, motionless, in front of the sink. When he didn't answer, I cleared my throat. Nothing. Then he stumbled to his feet, not even meeting my eyes when his shoulder slammed mine. Crouching low, he rummaged through one of the cupboards.

"What are you doing?" I asked, my voice hardly more than a whisper. There was a clatter of pans. My father sat back on his heels.

"I *wanted* it to be a nice morning for us." His voice sounded mechanical, rusty at the edges. "I was going to make you breakfast. I was going to give you your momma's book."

Her book! My mind flashed upstairs to where the journal slept wedged between my mattress and bed. Good thing I kept my door locked.

"What are you talking about, Abba?" I asked. My words were the words of a little girl. They sounded so *afraid* that I was sure he would be able to hear the lie in them. But it didn't really matter—he was hardly paying any attention to me. Instead he just stared into the darkness of the cupboard, like it was our dented metal mixing bowls that had spoken.

"The book. She told me to give you the book. The one her mother gave her on the day we had our bloodlines read." He let his eyelids slide closed. "I've looked everywhere for it. She told me about it on our wedding night. Told me she wanted our daughter to have it. I've looked everywhere."

His head swiveled sharply around.

"No one else has been in our home. I know you must have it."

"I don't know what you're talking about. I haven't seen any book." Lies fell easily from my lips. I had touched the book's leather cover every night before bed, cracked open the spine and breezed my fingertip down the list of names written there. The flyleaf bore the name of every woman in my family, ending with Momma's.

But I wouldn't tell my father. *No friend of Abel*, that's what Van had said. I knew that my father could never, ever be trusted. He wasn't one of us.

He stalked toward me across the narrow kitchen. I leaned my spine away as he reached out his big hands and gripped me by either shoulder. I braced myself, waiting for him to give me a hard shake. He'd done it plenty of times before. But he didn't. He held me at arm's length.

"It doesn't matter," he said, nearly whispering. Abba didn't even blink—just stared intently down at me. "So much like your mother, Terra. She was my heart's twin. Did you know that? Remember that she was my *bashert*. No matter what anyone tells you, I want you to remember that."

And with that he bent down and planted a kiss on my forehead. I stayed very still, waiting for it to be over. But for a long time my father didn't move. Like he didn't want to let me go.

"Sure," I said at last, prying my body away. My arms shook as nervous words poured out of my mouth. I hoped he didn't notice. "Your destiny. Sure. I should go. Mara will kill me if I'm late." I took a few steps through the messy galley. When I stopped to look at him, he was watching me, his eyebrows furrowed.

"Good luck today," he said. "At the reading of the bloodlines."

"Won't you be there?" I asked. "It's a mitzvah, after all."

"No, Terra," he said. His lips fell gently open. "No. I'm sorry."

"Oh." For a second I just stood there, pawing at the doorknob. Finally I cracked a weak smile. "Have to work late?"

One corner of my father's mouth lifted. He nodded.

"Okay," I said. I grabbed my lab coat from the hook by the door. "See you later, then." I threw the door open, stepping into the cold air. I almost didn't hear my father's voice past the rush of the constant winter wind.

"Good-bye," he said.

There was no use stopping home after work. I wouldn't find my father there, with his wavering smile and intense gaze. There would be only darkness to share between myself and the cat. So when Mara dismissed me for the evening, I just threw my overcoat on over my uniform, brushed my lank hair up under my hat, and marched off toward Koen's quarters. As I crossed through the commerce district, I greeted no one, my hands stuffed down into my pockets to keep the cold air from biting at them. If Koen was going to marry me, I decided, he'd have to take me as I was. Rough. Grubby. Hair unkempt. Because part of me wanted to be like the botanist, as much as I couldn't stand her sometimes. I wanted to be excellent. Unapologetic. Hard. If he was going to love me, he'd have to love that part of me too.

Standing outside the front door to the Maxwells' quarters, I sucked in a deep breath of frozen air. Then I gritted my teeth and knocked three times.

Only Ratty answered me, his shrill yelps penetrating the wooden door. When it didn't open, I knocked again, louder. This time it cracked open, revealing a sliver of dim light. Stella's brown eyes gazed out at me.

"I'm not supposed to answer the door when no one is home."

"Stella." I sighed. "It's me, Terra. You know me." I smiled helpfully—hopefully. The girl stared at me.

"Terra. You were here on Orbit Day. With your dad."

"Yes," I said. "You remember."

She finally opened the door.

Stella was hardly anything more than a round-faced girl. But I could see in the way that she stood, her small chin held high, that she didn't think of herself as a child. She thought she was grown-up—important. When I spoke, I was careful to make it clear to her that I considered her grown-up too.

"Koen and I are supposed to have our bloodlines checked today. So we can marry." Her eyes widened at that. "He's expecting me. Can you go get him?"

Stella just clutched at the door. "I *told* you. No one's home."

"He's not home?" My resolve wavered. But I forced my doubts down deep inside me and somehow managed to hold my head firm. "Do you know where he is?"

"I think he's in the atrium. He always goes there after work when he's not out with you." She waited a beat, like this was significant. "On the lower deck."

"The lower deck," I repeated. "Thanks, Stella."

I turned and started down the street again. As I did, Stella's voice called out to me. "Terra, wait!"

I looked over my shoulder. Stella just stared, not blinking at all.

"Good luck," she finally concluded, lamely. Then added: "With the bloodlines and all." I nodded one more time.

"Thanks," I replied.

17

I made my way to the lower deck, where I'd walked with my mother so many times before. It had been different then, green and bright and alive. I'd been there with Koen only once, that evening we almost kissed. Since then the few bits of autumn brown that had scattered through the landscape had disappeared completely. Everything was bone gray now, dead. Black branches craned their fingers up through to the upper levels of the dome. Vines, as brittle as white ribbon candy, grasped at the tree trunks. I hustled down the path, my breath coming out in steaming bursts as I called Koen's name. But there was no answer—only the sound of squirrels rummaging in the hard-packed soil, and crows calling to one another in the branches above.

I don't know what made me leave the path. I moved like I did in my dreams, as if my limbs were powered by some invisible clockwork. But in my dreams I was always happy—mindlessly, stupidly happy. Now, awake, I felt only a knot of uneasiness twisting my stomach. *Just nerves*, I thought as I pressed forward across a dry, ice-slick riverbed.

I heard movement in the tangled bushes ahead of me. The dumbest thought I'd ever had crossed my mind: *Maybe it's a fox!* And so it was with a sort of frantic, giddy excitement that I reached out to part the branches, and stepped into a shadowed glen.

There was a rustle of movement on the forest floor. Then a moan. I pressed forward, peering between the brambles.

It was not a fox.

"Koen!" I lifted my hand to my mouth. "Van!"

They stopped, staring—two pairs of eyes, one as brown as maple syrup, the other as green as spring buds. The boys were pressed up against a tree. No, *Koen* was pressed up against a tree, and Van pressed up against him, his hands knotted in Koen's hair. Their lips were bruised pink and slick with saliva. I had interrupted something— Koen had just begun to lift the librarian's shirt, exposing the bronze skin over his hip. But they were both frozen now, save for the heavy rhythm of both their chests.

My voice broke out into an incomprehensible syllable. I wheeled back—away from the tangled heart of the forest, away from the boys and their tryst. I saw Koen untangle himself from Van. He reached down to grab his coat from the muddy ground. That's when I turned and ran.

I didn't know where I was going, but it didn't matter. I knew that I could outrun him. After all, I'd done it before. The ground was soft with pine needles. It seemed to fall away as I ducked between the trees, tears streaming down my face, my coat flaring up behind me. I told myself that I would run far, far away from him, lose myself in the forest at the heart of the ship, that I would never see him ever again as long as I lived if I ran fast and far enough.

It was a stupid, stupid hope. For one thing, the *Asherah* was so little. There was no avoiding *anyone*. For another, after only a few minutes of running, I heard the approach of pounding footfalls. A pair of strong hands reached out, grabbing me by both shoulders. I was pulled to the ground.

"Get off me!" My words came out in a screech. It was Van who grappled with me, locking his muscular biceps around my arms in some sort of wrestler's hold. I could smell the pine on his hair and the cedar on his breath. Koen's smell. The smell of kissing Koen.

"Get off!"

"Tsssshhhh." He let out a soft hiss of sound, giving me a firm, strong shake. It reminded me of how my father would grab Pepper by the scruff when the cat swatted at him. It wasn't a violent gesture; it was supposed to be calming. Now I was the animal. I gritted my teeth.

"There," Van said. "There."

Koen came running up to us. He stumbled over a few gnarled roots, reaching out to steady himself on a branch. Then he stopped, watching me fearfully. At the sight of Koen, I felt Van's grip loosen for just a moment. That was my chance. I squirmed out from his strong arms.

"What are you doing?" I demanded. Part of me wanted to strike out, to come at them all furious teeth and nails. I was better than that, but just barely. I struck a nearby tree trunk with both fists instead. The bark burned the heels of my hands. "What are you doing? I was going to marry you!"

Koen didn't look at me when he answered. He didn't dare. His voice was no more than a whisper. "We weren't doing anything. You still can."

I let out a howl. Collapsing on the cold ground, I drew my knees to my chest, braying, my hands pulled up over my head. Koen called my name. But then Van said: "Let her cry it out." I heard the soft crunch of leaves as he stepped over me to get to Koen.

I don't know how long I rocked myself on my heels, crying into my arm. It seemed to take a lifetime for my breath to slow—I kept seeing it in my mind's eye, how their hips had been pressed together, how Van had wrenched his hungry mouth away from Koen's only at the sight of me. Maybe I should have realized it a long time ago. The silence in the library. The odd friendship between the *talmid* clock keeper and the young librarian. But I hadn't.

"*Faygeleh,*" I said, the word bursting breathlessly past my lips. That must have been what my father had meant all those weeks ago when he'd warned me of rumors about Van. Abba didn't know anything about the Children of Abel—but somehow he'd known about this, about the curve of Van's hip as it pressed to Koen's.

Men didn't love men. Sure, some *boys* had flings with one another. In school we called them "*faygeleh,*" a word that meant "little bird." But that was something you gave up when you were grown so that you could be a good husband, a father.

It made sense. It made so much sense.

Sniffling, I lifted my head; they both watched me. Koen clutched Van's hand in his. I remembered the cool, loose pressure of his fingers around my fingers and fought the urge to look away.

"You love him," I said. It wasn't a question, not really, and Koen answered more quickly than I liked.

"Yes." He looked relieved to say it. But then he added: "I can learn to love you, too, though. Like Van loves Nina. I still want to marry you."

Slowly, painfully, I pulled myself to my feet. When I answered him, my voice cracked.

"Why?"

I saw something pass between them—unspoken words in a language I wasn't privileged enough to speak. Van shrugged; Koen turned to me again.

"Because it's my duty. Because it's a mitzvah. Because . . . because your dad asked me to. On the first day of work. He went on and on about how much he worries about you. And you know, he's *right*. I think . . . I think you need someone to take care of you. And I can do that. I love Van, but I can love you, too."

"You'll never love me like you love him." The words hung between us, as ugly and as undeniable as a tumor. And we all knew it was true. He would never kiss me. Not like he'd kissed Van. I saw the librarian squeeze Koen's hand, a tiny gesture not meant for me.

"And what about Nina?" I demanded of Van. "Do you love her?"

"I love them both." There was no hesitation there. "It wasn't easy to tell Nina about falling in love with Koen. It hasn't been easy for her to share me. And it hasn't been easy hiding it either. But life wouldn't be worth a thing if I couldn't have both of them."

"Falling in love with him," I echoed. The words felt hollow. "That's the thing, though, isn't it? You'll take care of me, Koen. But you'll never fall in love with me. You'll never be my *bashert*."

"There are different kinds of love," Koen declared. "And it's not like we *have* to love each other that way to get married. It's not like my parents do."

"But I *want* . . . ," I began. Koen stared at me but didn't speak. A lump rose in my throat. I stumbled toward the main path, through the growing shadows of dusk.

"Terra," Koen called as I walked by. He tried to reach his hand out, but Van warned him back.

"Don't," he said, and I was grateful for that. Still, I stopped just a few meters beyond them. They were still holding hands as they watched me. They'd never stopped.

"I have a question," I said. Koen looked afraid of what I might say—but he nodded anyhow.

"Sure."

"I wanted to ask you about the Children of Abel. I guess—I guess this is why you joined, isn't it? Not because of the vocation system or the Council. But because . . . you'd marry *him* if you could, right? He's . . . *he's* your destiny?"

As their gazes met, I saw Koen's soften. He didn't look at me. That was as good as a confirmation.

A million arguments swam through my mind. A man couldn't be another man's *bashert*. They weren't even supposed to touch one another, not like *that*, let alone fall in love. But looking at the two of them standing there with their fingers intertwined, I couldn't bring myself to say it. Because they stood side by side, leaning into each other. I had the unnerving feeling that everything I'd ever been taught about love was a lie.

"I thought so," I muttered, and with that, I turned through the dimming woods and began the long walk home.

should have put the pieces together about Koen and Van. The way Koen pulled away from me when I leaned into him as we walked. The way his hand felt in mine, slack, no different from how it had felt when I'd held my brother's hand as a little girl. The way Van had looked when Koen had defended me—like he could have cried, like his heart was breaking.

But I hadn't. I thought I was perceptive, but I wasn't. I thought I was smart, but I definitely wasn't that, either. I had missed so many clues. Not just about Koen. About everything.

That night I came home to a dark house, hung my coat on the hook, and flicked on the galley light. From upstairs I heard Pepper's cries—long, mournful howls.

"Couldn't even feed the cat, huh, Abba?" I muttered to myself, and went to the icebox to get Pepper his supper. As I peeled away the wax paper that covered his food, a vision flashed inside my mind. Van's hands on Koen's hips. I forced it away with a shudder and set Pepper's supper on the ground.

"Pepper!" I called, but he didn't come running. There was a pause and then another low moan from upstairs, then a pause, a shuffle, and another cry. I felt my heart sink down into my stomach. I knew that something was wrong even then, but I did my best to ignore it.

"Pepper? Did I lock you in my room this morning? I hope you didn't piss on my bed." I forced a laugh at my own joke. But I took the stairs slowly, one at a time.

I reached the landing. Never before had our hallway seemed so long or dark; never had the way the shadows stretched across the scuffed metal floor seemed so sinister. There was light coming from under the door to my father's room—a long, thin vein of white. A flicker of shadows passed through it, and then I heard another yowl.

"Pepper?"

My hand was cold when I set it against the door. Colder than Koen's hand. Colder than ice. The heavy wood swung open under my palm. Pepper darted out before I could stop him. I watched his tail disappear in the halo of light that surrounded the stairs.

Then I turned to my father's room and brought my hands up to my mouth.

"Oh, no," I breathed. "Abba, no."

My father's bed was crisply made, not a single wrinkle showing, the sheets pulled taut under the mattress. His uniform had been left folded atop the coverlet. In the low buzzing light of his bedside lamp, strange shadows loomed. It took my eyes a minute to adjust—took my brain a minute too—to take in what was right in front of me.

My father had laced rope through the high, dusty rafters. He must have slipped it around his throat, climbed onto his desk chair, then kicked the chair down. My mind noted all of the little details—how his hands, blue and slack, sat against his thighs, how his leather shoes just *almost* touched the floor. I noted all of this dispassionately. It was like there was a hiccup in my brain.

It didn't hit me until I went to him and touched his ice-cold fingers. His body spun on the rope, and I saw his face. The open, hazy eyes met mine.

For the second time that night, I screamed.

．　　．　　．

It's hard to talk about what happened next. It's almost like it happened to someone else. All that screaming. Mar Schneider must have heard it. All those years when my father and I had fought, no one had done a thing. But that night, while my hands were still up over my head, my throat raw and stinging, the knocking came. I must have stumbled to my feet. I must have staggered down the stairs. But all I remember was how I tried my hardest not to look at the body that swung from the ceiling.

A guard stood on the front steps. I only stared at him, white-faced. Noise complaint, he said. Would have to keep our voices down.

That's when everything left me, all feeling, all fear.

"He's upstairs," I said, and collapsed just outside the front door. The guard streamed past me, a rush of blue wool and boots.

After that, more guards. Pepper tried to slip outside, and some neighbor caught him, then held him, staring at me. Speaking to me, but I didn't hear him. The men were in and out with their boots and their knives.

Koen came. Alone. Without Van. I don't know why. It was too late to change anything.

"I heard," he said, taking Pepper from my neighbor.

I didn't say anything. I was listening to the heavy footsteps on the stairwell. Then I was jostled. A line of guards streamed out, holding my father's cloth-enveloped body.

The crowd that had gathered went silent. They each raised a pair of fingers to their hearts—a salute. But I didn't do anything. And neither did Koen.

He just stood there, looking pale and afraid as he clutched my cat to his chest. Eventually the crowd thinned. My father's ghostly figure had faded down the boulevard by then, disappearing into the darkness.

"Terra," Koen said at last, stepping close.

When I finally answered, I could taste blood in my throat.

"That bastard!" I said. "That selfish bastard! He left me here! That bastard!"

Koen let out a thin sigh. He carried my cat up the front step and left him inside my empty house. Then he leaned out the open doorway.

"Come on inside," he said. "We have to get ready for the funeral."

I picked myself up.

"He left me here. That bastard!" I said again, but weaker this time as Koen closed the door behind me.

Down in the pasture funeral goers drifted like ghosts, looking gauzy and grave in their white cotton. They held hands. They sang. Some of them looked down at the wrapped body of my father and wondered why anyone would do such a thing. Perhaps a few of them understood. But they all cast down fistfuls of soil, frigid and dry from the frost, and then tried to stop themselves from wiping their palms against their trousers.

Or at least I assume that's what happened. I didn't see it.

Instead I lay on the cedar planks on the floor of the clock tower, staring up into the rafters as Koen rang the bells. The sound sank deep into my body, reverberating in my rib cage, making my molars vibrate. It almost hurt. But at least I felt something.

Gone, was all I thought. *My father is gone. I will never see my father again.*

But the air here smelled fragrant with the memory of him. I could remember sick days spent in the tower when he showed me the gears and cogs, when I sat in his lap, burying my face in the heavy corduroy of his uniform. Back then, when our faces were lit up amber from the dials, we were happy. I wasn't afraid of him yet. I never rolled my eyes or bit the inside of my cheeks to stop myself from complaining. No. Back then I thought my father was the smartest man on the whole ship.

But now he was gone. Gone, gone, gone.

Koen stopped ringing the bells. From the floor I watched as he plucked splinters of rope from his work-reddened palms. He was wearing his uniform. *Abba's clothes*, I thought, the lump in my throat thickening. But they fit him all wrong. The coat was both too loose and too short. The cuffs hardly covered his long arms.

He walked to the face of the big clock and bent at the waist. I watched as he peered out of the translucent amber glass.

"They're setting him in the ground now," he said, and then he turned his gaze to me. "Are you sure you don't want to go say good-bye?"

I didn't answer. I was sprawled there on the floor, my hands up near my head. When Koen put his palms on his knees, focusing his gaze on me, pressing for an answer, I only looked away.

"Okay. Okay," he said.

I don't know how long we stayed there, Koen leaning against the control panel, silent, and me on the floor. The words kept ringing through my mind, as sure as any bell.

Gone. Gone. My father is gone.

Finally I put my hands against the boards, felt the cold of the dusty wood beneath my fingers, and pushed myself up. When I stood, it was on uncertain feet. I staggered for a moment, put a hand to my head. My hair was a tangled mess beneath my hand, but I patted it down.

"Terra," Koen said. He was watching me, afraid I was going to fall. "You can come to my house if you want. You know . . ." He hesitated. Something in his expression told me that he doubted himself. And when he spoke, I knew that he was right to. "I'd still have you as my wife. It's . . . it's what *he* wanted, isn't it? To make sure you have some-one to take care of you. I'll take care of you."

I stared at him. Once, I would have wanted nothing more than to hear those words, to know that Koen still wanted me to be a part of his life. But something had changed for me in the forest.

"Why?" I said at last. "Why are you so hung up on this marriage thing? You don't even *want* me."

He looked down at his trimmed nails, at the broad fingers that clutched at one another in front of his stomach. In a low tone he said, "I just want to be normal."

My gut gave a lurch. It was too much for me then—the tears that racked the new clock keeper's voice, the ones that seemed to tighten my own throat but still wouldn't come. With a slow shake of my head, I staggered down the stairs. I took them one at a time, the rhythm plodding inside me.

Gone. Gone. Gone. Gone.

Koen followed. He kept his distance, but I could hear his feet on the steps behind me.

Gone. Gone.

We reached the open air. I sucked it in, letting the cold burn my lungs, letting the constant wind that cycled through the dome from fore to aft strike my face. I didn't even bother to button my coat against it.

As we stepped into the pasture, I felt what must have been a thousand eyes turn to me. All those Asherati in their funerary whites. We were the only ones dressed in color. I was still in my work clothes. I hadn't been able to bring myself to change. I wore my brown trousers, the hems torn around my heels, and one of Momma's old unraveling sweaters, which was a deep pine green. Koen was in his clock keeper's clothes. Abba's clothes. *Gone. Gone.* I guess we attracted attention. We stepped out across the field.

As I moved through the crowd, I kept my head high. People murmured their consolations, but I didn't look at anyone long enough to know who spoke to me or what they said. I didn't stop when they began to reach out, touching their hands to my shoulders. I walked right through them.

"Terra!"

Koen's voice reached out to me from somewhere in the thick of the crowd. He must have gotten lost in it. He must have lost me. I didn't stop. People put their hands on my shoulders, my arms.

It was Captain Wolff who halted my progress across the field.

One moment I was marching forward. The next, the woman was in front of me, her silver hair sparkling in the artificial moonlight.

"Terra," she said, gripping my hands in her hands. Inside I recoiled. I wanted to pull away, to snatch my hands back. But instead they just lay limply in her grasp. "The Council would like to extend to you their deepest apologies at the losses you've faced. Please feel free to come to me if you need anything."

I tried to imagine it—pounding on Captain Wolff's door in the middle of the night, crying on her shoulder as if she were my mother. Giving her every opportunity to plunge a knife into my back. I managed only a coarse syllable in answer—"Yeh"—and drew my hands away. Balling them into fists, as if the warm touch of my own palms would obliterate the sensation of Captain Wolff's fingers, I stumbled away, looking only once over my shoulder to the crowd that watched me.

That's when I spotted Silvan. He was standing off to the side, alone again, unguarded. With his arms crossed over his broad, white-clad chest, he gazed out into the foggy evening. Then he turned and looked over his shoulder at me. He squinted at me like he was trying to figure me out.

I stuffed my hands into my pockets again and hustled away.

My brother and Hannah managed to find me before I reached the pasture gate. Hannah clutched the baby to her chest. Even Alyana was dressed in white—a long gown of eyelet lace that looked clean against her peachy skin. Ronen grabbed me by the shoulder. I was surprised by the lines that deepened his features. Though he was barely twenty, he looked so old. And very much like my father.

Who is gone. Gone.

"You're coming to our quarters, aren't you?" His lips were pursed, worried. He still couldn't bring himself to tell me what to do. Which meant that I didn't have to agree to it, right? So I didn't. I walked off through the field, my boots sinking into the mud.

20

Our quarters looked the same. The same doorjamb where Momma had marked our heights with a pencil. The same familiar galley counters, where she'd kneaded dough while Abba cooked. The table where Ronen and I had fought— where he'd brandished a fork at me and I'd stuck out my tongue— until Abba had slammed his hands down and bellowed, "Enough!" In those days it hadn't been scary. Not with Momma there. When she rolled her eyes, we all just giggled. Abba gave her a withering look. Until his expression lost its icy edge and he smiled too.

It wasn't the same place, not anymore. It no longer had the same heart. The people I loved were gone, and they'd taken my home with them.

I went to my room. There was a basket under my bed where I kept my old school papers, notes from Rachel, a certificate I'd gotten when I was seven, for the highest marks in math, the only school honor I'd ever received. I dumped them all onto my blankets and then, working in silence, began to fill the woven container again.

I took my pencils, of course. And my sketchbook. My work uniforms. The few sweaters that still fit me. Momma's dress. And then I peeled the case from one of my pillows and got down on my hands and knees. Pepper was hunched up beneath the bed, his shoulders big and craggy, tensed in anticipation of my grasp.

"Come on," I said. The sound of my voice against the empty walls seemed to startle him. Pepper flinched, his tail arching up, and scrambled along the wall. I let out a sigh. Fetching Pepper would have to wait. Instead I slipped my hand between the mattress and rusted bed frame and pulled out the journal.

My father had been looking for it just this morning. When he was alive. Now he was gone, and all that was left was the stupid book and the lie I'd told about not taking it.

Black thoughts. My mind was flooded with black thoughts. They blotted out everything else like clouds of ink spreading across damp paper. I don't remember falling to the ground, setting my head on the cold floor, and crying into my hair. But it must have happened. Because later, much later, I picked myself up, my face a snot-slick mess, dirty-blond tendrils sticking to my cheeks and my lips.

I put the book in my basket. And I reached under the bed and grabbed my cat, ignoring the way his claws flexed as I stuffed him down into the pillowcase. I tied it closed behind him. Then I gathered my things and left the only home I'd ever known.

It was nearly dawn. The streets were dark and cold but not quite empty. Mar Schneider, dressed as he always was in a woolen tunic and a dusty tweed cap, sat on his front steps.

He must have seen me, how my tears shone in the streetlights, how my hair was a tangled knot. Because I saw him. I braced myself, waiting for his apology. "So sorry about your father," that sort of thing. But none came. He only touched two of his wrinkled fingers to his heart, saluting me. Then he turned away.

I walked briskly. Not forward, to where Rachel and her parents lived in a bright home full of fashionable wall hangings and warm conversation. Not to the starboard district, where Koen and his parents fought over their galley table. Or aft, where Ronen and Hannah were probably pacing while Alyana screamed and screamed. No, instead I walked down the straight, narrow roads of my own district, the port district, the place where the specialists and teachers and librarians and lab workers lived. My feet found the path easily, though I hadn't ever visited the quarters of this particular specialist before.

I'd forgotten my gloves. When I pounded the heel of my hand against the door, the cold metal bit at my skin. Pepper let out a meow through the fabric of his pillowcase. But no one answered us. I knocked again, and this time I didn't stop at three. I pounded and pounded and pounded, until at last the door swung open.

In the dim light from the streetlamp, dressed in her pajamas and a too-big robe that had to be her husband's, Mara Stone's face seemed to be carved out of concrete. Her skin was gray and pebbled from lack of sleep. She just stood there, blinking at me.

I opened my mouth, drew in a breath, and readied myself for my own sob story: I was alone now. I had nowhere else to go, not really, not anywhere with anyone who understood.

"I need—" was all I managed. Mara held up a hand. She spared me that, simply motioning for me to come inside.

Then she closed the door behind me.

Dearest Terra,

We weren't alone in our nostalgia, your father and me. By the time you were a child, I noticed how the ship's passengers had begun to pepper their speech with snippets of Yiddish and Hebrew—the language of our parents and their parents before them. It was a comfort to recall our baby names and the songs our grandmothers had sung to us. Our nostalgia tied us more firmly to Earth than any decree ever could. Even I found myself guilty of this, singing as I combed the snarls from your hair: "Shaina, shaina maideleh."

The Council would tell you that this was natural and right—the perfect execution of the contract we had signed. We were preserving our culture, saving these ancient tongues from certain death.

But I wonder if we shouldn't have been more vigilant, if we shouldn't have kept our minds on the future and our words circumspect. The past is a distraction—the Earth we left behind, kaput. All we have now is the present and the bleak, endless journey ahead.

My Terra,

Perhaps the world within these walls won't kill you like it does me.

On Earth, even before we knew of the asteroid's approach, there were several closed biomes. The TeraDome. The Arcosphere. BIOS-6. Experiments, populated with earnest students who were certain that their contributions would someday have a tremendous impact on the world at large.

Little did they know that the world at large would soon no longer exist.

I was asked to join one of these communities when I was in college. The ArcLab II. They needed psychologists—the first ArcLab project dissolved because of discord among its inhabitants—and offered me a scholarship in exchange for my services. I accepted, but then a few weeks later I met Annie. I dropped out. I couldn't stand the idea of being apart from her for eight months. I thought that I had abandoned life under a dome forever.

Will you laugh when, grown, you read of that? Clearly, we both know better now.

Perhaps if I had lived in the ArcLab II, I would have never boarded our ship. I would have known the claustrophobia that presses

down on me whenever I let my gaze drift up above the treetops, the way that I have to swallow the water quickly here before I can think of how many times it's been recycled, the way that even the air smells overused—stale. But I knew none of these things until we launched, and by then it was too late.

I'll be honest: There were times when I wanted nothing more than to hijack a shuttle, to trade this small space for another even smaller space. Times when I wanted to throw myself out of an air lock and go swimming in the airless stars.

But I had you to worry about—my child. And your brother, too. Perhaps that's why the Council demanded that we all be parents. Perhaps they knew how our children would tether us to this place.

I've fulfilled my duties. But that doesn't mean that I've grown obedient.

Seven years into our journey I noticed how listless and sad the other citizens were becoming. Purposeless. I petitioned the Council to let us use animal DNA from storage.

At first they denied my request. "What need do we have for pets?" they asked. They called the idea frivolous. I explained to them all the ways that animals could be therapeutic—how caring for creatures has long been known to lead to longer life spans, better health. They denied me again. I was enraged. This was my vocation, my job—the job they had given me. And they wouldn't even let me do it.

Finally your father intervened. He started a petition. Staged protests. Soon citizens were visiting us to speak of the animals they'd left behind. They were so lonely without little Barney, without Sampson, without Tilly, that good old mutt.

Daughter, you might scoff. It may seem like such a minor thing to you. Pets. At first the Council thought so too. Until we stormed the Council antechamber with our demands.

Only then did they give in. Of course, even then they insisted that these creatures be useful in other ways—pest control.

At long last we awoke fat calicos. Rat terriers. Dachshunds. Companions. Creatures we could care for and care about. Creatures that would depend on us and give us something to look forward to on every new, dark, stifling morning.

Daughter, heed my warning when I say this: Don't trust the Council.

Every comfort you've had was one for which we had to fight—even Alfalfa, your yellow dog who curled at the foot of your bed every night until he was old and gray-muzzled. If the Council had their way, we would live a life of bread and water and nothing else. They'll tell you that they have your best interests at heart. I've come to suspect that they truly believe this. They can lie to themselves. Please, daughter, don't let them lie to you.

PART THREE

ARRIVAL

PART THREE

21

slept on the floor in Mara's daughter's room. Her name was Artemis and she was only eight, and she talked in her sleep every single night, calling out for her mother, who never came to comfort her. Pepper was able to sleep through it, but I never could. I stared up at the ceiling, counting my breaths up through the thousands. There was no one left for me to call for.

In the morning I ate breakfast with them. Mara's husband, Benton, was a dark-skinned man with bone-white hair, and he read books every morning at the table through a pair of tiny spectacles. Artemis was more like him than like Mara—dark and soft-spoken and polite and largely distracted. But Apollo, who had just been bar mitzvahed, was cut from the same cheap cloth as his mother. At the rare times I tried to speak to him, he'd just roll his pale eyes or let out exasperated syllables. Once his father chastised him when the boy called me "a speck-brained fool." Mara smiled wryly at that, even as she let her husband scold him.

It was the only time I ever saw her look pleased to be a mother. After scarfing down her breakfast, she'd leave her dishes steeping in the gray water for her husband to wash, and rush off to work before I'd even finished my coffee.

That didn't matter, though, because I'd stopped going to work when my father died. I didn't ask to play hooky, and Mara didn't offer. It just happened. Every day she rushed off. Benton bundled up his kids and then went to work himself. He was a fieldworker. I couldn't believe that. The Council had paired Mara Stone with a *farmer*. I was left alone to consider that every morning at their kitchen table.

I developed a kind of routine. After breakfast I fed Pepper. Then I'd go up to Artemis's room and curl up on my sleeping roll. I wouldn't shower; I almost never changed my clothes. I'd take the ancient journal from my basket of belongings, clutch it against my body, and sleep.

I hoped to dream of Momma. I wanted her to take me by the hand, walk with me through the dome, and tell me what to do now that I was alone. I wanted her to give me answers: Why had my father taken his life? What had she been doing with the Children of Abel?

She never came. Instead I would be plunged into whiteout storms, the snow piling deep and burning cold around my bare knees. My dreams always started the same way: I'd stumble forward barefoot, lost, the wind doing a fickle dance around me. And then, just as I was sure I'd be swallowed up, a hand would reach out, grasp mine, and pull me forward. Lips would meet lips, and it was summer inside me, the smell of clover and magnolia sticky on the air. In my dreams we burned the winter away.

I woke only when Artemis stumbled into her room after school to put away her bag.

"Oh," she'd say, giving me a polite smile as she ducked out. "Sorry."

But there were other days. Dark days. Days when I couldn't sleep, much less escape into dreams. I'd leave that ancient book sitting on the floor, and let Pepper sit on the pages, and wheeze out tears. There were no kisses. There was no love. There wasn't even snow. All that was left was me, and I was alone.

On those days, on those low, dark days, Artemis would open her door, hear my sobs, and let it shut again, leaving me to my pain.

.   .   .

One afternoon Mara came home early.

I didn't hear her come in. It was one of my good days, and I'd been dozing, flashes of lilac and fuchsia exploding beneath my eyelids. Mara grabbed my shoulders and shook me hard. I let out a cry. The space inside my covers was warm and welcoming, while both the air outside and Mara's grimace seemed dangerously cold.

"No," she said, gripping my shoulders, pulling at the fabric of my shirt. "Wake up, Terra."

I tugged the blanket over my head. But Mara just snatched it down.

"Hey!" I whined. I tried to wrestle the blanket from her clutches. But she held on tight. At last I sat up, staring at her. "What do you want, Mara?"

"It's time for you to get up."

"My *father* died." I spat the words at her like they were made of acid. But she didn't even flinch.

"It doesn't matter. It's time for you to get up and tend to your duties. It's been two weeks. You have work to do." When I didn't answer, crossing my arms square across my chest, she gritted her teeth.

"What's that term your father was so fond of, girl? *Mitzvah?*"

I could feel it, how my gaze flickered when she said it, how tears suddenly stung my eyes. But I didn't want to give in. I couldn't! I couldn't imagine going out there and facing the light of day. "What good works can I possibly owe the people on the ship?" I asked through my scowl. "Why should I help them fix the whole damned universe? What did they do to stop my father from—"

I stopped midsentence, unable to make the words move past my mouth. For a moment, too long a moment, I sat slack-jawed. Then I found myself bringing my hand to my cheek and smearing away a long stream of tears.

"Oh, Terra," Mara said, tipping her head to one side. I hadn't wanted to do this in front of Mara. So far, other than that the first night, I hadn't. But here I was now, weeping openly while she forced a smile of sympathy across her sour mouth.

"I don't know why it happened to him," I said at last. "And Momma. I don't know why. No one else's parents . . . It's not supposed to happen here. Every other family is just perfect. A mother. A father. Two kids. Even *your* family. But he . . ." I sucked in a sharp breath.

"You know, Terra," she began, speaking slowly. "The founders of our society were very careful to control for certain things. So you're right. What you've faced in life is rare—in our entire history few Asherati have ever had one parent struck down before they've reached marrying age, much less two. But no matter how carefully the original passengers were selected for resilience, no matter how many counseling sessions I'm sure they made your father attend after your mother's death, you can't control for sadness, not totally. You can't control for grief."

"Or cancer," I said, not wanting to mention that my father had stopped attending counseling after only a few weeks. He'd pulled me and Ronen out too. *We're fine*, he'd told them. *I know what's best for my family*. "Momma's cancer. They couldn't control perfectly for that, either, right?"

Mara pressed her lips together. "Mmm," she said. After a moment she reached up and cupped her fingers around my chin. Part of me wanted to squirm away, escape her touch.

But I didn't. I let her run her thumb along my tear-slick jawline. "You've lost something. We can't deny that. But this loss will make you a stronger person."

"No!" The protest came out weak, shaky. Mara squeezed my jaw a little more firmly with her fingertips.

"Yes, it will."

With that, she stood, staring down at me. I wanted nothing more than to sink down in bed, snuggling into the blankets and closing myself to the world. But I couldn't—not with Mara watching me.

"Now," she said. "We'll start slowly. You're going to get up. Shower. Get dressed. And then come to the lab with me. That's all you have to do. Come to the lab."

She spoke easily, but we both knew that it wasn't a suggestion. It was a command. I *had* to obey. Without another word Mara turned and walked out. I waited a moment, sighed. Then I stumbled to my feet.

That day in the lab I sat behind Mara as she fiddled with her microscope and entered numbers into her computer terminal. At first I felt nothing but anger at my return to the messy, cramped laboratory. The only place I wanted to be was deep under the covers, hiding myself away from the world. But Mara didn't push. In fact, she didn't even speak to me. Instead she went about her work in silence, pecking steadily away at the keys.

"You're not going to give me something to do?" I demanded.

Mara didn't lift her eyes from the screen. "There are always slides to prep."

I had no desire to prep slides, and Mara knew that. But I went to my work desk and began to set out my supplies anyway, making a show of slamming my desk drawers, hard, rattling the tools within them. I stooped over, blade in hand, and set to work.

Soon my anger receded. But it was only replaced with interminable boredom. Setting my knife down, I rolled my head on my neck, counting the rivets on the metal ceiling. I turned to stare at Mara's bookshelves, trying to make poetry from the titles on the spines. But there was no poetry to be found in *Varieties of Lichen in Eurasian Boreal Forests*. At last, unable to stand it anymore, I pulled myself to my feet and dragged myself over to Mara's desk.

I stood there for a moment, watching her type. Generated on one monitor was a picture of two ribbons, intertwining each other. I watched as they slowly rotated.

"I hate it when people read over my shoulder," she said. I didn't answer, only watched as the ribbons twirled around and around. They were linked together by short chains. It looked almost like a ladder.

"What is that?" I asked.

Mara punched a key. After a moment the image changed. It was a single stalk of wheat—a familiar enough picture. On the end the long grass parted to reveal the spike, lined with fine hairs. But there was something strange about the proportions. The chaff was much rougher and thicker than that which encircled the wheat out in the fields.

"I call it *Triticum mara*," she said in a grave, important voice. I looked at her—and burst out laughing.

"Mara's wheat?" I asked. "You've designed your own *wheat*?"

She glowered at me, then punched another key to make the screen go blank. "Of course I have. I've based the gene sequence on einkorn wheat. Salt tolerant and hardy, but I've adapted it to the cold weather conditions we'll find on Zehava. Assuming Zehava's molecular environment is even compatible with our own. We'll find out soon enough, when that damned probe returns."

"I didn't know you were making your own plants," I said quietly. Mara frowned at me, her eyebrows low.

"Of course I'm making my own plants. What do you take me for, a gardener? We'll have a colony of hungry mouths to feed soon enough. Now, back to your desk, girl."

"But, Mara—"

I don't want to hear it!"

"But, Mara, I want to *learn*!"

My own words surprised me. But after all these weeks spent wallowing in the gray space of my mind, I felt desperate—starved, even—for something, anything, to fill that hole inside. There were tears in my eyes again, threatening to spill over—easily, as they often did those days.

"Please, show me what those ribbons are?"

Mara stared at me for a long time. At last she sighed and turned the computer monitor on. The two spiraling structures returned. "Fine," she said. "Pull up a chair. But no more laughing at my work. Someday, Terra, your life might depend on it."

Over the days that followed she taught me about RNA, about chromosomes and genomes and recombinant DNA. A few days into this second, stranger phase of my training as a botanist, we visited the hatchery—not to see the eggs, which hung empty now in preparation for our arrival on Zehava, but instead to speak to the genetic engineers. They not only manipulated human life on the ship but would also someday create the crops that Mara had designed to seed the fields and forests of the alien planet. One of them was a young woman, dark haired and kind eyed, who, when I asked her what her job could *possibly* have to do with mine, grinned at me.

"Nearly every single Terran organism had the same number of genes," she said, glowing at the prospect, "about twenty-five to thirty thousand. It's mind-boggling, isn't it? To look outside at the grass in the dome and realize it has as many genes as you do."

I expected Mara to roll her eyes at this, but instead she nodded fiercely. So I thought about it for a moment longer, the similarities between me—a girl, grown in one of the now-fallow eggs down on the hatchery floor—and the wheat we ate, and the wine we drank, and the flowers that would someday blossom across our new home.

"Thank you," I said, before Mara and I turned and walked out to the dome.

In the lab and at home over dinner, Mara told me how she planned to build crops that might save us from ever going hungry. Fortified rices and quinoa and soy, nutrient-dense food that would sustain us even if our population of livestock failed. For the first time in a long time—perhaps for the first time ever—I felt my mind begin to spark, stretching to accommodate these new ideas. It wasn't that I forgot about Abba, or what I'd lost. Of course not. On most days my heart still felt heavy and lonely in my chest. But now my mind swarmed with thoughts of the plants we might build on Zehava—strange plants, like the ones I dreamed about, whose leaves and stalks had never been seen on planet Earth.

Once, I had told my father that *his* job was like an art. For the first time I realized how Mara Stone was an artist too. Sure, her work would never hang on gallery walls. But it would fill up our bellies and be carried on the wind. It would shade us from the alien sunlight, and its leaves would paint the ground a thousand colors in autumn too.

One night, as Artemis snored in the bed above me, I reached for my pencils and carried them downstairs. For the first time in weeks, I cracked open my sketchbook. Sitting at the Stones' galley table, I began to sketch. Now I didn't just draw what I saw in front of me— the trees in the dome, the flowers or the vines. I drew whole new flowers, brand-new trees. As I rubbed the pigment into the rough-hewn paper, I felt myself wake to life.

I could have been happy like that, working with Mara, working, for the first time, toward *tikkun olam*. But I wasn't allowed. If there's one thing that I learned from the Children of Abel, it was that happiness was fleeting—*my* happiness most of all.

I tried to escape the Children of Abel, but I couldn't. No matter how I tried to push them into the back of my mind, no matter how hard I tried to forget it, the truth was that the world around me had changed. One night after dinner a knock came on the Stones' front door. Mara was hunched over her research at the galley table. I was helping Artemis clear the plates, scraping the food off their dented surfaces and into the composter, dropping them into the sink and letting the murky water run over them. When knuckles sounded against the front door, Artemis spun on her heel, her dark braids flying behind her.

"I'll get it! I'll get it!" she exclaimed. She was at that age when the idea of *visitors* was thrilling.

But when she answered, she stood there frozen for a moment in the open doorway, blocking my view.

"It's the . . . librarian?" she said, her perplexed voice lifting at the end. "And the new clock keeper?"

From outside I heard a loose, familiar laugh. Koen's laugh. And then his voice came tumbling in with a gust of air. "We're here to see Terra."

I dropped a dish into the sink. It echoed against the steel sides.

Mara barely suppressed a smile as she rose from the table. Standing behind her daughter, her firm posture was somehow menacing despite her stature.

"Come in, gentlemen," she said. "Make yourselves comfortable." She put her hand down on Artemis's shoulder, drawing her daughter away.

"Let's go, Artie." It was the first time I'd heard the little girl's nickname, but Mara's tone was more wary than fond. "We'll go upstairs and let Terra talk to her . . ." A pause. Her eyes flickered over the men as they moved inside. Koen and Van were all bundled up, stamping the cold from their boots. Finally she concluded: "Friends."

Artemis protested, but it didn't do any good. Mara dragged the girl upstairs, leaving me alone with Koen and Van as the sink water dripped from my pruney hands.

"Close the door," I said finally. "You're letting all the cold in."

For a moment Koen only stared at me, his hands deep down in his pockets. Then he let out a laugh. That strange, familiar bark of laughter, like he knew no other way to fill the silence. It hurt me to hear it, like a knife sliding down into my gut.

"Sorry!" He pressed the door closed with his hip. I exhaled. I thought that the long, slow release of air would still the way my heart was beating. It didn't, but if the men noticed my barely concealed panic, they gave no indication. They only stood there, fat in layers of clothing, smiling at me.

"If you're going to stay," I said, "you can take off your coats."

Before they could answer, I turned away from them. I thought if I kept my hands busy, then they wouldn't see how I shook. I fetched three mugs, put a kettle on for tea, and then began to clear the table, still half-scattered with supper plates and Mara's books. The men peeled off their layers, unwound their scarves from their throats. I could smell the cold rising up off them, and beneath that the musky scent of their bodies. Cedar wood and old pages. Dust and something else. I saw an image in my mind: their bodies pressed together in the forest. Ashamed at the thought and the strange, muddled way it made me feel, I sat down, with my hands in my lap.

"So what do you guys want?"

"What?" said Van. He pulled out a chair at the far end of the table and draped himself across it. "We're not allowed to come visit our dear friend Terra?"

I glowered up at him.

"I came looking for you after the funeral," Koen said. At first I could hardly hear him. He spoke in whispers. "First I went to your house, then your brother's, then Rachel Federman's. When someone told me you were staying with Mara Stone, I figured you didn't *want* to be found."

"Maybe I *didn't*," I said, not wanting to think about the deeper truth behind his words: that he'd looked for me. That I'd been on his mind. Koen stared down at his cold-chapped hands spread out on the tabletop.

"You're still one of us, you know," he whispered. I studied his face. It didn't feel true, not anymore. If I'd ever held anything in common with the Children of Abel, it had disappeared that night in the dome.

"Look," Van said. "We're not here to see you for the pleasure of the experience. There's something we need to talk to you about."

I looked over at him. Koen did too, a sort of dread lurking beneath his eyes. But Van just glared at me, his arms crossed firmly over his chest.

"It's time that you pay up on your promise. We need the foxglove."

"No!" I cried, looking between them. "I can't!"

"Can't?" Van asked. "Or won't? You wanted to be one of us, didn't you? To do justice to your mother's memory and the memory of your ancestors?"

"Van . . . ," Koen said, a warning in his voice. Van's lip trembled, but he went on.

"You want liberty? This is how we achieve it. Not through meetings or whispered conversation but by taking action."

I stared at them, my heart falling to pieces in my chest. But then there was a rustling on the stairwell and tittered laughter. I swung my gaze over to the librarian. "There are children here. That's your rule, isn't it? That we don't involve children?"

Van glanced up the stairs. For a moment his mouth was a hard line. But at last his lips softened. He sighed.

"Fine," he said. "But this isn't over. Come on, Koen."

Together they rushed to put on their coats and took harried steps toward the door.

Van went quickly, ducking out without another word. But Koen paused for a moment on the front steps, holding the door open. His brows were furrowed up so high that they disappeared beneath his bangs.

"I'm sorry, Terra," he called. "I *told* him this was a bad idea."

I went to the door. The air outside was sharp, and I could see how the blood was rising to Koen's pale face.

"Yeah, yeah," I said. I didn't have the strength left to spit the words. Koen nodded. Then he stuffed his hands into his pockets and turned toward the darkening street.

I shut the door behind him. As I finally went to fetch the kettle from the stove, I spotted movement on the stairwell. It was Apollo. He stood at the top of the stairs. His sister sat two steps below him. She was holding Pepper tight against her chest. Both watched me.

"Want some tea?" I asked cheerfully, and poured the three mugs full of steaming water.

Most mornings I took my time, milling through the crowded streets even after the clock bells rang out nine. It was the last luxury of mourning Mara still allowed me—or maybe she knew it wasn't worth a fight, I don't know. The day that the second probe was due was no exception, though the energy on the ship was different, jangly and electric. As I neared the lab buildings, I had to duck around white-coated specialists as they laughed and drank. They spilled right out the sliding doors, crowding the fields, trampling dead plants.

"It's really crass, isn't it?"

A voice reached out to me from across the path. It was Silvan Rafferty. He sat on the rail of the footbridge that led to the labs, idly swinging his legs. "Doesn't take much to excite them."

I frowned, reaching down to jostle the seeds in my pocket. "Well, sure," I said. "The probe results are due today. Aren't you excited?"

Silvan gave a shrug. Then he pushed off the rail. He landed with surprising grace—moved with it too. He swaggered toward me.

"Some might be excited by the mystery of Zehava." His black eyes glinted as he spoke.

"But not you?" I asked.

"No, I'm more interested in our actual arrival."

Silvan stepped closer. He stood only an arm's length away, smelling like jasmine flowers and clean hair.

"Why?" I asked. Silvan's mouth twitched up. He had a dimple—just one—in his left cheek.

"Because it's our destiny to inherit an entire *planet*, Terra. It will all be *ours*. Doesn't that interest you?"

"Sure. I guess. As much as anything interests me." I spoke fast, all flustered. I didn't want him to know about the drawings I had hidden in the sketchbook in my bag—about the things I'd learned from Mara. I didn't want him to know how I'd changed, softened. So I spoke quickly. "Mara's waiting for me."

Silvan held his strong chin up. "Sure," he replied. "Wouldn't want to keep the botanist waiting."

A sly smirk lurked behind Silvan's eyelashes. I couldn't stand to look at it any longer. I spun on my heel, rushing past him on the bridge and through the sliding doors.

Even when the doors closed behind me, I could practically feel him there, standing on the path with his hands on his hips. I jogged down the hall and, when I reached our door, pounded my palm against the panel.

I was greeted by the clatter of a clay pot striking the wall. Soil scattered across the floor. Then Mara's terse voice came calling.

"Terra, is that you?"

"Who else?"

"You're late," she said. "As usual." I heard another crash of terracotta, another shatter. I edged toward the rear of the lab.

She stopped throwing things for a moment and stooped over her desk, rubbing soil into her eyes with dirty hands.

"What's going on?" From the sinking feeling in my stomach, I could have probably guessed the answer.

"The probe! The probe!" she cried, casting her head back. I was afraid for a moment that she'd throw something again, but instead she just clutched her hands in the air.

"Bad news?" I asked. "We won't be able to land there? Stuck in our happy little prison forever?" I wanted to shudder at the words, but treating them like they were a joking matter somehow made them easier to say.

"No, Terra. No news. That's the problem. There is no news. Again. Once again. They've lost the probe."

I felt a stab of pain just above my gut, like someone had kicked their boot into my stomach. But I didn't want Mara to see. So I just leafed through the papers on my worktable, looking distracted. Then a flash of realization went through me. I turned to Mara, my mouth tight.

"That explains why Silvan Rafferty was outside," I said. "He was gloating over the specialists."

"I'm sure." Mara paused. She rubbed her hand over her forehead. "You know what they propose to do? Send a shuttle of specialists to study the surface."

I sucked in a breath. "But if they destroyed two probes . . . They wouldn't sacrifice a shuttle full of citizens for their plans?"

"Who knows *what* Wolff will do? She's power hungry. She'd throw her own children to the wolves if it would secure her place. It was one thing to stand and watch while she diverted my work. But now . . ."

"What?" I prompted.

"People, Terra. People. She's not just destroying machinery or work. She's going to murder her own citizens."

She was watching me closely. I could feel my defenses rising, like a second skin was lifting up over my own. "Well, we can't do anything about it," I said, speaking quickly. "Botanists aren't joiners, right? It's not my problem." I turned toward my work desk, staring down at the sketches of adapted plants that were scattered over it. But I could feel Mara's eyes on my back.

"She's done it before."

"Yes, I *know*," I said, speaking in a rush as I turned. I was being messy, not watching my words. "Mar Jacobi. I was there. I saw him die."

Something behind Mara's gaze flickered. "They killed the librarian, then? What, was he threatening to incite the population with his *books*?"

I lifted my hand to my mouth, speaking through a net of fingers as if I hoped to catch my words and pull them back in. "Oh. Oh, I didn't mean—"

"Don't worry, girl," she said. "I won't go spilling your secrets, even if you do. But I didn't mean the librarian."

I thought back to the funerals my father had dragged me to over the years. All for older citizens. There was nothing out of the ordinary there. Old men and women had died in their sleep. Except for one. I dropped my hand. It fell against my hip like a deadweight.

"I hoped I'd never have to tell you this. I thought I could just teach you how to do good work and keep you out of this rebellion rubbish."

"Tell me *what*?" I was still trying to pretend that I was very interested my own drawings—trying to pretend that I didn't already know them by heart. I felt Mara come closer.

"Years ago I found a flower in the atrium. Buried beneath a hedge. I thought, 'That's odd. What's that doing there?' I knew that I hadn't planted it. *Digitalis purpurea.* Foxglove. It shouldn't have been there. I certainly hadn't gone spreading it through the dome. Far too dangerous. And I'm the only one who has access to the herbarium. But the doctors, now, *they* have several of the plants.

"I realized—" Mara paused a moment to take an echoing breath, then began again: "I realized that a member of our senior medical staff must have planted it. A foxglove plant that wouldn't be missed if he chose to utilize any of its parts. And I remembered something. A recent death. A very unusual death."

I could feel the beat of my heart in my throat and against my tongue. I swallowed it.

"Four years ago," she said. "This was four years ago."

"That's when Momma died." My voice was suddenly childish and soft.

"Terra, most cancers were eradicated by the middle of the twenty-first century. A few remained on Earth—genetic strains, unavoidable, I suppose. But our ancestors were carefully screened for that before they were ever allowed to board. And it was effective. Oh, there have been early deaths now and then. The flu pandemic of my grandparents' generation killed one-sixth of the *Asherah*'s adult population. But in five hundred years in space? Your mother was the very first cancer victim."

I couldn't look at her anymore. Instead I studied the pattern of scuff marks on the floor.

"I realized that it had to be a doctor who did it. A powerful doctor. Slipping bits of *Digitalis purpurea* into the pills your mother took every day. And there's only one doctor who oversees those pills. Mazdin Rafferty. Head doctor and member of the High Council."

I closed my eyes then, squeezing them hard. But Mara went on.

"I thought about that poor baker. The one who had come to me years before. A rebel, a member of the Children of Abel. And I thought I'd been right to turn away from them then. Who knows? Perhaps I was. Perhaps Mazdin Rafferty might have poisoned *me* if I'd joined her cause."

"But, Mara," I said, "I'm like you. I'm not a joiner. I . . ." Mara watched me closely. There was no escaping her gaze.

Mara let out a grunt. "If we don't act, people will *die*. Innocent people. You might be my *talmid*, but you're your mother's daughter, too. It's time you acted like it."

She threw something at me. Something small and shining—

something that she'd had ready, hidden in her coat pocket. I caught it. It was a bottle, made of old amber-colored glass.

"What is it?" I asked. Even through the foggy glass I could see that it was filled with white powder. There was no label on it—no skull and crossbones warning me away. But still the sight made me uneasy. Mara grimaced.

"I told you. *Digitalis purpurea.* Purple foxglove. Can you imagine? Your mother ate pills made out of it every day and never had any idea."

Clutching the bottle in my hand, I remembered. She was always forgetting her pills. Abba was the one to remind her, passing her the case filled with her rations. Standing over the sink, she'd swallow them down with a handful of mud-colored water, grimacing. And then she'd wink at me, urging me to do the same.

"You want sweet dreams tonight, don't you, Terra?" she'd asked. I'd gone to the sink and swallowed my pills too. I didn't want to upset her.

Little did I know that they were killing her.

"Okay," I said. I still grasped the bottle in my sweaty hand. "I'm in."

The corner of Mara's mouth lifted. "Good," she said. "Tell those rebels they can poison every member of the Council for all I care. Mara Stone isn't going to just stand by and watch idly as they kill their own citizens."

I could hardly hear her voice. I looked down at the thing I held in my hand, at the way the light reflected off the amber surface. I felt the sudden urge to say something, to make my commitment clear.

"Liberty on Earth," I said. The words didn't fit my lips quite as comfortably as they once had. Still, a bemused smile crossed the botanist's mouth.

"Liberty on Zehava," she concluded.

In the dim afternoon the library seemed to gleam like a bright tower. I shouldered the iron doors open, revealing a dark space mottled by filtered light. Van stood behind the counter, chatting with a guard member. As I drew near, I saw the severe line of her profile, the sharp, hawkish features.

Aleksandra Wolff.

I hung back, hesitating as she and Van completed their conversation in low tones. Each glowered at the other. Meanwhile my heart seemed to have leaped up into my throat. I eyed the knife that she wore even now, tethered to her slim hips with a knot of leather.

Finally she spun on her boot heels and stalked off.

"Is everything all right?" I asked Van when I reached the desk's edge. I kept my voice at a whisper. I don't think I could have spoken any louder than that if I'd tried.

"Yes," he said peevishly. "Why?"

"Because Aleksandra is the *captain's daughter*!" I said, turning to watch as the guard slipped past the library's heavy doors.

"Don't worry," he said. "She's one of us."

He might as well have slapped me across the face. I stood there with my mouth open, not quite believing it. Captain Wolff's own daughter, a Child of Abel.

"But she was there the night Mar Jacobi was—"

Van's hand cut through the air, intercepting my words.

"A double agent learns to keep their mouth shut even at the worst times," he said. "And you know, there's a reason why we don't publicize our rosters." His words were meant as a warning. I pressed my lips closed.

"Yes, yes," I said. "Of course. I won't tell anyone."

Van stared at me. "What do you want, Terra?"

I reached down into my pocket, feeling the cylinder of glass deep inside. Then I pulled it out and slammed it down on the counter in front of me.

"What is that?" Van asked. A smirk curled my lips.

"Digitalis purpurea," I said. "Common foxglove."

Van stared at the bottle, green eyes gone wide. "You did it?"

I nudged it toward him. "I did."

Reaching out a hand, Van set his fingers against the glass. But then, to my surprise, he merely pushed it toward me.

"You hold on to it," he said. My fingers hesitated.

"What? Why?"

As if afraid he'd find someone there, Van looked over his shoulder. "Our leaders were hoping that you would be the one to carry out the task."

"Me?" I whispered.

"You have nothing to lose, Terra. No family. No intended, not yet. And there have been rumors that our target is . . . fond of you."

I stared at Van. My hand was still poised against the amber glass. It felt ice cold beneath my fingertips. "Fond?" I said. My mind raced. I ran through the options: The rebels wouldn't have me kill Koen, nor Mara. And certainly not Rachel. Who else ever gave a single glance in my direction?

"Silvan Rafferty," I said, my gaze dropping down. I thought of the way that he'd smiled at me when he'd found me in the dome, and the way that he'd grinned when he'd asked if I had my mind on anyone. And then I thought of the kiss, long past—a secret shared only between the two of us, never whispered to another soul.

I thought of my dreams.

"I don't understand. He's not even captain yet. What good would it do—"

"We need to get him out of the way," Van said, licking his lips. He looked hungry for it. "Without Silvan to take up her mantle, Wolff will be vulnerable against our plan."

"And what's your plan?"

He didn't answer at first. His hands were flat on the wooden desk, still—like he was waiting for something. "To incite the people to riot. Once we've pushed them toward it, they'll be easy to sway. In the chaos, we strike down Wolff. Then we install our leaders in her place."

I didn't want to look at Van's face. But out of the corner of my eye, I could see how his mouth was set in a grim line.

"I would think that you'd be eager for an opportunity to help us, Terra. After all, he's Mazdin Rafferty's son. And we all know what the doctor did to your mother."

"You know about that?"

"Of course. Your mother was one of us. The loss of her was a grave setback for the Children of Abel."

My throat felt dry, tight. I swallowed hard, but it didn't help at all. "And how am I supposed to get to Silvan, anyway? We're not even friends."

"Mmm," Van replied. "Aleksandra has heard him speak of you several times in complimentary tones. And since that merchant girl was turned down by him, the others have stayed away. He has no suitors. It would be easy for you to insinuate yourself into his life. You'll ask for his hand. He's sure to say yes."

"You want me to marry Silvan. Then poison him?" It felt ridiculous to say it. But Van's expression remained cool.

"Whether you marry him or not, we need you to get close enough to do it before we settle on Zehava. We need our people in place before the Council forces us to stay here"—his eyes searched the dusty rafters, reaching for the dome ceiling beyond—"in this prison."

I didn't know what to say. My fingers still rested on the cool glass. I *couldn't* do it—couldn't do what they were asking of me.

Couldn't kill Silvan.

"Terra," Van said, his voice dropping low. At last he reached out, touching his fingertips to mine. "Your mother wanted you to live a better life. She wanted you to be free on Zehava. You can help us ensure that she didn't die in vain."

I thought of Momma. I thought of her death, how long it had taken her to gasp out her last breath.

Then I snatched the glass bottle back, dropping it down into my pocket. I gave three rapid nods.

"Fine," I said, spitting the word. "Fine. But I'm not doing this for you. I want you to know that."

And I wasn't. Once, I had thought I'd be able to become one of the rebels, to fit among them easily, blending in at their library meetings, joining them in their treasonous words. Now I knew better. There was only one person who owned my loyalty.

"I'm doing this for my mother," I said. Van's eyes glinted.

"We don't care who you're doing it for, girl." His fisted hands were as still as stone against the counter. "Just as long as you do it."

Hours later I paced across the tiny room I shared with Artemis. She was stooped over her schoolbooks at the center of her threadbare rug. Every time I passed, I had to step over her. From the girl's bed Pepper watched me, befuddled. But I hardly paid him any mind. My thoughts were on the bottle of powder that I'd tucked into the bottom of my basket of things.

As I reached her desk once again, I paused. Most of Artemis's room was stark, clean except for her little metal desk—that's why she had to work on the floor. Amid the clutter of papers and pens there, I spotted a mirror, no bigger than my palm. I picked it up, ignoring her protests.

"Hey! My granma gave me that!"

I angled it to my face. Pale eyes gazed at me, but the circle of glass was too small, really, to let me see the rest of myself. I dropped my hand to my side and gazed at Artemis.

"Do you think I'm pretty?" I asked. Artemis lifted her shoulders and then let them fall again.

"Sure."

"No," I growled. "I mean *really* pretty. Like, do you think that a *really* good-looking guy would marry me?"

She began to smile. But it wasn't a confident smile—the edges were all wobbly as she forced them up. "Sure?" she said again, and this time she sounded less certain.

I dropped her mirror down onto her desk. The circle of glass tipped and spun. Artemis watched closely, waiting for the spinning to stop. She was afraid the mirror would break. Without another word I ducked out of her room.

"Make me pretty."

I stood in the center of Rachel's shop as the night's blue light spilled across the old carpet. It was quiet there. All the customers and the other shop workers had long since gone home. But Rachel, of course, was working late.

She'd let me in with only a small frown at my unexpected visit. It had been ages since we'd seen each other. But she was the same old Rachel.

"Pretty?" Her sweet voice was soft. "I've told you before. You *are* pretty."

"No," I said. "I might be passable. But I'm not like you. We both know that." Something behind her eyes flickered. She agreed with me, even if she didn't want to say it.

"Is this about Koen?" she asked, a gentle smile lifting her lips. But I scowled at her, and her smile fell.

"No. Didn't you hear? I told Koen I don't want to marry him. It's not about Koen."

Her forehead wrinkled in confusion. It was an unfamiliar expression; Rachel was usually so sure. Her uncertainty made her look odd. Older. "Someone else, then?"

"Yes, someone else." Even I could hear the rough edge to my voice. I forced my lips to soften. I tucked my hair behind my ear and let out a small, unhappy laugh.

"I need to find someone else. Someone who will really care for me. I don't think that will happen unless I start, you know, dressing nice and stuff. But I'm terrible at that. You know I am. I have gelt, if it's that. I can pay you. Please?"

"Oh, no." Rachel reached out and took my wind-cold hands in hers. Her pinkie fished for mine. I hadn't expected the small, familiar gesture. It had been so long. Guilt peaked within me. "I can't take your money. Of course I'll help you. We're *friends*. I'm glad you came to me. Only . . ."

She hesitated, looking at me sidelong. I couldn't help but frown as she examined me. "What?"

She reached out with both hands, pulling a handful of my long, sallow hair from either side of my shoulders. The frizzy waves nearly reached my waist. She played with them, tugging the soft locks straight. Her expression was thoughtful. "I think we should start with a haircut. When's the last time you cut your hair, anyway?"

I tightened my lips as I thought back to it. I'd been almost twelve. Momma had trimmed my then shoulder-length locks in our galley, as she always had. The split ends of my hair now were the same strands that her hands had touched.

"I dunno," I said, shrugging. For some reason that made Rachel giggle.

"You wouldn't," she said. At last she dropped my hair. Then she went to the register and fetched a pair of scissors. They were the kind you cut cloth with, all metal and gleaming sharp. I wondered if it would ruin the edge to use them.

"Are you okay with this?" she asked, reaching out to smooth down the rumpled locks of hair once more.

"Yes," I lied. "I'm great."

Rachel grinned. She tangled her fingers in my fingers and led me toward the rear of the store. "Good," she said, and then added, in a whisper: "I've wanted to do this for ages."

Without the heavy weight of my hair, the whole world felt different. Though my stomach had turned somersaults as Rachel had made those first tentative cuts, I had to admit that this was an improvement. When I looked at myself in the mirror, I could see how I'd transformed into someone new—a grown-up. And now, walking through the commerce district, watching as men turned their heads toward me to follow my progress, I had to admit that it had been a worthwhile sacrifice.

But it wasn't just the haircut. The makeup and clothes that Rachel had chosen for me changed things too. She'd given me the best stock in her store: a pair of dark purple stockings, a pleated skirt, a pale yellow sweater that was too big on me. It kept spilling down, exposing the blue veins over my shoulders. I'd tugged the sleeves up, but then Rachel had flicked me on the ear.

"Stop it," she'd said. "It's supposed to look like that."

She'd lent me her coat, the olive-green one with the brass buttons. And a cream-colored scarf so soft that it felt like it was spun from the down of a baby bird. The only thing I owned that she'd deemed acceptable were my boots—the ones she'd helped my father buy. Still, even though I wore her clothes, I didn't quite look like Rachel as I gazed at myself in the mirror. I looked like me, but a new me, a different me. A Terra I'd never met before.

"Are you sure you don't want money for this?" I asked as I stood in the doorway of the shop. Rachel just shook her head.

"No, just . . . just come visit me more, okay?"

I gripped her and hugged her then, squeezing her tight.

"Thank you," I said fiercely.

My steps were light down the pavement. It was bitter cold outside, and my naked ears burned against the wind, but I didn't care. I just smiled and said hello to the boys who nodded at me as I passed. The weight of their attention was so new, so strange. I almost felt optimistic, but I didn't allow myself the luxury of that emotion. What I was about to do was terrible. I had no reason to be happy.

I headed to the aft district, where the Council quarters all stood in an orderly row. It was just about suppertime now. People would be sitting down to eat potatoes and cabbage and handfuls of pills to keep them awake until the ship's lights dimmed overhead. The thought of the pills put a bitter taste in my mouth. Of course, I'd still have to take them every day for the rest of my life if my body was to obey Zehava's long days and even longer nights.

But I'd never trust them again.

I reached Silvan Rafferty's front door. They had a buzzer—all the high-ranking families did. It felt odd to jab my index finger into it instead of knocking.

But sure enough, soon the door cracked open to reveal Silvan's dark-eyed mother.

She didn't smile. Her red-painted lips were pursed. "Can I help you?"

"I'm here to see Silvan," I said. His mother tilted her head, dark curls tumbling over her shoulder. Her son took after her—beautiful but spoiled. I drew in a breath. "I'm here to ask for his hand."

24

I'd never seen the inside of a Council member's home before. Though the gray-faced town houses looked the same from the outside as every other house, from within I could see how the rooms stretched back twice as deep. Past the entry hall and the galley—whose wood-block counters were newer and less deeply marred by generations of dull knives—there was another room. I could see the polished surface of a fine dining table there and, beyond, a long sofa made out of animal leather. It was a sitting area, a new notion for me.

Gatherings on the *Asherah* took place in bedrooms or workplaces or, at best, over meals. And yet Mazdin Rafferty and his wife had a whole separate area of their home for *sitting*.

It was suppertime, but you could hardly tell. Their galley was clean, dim, and empty. I stood by the door with my hands in my pockets and watched as Silvan's mother went to the stairwell. As she called for her son, I became intensely aware of my tongue. It felt much too big for my mouth. I wondered if this was how Koen had felt the day he'd come to declare his intentions to me.

"Silvan?" his mother called. She looked at me sidelong, arching her plucked eyebrows at me. "Sil? There's a girl here to see you! That Fineberg girl!"

She waited, her head inclined. I waited too, for the pound of adolescent feet against the stairs. But no footsteps came. She let out a small sigh, lifting her hand from the banister.

"Go on up," she said. I hesitated, peering up the stairs. Part of me couldn't quite believe that I was going to do this—was going to ask a boy for his hand. And Silvan, no less. I glanced at his mother, but she'd already walked away, leaving me alone there gripping the rail. So I made my way up the narrow steps.

Strains of music whispered through the gap beneath Silvan's bedroom door. I knocked once, twice. That's when I saw the panel next to the door, the same kind we had in the labs. I pressed my palm against it. The door was unlocked, and it shivered open.

Silvan's room was massive, almost as big as the entire lower floor of my childhood home. Most houses had metal furniture built right into the walls. But Silvan's room was full of dark, sturdy wood—a four-poster bed, a polished desk, and a dresser. Embroidered hangings of flowering gardens shadowed the walls.

He sat in the middle of all of it, nested within his bed, clutching a small guitar against his chest. Broad fingers ran aimlessly over the metal strings. Every note sang out as if he had plucked it from the air just for me.

At my arrival he lifted his chin. His fingers froze on the strings as the notes rang out, then faded. Then his smile grew.

"Terra!"

I couldn't help it. I grinned at the sound of my name. Then, remembering myself, I gave my head a solemn nod.

"Silvan," I replied. I watched as he set his guitar down on his bed. Finally, in one single, graceful motion, he jumped off it. As he sauntered over, I felt myself flush. I could smell him again, feel the sharp heat of his body. It made me want to lean into him, to touch my lips to his neck.

I fought to remember that Silvan's father had killed my mother. This was no time to wax poetic about the way he *smelled*.

"You cut your hair."

He reached out. I saw the hazy shape of his hand in the corner of my vision. His fingers were broad and strong. And they moved as if the world belonged to them.

"I did," I said, leaning back even more. My hair fell out of his grasp, but a smile lit his lips nevertheless. I saw how straight his teeth were, and how very white.

"I like it," he concluded. Then he turned, sauntering toward his bed. He perched on the end of it. "To what do I owe the pleasure of your visit? Come to complain about the probe? You should get in line for that one."

Silvan sat with his shoulders squared, his heels striking the footboard. Glossy curls cascaded down his shoulders. Normally, I would have drawn a steadying breath, trying to calm myself. But looking at him, at the way he smirked at me, it didn't feel necessary. Standing there in Rachel's coat, my hair tucked behind my ears, I felt for the first time as if my whole life had been headed for this moment. Like something made sense.

I would marry Silvan. And then I would poison him.

"No. I don't care about the probe," I said, lying like it was nothing. "I'm here to declare my intentions. Silvan, if you'd have me, then I would be honored if you'd consent to marry me."

Part of me expected that he'd be shocked—or that maybe he'd recoil, disgusted by the thought. But Silvan's eyebrows only lifted.

"When did you decide you wanted me? Was it our vocational ceremony? When Wolff made me the next captain? Or was it today, outside the labs?"

My voice was flat, but I was surprised to find myself telling the truth. "I always wanted you. But I missed my chance, and then you belonged to Rachel."

A grimace crossed Silvan's features. "Oh, that rubbish. Poor girl. It's not her fault I could never marry some shopgirl."

I made myself nod, as if I agreed—as if I even understood. But how could I? I'd never been the son of a Council member.

"And what about Maxwell?" Silvan asked. "The clock keeper. Aren't you promised to him?"

"No. Almost. But then I told him how I felt about you, and we broke it off."

Silvan pushed himself off his bed again. He swaggered close, standing so near that I could practically taste him. When he spoke, his voice was husky.

"And how do you feel about me?"

I couldn't lie. Not with him this close, so close that I could see the dark stubble shadowing his cheeks and the way his black eyelashes trembled. I told him the only truth that would do any good now, the only one that would help me.

"That you're beautiful." It was the truth. *Oy gevalt*, it was the truth—but only a tiny part of the truth, the smallest sliver. My words didn't alight on the Children of Abel, or the poison, or Momma. They didn't touch upon the boy I dreamed about or anything that had happened with Koen. But before I could think of those things, before my lies showed in my face, Silvan crushed me in a kiss.

It's all part of the act, I told myself as his soft, full lips pressed to mine. But the truth was, I was starved for this—his hands, warm through layers of wool and cotton, firm against my lower back. I'd waited so long to be kissed and had been touched only in dreams, and it was never enough, at least not compared to this, his hot, panting mouth on mine.

He finally pulled away.

"You could have said something sooner, you know," he said as I pressed my hand to my mouth.

"Could I?"

"Yes. I've been watching you. You've grown quite lovely. And a botanist. That's a specialist position. A worthy match for a captain."

"Unlike Rachel." An ugly accusation rang in my words. But I kept my gaze hard, afraid that if I let it soften, then the rest of it—the whole truth about my purpose there—would become clear. Silvan's mouth twitched.

"Unlike Rachel," he agreed. But what he said next surprised me. "Rachel's a good person. I cared for her once. But we were children then. We're not now."

Guilt clenched my stomach. I thought of the bottle that waited for me in Artemis's room.

"No," I agreed. "We're not."

Silvan watched me for a moment, his expression surly. Then he gave his curls a shake. "I have an idea," he said, cracking a bright smile. "Why don't we wed the day we enter orbit? We can be married in the captain's stateroom, Zehava dawning above."

I saw it in my mind. Silvan would look handsome in his uniform, his long hair tied back. But it was still hard for me to see myself dressed in harvest gold standing beside him. Still, I knew which answer was the right one. I gave my swift reply. "That sounds perfect."

Silvan took my hands in his. For some reason I expected them to feel cool, like Koen's always did. But they weren't. His skin was warm, as soft as a baby's. He had the hands of someone who had never worked. He pulled me to him and kissed me again, no less deeply than before.

"Good," he said, panting. "Good."

The next day after work I sat on Mara's front stoop. The light was better out there than in Artemis's room, even as the artificial sunlight faded from the overhead panels. I could hardly feel the cold of the day—I was too busy for that. My sketchbook sat on my knees, my pencils spread out around me on the step. I picked up a dark red pencil and layered it over the crosshatched blue I'd already set down.

I was drawing a new variety of foxglove. If Mara could build high-protein wheat, I saw no reason why I couldn't reimagine a version of the pretty flower, its heavy bells laden with pollen, that wouldn't be quite so dangerous to grow. As I shaded in the delicate blue that lined the inside of the petals, I heard footsteps on the path.

"Hello, Terra."

There stood Koen, wool scarf knotted at his throat. The smile he gave me was grim—but hopeful, too. I felt a wave of emotion crest inside me, but I stuffed it down. I did not speak.

"What's that you're drawing?" he asked.

I slammed my sketchbook shut, holding it in front of my body like a shield. "Nothing," I said. "What do you want?"

Blushing, Koen lifted a hand and touched his tangled hair. "Marry me?" he asked, his voice lifting weakly at the end.

"You don't want to marry me, Koen. You don't. I know you don't."

"But I do!" he protested. He held his hands out to me. "If we were married, then you wouldn't . . . you wouldn't have to marry Silvan. And, you know, do what the Children of Abel asked. Van would stop them from doing *anything* to you. He'd protect you, if you married me."

I sighed.

"And then you can pretend like you're a normal person. A normal boy. But you're not, are you?"

The heat over his face was bright and high. His mouth formed a small, wavering line. "Maybe I'll never be normal. But you wouldn't be normal either. It would be okay, though. We could be friends. I miss—I miss being friends."

Sometimes I missed it all too. Not only Koen but those meetings in the musty library, touching my hands to my heart and pretending like I was fighting for something pure and just. But the wounds were still there, raw and festering underneath my hard skin.

"I want to be friends too," I murmured. "But I don't think I can, not yet. And I know I can't marry you."

Koen stared down at the paving stones that lined Mara's front walk.

"Okay," he said, and shrugged. "I tried."

"You *did*," I agreed. He lifted his lips in a tiny, feeble smile.

"You don't have to do it," he said. "You don't have to k—"

I shook my head. "No, I do. You said it once: These aren't people you want to cross. There's no telling what they might do. Besides, I *want* to. Silvan's dad killed my mother. I need to set things right."

"Are you sure?"

"Yes," I said. "I am."

Koen nodded finally, apparently satisfied. Without another word he started down the road toward his parents' quarters, leaving the way he'd come. I watched him go. Then I opened up my sketchpad, scribbling hard across the page. I hoped to distract myself from the queasy feeling in the pit of my stomach, the feeling that just wouldn't abate.

Because the truth was, I *wasn't* sure if I could kill Silvan Rafferty. I really wasn't sure at all.

Silvan wasn't like Koen. He had no patience for evening strolls through the dome or holding hands. He demanded that I meet him in his room every night after supper so that we could talk about our wedding. But we hardly ever talked at all.

Instead we rolled around on his wide bed, getting all tangled up in the sheets, mashing our bodies together. I laced my hands through his hair, and his fingers, hot and clammy, worked their way over my belly. With his body heavy on mine, I didn't think about my father. I didn't think about Momma. I didn't even think about Benjamin Jacobi or all the people who were counting on me. It was just heat, mouths, skin, lips meeting lips until mine were raw and peeling. Those nights in his bed brought me closer to my dreams than I'd ever been. Sometimes, when we rolled away from each other, I'd touch his soft hands and think about how they must be the hands I'd been promised.

Silvan, I thought, ignoring the ridges over his fingers, the long life lines on his palms, *my* bashert.

Did his parents know what we were doing up in his room at all hours of the night? They must have. I'd sometimes see them as I passed through their galley on the way to the stairs, and I blushed as I followed Silvan to his room. But they didn't say anything. They didn't even say hello.

I knew why. Plenty of kids messed around before marriage. But there were unspoken rules. Couples went for walks when they needed to be alone. They hid in the tall rows of corn or out in the alleyways between the shops. They didn't burn off young lust under their parents' roof.

The only thing that saved me from feeling terrible about the whole thing—feeling anything, really, other than the white-hot burn of lust—was the way that Silvan always pulled away at the last moment, before we went all the way. He'd squirm away from my hands or arc his body away from mine. At first I worried that he might be like Koen. But he wasn't—he *wanted* me, I could tell. So when he'd lie in his bed, breathing heavily and smiling at me, when he said, "You really should get going. It's getting late," I thought that maybe he was just trying to be good. To wait until landing. To wait until we had our own home.

Exhausted after our trysts, I headed to Mara's quarters under the gray light of dawn. The early morning was dim and cold; my hot breath fogged the air. For a moment, just a moment, the ship seemed to have taken on a new clarity. I could see every crack in the old metal pathways. I could hear the birds calling to one another. It was so cold. It seemed like there shouldn't have been any birds. But there were, and I thought that maybe, for the first time ever, they were calling to me.

Then one morning I stepped inside and saw Mara sitting at her galley table, a deep frown wrinkling her face.

"You're still up," I said, pulling my boots off, ready to duck up to Artemis's room to sneak in a few precious hours of sleep. Mara didn't smile at me. She didn't laugh.

"You were gone so long," she said, pushing up from the table, "that I thought you might have forgotten your work."

She took something from her pocket. A bottle made of amber glass, filled with white powder. Then she set it on the table.

"I thought you were going to give that to the rebels," she said.

I took the bottle from her, staring down at its red-gold glass. My mouth groped for words, but Mara didn't wait to hear them. She only rose wordlessly from the table.

"You need to be more careful," she said at last, clutching the banister beneath her hand. "There are children in this house. If one of them got into that—" Her voice gurgled strangely, a strained sound. It was the only sign I'd ever seen her give that she cared about her children.

"I'll be more careful," I promised, clutching the glass bottle in my fist. Mara nodded once, twice. Then she disappeared up the stairs and was gone, and I was alone beneath the buzzing galley lights.

Before we set a date for our marriage, we needed to schedule a time to get our bloodlines checked. I mentioned it to Silvan in bed one night as his hand skimmed over my bare hip. We'd already tumbled away from each other. My body was spent, tired—but still responded to his touch like it always did. Goose bumps lifted over my arms.

"We need to make sure we're not related, don't we?" I asked. He smirked at me.

"I'm sure we're not. I know your family has risen up in the ranks only recently."

"So?" I said, feeling his fingers trace gentle circles on my thigh. "How do you know my great-grandma didn't wear a gold cord? Maybe we're distant cousins."

"Terra, I would know if that were the case."

"How?" I demanded.

Silvan gave his muscular body a twist, springing on me, grabbing my hands in his. He pressed my body to the mattress. His lips formed a toothy grin.

"I can tell," he said. "It's the way you walk, swinging your hips like a common girl." He pressed his stubbly chin against my neck, leaving a trail of rough kisses on my throat.

"Besides," he said, barely lifting his mouth from my skin, "it's not as if it matters."

I squirmed away from his kisses. "What do you *mean*?"

"The bloodlines are a farce," he said. "You *must* know that already. We make our children in a lab. If they have any genetic flaws, we select out for them anyway. What would it matter if cousins married cousins?"

I struggled to sit up. "But then why read the bloodlines at all?"

"Because it lets us ensure that only the *right* families marry into one another. If the Council decides it's not meant to be, then we falsify the results. If you ask me, it's a bit unfair. People should marry whoever they want—within reason, of course. I might even change things once *I* become captain. But Abba says that it's the best way to ensure that commoners stay in their place. Of course . . ."

He hesitated. I finally sat up, gawking at him. "Of course *what?*" I demanded.

Silvan looked thoughtful for a moment. Then he gave his head a shake. "Nothing." He scooted close, kissing the corner of my lips. "Come on, Terra," he prodded. "Surely you realized all this?"

I hadn't. I should have, but I hadn't. I swallowed hard, forced a smile. "No," I said smoothly. "But it makes sense."

Silvan eased my body down into the bed again. I turned my head away from him, to the pile of clothes on his bedroom floor. The bottle of poison was buried in one of the pockets. Waiting for Silvan. Waiting for me.

In the genetic archives neat volumes lined the shelves on the walls. I couldn't help but wonder now if all the books on the shelves were just for show—or if, perhaps, the words inside were nothing but lies cooked up by the Council. Still, the woman who sat behind the curved desk didn't look much like a Council stooge. She was short haired, plump with middle age. She smiled up at me.

"Good evening," she said. I set my hands awkwardly on the desk.

"Hi," I said. There was a long cricket of silence. Her smile grew just a little—thin lips belied her amusement.

"Can I help you?" she offered. I let out a coarse laugh.

"I need to make an appointment for me and my intended to have our bloodlines checked."

"Mazel tov!" the woman said. "And what's your name?"

"Terra Fineberg."

Her trim nails clacked against the keys. "Let's see . . . ," she began. But then her expression changed. "Your bloodlines have been run already. A match between you and a Mar Maxwell." She hit a button, and a noisy printer at the end of the desk began spewing pages.

My throat tightened. That must have been my father's doing. "The match was never made," I said. "We broke our engagement."

The woman stared down the desk at the scroll of pages unfurling from the printer. "That's strange."

"What is?"

"Our records indicate that someone came to collect the record. An Arran Fineberg." She walked over and tore the pages off. Then she set them on the counter between us. "Usually if an engagement is broken before the contract is signed, we simply discard the results."

I gawked down at the printout. "My father," was all I could manage to say.

"Yes, well." A furrow had deepened between the woman's eyebrows. "He must have been quite excited about your match."

I stared at her bleakly.

"Ah." The woman forced a breezy tone. "I suppose it's for the best, if a new love has found you. What's the name of your intended?"

"Silvan Rafferty."

His name changed the air in the archives. The silence felt sharp, electric. Or maybe it was just my blood pressure skyrocketing.

"You're the girl . . ."

"Who is marrying the new captain," I said carefully.

"Yes," she said. Hastily she turned to her screen. "Well, *Talmid* Fineberg, if you come back in one week with your intended, we'll have the research all done for you. Here's a reminder card."

She jotted the date down on a tiny rectangle of paper, then dropped it atop the printout. I scowled down at both.

"Oh," she said. "I can shred the other report for you if you'd like. . . ."

"No!" I said. My hands darted out. They moved with a frightening hunger, grabbing the card and printout both. I clutched them to my chest. "No, thank you." I felt myself blush as the woman regarded me.

"Of course," was all she said.

I started to turn to leave. The woman's voice reached out.

"Terra?"

When I looked over my shoulder at her, I saw that she'd lifted two fingers to her heart. "Liberty on Earth."

I wondered how this woman knew. Maybe she was one of the rebellion's leaders. Maybe she'd been the one who'd decided to push me down this horrible path. I heard myself answer her, but my voice sounded distant, like it belonged to someone else.

"Liberty on Zehava," I said.

I sat beside Artemis on her bed, running my hands over the printed text.

"He did this for me," I said to her. The child watched me with saucer eyes. "Checked my bloodlines to ensure we'd make a match."

I looked down at the printout. It traced back Koen's line and mine. The two threads went back and back but didn't touch, not yet. And they wouldn't, either. No matter what my father had believed on the day he'd . . .

"He wanted to take care of me," I told her.

"Sure," Artemis said. "I bet he loved you lots."

I turned to her, considering her features. Her aquiline nose was her mother's, but that was the only thing. Otherwise she was tall and strong-bodied like her father. Artemis was kind, but not particularly bright. So why was I looking to her for answers? Habit, I guess. For years I'd turn to Rachel for help or to Ronen. When I saw Benjamin Jacobi die, I leaned on Koen. Even years ago, when Momma passed away, I'd reached out for my father, expecting him to comfort me. And where had it gotten me?

It was time to look for answers in myself.

"You know, he did love me, in a way," I said. For the first time I spoke to her like she was the child—and I the adult. "But I don't think that was the whole story. I was an obligation, too. My father valued nothing more than doing his duty. I was part of that. That's why he pushed me toward Koen. He couldn't leave until his duty was fulfilled." I felt a lingering flash of anger as I said it. Left me. He'd *left* me. But I pushed that thought away. This was the *truth*. And my father was gone, and it wouldn't do any good to be angry with him.

"I'm sorry, Terra," Artemis offered. I smiled faintly, then looked down at the list of names. Just above my name was Momma's. Alyana Fineberg. I touched the square letters and felt something go to stone inside me.

But my tone was gentle, for the girl's sake. "That's okay, Artemis," I said. "That's okay."

told myself that Silvan knew only my body—that he didn't know my true self, not really. I told myself that if he had, he would have known how I'd been transformed, how every part of me that had once been soft and gentle was going to concrete. I watched him press kisses into my collarbone, drawing his soft hands over me. He took my laughter and my goose bumps to mean something deep and loving and true. I told myself that the only emotion that ran beneath my pleasured skin was anger. Anger at him and the Council.

No matter how warm and urgent his fingers, I reminded myself of how he'd reaped the harvest of my mother's death. Power, and lots of it. Silvan was complicit—wasn't he?

Sometimes I'd gaze into his black eyes, find myself reflected back, and think: *You're so stupid. You have no idea.* But deep down I knew that wasn't fair. I'd always had secrets, and not just the poison I carried with me wherever I went. There were dreams, too, wine dark. They still came every night. When Silvan kissed me, I thought of snow and the wild perfume of summer flowers. I was always naming them in my head, even as I sprawled out by his side in his wide, luxurious bed—even as I let him whisper sweet words into my ear. I couldn't hear them. All I heard was *Magnolia virginiana, Syringa vulgaris*, and the names of a thousand different species of rose.

I was never really *with* Silvan, never really fully myself.

So how could I blame him for his honey-sweet kisses, the way he spoke to me—syrupy, empty words? I was a creature of artifice, like the jewel-toned sundew plants that caught insects in the dome. When he tangled his big hand through my hair, cupped the crown of my head in his palm, and said to me, "My parents want you to come to supper tomorrow night. Captain Wolff will be there," I gave a gentle smile and said, "Of course. I'd love to do that."

Even as a white spark of fear traveled down my spine.

•   •   •

Supper turned my stomach. We ate lamb and potatoes and shallots all cooked in a red, tangy sauce. I wasn't used to so much butter or fat, but I think it was the memory of my family's own meager meals that did it. After Momma died, we no longer had her half-stale bread from the bakery to supplement our rations. Meat—always lean and tough with sinews—was a rare pleasure. But at Silvan's house each serving was the size of what my entire family might share on a harvest day. Luckily, no one noticed how green I'd gone as I cut into my chops. They guzzled wine, sweeter than the vintages my father had once drunk. Silvan's father drank especially deep. That was something our families had in common.

"He cares about his wine more than me," Silvan had once told me with a sulk. And now I saw that it was true, as the doctor who'd killed my mother uncorked one bottle after another, careful, even in his drunkenness, not to spill a single drop. They were all jolly as they drank, flashing smiles, cracking jokes. But sitting at the table across from Silvan's father and Captain Wolff, all I could think was, *You killed Momma. If it hadn't been for you, she'd still be here—and Mar Jacobi and Abba, too.* I kept playing with my food, stirring it around on the plate.

"Well, Terra?"

I dropped my fork against the china with a clatter. Across the table Silvan's mother's mouth twisted, though I couldn't quite be sure if it was with amusement or disapproval.

"W–what's that?" I stuttered. Captain Wolff's off-kilter smile was stiff. She took a long draw of wine, swallowed, then asked again.

"Do you enjoy your work with our botanist?"

"Sure," I said. "She's great."

Doctor Rafferty gave a coarse laugh. Captain Wolff glowered at him.

"The woman is her teacher, Mazdin. It's natural that she feels some fondness for her. No matter how troublesome she's been for *us*." She gave me a sidelong glance. "She doesn't know any better."

Anger flashed up in me. I stuffed it down. Nobody noticed. The doctor just looked down at his glass, swirling the wine at the bottom.

"Stone's always done her job well. I'll give you that. It's not her *work* that's ever been an issue."

"Yes, yes," Silvan's mother said. "Stone is a true Asherati. She's always been a dedicated worker. But she's a wild card, still. Terra, you will tell us if she ever seems ready to stir up trouble, won't you?"

"What do you mean by that?" I asked. The words sounded harder than I'd intended. But Uvri Rafferty's smile was serene. Unperturbed.

"I'm not really sure *what* I mean," she said. She forced a cascade of laughter. And then she turned to her husband and inquired about the last clutch of newborns.

I slumped low in my seat.

. . . .

The adults were content to make small talk long after the dessert plates had been cleared. I was crawling out of my skin, of course. But Silvan didn't notice. He sat with his elbows propped against the polished galley table, watching the captain, waiting for his moment to jump in.

"I see you, Silvan," the captain said, pouring herself more wine. All the adults laughed, but the corner of Silvan's mouth ticked up in annoyance. Still, Captain Wolff waited.

"Go ahead," she finally said.

"Well, if you insist," he began. Though his tone was smooth, his complexion had darkened. He was blushing. I'd seen him nearly naked, but I'd never seen him blush before. "I know that you and Abba have been eager for me to come up with some ideas for the colony."

"And finally pull your weight," Doctor Rafferty grunted. I had no idea what kind of training Silvan had done with the captain. It couldn't have had the intensity of my training with Mara—he spent too much time wandering around the dome for that.

"I *want* to pull my weight, Abba. That's the point!" He paused just long enough to suck down a mouthful of wine. "I was thinking about how we go about selecting the guard. I know the Council picks guards only from the high-ranking families, but—"

"This ensures that we can trust them. I know my daughter won't betray me—nor will the children of the other Council members,"

Wolff cut in. I felt a shiver at her words. The Children of Abel kept their secrets well.

"Y-yes, well," Silvan stammered, "that's fine. But once we reach the surface, we'll need more guards, won't we? To protect our colony?"

I gaped at Silvan. Didn't he know of the Council's plans to keep us captive in the dome? How much protection could we possibly need if we were still trapped inside the *Asherah*?

"I thought we could institute a general draft," he went on. "Raise an army. And I could lead it."

Silvan's father snorted on his wine. His mother giggled too. Even Captain Wolff's eyes held laughter.

"You *do* aim high, *talmid*," she said. "However, there's a problem with your little plan. A general draft would mean inviting the general populace into the guard."

Silvan slammed his glass down. "So? What's wrong with commoners? If they trained under me, you can bet they'd know better than to commit treason. They'd be loyal!"

Doctor Rafferty was the one who answered. He spoke to Silvan as if he were much younger than sixteen. "Son, it's not a matter of loyalty. The common Asherati is too temperamental to be trusted with *weapons*."

The anger that had been simmering inside me flamed brightly. I gripped the stem of my wineglass, resisting the urge to throw it at

Doctor Rafferty. I clutched it so tight that my knuckles went white. No one noticed.

Captain Wolff shook her head. When she spoke, it was in a patronizing tone—like she didn't quite expect Silvan to understand. "No, don't give him the wrong idea, Mazdin. Oh, there are dependable people among the lower classes. But we must protect them from the dangers that await us on the surface. Their safety is too precious to put in jeopardy like that. That's why the Council rules for them, with the captain's guard standing watch. It's in their best interest."

"But, Abba," Silvan said, "if we got them early, maybe we could get them on our side. Then we wouldn't risk losing them to the Children of Abel."

"Silvan!" Captain Wolff snapped, a stern warning in her voice. She slid her gaze sideways, to me.

"What?" Silvan said. "We're getting *married*. She'll have to find out eventually." He turned to me. When he spoke, his tone was a perfect echo of Captain Wolff's. Paternalistic. Condescending. "The Children of Abel are this stupid group of commoners. They think they can bring down the Council."

"Oh," I said, doing my best to sound bored. "I see."

"Anyway, I don't know why you're so down on my idea, Abba. I'm going to be captain, after all. You'll have to get used to the idea of listening to me someday!"

"Enough, Silvan." I heard the danger that lurked beneath Mazdin's words. It was the same sort of warning my father would issue—the same sort of warning that I always mistook for a challenge. Apparently, Silvan did too.

"But, Abba—"

"I said *enough!*" And with that roar Mazdin Rafferty pounded his fist against the table.

The dishes rattled like bells. Silvan's mother reached out and gripped her glass, silencing it. But Silvan sprang to his feet.

"Come on, Terra," he said. I watched in confusion as he went to the door, wrestling our coats from the hooks. The adults sat in mortified silence. I couldn't bring myself to look any of them in the eye.

"Thank you for the lovely dinner," I said stiffly. Neither of Silvan's parents even dared to look at me. But Captain Wolff gazed up.

"You're welcome, Terra," she returned, the scar tissue on the bridge of her nose crinkling. I was surprised by her tone—kind, sympathetic. But there was no time to contemplate that. I scrambled to my feet and followed Silvan out the door.

He thrust my coat at me, then hustled down the road. He held his own wool jacket in his fist, letting the sleeves drag over the cobblestones. He didn't need it. The heat of his body seemed to broil the air straight through his sweater.

"I can't believe them. Treating me like that. When Wolff kicks the bucket, they'll see."

I buttoned my coat. "But, Silvan," I said, picking each word very deliberately, "your parents are Council members. The captain is subject to the Council's whims. You'll always have to listen to them, won't you?"

He stalked ahead.

"Hey!" I called. I ran down the cobblestone street. When I reached him, I matched his strides, slipping my arm into the crook of his. But I could tell that he was closed to me. His strong body was hard, tense against mine.

"Hey," I said, pulling him to face me. For a moment Silvan refused to look me in the eye. So I touched my hand to his chin. His skin was dark against my hands, almost the color of mud.

And then his gaze softened. I saw, for a passing second, the proud little boy inside him. He was just a kid, really, a kid who had gotten his way about a lot of things, but nothing that counted.

He isn't so different from me at all, is he? I thought, though my stomach clenched with guilt at the notion. The sympathy I felt for Silvan—this small, confusing affection—was wrong, all wrong. I needed to be hard to him. I needed to *hurt* him.

I needed to look away. But before I could, he caught my face in his hands, leaned down, and kissed me deeply. Soon I was leaning into it, our bodies drawn so close together that there wasn't any space between them at all.

It was a voice that drew me out of the kiss. A familiar voice. Rachel's voice.

"Terra?"

Even in the tight crush of Silvan's arms, shock rang through me. Rachel stood in the golden circle cast down from a streetlamp. Koen stood beside her. His posture was slumped, uncomfortable. Like he was trying to make himself small. Though Rachel was almost a full head shorter than he was, she took up so much more space.

"Rachel!" I called, and without a second thought I broke away from Silvan's arms. But she hustled off in the other direction.

"Rachel, wait!" I reached out for her, touching her hand. But she tore it away. I matched her pace, but she refused to look at me.

"Terra Fineberg," she muttered in a low tone, "you are the *worst*. You're a lying, boy-stealing—"

"I'm not *stealing* him!" I said. I wanted to let it all spill out—the Children of Abel, their plot. But when I glanced over my shoulder, I saw that Silvan and Koen were trailing behind us. And both were still within earshot.

"What do you call what you're doing with him, then? I heard rumors about the two of you. You know how people talk. But I *defended* you. I told them that my friend would *never* do such a thing.

Oy, I can't believe I helped you. Giving you a haircut. Telling you you're pretty. Well, you know what? *Koen* has just asked me to marry him. Our wedding's in two weeks. The day we arrive in orbit around Zehava. So how's it feel?"

I felt a lump rise in my throat. Rachel was still marching forward, taking wide, wild strides. I grabbed her by the arm, turning her to face me.

"Rachel!" I said. "Don't you know? Don't you know why I didn't want to marry him?" I could see it then—the flash of Koen's hands against Van's waist. Skin meeting skin. My gut clenched at the thought.

"Why?" Rachel's question cut me open.

"He'll never love you," I said. "He's a *faygeleh*." I'd wanted to defend myself, to show her that *I* had been the one to turn down Koen. But it was selfish, telling her the truth. I regretted my words instantly.

The pronouncement hung heavy on the air. Rachel turned, looking at Koen. I followed her gaze. Silvan did too. The young Council member slapped both hands against his thighs. He seemed to find this the funniest notion in the world.

"You?" He let out rough, humorless laughter. "You schtup men? Just wait'll the Council hears about this!"

"No, no, I don't mean it!" I said, and clamped my hand over my mouth. But it was too late. The words were out, and no one heard me take them back anyway. Rachel was staring at Koen, tears welling.

"Is this true?" she asked.

Koen gave his head a frantic shake. "No," he said. "It's not true! It's not!"

He rushed over to where we stood. I could feel the panic rising off him, like a trapped rabbit about to be felled. His hands shook as he grabbed Rachel roughly by the wrists and pulled her to him. He smashed his mouth to hers, a kiss that seemed to be all spit and tongue.

I wasn't sure what to do, what to say. I glanced to Silvan, curious as to whether he was buying this outburst. He just rolled his eyes as the pair parted, a silver thread of saliva trailing between them.

Rachel turned to me, glaring. Koen still held her hands in his.

"I can't believe you, Terra," she said. "I just can't believe you. Why would you make up such lies? You're such a sad, miserable person. Always looking down your nose at everyone else like you're better than them."

"No, Rachel . . . ," I protested. But then I felt another wave of terrible, toe-curling guilt. Because I'd let out Koen's secret. Because I'd been kissing Silvan just minutes before, and it hadn't had a damned thing to do with the rebellion, or the Children of Abel, or setting things right. I'd done it just because I'd wanted to be kissed.

When my words faded, Rachel let out an exasperated sound. "You wanna know why Koen didn't want to marry you?"

I didn't answer, but she went on anyway.

"He didn't want you because you're just as screwed up as your crazy dad."

The words sliced into me like a ceremonial knife. I let out a cry, but Rachel didn't care. As I lifted my hand to my mouth, she threw an arm over Koen's shoulders and dragged him down the dark, curving streets.

Silvan came to me. He drew me to his chest.

"Just ignore her," he said. "She's a bitch."

That's when I knew I was a bad person. Because I didn't defend Rachel, not when Silvan called her that horrible name, not after everything she'd done for me—after nearly a lifetime of friendship. Instead I only cried into his sweater and let him lead me off toward the dome.

In my dreams kisses were simple, uncomplicated. There were no expectations. No promises. No specter of rebellion hanging over my head. There was only affection. Warmth. Desire. Against my body, that three-fingered hand looked as bright as a jewel and nearly as translucent. My own fingers were ghastly pale and unfathomably solid against his.

The boy who visited me in dreams could do things that no other boy could. He'd call to the trees, ask them to throw down their purple leaves for us. The thorny brambles would flee at the sound of his voice. Silvan couldn't even stand to hear me talk about my work with Mara. But this boy didn't only talk *about* the forest that surrounded us—he seemed to talk *to* the forest too.

I tried to find that same sense of wonder when I lay down beside Silvan. I let my body melt into his; I let my lips part and his tongue trespass on mine. When his hands would ease over my hips, tugging my clothes away, I let myself believe that these were the same graceful movements that I found every night in sleep.

There were differences, of course—differences as innumerable as the stars. Silvan's face was lined with stubble. His irises were dark, but ringed with white. And though he often smelled like flowers, they were the wrong flowers. Jasmine and lilies, and their scent bottled and preserved. In my dreams the smell of pollen was everywhere, and those exotic flowers grew wild, unchecked. But Silvan's body, hot beside mine, was the closest I'd ever come to that long-promised oblivion. And so when we tumbled together, I ignored everything about him that wasn't flawless and perfect and true.

Because Silvan was real, not a fantasy. His lips. His fingers. The way my mouth would be raw from stubble after hours spent kissing. His body was the only thing tethering me to the floating ground of the *Asherah*.

On that night, I pushed my guilt away as I clutched Silvan's hand in my hand and let him drag me toward the forest.

We reached a grove that was all prickly briar bushes and brittle vines. Silvan spread his white coat out on the frozen ground. He eased me down against it, scattering kisses over my face and neck, peeling my clothes off one layer at a time. My own hands bumbled forward, twisting his sweater over his head. His underclothes were made of silk. They were white, of course. Through the shimmering fabric I could see the dark curve of his shoulders and the heat rising off him, fogging the air.

My fingers traced the shape of his hip bones through the white cloth. I tugged at the waistband of his pants, drawing him close.

That's when he pried his body away.

"No," he said, even though I could hear how his voice was still gruff with lust. I propped myself up on my elbows, felt the chilly air set in against my bare skin. Silvan was squeezing his eyes down to narrow slits. They looked hazy, unreadable. I reached out and hooked my finger into one of his belt loops, giving him one last halfhearted tug.

"Yes," I said, trying to force any uncertainty from my voice. I needed him tonight—needed him to wash away any memory of Rachel, of Koen, of dinner, of the poison tucked into the breast pocket of my jacket. But Silvan only swayed a little.

"I can't," he said. "It isn't safe."

"Safe?"

I clutched his coat around my shoulders. Silvan squatted on the ground in front of me.

"There's something you should know. I . . . The sons of Council members . . . We never had our bar mitzvah. If we go too far, you could get pregnant."

Pregnant. I clutched the coat tighter around my chest like it could shield me from the danger. I knew about the natural order of things. How the sheep birthed their babies live in the pastures. How someone's cat was always going into heat in the district, drawing all the toms out of their quarters. But I'd never thought it was something that could happen to me. We were humans—above such things. Weren't we?

"No," I said. I was speaking fast, panic mounting in my voice. "It's not true. You told me that the bloodlines don't matter. We make our babies in a lab. . . ."

"Most citizens make their babies in a lab. Even my parents. But we—we'll be *different.*"

"You were sent away that year just like all the other boys. I remember. You weren't in school."

Silvan sighed. He fell against the hard ground. "Right. No one could know. So me, and Doron Smithson, and Edan Finkus all just went and hung out for a week. We went fishing. Or played cards in Edan's quarters. That kind of thing. We did our best to keep out of sight."

"Why?" I demanded, but I knew the answer even before the words were out of my mouth. "Why wouldn't the sons of the

Council members be sterilized? We need to control the population on the ship. If girls start having babies—"

Silvan shrugged. "On the ship, sure. But we'll be leaving the ship soon. Population control is fine for commoners. But we're going to be the leaders of our society. Our children will inherit Zehava, wear the gold cord, grow up to be Council members. It's up to our generation to ensure that there will be enough strong, high-ranking babies to survive."

I could hardly hear Silvan's words. My mind had gotten stuck on one of them: *commoners*. Momma had been a baker. Abba's father, a metalsmith. I didn't know what fluke had brought Abba up to the rank of specialist, but I knew my people. And we were common to the bone.

"Silvan, *I'm* a commoner!"

"No," Silvan said. He gave his head a fierce shake. "You're a specialist. And soon you'll be a Council member. You'll get your cord on the day we're married. And then we'll land and we can get to work making new citizens."

Was this what our midnight trysts were all about? I remembered what Mara had said about the dangers of giving birth. I had a terrifying vision of my body broken by childbirth.

"Silvan," I began. He put a finger to his lips.

"Shh." He leaned forward, cupping his hand against my face. "I know this is a lot for you, Terra. But I know you'll make a wonderful wife, too. With you by my side we can ensure that the Council rules Zehava for years and years and years. Abba says it's the best way."

Waves of nausea rolled over me. But Silvan didn't notice. He only drew close, the heat of his body trespassing on mine. He smiled wickedly.

"Now," he said. His tone was playful, coy. Didn't he see how I couldn't bring myself to look at him? Couldn't he tell that I didn't want him anymore? "We may not be able to rut in the grass like the other *talmids*, but there are things we *can* do."

In his white underclothes his body seemed to glow. He knew what he was doing as he laid me down against the cold ground, as he kissed a line down my throat.

I let him do it. I let his mouth meet my belly, my hips. But all the while, as I felt the warmth of his mouth against my skin, my mind was frantic with unhappy thoughts. Though the poison waited for me in my pocket, I'd sometimes been tempted to just go ahead and *marry* him, to steal a little slice of happiness for myself. I'd wanted to see my dreams come to fruition, rebellion be damned. But now that I knew what waited for me, I could see no other path out. I cast my head against the ground and felt my heart turn to stone in my chest.

woke in the crook of Silvan's brawny arm, wrapped in his woolen
coat, my body sticky with sweat and dew and aching at the points
where it had touched against the cold ground. The light in this early
hour was blue and gold overhead, the sky shadowed with crows.
The clock tower bells rang out. Seven in the morning. I winced at the
sound—the tolling bells a reminder of the boy who pulled their ropes.
I'd spilled his secret, betrayed him.

I peeled myself from Silvan's hold. Then I went to fetch my outer layers. The fabric of my sweater felt cold against my rubbed-raw skin. All of me felt raw. Even my eyeballs hurt as I blinked away sleep.

"Going somewhere?"

I turned. Silvan was sitting up on his elbows, gazing at me. A sultry smile played on his lips.

"*Some* of us have work to do," I said. I couldn't really help it—I sounded jealous, and was. I knew that he slept in most days, tucked inside his down comforter. But Silvan didn't mind. He only shrugged, still smiling.

"Tell the botanist I said hello," was his only reply.

I stumbled away from him through the brambles. The day was crisp and bright, and the air held a sharpness that you find only in winter. On the lift up to the main level of the ship, a bunch of school children shoved one another and cracked jokes, but went silent at the sight of me. I couldn't really blame them. I'm sure my eyes were shadowed, and my hair a nest of snarls.

I still had two hours before work. Not long enough to sneak in real sleep, but just enough time to slip into Mara's little shower stall and let the hot water wash the night away. As I made my way through the districts toward her quarters, I couldn't help but walk a little more briskly at the thought of it and the thought of wrapping myself in the warm, clean clothes that would shield me from the morning. But then I saw a figure on Mara's doorstep, tucked against the entryway, asleep in a heavy coat and scarf.

"Ronen?" I stood at the bottom of the stairwell, staring up at him.

"Terra." My brother blinked the sleep from his eyes. Beneath the line of his wool cap, a frown creased his brow. "What time is it?"

"After seven. What are you doing here?"

Ronen gripped the jamb with his gloved hand, pulling himself onto unsteady feet. He answered my question with a question. "Where *were* you all night? Oy. Our father was right. Running around without any supervision. I should have known that Mara Stone is unfit as a guardian—"

"I was with Silvan," I cut in, my voice stern. I didn't want to hear what my father was right about or what Ronen thought of Mara. "Silvan Rafferty. We're intended, if you didn't know."

My brother stuffed his hand down into his pocket, as if that would hide his surprise. "Silvan Rafferty. The captain's *talmid*? I heard rumors, but I didn't really think—You're marrying the next captain?"

I shrugged. Meanwhile my brother let out whooping howls of laughter, laughter that soon turned into a raspy cough in the cold air.

"What's so funny?" I demanded.

"It's just funny—you, the captain's wife!" When I didn't crack a smile or laugh back, Ronen gave a wince, concluding, at last, "Mazel tov."

"What are you here for, Ronen?"

He staggered down the stairs, coming to stand before me. There was a time when he'd seemed insanely tall, like a skinnier clone of my father. An adult. Now he couldn't have been more than half a head taller than I was.

"They're sending Hannah away," he said. "She's to join the shuttle crew for Zehava tonight."

"No," I replied. "Her father's a Council member. He wouldn't make her join the crew. . . ."

My words died out. Of course Hannah's father would give her up. There was no end to the Council's villainy. Ronen frowned. "What are you talking about? She's a cartographer. They need her. What does her father have to do with this?"

"Nothing," I said quickly. "Never mind. Go on."

Ronan's tone was sharp—reproachful. "I was going to ask you to come home with me. I need someone to help me care for Alyana."

"I can't, Ronen. I have my own job."

My brother's hand darted out. He gripped my forearm, squeezing it through my coat. There was something almost menacing in his gesture. It reminded me of my father. But his tone was sad, pleading. "Please. Just until we land. Until Hannah returns."

Then his voice shifted, changed. Broke. For the first time in a long time, he seemed *present*. Not only that—for once he looked nothing like my father. His lips, furred with a hint of a mustache, were trembling. They were asking me for something. They were asking me for *help*.

"Okay, Ronen," I said. The words came out coarse, choked with tears. I think we both knew that this was a death sentence. His wife might never return. But I told myself I wouldn't cry. When had Ronen ever cried for me? "I'll get my stuff."

At first I moved quietly, mindful of the girl who slept in the narrow bed as I gathered my things. Into my basket I piled Pepper's catnip mice, my work uniforms, and my pencils. I fished my sketchbook out from under Artemis's bed. But just as I was about to turn to leave, hefting the basket in both hands, I realized something was missing.

Momma's journal. I dropped to the floor, my legs sprawled out as I rifled through my belongings. In my head I kept a silent tally: catnip mice, dirty lab coats, a dozen pencils with the erasers chewed down, sketchbook. But I'd been right the first time. The journal was gone.

I spun around as quick as a cat, gripping Artemis by both shoulders. She let out a cry at the way my fingers dug into her arms through her nightgown.

"Mommy!" she whined. Then she opened her eyes. "Terra?"

"Give it to me!" I hissed. Artemis drew away. I couldn't blame her. Even I was surprised by the heat in my voice. "Give me back my mother's book!"

"I don't know what you're talking about!"

I knew the book had to be around here somewhere—pressed under her mattress, tucked into her underwear drawer. I dropped her down against her pillow, went to her dresser, and threw the top drawer open.

"Tell me where it is!" I growled, throwing her undershirts onto the floor. Artemis was sitting up in bed now.

"Where *what* is? Terra!"

I whipped my head around, scowling at her. "The book! The one with the leather cover!"

"The one you sleep with?"

I sneered. "No, the other book with the leather cover." Artemis didn't answer right away. She rose from bed and stumbled toward the basket.

"Isn't it with your stuff?" she asked, then reached in and pulled out one of my lab coats. I stalked over to her and snatched the coat from her hand.

"I *looked* there already."

Artemis stared up at me. Then something happened. Her chin started trembling. Tears began to streak down her cheeks.

"I'm sorry, Terra!" She gave a hiccuped breath. "I don't know what happened to it. I promise I'll find it for you!"

Once, I would have set a hand on her shoulder, drawn her to me, given her a hug. But looking at her, at how she cried like a child, I felt my stomach turn. Taking my basket in both hands, I gave my head a shake. I left her weeping, alone in her room.

The shuttle was leaving that night. I had one supper with Ronen and his family before we made our way down to the shuttle bay. Hannah did her best to act like everything was normal as we ate. She cooed at her daughter, rocking her. Then she pressed the baby into my arms. I whispered soft words, comforting words, but when I looked up, I caught worry in Hannah's eyes. She stuffed it down, smiling at me.

After all, according to the Council, the shuttle crew had nothing to fear. Hannah and my brother acted like it was true, and I played along. What good would it do to tell them the truth, how Captain Wolff had destroyed the results of two probes already, how the Council thought commoners like Ronen too stupid to think for themselves? So I sang my little niece songs that my mother had once sung to me and tried not to think of everything that must have once weighed heavy on *her* mind too.

When supper was over, Hannah showed me how to knot Alyana's sling over my body. I cradled the baby against me as we meandered through the district. As they made their way through the winding streets, they silently held hands. The citizens we passed touched their hands to their hearts, nodded. It was a brave thing that Hannah was doing. Everybody knew that. What I didn't understand, or want to understand, was why some of the citizens caught my gaze as I trailed behind the couple, and saluted me, too.

I refused to look at them. What if someone saw? Besides, I hadn't done anything yet. So I only set my jaw, holding my head high.

We took the district lift down. It made me feel strange to see my brother reach out and hit the number zero on the panel; stranger still when the lift gave a beep of protest and waited for Hannah to press her finger against it instead. I'd never been down to the shuttle bay before. None of us had. It was one of those places you read about or heard stories of but never, ever saw. The lift lurched downward. I clutched Alyana against me, pressing my lips to her baby-soft hair.

"Is she all right?" my brother asked.

"Yes. She's fine."

We stepped out into the dimly lit bay. The walls surrounding the lift exit were black. At first I thought it was dirt that darkened them. But then I realized that the walls and ceilings and even the floor beneath us wore a coat of rust.

The rest of Hannah's team waited in a loose circle around one of the air-lock doors. It was a shining pane of black glass, and it reflected their brave expressions. Their families waited too, hanging back as if afraid to come too close. I watched as Hannah spotted her parents among the crowd, dropped my brother's hand, and went to greet them. He waited with me.

"I should give her space," he said. "They must be worried about her. They'll want to wish her good luck."

I saw Hannah's father reach out and touch the cord on her shoulder—specialist blue, threaded with gold. He looked proud, a little wistful. I felt a strange pang in my chest.

"If he's so worried," I said, "then he should stop this. He's a Council member. He has the power."

My brother wouldn't look at me. His tone was flat. "Terra, that's treason," he said, and then he went to join his wife, leaving me there with his child by the mouth of the lift.

After a moment the door opened again, and the captain's guard paraded out of the lift. Someone jostled my shoulder, and the baby stirred. She let out a cry. Across the room I saw Hannah's clear eyes snap up at the sound. But before she could rush over, Captain Wolff exited the lift, Silvan at her side.

"I didn't expect to see you here," he said as the captain marched by me, her ice-cold eyes fixed ahead of her. Silvan ignored how I jiggled and shushed little Alyana. I grimaced at him.

"My brother's wife is on the exploratory team."

"Ah, yes," Silvan said. "The cartographer girl. She comes from a good family."

It was too much for me. I'd had too little sleep, and the baby was bawling in my arms. "Why would you send a Council member's daughter out there? It doesn't make any sense."

Silvan's unruly eyebrows knitted up in confusion. "What are you talking about? We need someone to draw us maps. It's her *job*."

At this I only snorted. Silvan's words revealed that he really *was* the innocent I'd long suspected—swallowing Council rhetoric without a moment's hesitation. But I knew better. Hannah would never have a chance to do her job. This was all just for show.

But before I could say that, Ronen came over. He lifted Alyana from her sling and cradled her in his arms. She was almost instantly quieted. I let out a ragged breath.

Then I was surprised to feel a hand settle in between my shoulder blades. It was the unmistakable pressure of Silvan's fingers, broad and warm. He drew me against him, planting a kiss in my hair.

"I know," he said, and let out a small laugh. "I'm tired too."

My heart swelled painfully in my chest.

I could hardly listen as Captain Wolff stood before the shuttle crew and made her formalities. She lifted her hands. The guards beside her looked purposeful and proud. There was yet another speech, this one on the importance of their mission, of how the shuttle crew would be the first noble step toward *tikkun olam*. Yadda yadda yadda. I leaned against Silvan, feeling sad as he raked his fingers along my back. And guilty, too. I should have been thinking about my brother, my niece. And Hannah. But I thought only about myself. In a few weeks we'd be landing, and I'd poison Silvan. And I'd lose the last small comfort I had.

We watched as Captain Wolff opened up the air lock. The glass door rolled aside, letting out a rush of musty air. One by one the shuttle crew filed in. Then they disappeared up the narrow stairwell that led to the shuttle. Soon the door rolled over again, closing. All we could see was the panel of shining glass.

"I hope the shuttle still works," Silvan joked. But his tone was grim. I hoped so too.

There was a sound—the massive roar of engines igniting. It seemed to go on for a very long time, growing louder and louder still. Then it was done, and there was only silence.

There was a smattering of applause from the crowd. Even Silvan clapped, and he let out a whistle.

Not me, though. I was watching Ronen. My brother rocked his daughter in his arms almost frantically. Then I realized he was doing something that my father had never done. Crying. Big, sloppy tears ran down his cheeks.

27

After the shuttle departed, something changed, shifted, about the mood of the ship. I'd walk through the districts and hear how nobody spoke except in whispers. In the cool, stirring air of the dome, the fieldworkers went about their business in silence. Even the merchants spoke in low tones. When I walked by the shops in the morning, nobody shouted "Sale!" at me. At the counters citizens paid their gelt, took their packages, and were gone.

I think that everyone was holding their breath. I know I was. For one thing, I was waiting to hear what kind of disaster would befall the shuttle. I was sure that at any moment Captain Wolff would call us to gather in the pastures and announce that there had been an accident—an explosion, maybe, or a crash. Then we'd all hang our heads and sing.

But I don't think that was all of it. We worried about the shuttle crew, sure. Every night I watched my brother rock his daughter and promise that her mama would come home, and my heart broke a little more. But there was something else, a sort of breathless excitement in the way we all looked up as we walked through the dome, watching Zehava grow bigger and bigger in the sky overhead.

We were almost there. For five hundred years the planet had been nothing more than a story parents would tell their children. I'm sure there were times when nobody believed we'd ever *really* get there. It was just a myth, a fairy tale. But now things were different. Nine Asherati were bound for the surface, even if their mission was a farce. Soon we would arrive. And then maybe—just maybe—we'd finally be free.

Two weeks. Only two weeks remained. I went about my business like my life would always be this way—I walked to the labs in the morning, talked genetics with Mara, spent my afternoons dreaming up new plants or digging through the dirt. Then I came home to eat supper with my brother and his baby before frittering my nights away with Silvan. But part of me was always looking up at the glowing sphere of blue and white that grew bigger and bigger in the black distance. Soon we would arrive. Soon everything would change.

But not for Silvan.

He was the only one who seemed unaffected by our journey's approaching end. When I joined him in his parents' quarters at night, he joked and cuddled with me like he had no worries at all. Since the blowup with his dad, the only thing he fretted over was our wedding. He was *very* concerned that the day go off without a hitch.

"You'll ask Mara for flowers from the greenhouses," he said. "I like lilies. White lilies. Ask her for those."

"Silvan," I said, turning over in his bed. "She's not a florist. The greenhouses are for *research*."

"But we can't get good flowers from the florists anymore. It's too cold. Besides, you want flowers on our wedding day, don't you?"

I arched an eyebrow. His smile was sweet, showing only the smallest line of his white teeth. I almost couldn't stand it. I pressed my face into his neck, disguising beneath a giggle the guilt that twisted my stomach.

"Oh, all right," I said. I felt his fingers work their way through the cowlicked locks of my hair.

"Good. I was thinking about something else, too. Thinking maybe we should both wear white."

My body went stiff beside him. I sat up, struggling to keep my frown from warping my expression. "What? No. I'm not wearing the color of death at my wedding. Besides, wedding dresses are supposed to be *gold*."

Silvan scowled. "Says who? Just because it's tradition doesn't mean you *have* to. It's not like it's in the marriage contract."

"No!" I spoke the word decisively, clearly. Silvan gave a small shrug.

"All right," he said.

I fell down onto the bed beside him. "I don't see why you're so hung up on the white thing, anyway," I said, a note of sulkiness seeping through my voice. Since Silvan had become Captain Wolff's *talmid*, the only color he ever wore was his purple and gold rank cord. Even now, his silk underclothes were as white as new paper.

"What, you don't think I look good in white?"

I bit the inside of my cheeks. I couldn't deny that he did. Silvan grinned.

"I wear white because I like it and because I have the gelt for it. You know why most people save white for funerals? It's because it gets dirty so easily. Most clothes can be worn again and again and again for generations, and no one can tell the difference. People think they're doing a mitzvah by saving their whites for funerals. I think it's a waste."

I'd never heard Silvan talk about mizvot before. My stomach clenched again. It was like he was taking the memory of my father and stomping on it. And his smile never faltered for even a second.

"A waste," I said.

"The dead don't care that you save your best clothes for them!" I could tell that Silvan had spent a lot of time thinking about this. The way he said it sounded almost rehearsed. "The dead are *dead*!"

I felt anger flare up inside me. Red-faced, I muttered, "Fine. But don't expect me to wear white to *your* funeral."

Silvan thought I was joking. He locked his arms around me in a bear hug, rocking my body as he mimicked my words. "Fine! Then don't expect me to wear white to *yours*!"

Those days, work was a necessary release for me, the only place where I wasn't "Terra, Silvan's intended" or "Terra, the secret assassin of the Children of Abel" but simply Terra—a girl, a botanist, a person who did good work when she could and who lived and changed and grew. I'd already shown Mara my drawings. She laughed and told me it was a wonderfully backward way to design plants—function to follow form—but then she let me sit down beside her at her computer and watch as she put one of my designs into practice, rendering its gene structure on the dusty, fingerprint-streaked monitor.

We didn't talk about rebellion. We didn't talk about Silvan Rafferty. In the lab we could pretend like the world outside didn't exist—that Zehava didn't loom overhead, an ever-expanding circle beyond the dome glass.

But I couldn't just keep my head down and pretend like nothing was happening. One morning I arrived at the labs to find Mara perched on the edge of her desk.

"Good morning," I said as I went to hang my coat on its hook. But Mara held up a hand, stopping me.

"Not so fast. Someone came looking for you this morning."

"Was it Ronen?"

I'd been up all night with Alyana, rocking her, feeding her. It was supposed to be his turn to care for her now. *Leave it to Ronen to come bother me at work*, I thought bitterly. But Mara only lifted her eyebrows.

"Hmm? No. It was that redheaded man. You know the one—the librarian."

"Van Hofstadter?" I hated saying his name.

"Yes, that's the one. He wanted to speak to you. I suppose this has something to do with the Children of Abel."

"I suppose it does," I agreed. I reached for my coat again, slinging it over my shoulders. But as I turned to leave, Mara called out to me one more time.

"Terra!"

When I turned, I saw that Mara grimaced.

"You're still involved with the Children of Abel, aren't you?" she asked. "This didn't end with the common foxglove."

I hung my head. The bottle in my lab coat pocket felt suddenly very heavy, as if the glass had been blown out of ancient lead. I suppose my silence answered for me.

"Are you comfortable with your role in this?" Mara demanded, rising from the desk and walking close to me. I bit my lip, hard. Tasted blood.

"I don't see any other way," I said. "If I don't kill Silvan—"

"Silvan? Everyone knows that boy is a milk-fed fool. He's only a pawn for the Council. Is this what your engagement is about?"

Of course, that wasn't *all* it was about. It was about kisses, too, shared under a canopy of empty branches and stars. It was about hands and heat.

But none of that mattered, not really. What mattered was the poison weighing down my pocket.

"Yes," I said bleakly. "I'm marrying him so I can kill him."

Mara sighed, turning away from me. When at last she spoke, it was over her shoulder. "It's hard, on this ship. So few choices. Such claustrophobic air we must breathe."

"You've made your own choices," I protested. Somewhere deep in my heart I'd become convinced that I'd been doing the same— forging ahead on a whole new path, exacting revenge for my mother's death. Now I didn't feel so sure.

Mara gave a snort. I could see how her lip curled even in profile. "I fought for every choice I made. And I'm a better mother at sixty than I ever would have been at twenty, like the other sweet young things from my clutch. I never wanted to be married. Never wanted to be a mother. But the Council saw to it that I married and had children, whether I liked it or not."

"You could have joined the Children of Abel. Momma asked you—"

"And trade the Council's goals for the goals of the unwashed masses? That's the problem with picking sides, Terra. You end up fighting for someone else. But who is to say that someone else has ever been fighting for *you*?"

I pressed my lips together, unsure what to say or do to make Mara understand. She was right—I didn't have any choices, not really. So long as I was trapped under the glass of the dome, I'd be living the life that either the Council or the Children of Abel chose for me. But I was doing my best, wasn't I?

"You should go," she said at last. "The librarian's waiting."

I gave a small, sad nod and hustled out through the laboratory door.

"I despise you, Terra Fineberg."

Van glowered at me across the library's checkout desk. His hands were making quick work through a pile of returns. In the morning light of the library, his copper hair looked as dark and shiny as blood. I blanched, stuffing my hands down inside my pockets.

"What did I do? I'm doing—" I glanced out at the people browsing in the stacks and lowered my voice. "I'm doing what you asked of me, aren't I? I got the poison from Mara. I'm marrying Silvan."

"Yes. Silvan." Van's lips tightened. "Seems a little bird told Rafferty about my friendship with the clock keeper. Did you know that Koen refuses to speak to me now? Says he's going to marry that Federman girl. Says he deserves a chance to be normal."

Van's voice changed as he spoke, revealing deep emotion. I had the sudden disarming suspicion that Van had spent most of the last few days crying.

"I'm sorry," I said, and then I repeated it for emphasis, to show that I meant it. Because I did. Whenever I thought of what I'd done, I felt halfway ready to puke. "I'm very, truly sorry. I didn't mean to tell Silvan. It was a mistake. Rachel—"

Van let out a sound of disgust. "I know all about Rachel," he said. "I know the whole gruesome story. I suppose he'll forget all of this eventually. He won't be able to hide his true self for long. But to be honest, Terra, I find it difficult to abide the sight of you right now."

My cheeks burned. "So why did you ask me here, then?"

"Because people are talking. About your early morning walks to your brother's quarters. About how you and Silvan Rafferty have been rutting in the fields."

Heat rose to my face. "We have not *rutted*!" I said, but then Van lifted his fingers to his lips and let out a soft hiss of air. I guess that was fair. We *were* in a library, after all.

"We didn't *rut*," I went on, whispering. "It hasn't gone that far. Besides, how am I supposed to make him believe we're to be married if I don't return his affections?"

Van gave a shrug. "Conduct yourself however you want. I don't care if the two of you screw like bunnies. The only thing I care about is the Children of Abel. I need to know you're on our side. I need your promise that your little romance with Rafferty is only an act."

Van spoke like he thought I was some silly girl, helpless before Silvan's charms. But the flash of anger that I felt was accompanied by a hearty side of guilt, too. My emotions had been fickle lately. Even I wasn't sure that I could trust them.

"I promise!" I said, forcing the words.

"Good. You know, it won't take much to set them off." With a tilt of his head, he indicated the people who browsed through the stacks. "Once you've done what we've asked of you, there will be chaos. We're not just a scattered band of rebels anymore. I'm talking ship-wide mutiny."

Mutiny. My hands went cold at the word. I balled my fists, then thrust them down deep into the pockets of my lab coat.

"That's what you wanted," I began, "isn't it? Riots? Chaos?"

"The people of the *Asherah* have been complacent for too long," Van agreed. "As dead as the engines of this ship. Everything's finally changing, Terra. Thanks to you."

I looked up. There, in the shadows of the towering bookshelves, in the light that glinted down at us from the stained-glass windows, people watched. Little children grew quiet as their gazes met mine. Old men squinted up from their reading, nodding their gray heads. People touched their fingers to their chests, saluting me. As I looked, Van spoke.

"The citizens are growing restless. They've been waiting for something like this for a very long time. And they've been patient. But now, with that planet looming overhead? We know we don't have to wait much longer. And it's all because of you. Haven't you seen it, the way people look at you?"

"Maybe," I mumbled. Then I reconsidered. "I've been trying to ignore it. I've had other things on my mind."

Van's haughty eyes flashed, as bright as jade. "Yes. Exactly. You've been *distracted*."

I scowled. When I didn't reply, Van returned to his work, scanning in the returns one by one. I reached over to a nearby cart, idly running my finger over the rows of spines. Some of the books had water damage, the pages rumpled even as they sat wedged between other books. Some had crumbling covers. Most had been mended over and over again, the book cloth coated with library tape. All were very old.

"Van?" I called, my hand lingering on the top of one of the books.

"What do you want?" he asked with a scowl. I didn't flinch, not this time.

"What's going to happen to all these books when we land?"

Van looked down at the volume in his hands.

"We'll bring what we can to the surface. A shuttle's worth, maybe. The most important volumes only, of course."

"But what about the rest? And the library itself?" I gaped up at the stained glass. Planet Earth was cerulean and emerald. Golden stars winked and twinkled behind her. Those windows had always been one of my favorite things on the ship "Do we just . . . leave it here?"

"You know, I used to worry about the same thing. Oh, Benjamin tried to teach me it was a trifle. The library was included in the original manifest only because one of the first Council members insisted on bringing his books along. Argued it would help us preserve Terran culture. Really, it was a luxury our ancestors shouldn't have been able to afford—books." He set the book down on the counter, tapping its surface with his index finger.

"We learned of that donor's wisdom only after the last uprising. A hundred and seventy years ago, the Council deleted our digital archives as a punishment. Within seconds, thousands of volumes . . .

gone." He gestured expansively with his fingers how—*poof!*—all that information had just disappeared.

"Benjamin and I used to argue about it. I said we needed to bring every volume to the surface even if it took a thousand shuttle trips. We needed our legacy, I said. Then, when he told me about the Council's plot to keep us in the dome, I told him I hoped the Children of Abel would fail. I told him I didn't want to leave my home behind. Or the library. The pretty windows. And all these *stupid* books."

"But not anymore?" I asked. Van's expression was bleak.

"I was a child then," he said. "What did I know about anything? I hadn't even been in love."

The frown that creased the corner of his mouth was deep. I felt a lump tighten my throat at the thought of it—of Van falling in love with Koen and then losing him because of me. But I swallowed that thought. "Now how do you feel?"

He laughed. Desperate, hollow laughter. "I don't care about books. I don't care about buildings. Freedom. That's what matters. So I can love whomever I please."

In the darkness of the airless library, Van's gaze searched mine. He was looking for promises. Vows. My throat grew even tighter. I looked up at the light that passed, green and blue, through the stained glass Earth. Then I looked away.

The day arrived when we were to have our bloodlines read. This time Silvan met me at *my* house—or Ronen's house, at least. There was no way I was going wandering through the dome in search of him, not after what had happened with Koen.

He arrived early, while I was still brushing the postwork snarls from my hair. Ronen appeared at my bedroom door, jiggling Alyana in his arms.

"Your intended is here," he said. His smile surprised me. I hadn't expected any kindness from Ronen, though things *had* been going better between us lately.

"Thank you." I set my hairbrush down. Shifting Alyana from one arm to the other, Ronen's smile grew.

"You know, Abba would be so proud of you. How you've risen. The captain's wife!"

I fought the urge to grimace. I didn't want to think about Abba or what he might have thought of my match. But Ronen didn't mean the words to be an insult. So I kissed his cheek as I passed.

"Thanks, Ro," I said. I hadn't called him that in years, since we'd both been kids. My brother just grunted in embarrassment.

I headed downstairs, grabbing my coat from the hook by the door and tossing it over my shoulders. I ignored the familiar weight in the pocket—the little bottle of poison, waiting for the day it would be used. Well, it would have to wait a little longer. It wouldn't be used today.

Silvan stood straight, grinning at me, looking beautiful. He wore a long tunic. At first glance it looked simply white. But when I came closer, I saw that it was embroidered with tiny flowers in threads of violet and gold. It matched his rank cord perfectly. It was a beautiful, fine outfit—and it must have cost a fortune. Seeing how I regarded him, he flicked his curls off his shoulder, preening.

"Do you like it?"

"You look nice," I admitted, not really quite sure what else to say.

"I wanted to wear something special," he said. "Since you and Abba won't let me wear what I want on our wedding day."

We stepped out into the cold together. It was almost suppertime. The districts were crowded as people went from the butcher, to the baker, to the greengrocer, collecting their rations. I couldn't be sure, but I thought their voices seemed to ebb as we passed. Each citizen lifted two fingers to his or her heart. Silvan looked smug, his posture firm and straight. He thought they were saluting him. I let him think that. In a way, I would have preferred it too. It would have been simpler if we were just the rising captain and his intended, going to seal our engagement.

But of course I knew the truth. As they touched the pads of their fingers to their chests, all eyes were on me.

Every day we neared the surface brought me one step closer to executing the terrible task. To killing Silvan. He viewed the passing days eagerly: Soon we'd be on Zehava, and I'd be fat with his babies. But I didn't have the pleasure of that fantasy. I knew the truth.

We stood in the gleaming record room as the archivist read down the list of names. She was a better liar than I was, giving no indication that she knew that soon Silvan would be dead. I stood stone-still underneath the weight of his arm. He clutched me to him, a broad grin plastered across his face.

At the end of it she gave us a pen and made us sign on a dotted line at the bottom of the page. Our signatures were our pact, our promise to each other that we would be wed. My name was writ small, in cramped letters that hardly took up any space at all. But Silvan wrote his own name in huge, loopy script.

If only he'd known what he was signing up for.

After it was all over, we gathered in Silvan's quarters for wine. My intended had orchestrated the whole gathering especially on my behalf. His older sister and her husband stood there, bored, rolling their eyes at everything Silvan said. His mother's mouth was tight with disapproval. Silvan didn't pay them any mind, though, hustling about to fetch glasses and pour drinks. Only Silvan's father looked at all pleased with the idea. When Silvan went to fill my glass, Mazdin stopped him.

"No, Son," he said in his rumbling baritone, "your intended should drink something special tonight."

He went and fetched a bottle from the wine rack. As he worked the corkscrew into it, Silvan lowered his brow.

"But, Abba," he protested. "That bottle's almost fifty years old. You've been saving it—"

"For a special occasion," he said, sloshing my glass full. "Terra's joining our family now. She deserves the good stuff."

There was something in his voice that I couldn't quite read.

"You'd better not let that go to vinegar," his wife warned. She was scowling at me. I don't think she'd ever warmed to the idea of my marrying her son. But Mazdin just laughed. He filled his own glass, then jammed the cork into place and returned the bottle to the rack.

"I think I can handle leftovers," he said.

At long last Silvan grew tired of waiting. He cleared his throat, lifting his glass for his toast.

"To my new wife and the line our union will create," he said, hoisting the goblet high. "To life and to Zehava. *L'chaim!*"

"*L'chaim,*" we all murmured, touched edges, drank.

The wine was delicious, dark and rich with a hint of fruit behind it—nothing like my father's sour, acidic stuff. I choked it down. Silvan watched me proudly, then leaned over to kiss the crown of my head.

"I can't wait till next week," he said fondly. He didn't even seem to notice how his sister and brother-in-law were already rushing to get their coats.

"Off so soon?" I called to them, eager for a distraction. If I thought too much about Silvan's words, I was sure that the guilt would show in my face.

"Yes," she said, then gave a rude smirk. "Other things to do."

They were out the door, gone.

"I have things to do too," Silvan's mother said with a yawn. She started up the stairs, but hesitated for a moment at the bottom, looking at her son.

"Silvan," she said, "I believe your father would like to have a word with your intended."

"Abba?" Silvan put his arm around me again, pulling me close. "Well, whatever you want to say to Terra, you can say to me."

Mazdin set his glass on the counter. "Please, Silvan," he said gently, "can't I have a word with my future daughter-in-law?"

Silvan let me go. "Fine!" he said, huffing toward the stairwell. Then he paused, giving me an amorous smile. "I'll see you later, Terra."

"See you, Silvan," I said, but my gaze was fixed on Mazdin Rafferty. In my ears I heard my heart beat a wild rhythm.

Silvan and his mother made their way up the stairs together. At last I heard bedroom doors click shut. That meant I was alone with Mazdin—my mother's killer. He watched me carefully even as a smile played on his handsome, hungry lips.

This man's not a doctor, I thought. *He's a hunter.*

"Terra," he said, "come sit with me."

He gestured to their sitting area, which, so far as I'd been able to tell, mostly went unused. My glass was almost empty, but I still clutched it in one hand. It gave me something to focus on as I made my way over to the leather sofa and sat down. I fought the urge to leap up, to bolt toward the front door.

Instead I sat, smoothing my trouser legs against my thighs with my palm. Then my gaze fell on a book that sat squarely on the coffee table. It wore an ancient cover, gold letters stamped into the leather.

"That's mine!" I cried. I grabbed it, crushing Momma's journal against my chest.

Mazdin chuckled as he sat down.

"Is it?" he asked. "A little boy by the name of Apollo brought it to Captain Wolff. He found it in his quarters, in his sister's room. Read a few pages and it troubled him. And I can see why. Can you imagine being a child and stumbling across such treacherous words in your own home? He knew he was doing a mitzvah, bringing it to her."

A mitzvah. Apollo, who'd called me names and vied for his mother's attention, knew what he'd done. The boy wasn't stupid, but he *was* jealous. Holding the book against my body, I saw how Mazdin's lips—full, like his son's—twisted angrily.

"One of the benefits of living on such a small ship," Mazdin said, "is that petty disagreements easily run amok. And it's always only a matter of time before one citizen betrays another."

His words reminded me of Koen. I hadn't meant to let the truth slip out about his love for Van, and certainly not in front of Silvan. But it had. I hadn't meant to hurt anybody, but the boys would pay the price anyway. I closed my eyes against the pain and the fear that was boiling over inside me. Mazdin didn't seem to notice.

"Now, Terra," he said, "don't feel bad. This isn't the first time such a thing has happened, and it won't be the last. Why, four years ago I ran into our clock keeper at a pub down in the commerce district. He looked so *sad*, so I bought him a drink for his troubles. And you know what he told me in return?"

Abba, I thought. *Oh, Abba, what did you do?*

"Told me he'd caught his wife with the librarian. Lying together, in his very own bed."

My mind resisted his words. My mother and father had loved each other, hadn't they? He had called her his *bashert*. But had she felt the same way about him? I couldn't remember, not really. What I *did* remember was the expression on Benjamin's face at Momma's funeral and then again on the day I received my vocation. Like he'd lost something precious. Like he was searching me for some shadow of my mother. I set the book down on my knees, staring down at the cover. I couldn't bring myself to look at the doctor.

"He didn't mean to betray her," he said, his voice syrupy. "He was in pain. Why not talk to a Council member about it? Of course, it was easy after that to find out what had brought the star-crossed lovers together. The Children of Abel. Your mother was one of their leaders, you know. And Jacobi their messenger. I imagine that it all seemed terribly romantic."

There was a long pause after that. I guess I was supposed to say something, but I couldn't make my lips move. I only stared down at Momma's book. Mazdin reached out and snatched it from me. He glowered at it, then tossed it down onto the table.

"What do you know about this book?" he demanded.

I wanted to blurt out that I knew nothing, to beg for forgiveness, to throw myself on my knees. I wanted to save myself from the gleam in his eyes. But the gleam in Mazdin's eyes was too much like my father's. I was frozen in fear where I sat.

"The writer's name was Frances Cohen," he said. "She was the ship's first psychologist. A specialist, like you. She even tried to start an uprising. Seems to be common in your family. Though I never did understand why her journal was considered a document of the rebellion, myself.

"Frances might discuss freedom. But in the end she gave in, as they always do. She had her babies. Obeyed the Council. Became a true Asherati. That's how it always goes. Well, either that, or you die."

I hadn't moved a centimeter from where I sat, hadn't even looked up. Without a word Mazdin rose from the sofa, leaving me there alone. But he stopped at my side as he passed me, and bent at the waist. When he spoke again, his words were whispered, hot against my ear.

"I'd hoped my son would choose better," he said. "But Silvan's never been bright. I have to let the spoiled child have his marriage. Still, I'm not worried. You're just a broken little girl, aren't you?

You might have dreams of rebellion, but you're not a threat."

I watched him as he started up the stairs.

"You pose no danger to me or my son," he called out behind him.

He disappeared into the darkness above. I heard a bedroom door slam. Soon silence followed. I was alone, all alone, in his living room.

My body thought for me. Trembling, I rose, taking the journal in hand. I shuffled toward the door, groping for my coat. Numbly I slung it over my shoulders. My fingers moved mechanically, fastening the buttons.

It was the weight in my breast pocket that brought me back. I reached in. My fingers found a red-gold bottle, heavy with white powder. A grin curled my lips.

My body moved with sudden anger, my limbs propelling me across the galley and right to Mazdin Rafferty's wine rack. My hand flashed down to the bottle he'd just uncorked. It moved with purpose. His smug words echoed in my brain.

I think I can handle leftovers.

Handle this, I thought, gripping the cork and tugging it out of the bottle's mouth. The galley echoed with a resounding *pop.* I unscrewed the cap from the bottle of poison and began to pour it in.

It's funny. I had spent so much of my life sad or scared. But my hands didn't shake as I emptied the powder from the bottle and watched it sink into the dark liquid. I couldn't even hear my heart in my ears. Instead I saw the moment with perfect clarity: the white of my hands in the galley light, the bloodred of the wine behind them. It was a rash, angry, terrible thing that I was doing. But I didn't feel angry. Only strong, decisive.

Because I wasn't acting for myself or for the Children of Abel. No, the poison I put in Mazdin Rafferty's wine was for Momma, and my father, and even for Mar Jacobi. It was for everyone who had died, everyone I had lost.

I shoved the cork in and gave the bottle a few fierce shakes. I was strong, whole. Someday soon Mazdin would learn.

Other than a few frothy bubbles, you couldn't even tell the bottle had been disturbed. With satisfaction I slid it into place on the wine rack. Then I turned to where I'd set the bottle of poison on the counter, and froze.

It wasn't empty, not quite. But no more than a sprinkle remained, clinging to the amber glass. As I slipped the bottle down into my pocket, I realized that there was no way I'd be able to do what the Children of Abel had asked of me, not anymore.

I buttoned my coat up the rest of the way and left.

That night, as the clock tower bells called out across the pastures, I climbed the tower's steps alone, only the ghost of my memories by my side. At the top I found Koen. His silhouette danced across the floorboards as he threw his weight against the ropes. The rhythm stuttered when he saw me, his face an unreadable mask. But he had to finish his work. So I waited there at the top, watching his lean body move until his shoes touched the floor again and he once again found solid ground.

"What are you doing here?" he asked.

I reached into my pocket and pulled out the bottle. Then I crossed the floor and handed it to him. Under the shadow of the bell, Koen frowned at the empty glass.

"What's this?"

"What's left of the poison. Tell the Children of Abel that they can find someone else to murder Silvan Rafferty. I'm out."

I started toward the stairs.

"Terra!" he called. I turned, searching his face. His thin eyebrows were arched up under his unruly mop of hair. His broad lips were twisted in a question. At last he said, "You know, I'm mad at you, but I don't want to see you *die*."

"I don't want to see me die either, Koen. But I don't see any other way out." I spoke down into the dark stairwell now, my voice echoing off each dusty step. "The way I see it, so long as we live under dome glass, I have one of two options: kill Silvan Rafferty or marry him. And he doesn't deserve to die."

"But . . ." Koen's voice was strained, sad. "You don't *love* him."

"So? You don't love Rachel."

"That's different! I'll *never* get what I want. Marrying Rachel is my best chance at living a normal, happy life. What am I supposed to do, be alone forever?"

"What, am I?" I asked.

"Oh," was all that Koen said. He stared down at his cradled palm, at the glass that rested within it. He looked so *sad*. So I took quick steps across the cedar floor and put my hands over his.

"Koen," I said gently, "I'm sorry I told your secret."

He shrugged. "It'll be all right. What I had with Van, it . . . it was just kid stuff. Messing around. We weren't meant to be together forever."

I felt his fingers beneath mine. They were ice cold, lined with blue-purple veins that I could see even now in the tower's dim light. I remembered a time when I'd thought those hands might be the ones that haunted my dreams. I knew better now, but I couldn't help but feel some fondness for the boy who owned them.

"I think *you* should decide that," I said. "Not the Council. Not the Children of Abel. But you, and Van, and Nina, and Rachel. You're the ones who matter here.

"Besides," I said, squeezing his fingers, "I don't want to see either of my two best friends get hurt. Okay?"

Koen didn't answer. But he blushed suddenly, furiously. I felt my throat tighten in response. I needed to go—before the tears came, before I made a fool out of myself. I headed toward the stairs.

"Terra?" Koen called, just as I started down the steps again. I glanced at him.

"Yeah?"

"I hope . . . ," he began. Then he sighed and tried again. "I hope the Children of Abel don't hurt you. I'll do what I can to see to it that they don't."

What could Koen do? He was only a boy, really, hardly more than a child. The smile that trembled on his lips was sweet and hopeful.

"Thank you, Koen," I said. I headed down the stairs and out into the freezing night.

A dome hung low overhead, but it wasn't our dome. The sky—viewed through smooth, solid glass—was a bleak, pale yellow. Moons waxed against the horizon, just visible through the afternoon light.

The vines of the forest had already enveloped us. The flowers blossomed brightly against our skin. He held me in his arms. When he spoke, his words were as hot as summer against my ear. I couldn't tell you what language he spoke. But I *could* tell you his meaning.

Who are you? You weren't supposed to be here. But I think . . . I think I would have been dead by now if it weren't for you.

I turned to him, but my own hair veiled his face. All I could see was a shadow of black—his eyes endless, pupil-less. When I reached up to cradle his face in my palms, it was blindly. I felt skin, the impression of a mouth.

You're my bashert, *aren't you?* I asked him. In my dream my chest was tight with the promise of tears. *I never believed in them before, Silvan.*

He laughed. Both our bodies shook with the force of it. *Who is Silvan?*

Silvan. We're to be married. And I'm supposed to—

But he cut me off before I could say it. It was as if he weren't listening—like he was lost in his own troubled thoughts.

There are always two, he said. *But after a loss? No, there's never another.*

I didn't know what to say. I tucked my face in against his chest. His skin was ice cold. He hardly seemed to breathe.

Who are you? he said again. His voice faded. *You weren't supposed to be here. Who are you?*

There was a sound like a million bones breaking—a crackling, a snap, a shudder. We looked up. The dome was dissolving into scattered darkness. When I looked down, turning to see him again, he was gone.

There was only the scuffed wall beside my bed.

Even after I startled myself awake, I heard a groan move through

the ceiling rafters. There was a great shudder, the sound of metal lurching. I reached out and touched the walls, sure that I had imagined it. But I could feel the cold steel moving beneath my palms.

The thrusters. I'd almost forgotten. Somewhere on the ship Captain Wolff must have turned them on, slowing the ship to a stop. I told myself that this was normal. I told myself to stay calm. But the noise went on, and I could feel the vibration down into my bones. In the distance Alyana woke and began to bawl. This wasn't just *my* nightmare.

In the spare bedroom of my brother's home, I turned over on the narrow mattress. My eyes adjusted to the dark, but my mind couldn't accept the sensation of my body moving beneath the sheets. Or the sight of Momma's wedding dress hanging, wrinkled, at the far end of the room.

In the morning we'd be frozen in Zehava's orbit. In the morning I'd be wed.

It seemed to take ages for the noise to stop. In truth, only an hour passed, maybe two. But by the time silence came again, I'd become so accustomed to the terrible sound of the thrusters that its absence startled me. Down the hall there was a hiccup of quiet, then Alyana started wailing again. When I didn't hear Ronen's footsteps in the hallway, I sighed and flicked on the light.

I got up and plodded down the hallway to Alyana's room. Pepper darted after me, circling my ankles again and again in a panic. I guess he didn't really understand stuff like "thrusters." The baby didn't either. When I reached the pitch black of her bedroom, she paused for only a second before she started screaming again.

I lifted her into my arms. Her wailing faded but didn't die. I carried her down the stairs into the galley to fix her a bottle.

The three of us waited for the water to heat. Pepper sat on the table, flicking his tail. By then Alyana's cries had steadied. Still, she windmilled her tiny fists against my body. I lowered my arms, looking at her for a long moment. Red-faced and bald, she looked more like my father than she did either of her parents.

"There, there," I whispered. As I spoke, I bounced her gently. "There's no need to be sad. Don't you know what today is? Today's the day we go home. To Zehava. Just wait until you see it. The snow-capped mountains. The frozen oceans. It's all blue and white and beautiful, and someday, when you're bigger, you'll go outside and look up at the dark sky and see a million stars sparkling. And then you'll realize that some of the stars are really snow, little pieces of the night that have broken off. And you'll stick your tongue out and catch them in your mouth. And then your momma will call you inside, and she'll wrap you in a blanket, and you'll be warm and safe."

I heard movement behind me. Ronen stood on the stairs dressed in his striped pajamas and my father's ratty bathrobe. I wondered when he'd gone to take it from our old quarters. In a way, I felt relieved to see it as he sloped across the galley floor, yawning, and went to turn off the stove. Deep down I was happy to see bits of Abba in my brother, in the way he carried himself as he prepared the bottle.

Maybe that's what I hadn't realized before, in the years after Momma died. How life moves on whether you want it to or not. How we carry the dead with us. How death is an ending only for the person who died.

Ronen came over and took Alyana from me, offering her the bottle. As she suckled, I rose from the table, hefting my cat under my arm.

"Hey, Terra."

Ronen called for me as I made my way toward the stairs. When I turned, I saw a thin, tired smile playing across his mouth.

"That was crazy, wasn't it? The thrusters."

"Yeah," I said. I hesitated at the bottom of the stairs, knuckling one of Pepper's silken ears.

"I can't . . . ," Ronen began. His expression was pained as he nursed his daughter. "I can't believe Dad missed it."

I frowned. "Yeah," I agreed, but then added: "His loss, though, isn't it?"

To my surprise, Ronen didn't argue with that. He only grinned. "Yeah," he replied. "Seriously."

I gave my brother a weary smile and trudged up the narrow steps.

. . .

There was no one to help me dress for my wedding.

Tradition was that a girl's mother dressed her in gold silk. Her aunt and sister-in-law would lace flowers through her hair. But my father's sister hadn't spoken to any of us since years before he died. And Hannah was down on the surface of the planet, gathering data. Even my brother begged off helping. He'd see me later, he said as he fixed Alyana's sling to his back. Later, he said, at the wedding. Right now he had work to do. But I knew that in the dome, celebrations raged. Zehava was dawning overhead. No one was working. Not today.

I went to the shower and slathered myself in the ceremonial honey and salt wash I'd purchased the night before. The water was lukewarm and briny, as always. Still, I did my best to scrub myself clean. The pungent scent made me wrinkle my nose, but I had to go through all the motions of tradition. After all, today was the day I made my choice—the day I married Silvan, whose father I'd killed. The day my heart withered and died. Because I had no other option.

I crossed the hallway of my brother's home and reached my spare, undecorated bedroom. Momma's wedding dress was the only bit of light within those steel walls, but it was a feeble one. After all, I'd mended the old gown myself, looping crooked stitches through the torn silk. I'd never been very good at sewing.

I pulled it over my head. It didn't fit right, not really—not with the way that my arms and back had grown muscly from work. The fabric bunched and pinched around my armpits. I could hardly lower my arms as I fumbled for the buttons. But what could I do? I hadn't been able to afford a new dress, and I wasn't going to go asking Silvan's family for the gelt.

I was sucking in my stomach and trying to tighten the bodice cords, when a knock sounded at the door below.

Holding the bodice of my dress against my body, my wet hair dripping down my shoulders, I rushed to answer it. When I threw open the door, I found Rachel standing there.

Beneath her heavy winter coat she wore her own wedding gown. There were violets pinned in her black hair. In her arms she held another golden dress. She looked angry, a deep crease forming between her eyebrows.

"Rachel!" was all I could say at first, the syllables falling clumsily from my mouth. She just thrust the dress at me.

"Your brother bought this for you," she said. "I don't know *why* he wanted me to deliver it *today*, of all days. He must have known that it's my wedding day too."

Wordlessly I took the hanger from her hands. The dress was made from silk, like Momma's dress, but *this* silk was flawless and new. Nicer, too. The fabric shimmered against my hands.

"It's beautiful," I said. But Rachel was already halfway down the path. A sudden pang of desperation went through me.

"Rachel!" I called. "Wait! Please! I'm sorry!"

She stopped but didn't turn. So I did the only thing I could. I said it again.

"Please, Rachel. I'm so sorry."

I heard her loose a low, hollow sigh. "When asked for forgiveness, one should forgive with a sincere mind and a willing spirit," she began, her voice nearly swallowed up by the wind. "Forgiveness is natural to the seed of Israel."

"Israel?" I asked. I'd heard that word before, in Momma's book. Even then I hadn't been sure what it meant. A place, I guessed, maybe. But I had no idea why Rachel would go on about it.

She turned slowly. I could see that she was forcing the tight line of her lips to soften.

"It's in this book that Koen gave me. I was telling him about the electric candles that Mom lights. And he found me this book in the library about it. It's called the Torah."

I frowned, trying to stop my mind from reaching for the natural conclusions: that if Koen had returned to the library, then he'd returned to Van, too.

"It's an ancient history," Rachel went on, mistaking my expression for curiosity about the book, "of these people on Earth who live in a desert and stuff. Anyway, it talks a lot about how you're supposed to act. And it says if someone asks for forgiveness three times, then you're supposed to forgive them."

There was a long silence. I looked at Rachel. Though her jaw was tight, she still looked beautiful: long limbed, but not gawky. Strong, but still graceful. My best friend looked like such an *adult*. I knew in my heart, suddenly, fiercely, that I didn't want her to walk down that road without me.

"I'm sorry," I said again, almost shouting the words. The tears flooded my eyes before I had a chance to even anticipate them. "I'm so sorry! I didn't mean to hurt you with Silvan and all of that. I didn't mean to embarrass you. But I did and I'm so, so sorry."

Rachel cracked a smile. "That's more than enough, Terra. Three times. The book only said *three* times."

I sniffed tears. Rachel let out a laugh.

"Do you need help getting dressed?" she asked. And then, because I could trust her, always, to be honest with me, she added: "Because you're kind of a mess."

I gave a mute nod. Still smiling, Rachel followed me into the house.

Rachel helped me out of my old, ill-fitting dress and into the new one. It must have been made to my measurements. When the stays of the bodice were tightened, it fit my curves like a glove. It had long, narrow sleeves, a low boatneck. It wasn't flashy like Rachel's dress—

hers had flowers embroidered in the pleats and tiny beads sewn all along the top—but the plain, elegant style suited me. Even I had to admit that I didn't look half bad in it.

"Ronen picked this?" I asked, turning in front of the mirror.

"Well, he had *some* help," Rachel said, winking at me.

She sat me down on the bed, twisting my short hair into a braid. Her hands made quick work. In our silence Pepper padded in and settled on the hem of my dress.

"You're going to be covered in cat hair," Rachel said. I shrugged.

"I figure Silvan should get used to it."

Rachel gave a laugh. "Can't escape the cat hair," she said. "It's an indelible part of Terra Fineberg."

At first I laughed too. But her words swirled around in my mind. *Indelible part.* After another moment I gave her an uneasy look.

"About Koen . . ."

Rachel looked at me for a long time. "Honestly, I don't think he could stay away from Van Hofstadter if he tried. But that doesn't matter. Just because we're getting married doesn't mean he's my destiny or anything. This wedding is about survival. I'm marrying him because otherwise I'll have no choice in who I marry at all. Everyone else from our class is already married or intended. And I *won't* let the Council choose for me."

I darted my hand out, grasping her pinkie finger in mine. Her hand stayed limp at first. Then she gave my hand a little squeeze and smiled up at me.

"We're friends, at least. Koen and I," Rachel said. "But it's not like you and Silvan. It never will be. You're so lucky."

"Lucky?" I sighed, glancing in the mirror. My reflection was almost startling. With my hair back, I was almost another creature. Not the botanist who spent her days in a muggy greenhouse. And not the assassin who had poisoned a man in a fit of rage.

"I've done things I'm not proud of, Rachel. To you. To Koen. To Van." I turned to face her. "To Silvan's father."

She drew in a breath. "Mazdin Rafferty?"

It was his name that did it, sending a shock of anger through me even now. I thought of his dark hair, scattered with silver; his eyes, brown and lined and cruel. I thought of his sneering, laughing mouth. I thought of his delicate doctor's hands—hands that had been used to kill my mother.

"I had to do it," I said evenly. "You have no idea who he really is."

"Do what?" she whispered. "Terra, what did you *do*?"

I didn't answer, only stared at her with wide, wild eyes. I couldn't tell her the truth. So I kept my lips tightly shut. At long last Rachel looked away. She touched her hand to Pepper's back.

"I'm scared, Terra," she said. Her voice was full of tears. "About what comes next."

I went to the bed and sat down beside her. Holding my chin high, I made my voice sound firm. I couldn't let her know that I was just as scared as she was.

"I promise you, no matter what happens to me," I began, speaking slowly so that she would know that I meant every word, "that nothing bad will happen to you. I won't let it."

Rachel threw her arms around me and buried me in a hug.

n our gold wedding dresses we walked through the dome together. The fields were crowded with drunken teenagers who had all filched their families' wine rations. But I don't think anyone cared. Everybody was joyful, exuberant. The air was busy with wild energy.

Overhead, Zehava gleamed and twinkled. We were fixed into orbit now. For the first time we could see the shapes of her continents, mostly frozen and white in a sea of turquoise. There was one larger landmass on the planet's northern side, joined to the smaller southern continent by a narrow bridge of land. There, near the equator, the planet gleamed violet. The color was so familiar—the same shade as the tangled vines that spread through my dreams at night. The same color as the hands that had pressed, hot and wild, against my pale skin. I found myself staring up at it, speechless.

"Are you okay?" Rachel asked. I forced a smile.

"Sure," I said. "It's just amazing, isn't it? The universe and all."

"It is. You know, the Torah says—"

"Torah." I rolled my eyes. "What is it with you and this book?"

Rachel's cheeks darkened. She smoothed down the fabric of her dress.

"It made me feel good to read it," she said. "Not just because it explained the lights. Did you know that once, people didn't work one day a week? Not just work, but they didn't do *anything*. Write or draw or turn on the lights. Because that was the day that the universe was done being created."

"All of the universe? Created in a day?" I tried not to grin at the idea of it. We'd been traveling through the stars for too long for me to believe something as absurd as that.

"Well, the Torah says six days," she said, the smile on her lips tentative. "I don't know. Maybe it's a metaphor. It makes me feel good to think that there's a plan behind it all. A force driving us, just like the engines once drove us. Someone watching down over us, you know?"

I glanced at the purple-scattered continents overhead and let out a sigh. Looking at those white-capped mountains and blue seas, it was almost enough to make me a believer. Almost. But I'd seen too much in my life to have faith that there was someone watching down over *me*. I was alone, and always would be.

"C'mon," Rachel said. She took my hands in hers. "We're getting married on the same day. Just as we arrive on Zehava. That has to be a sign that there's a greater plan, right?"

I grinned. "Silvan's greater plan, maybe. Anyway, I just can't believe I won't be at your wedding."

"And I won't be at yours," she said sadly. I gave a shrug.

"Honestly? I never really thought about that. I thought about what it would be like when *you* got married. But not me."

"Really?" Rachel seemed genuinely surprised. "But we always talked about it."

"Just talk. Don't get me wrong. I always hoped I might find my *bashert*. But on a ship this small, what were the chances of someone loving *me*? I thought marriage was something that happened to other girls. Girls like you."

Rachel stood there, the wide pleats of her dress spread around her like flower petals. She cradled my hands in hers as she spoke. "Terra, you have to stop this. You're my friend. My brilliant friend." She paused, her bright smile growing fond. "Do you remember the day we met?"

"We sat next to each other in school," I said. But to be honest, that was all I could remember. Everything before my mother's death was hazy.

"Yeah. But that wasn't the whole story. It was the first day of class. And the other girls were making fun of me. My mother had dressed me in a ridiculous outfit, all blues and greens. That would be the style the next season, but that year it was all earth tones. They called me a fish.

"You turned around and *glared* at them. You were so angry. You told them to shut up, that I was beautiful. And then you reached down and grabbed my hand and held my pinkie so tight, I thought it might fall off. And I sat there thinking that if this smart, *brave* girl thought I was pretty, then I must not be so bad. We were always friends after that."

I couldn't help it. I crushed Rachel in a hug. She smelled like honey and violets.

"If you think I'm smart and brave . . . ," I said, pulling away. My voice was tight with tears. "Then I must not be so bad."

"No," she agreed, holding me at arm's length. "You're not. You're so courageous, Terra. I've always thought that. I might not agree with the choices you make. But I don't doubt for a second that you can do anything you set your mind to."

We stood there for a moment, grinning at each other in the

shadow of the clock tower. Then the bells began to chime. As the crashing sound washed over us, Rachel leaned in, shouting her words.

"I guess we should go get married," she said. I laughed, finally letting go.

"Sure," I said. "Why not?"

The lift doors slid open, revealing the polished floor of the captain's stateroom beneath dozens of well-dressed feet. I drew in a breath and stepped inside. My own shoes were a pair of silk flats that I'd bought especially for the day. Without my boots my calves felt naked beneath my dress; every step felt precarious, like I was walking on ice.

I searched for familiar faces. Ronen was there, looking awkward as he clutched Alyana to his chest. He stood with Mara and her family. I noticed that Apollo had dressed well for the occasion, in a dark tunic threaded with gold. He and his sister and his father, too, all beamed at me as I neared. But Mara only arched an eyebrow.

"You've cleaned yourself up," she noted. I felt myself flush and crossed my arms over my chest. Goose bumps prickled my bare clavicles.

"You haven't."

She wore her lab coat and muddy shoes. I noted the trail of dirt across the marble.

"My work is never done," she said, and, taking a long draw of her wine, she gestured up at Zehava. White clouds swirled over the landmasses overhead. "Did you notice? Purple vegetation. Perhaps their plants absorb retinal rather than chlorophyll, as Terran plants once did."

"Terran! Like you, Terra!" my brother barked, then let out a laugh at his own joke. Mara's children looked uncomfortable, shifting in their dress shoes.

"Yes," I said impatiently, "like me." A flood of red washed over my brother's face.

"Sorry," he said, chuckling as he jiggled his daughter. "I just never realized."

I watched him for a moment. I felt something, an alien twinge of sympathy. So I flashed him a smile. He grinned.

"By the way," he said. "You look great."

I felt myself blush furiously. "Thank you," I said, leaning into my brother, "for the dress."

Ronen gave a proud nod. "It's what Abba would have wanted."

I beamed at him. Then I heard the distant tolling of bells. "I should go find Silvan," I said, and slipped away through the crowd.

He stood at the front of the room alone, sipping wine. It was odd to see him in a dark color for once. His navy-blue uniform brought out the blue hues in his glossy curls. His shoulders were squared, proud as he gazed up at Zehava. I tried to swallow down the strange emotion that had begun to crest inside me—a small, instinctual joy at the sight of him.

"You look stunning," he said, bending down to press his lips to my neck. His family watched us from the edge of the crowd. I felt myself blush even hotter at the touch of his mouth. He said, "And you wore lilies. My favorite."

"Mara wasn't happy about it," I admitted. And then I forced my voice to sound haughty. "But she's only a specialist. And I'm practically a Council member now. It's *my* wedding. I'll wear my husband's favorite flowers if I want."

He laughed at that, at my lie. And then he handed me his glass. I took a gulp of wine so big that it seared my throat.

"We'll start as soon as Captain Wolff arrives." Silvan had decided that the captain would perform our ceremony. I didn't object. It seemed like a suitably dismal choice in light of the match we were about to make.

"Good," I said, and swallowed the rest of the wine. Silvan flagged down a waiter to bring us two more glasses.

As we waited for the captain's arrival, his family meandered over. His older sister offered me a limp handshake, holding out her hand like it was a piece of fragile glass. His grandfathers took turns at thumping him on the back. His mother watched me, gaze murky with disapproval.

"Mazel tov, mazel tov," one of his grandmothers said, clutching my hand in her age-marked paw. As we descended into small talk, I gave Silvan a weary look. But he was busy whispering to his father about something.

Mazdin wore a black wool suit with gleaming buttons. His specialist cord was bright against it. He and his son should have been a perfectly matched set. But despite his fine garments, something was wrong. His olive complexion had gone sallow; there was a sheen of sweat over his brow, and fat droplets tumbled down his cheeks. His skin had a waxy cast. Between sips of wine he gritted his teeth as if his stomach would not be calm.

I knew that look—sickly, nauseous. It's how Momma looked the day before she died.

I turned away. I wouldn't let myself think of it, of how Mazdin Rafferty's life was dwindling down before all our eyes. I wouldn't let myself feel guilty or sad. This was the fate he'd chosen for himself nearly four years ago when he'd killed my mother.

I drank down my second glass.

An hour passed like that. I was caught in a vortex, only able to keep afloat through one cup of wine after another. The captain's stateroom began to take on a glittery quality as the night dawned. In the distance I heard the clock bells chime out twenty o'clock. A frown darkened Silvan's features.

"Where the hell is Captain Wolff?" he asked his mother, who fluttered her lashes at him.

"Language, Silvan," she said. "I'm sure she'll be here soon."

"Ready to be married, Son?" Silvan's father said, setting a hand on his back. Then he broke out into a rash of hacking coughs. I winced, but before anyone noticed, a shout rose up from the crowd.

"Look!" someone called, and everyone turned.

Night was setting in across Zehava. A sliver of black shadowed the planet, enveloping the water and mountain ranges and mulberry-bright jungles. And on the northern continent, as the night blotted out all color, something was happening. The planet seemed to be flickering to life—sparkling pinpricks of light dotted the landscape in the darkness.

A hush fell over us. It was Silvan who finally spoke, whose deep voice lifted above the whispers of the almost-silent crowd.

"Lights," he said. "But that must mean . . ."

I sucked down the last of my fourth cup of wine and finished his sentence for him: "Zehava is inhabited."

The room erupted in conversation. But I didn't say another word. I just sank down onto the cold floor, my dress spread around me like a pool of gold. I watched Zehava flash and twinkle overhead as night made its progress across it.

Silvan's family drifted away, gossiping with the other Council members about this new development. Even Mazdin staggered off. But Silvan crouched at my side.

"People," he said, laughing coarsely. I think he'd had too much to drink too. "On Zehava. If we're not the first people there, it's not good for much, is it?"

I didn't know what to say. I only shrugged.

In our silence I didn't notice the captain's daughter approach. Not until her shadow was cast down over me.

"Captain Wolff needs to see you in the command center, *Talmid* Rafferty," Aleksandra said. "It concerns the shuttle crew."

Silvan scrambled to his feet, using my shoulder for leverage. For a long moment I just sat there, watching as he disappeared through the noisy throng of people. But then something shifted inside me, snapping. I stood too, holding my skirt in both fists as I ran.

"Silvan! Wait!" I cried as I slipped into the lift beside him. Aleksandra narrowed her eyes. I just cast my gaze away, ignoring the heat that spread across my cheeks.

"The captain didn't request your presence," she said. But I held my jaw firm.

"Silvan's my husband. I go where he goes."

"You're not married yet," Aleksandra said as the door slid shut. Still, she peeled off her glove and pressed the button with her bare finger. The lift gave a lurch, then began its ascent through the glass-walled shaft that tunneled up through the bow of the ship. As we lifted I could see the dome's topography laid out behind me like a map. The labs, their metal roofs gleaming purple in Zehava's light; the dark stone forms of both the school and library; the rolling fields and the clock tower at the center of the pasture; the forests, whose trees poked up from the lower levels; and the narrow, shadowed place in the distance where the districts were. I squinted at the glass. People were pouring into the dome in droves. They flooded the pastures and the fields, rushing the clock tower. From this far away they looked like ants—ants swarming the body of some dead thing, tearing it to pieces.

"What's happening?" I asked, my breath fogging the wall of the elevator. I hadn't been speaking to anyone in particular, but Silvan's answer came quickly.

"Celebrations, I'm sure."

Aleksandra snorted.

"What?" Silvan asked, with heat in his voice. He hated being laughed at.

"The commoners are revolting. The riots began as soon as night fell on Zehava."

"Riots?" I cast a worried glance out toward the clock tower. I remembered what Van had said about mutiny. I should have been happy. Everything was going according to plan. But Rachel was out there, and I'd only just sworn to keep her safe. . . .

No one spoke as the lift dinged into place. Silvan marched out, his shoulders straight. I began to follow, but then I saw how Aleksandra hung back.

"I'd like a word with your intended, *Talmid* Rafferty," she said. Silvan's brow lowered. I guess he was getting used to it, though—to people wanting to talk to me but not him—because he only sighed.

"Sure, be my guest," he said, then left us in the lift. I watched Aleksandra listen for the fade of his footsteps. Then she let the door of the lift close and didn't push any buttons. I was trapped in the tiny space with her. I stared down at the corner of the dark lift, fleeing her gaze.

"You can't hide from me, Fineberg," she said. Her hand touched the hilt of her blade. I braced myself—this was it, I supposed. Time for my own throat to be slit.

"No," I agreed. "I can't."

But to my surprise she didn't unsheathe her knife. Instead she only rested the heel of her hand there, letting out a deep sigh.

"We know what you did. Mazdin Rafferty's illness is unmistakable."

"I—" I began. Then I just closed my mouth again. Really, there was nothing to say. I'd done it, disobeyed the orders of the Children of Abel.

"Such a waste! It would have been easier to enact our plan without Silvan standing in the way. Boy fancies himself a leader. He's bound to fight me for control of the ship at some point. I told them we couldn't trust you. But Hofstadter insisted you had nothing to lose."

"Told them?" I asked. "Do you mean . . . the leaders of the rebellion?" I tried to imagine who *they* might be—muscle-bound field-workers, maybe, conspiring between rows of corn. But Aleksandra just regarded me carefully, a smirk curling her upper lip.

"I meant *my* trusted advisors."

I stared at her for a long time, feeling my heart drop into my gut.

"You lead the rebellion?"

Her confirmation was only a small, short nod—almost invisible. But unmistakable.

"I guess you could say that the women in my family have always craved power. Whereas the women in your family . . ." A hint of disdain twisted her mouth. "Well, you try, don't you? Even if you always fail."

She pressed a button. The door dinged open. But her words had settled into me like a stone. I reached up a hand, touching her shoulder.

"Please don't kill Silvan!"

I wanted to stop her—to make her understand how harmless he was. I knew that I had no right. He was in their way—in *her* way. But, to my surprise, Aleksandra gave her head a shake.

"Watching you kill the brat would have given me some satisfaction. Oh, it burned me when she named *him* as her successor." She gazed down the dark hallway, her pupils tiny pinpricks of determination. "But he's not the one standing in my way, not really. Mother is."

Aleksandra left no time for her words to sink in. She stalked off past me, disappearing down the hall.

I stumbled after her, past tiny windows that showed only a sliver of Zehava. Purple light mottled the floor. My steps were small—they had to be, because of my shoes—but hasty. At last I reached the sliding doors at the end of the hallway.

The doors opened onto a strange room, one filled with flickering panels and twinkling lights. Illuminated maps of the ship lined the walls, showing which systems were working and which had finally run down. The air was clouded with dust, and it smelled ancient, untouched. A soft stream of voices crackled through the silence. In my wine-addled state I didn't yet understand them.

Behind a podium, lit blue in the alternating light, the trio stood— Silvan, Captain Wolff, and Aleksandra. The captain's hair was twined in an intricate braid. She was dressed to the nines for our wedding today: dress boots, spotless wool, buttons bearing the pomegranate seal of the Council. My gaze flicked to Aleksandra. I had trouble believing it, that this woman, whose lean figure and proud posture were so like her mother's, was preparing to strike her down.

As I fell into place by Silvan's side, I heard Aleksandra's hushed words. "Rioting has erupted in the dome," she was saying. "They've taken over the grain silos and the labs. They'll likely descend on the hatchery next."

"They're liable to kill themselves," Captain Wolff replied, the corners of her mouth turning down. In her dismay her twisted face looked even uglier. "I want you to see to it that they're contained. Minimize the loss of human life."

Aleksandra turned and marched off. Her hard gaze flitted over to me for only the briefest moment and then away. She disappeared behind the sliding doors.

Captain Wolff stared down at the podium. It hardly seemed like she registered our presence.

"We should have anticipated this," she said, "when the probes disappeared. We shouldn't have sent the shuttle crew."

"What do you mean, *disappeared*?" I demanded. My heart pounded out a wild beat now. Silvan turned to me from his place beside Captain Wolff.

"Mara told you, didn't she?" he asked, his tone a touch impatient. "We've sent two now. They nearly reach the surface, but then the signal goes out."

"Yes," I said dully, "she told me."

But my mind went frantic at the thought. The Children of Abel were *wrong*—Captain Wolff hadn't destroyed any probes. She'd been telling the truth. They'd been lost, truly lost. Silvan was the one who finally brought me back to myself, pointing down at the screen.

"What's that?" he asked.

An image, black and white and occasionally crossed by a frenzy of static, was projected on a screen set deep into the podium. The quality was so low that I couldn't make out the image at first—only a dim impression of faces, people.

"That's the shuttle crew," Captain Wolff said. Her voice was low. There was sadness in it. "There's Hannah Fineberg. I'd recognize her anywhere. I watched her grow up. Every Launch Day, her family had dinner with mine."

Through the static I saw Hannah's face take shape. She was sitting in the corner of the screen. There was something dark—blood?— smeared over her forehead. I listened to Hannah's voice as it came thinly through the tinny speaker. She was repeating the same words over and over again.

"Mayday, mayday, mayday," she was saying. "Zehava is inhabited. I repeat, Zehava is inhabited."

"No," Silvan said. He pressed his hand against the glass, smearing away the dust. "I meant *them*."

That's when I saw them—people, standing behind Hannah and the rest of the crew. But there was something wrong with them. They were too tall, or too skinny, or something. The movement of their bodies just wasn't right.

I saw my sister-in-law, the mother of my niece, my brother's wife, turn to the crewman beside her. She spoke to him. Someone jostled her. A figure stood hovering over her shoulder.

"The inhabitants are demanding that we leave the surface. Please send a recovery shuttle. . . ."

Inhabitants. The three of us stared at the figures, trying to make them out. Their eyes were wide set and lozenge shaped and black, pitch black, not a single sliver of white in them.

I'd seen those eyes before. Eyes as dark and as endless as the space outside the ship. They visited me every night in dreams. *He* had settled down beside me, his cool skin as fragrant as a flower. He'd watched me, and I'd watched him, and we'd felt safe together—whole.

I saw Captain Wolff stroke her jaw with her gloved hand. "Our biologists have long known that there was a possibility of life on the surface. But we thought—"

I never got to learn what Captain Wolff thought. The sound of heavy footfalls against the metal floor interrupted her. Aleksandra had returned. Her boot heels clopped against the floor.

"Mother!" she called. "It's worse than we feared. We've been unable to contain them. Perhaps they'll listen to you."

The captain nodded slowly. "We'll deal with this later," she said, tapping the dusty screen. She turned to her *talmid*, regarding him gravely. "Silvan, you stay out of the fray."

Hannah's voice lifted up from the speaker, contorted with pain.

"Please send a recovery shuttle. Please . . ."

Captain Wolff glanced down again. Her black eyes had gone huge at the sight of the screen. For the first time I realized that her gaze wasn't cold, as I'd long thought. No, only proud. And now that pride had vanished behind her worry over Hannah, over her people.

"Wait!" I called, remembering Aleksandra's threat. The captain turned to me, her gaze softening.

"The Asherati need me," she said. The realization hit me like a slap. Captain Wolff didn't see herself as apart from the rest of us because she hated us—but because she wanted to protect us, as a parent might. She gave me a small, tight smile. "Don't worry, Terra. We're almost to the surface. Soon you'll be living the life your father always wanted for you."

The thought of my father made me sway. It was all too much for me—my memories of Abba, Zehava, the wine. Hannah on the view screen, blood trailing over her face. And the people behind her. So strange, so familiar . . . As I tried to steady myself on my feet, Captain Wolff disappeared behind the sliding doors. For a long, gaping moment Silvan and I were left alone in the musty room.

"Are you all right, Terra?" Silvan asked, stepping close to me. I licked my lips, groping for words. But they didn't come.

"I'm sorry," he said. I felt the warmth of his breath on my ear, noted the effort it seemed to take for him to get the apology out. I didn't think Silvan was a boy who apologized often. "I guess we won't be married today. You do look beautiful. We'll get married when this is all over, though. Right?"

I didn't answer. Instead I turned, letting my eyes linger on the strong, stubbly line of his jaw. My gaze drifted down to his shoulder and rested on the violet threads all tangled with gold. He and Captain Wolff were the only citizens who wore those colors. Soon Silvan would be the only one.

Unless I did something.

"Silvan," I said, my voice hushed, "stay here. Stay out of the fray."

With that, I stepped out of my silky wedding shoes. I couldn't run with them on. And I needed to hurry. I handed them to Silvan. He frowned at them—at me.

But there was no time for that. I took off running toward the lift.

"Terra!" I heard Silvan calling after me. "Terra!"

But I only slammed my hand against the panel, then stepped inside. The doors were already sliding closed when I shouted back. I don't know if Silvan heard my hysterical, echoing words.

"She's going to kill her!"

But I realized that it didn't matter if he heard me. Not one bit.

He was behind me now, left alone in that dark room as the lift plunged down into the ship. It was as if the taut string that had held us together had finally been severed. I'd expected it to hurt, but it didn't. It felt *good*. I knew then that I would never love him, that our marriage would never be sealed.

The doors slid open. What was revealed was nothing short of chaos. The stone pavilion around the lift was swarmed with citizens, who had descended upon the hospital and school and lab buildings in droves. They'd shattered every window, storming inside to liberate the computer terminals and gadgets and doodads from the oppression of their outlets. Only the library stood untouched, the stained glass dark and perfect in the evening light.

The crowd shifted and swayed around me like wheat stalks in a breeze. I waited until the crush of bodies parted—and then I surged forward.

The crowd stank of sweat and alcohol. Furious limbs surrounded me, jostling my body as I raced over the pavilion and toward the dome. At last my bare feet found the familiar cobblestone of the dome path. I jogged past the grain storage, barely noticing the people who poured out with arms piled high with ears of corn. Overhead, I knew that Zehava twinkled and shone—pinpricks of light illuminating the purple dark of her continents. I wanted nothing more than to stare up, to study the swirling blue oceans and the white clouds that passed over them. But there was no time for that. I ran forward.

At last I spotted a familiar face. Laurel Selberlicht. She and Deklan were running hand in hand across the green pasture before me. Each of them held sizable stones in their fists. Deklan's hands were bloody. I couldn't tell if the red that dripped from his knuckles was from his body or someone else's. I watched, stunned, as they vaulted themselves over the pasture fence. They'd almost run right by me, but I shouted out to them.

"Laurel! Deklan! Have you seen Aleksandra Wolff?"

Laurel stopped, turning toward me. The frantic smile that had lit her lips fell. She lifted one hand—the one that was weighted by the stone—and pointed toward the desiccated fields.

"They say she took her mother there," she said. I glanced doubtfully down between the rows of corn. Before I could answer, Deklan gave Laurel's arm a tug and dragged her down the path.

I stood on the edge of the field, my hands balled into fists. The last time I'd run through the corn, I'd been with Koen. Back then my only worry had been getting him to press his lips to mine. Now I had bigger problems. Captain Wolff. Aleksandra. That knife she kept tied to her waist. My bare toes curled into the soil. I threw my weight back, readying myself.

And then I bolted forward.

Most years the rows would have been plowed under by now in preparation for the long, cold winter. This winter, our last on the ship, they'd been left high. I almost cursed myself to realize it—how the Council would have never left the cornfields in such a state if they'd truly intended for us to stay in the dome. A contingency plan—it had only ever been a contingency plan. Captain Wolff didn't want to stay inside this dome any more than I did. Mara was wrong and Van was wrong and the Children of Abel were more wrong than any of them. How many little details had I ignored to believe the lies that Aleksandra had seeded among us so that she could put herself in a position of power?

The dry leaves rustled all around me, smothering every trace of noise beyond. There was no shouting. No sound of footfalls or glass shattering behind me. There was only my own breath and the papery-dry swishing of the stalks as I slipped through them.

And then, a voice. Captain Wolff's voice. I'd heard it lift up over the gathered crowds a hundred times before. Now it was low, grave. I slowed to a stop.

"You can't do this. Put the knife down, Alex."

My chest still heaving from my sudden sprint, I turned toward the sound of their struggle. There was a rustle, and then I heard something heavy strike the frost-hard ground. I parted the leaves, peering forward. Aleksandra had wrapped her mother's braid around her gloved fingers, forcing the captain down onto her knees. Captain Wolff lifted her scarred face to watch her daughter.

"They won't follow you," Captain Wolff said. "Not after they've discovered that you killed your own mother."

"Good thing they won't find out," Aleksandra said. I saw her free hand flash down to her hip.

Move. Move, I told myself. I pushed forward through the corn, cupping my hands around my mouth, letting out a scream.

"No! Stop!"

But the sound of my voice was buried beneath Captain Wolff's last gargled breath. Like a doll whose strings had been cut, she collapsed in the dirt. The last time this had happened, I'd taken off running. Now I just stood, frozen, staring down at her body. Her silver rope of hair lay twisted in an expanding pool of red.

Aleksandra didn't see me, not at first. She was too busy wiping off the edge of her knife against her mother's coat. I watched as she slid the blade down into her sheath. It fit neatly, as if it had never been disturbed at all.

Then she stood again, and her black eyes lifted. Once I'd thought that she was a younger, more beautiful version of her mother. But though her skin was indeed smooth and clear and without blemish, I now knew the truth.

"Oh, look," she said, her hand moving toward her knife again. "A little bird. Better catch her before she sings."

She took one step forward. *Now* I ran.

I ran harder and faster than I'd ever run before. My bare feet pounded against the cold soil; my breath came out in white bursts against the air. I could hear Aleksandra behind me, rattling the cornstalks as she passed. But I didn't stop to think about that. I ran, and I ran, and I ran.

Soon I'd spilled out of the pastures. The cobblestones felt like ice against the soles of my feet. The path had grown crowded. I decided to use that to my advantage. I dodged between the bustling workers, who had lifted up their voices in a thudding chant. Hundreds of fists pumped the empty air—

"Stop the Council! Free Zehava! Stop the Council! Free Zehava!"

—but this time my own fingers remained firmly at my sides. I pushed through the crowd, stumbling out again only when I squeezed through the slats of the pasture fence.

Past the lambs, across the dewy soil, I ran. It wasn't until I was half-way to the clock tower that I realized I had no place to go. The districts ahead were empty now. The people had taken to the fields, and they now followed Aleksandra, who would surely come for me soon. And I couldn't very well return to Silvan, not after what I'd done to his father. I stumbled to a stop, searching the dome for an escape. But there was nowhere to go. I realized, for the first time, that the glass above might as well have been bars. And then my eyes reached up past the glass, and beyond.

Zehava. It sparkled under its triple moonlight like a whole new field of stars. Each point of light was a home, safe from the frantic bustle of the crowds around me. I stared up at Zehava, my mouth open. I hardly noticed the gaggle of teenagers who had spilled by me or how they wielded wrist-thick branches like clubs. My mind was on the people I'd seen on the screen up in that dusty command room. Not Hannah and the shuttle crew—the other ones, the strange ones. Tall and slender, their bodies had bent like reeds in the wind.

I knew a body like that one.

This dome held nothing but danger for me now. I'd forever be at the mercy of Aleksandra Wolff, the Children of Abel, their knives and clubs and fists. But I'd be safe on the surface below. I'd be safe on Zehava—safe in *his* arms.

I took off running again. Not toward the captain's stateroom, where Silvan still waited for me, nor toward the clock tower, where Koen and Rachel had surely joined their hands already and said their vows. No, this time I plunged myself past it, through the trampled pasture and toward the districts beyond. There I'd take the rear lift down. The shuttles shone in the darkness. They offered my only escape.

"Wait for me," I breathed into the cold air. "I'm coming."

Darling Terra,

The first time I ever saw the Asherah was on the shuttle over.

From far away it looks like an insect. A lightning bug. You've never seen one of those, have you? No, I don't think they're on the approved list of pollinators. Perhaps one of our descendants will know their light, but you'll never catch one in the hollow space of your palms and watch it flicker on and off.

Like a lightning bug, the Asherah has a long, round body—and it's lit up from inside, lit by the light of the forests and pastures and fields, by the life that stirs inside. The head is where the labs and the captain's stateroom and the command center are. The insidious brain of our little ship. But the true light lies in its body, where the people live.

As I sailed beneath the Asherah in our shuttle, I felt a quiet awe come over me. She was shining and new then, but huge and silent and terrible, too. And resting there, in the dark stillness of space, she looked utterly and completely terrifying.

She's never frightened you. You know her too well. You visited every twisted, hidden path. You sat on the shore of her bays and got sunburned by her UV lights, and you think she is the whole world. And for you, she is.

I'm an old woman now. You've asked me so many times why I'm unhappy, why I speak up against the Council, why I let your father argue with those gold-corded beasts at meetings. You tell me that every choice they've ever made has been for our survival. And you're not wrong.

But know this: It's the dream of the world beyond our ship that has kept me alive. Not only Earth—though every bone in my old body aches for her. But some other distant place, one that the Council can't control. This thought of freedom, of a life without contracts or the net of glass above—this is what has sustained me.

Because someday, hundreds of years from now, one of our daughters will step outside for the first time—step into the air, the fresh, new air. And then she'll turn around, just as I did in my shuttle. She'll look back over her shoulder. And she'll see her world fade into the dark behind her.

I saw the dying, ancient Earth. She'll see the Asherah, her metal body darkened by hundreds of years of travel through the stars. And she'll abandon it. Because the entire universe is waiting for her, massive and strange and alive.

And full of hope.

ACKNOWLEDGMENTS

The following individuals get gold stars, love, and a thousand hugs:

Phyllis Ray Fineberg, my mother, who lent me her name for Terra's. Without her passion for science fiction—Sundays watching *Mystery Science Theater 3000*, *John Carter* movie dates—or her help with my bad Yiddish, this book would not be here. Or it might, but it would not be very much fun.

My sister, Emily North, who shares a birthday and a star sign and also shared a childhood with me. You're my favorite Capricorn. Thank you for being there.

My mother-in-law, Elayne Rudbart, my first and most fervent fan.

All the writers and early readers of this manuscript who offered both critiques and support: Patrick Artazu and Tarah Dunn; the Interrobangs—T. S. Tate, Jaimie Teekell, and Shannon Riffe; the ladies of YA Highway—Leila Austin, Lee Bross, Sumayyah Daud, Sarah Enni, Kristin Halbrook, Amanda Hannah, Kate Hart, Kody Keplinger, Steph Kuehn, Kristin Otts, Amy Lukavics, Emilia Plater, Veronica Roth, and Kaitlin Ward; and my dear, dear Bruisers—Douglas Beagley, Nicole Feldl, Wayne Helge, and Fran Wilde. Thanks for keeping me from going nuts, guys!

Special thanks to Kirsten Hubbard, who mentored me, helping me learn the ropes of this crazy YA book world; Rachel Hartman, brilliant belly dancer and book lover; and Sean Wills, who is just the best. Go make a thing, Sean. I'll get coffee.

Kelly Lagor, who fixed my science, made it deeper, better, and more interesting. Every sci-fi writer should have their very own plant biologist.

My amazing agent, Michelle Andelman. From the moment you stumbled across that raw paragraph of this book, you've been its greatest advocate and defender. Thank you for loving *Starglass* before it was even done.

Rob Shields, for so perfectly capturing Terra's sense of longing (and her sartorial choices). She—and *Starglass*—are so well-dressed thanks to your work.

My stellar team at Simon & Schuster: Lucy Ruth Cummins, Jenica Nasworthy, Karen Taschek, and Angela Zurlo. And especially Navah Wolfe, fellow geek, lover of Indian cuisine, and editor extraordinaire. Thank you for your tireless belief in this book and in my ability to make it *better*.

And finally, my husband, Jordan. Thank you for all your love and support, for all those elephants, and owls, and television nights, and movies, and books shared, and pages folded over. Thank you, Pookie. Thank you, thank you, thank you.

TERRA IS FINALLY ON THE ZEHAVA, THE PROMISED PLANET—BUT NOTHING IS AS SHE EXPECTED IT TO BE...

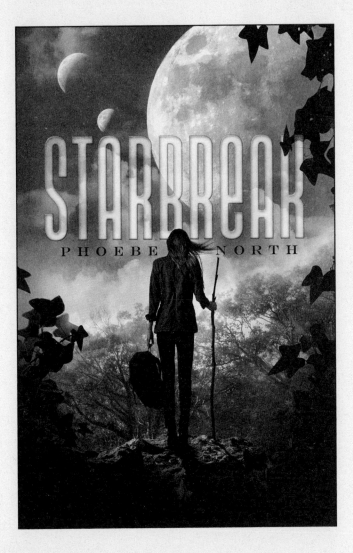

O n the night of the riots, I wasn't the only one who ran for the shuttle bay.

As I pressed across the frozen pastures, my hands balled into fists, my feet bare against the cold ground, I was joined by throngs of people. Citizens, their gazes drunk-dizzy and crazed, spilled out from the districts and the fields, clamoring for the aft lift. That day—my wedding day, the day we arrived on Zehava—was supposed to be a festive one. The citizens had been saving up their rations for weeks, stockpiling bottles of wine so they could drink from the first moment dawn cracked until the planet was stained black by the darkening night.

But the planet never went dark. Instead Zehava twinkled and glinted in the dome glass like a second sky. Lights. The northern continent was scattered with lights, clustered around the black oceans like gilt edging a page. Those lights could only mean one thing: people. There were people on *our* planet, the planet we'd journeyed five hundred years to find, the planet we'd been told would someday be our home.

Maybe they didn't believe it, those citizens who ran by me, jostling and shoving one another. Maybe they were so drunk, they'd convinced themselves it wasn't true. Zehava was theirs— their abbas had sung them songs about it; their mommas had told them about the good lives they'd live underneath the wide open sky. Maybe they thought the lights were something else, a trick of Mother Nature—phosphorescent algae or glowing rocks. Whatever the case, in their drunken fervor they'd convinced themselves that the path ahead would be easy. They'd take a shuttle down to the surface and find Zehava perfect and empty. It had been promised to them, after all.

I ran for a different reason, the pleats of my long golden gown clutched in my fists. Sure, I was just as starved as the rest of them. I wanted Zehava too; the Goldilocks planet would be our better, more perfect home. But that night? I mostly just ran for my life. When I squeezed myself into the crowded lift, the smell of sweat and wine and bloodstained wool all around me, I gave one last look back. I couldn't be certain, but I thought I saw her there. Aleksandra Wolff, leader of the Children of Abel. The captain's daughter—a woman so powerful that she'd kept her family's name for her own, defying all of the traditions of the ship. Her black braid swung behind her as she ran.

When the door shut behind me, I put my hands on my knees, panting. The air felt cold and sharp inside my lungs. I remembered the expression on Aleksandra's face—wild, hungry. I'd seen the whole thing, standing frozen in that cornfield as Aleksandra held that silver rope of hair in her hand and drew the knife across her mother's throat.

An old woman stood beside me in the lift. She touched her hand gently to my bare shoulder.

"Aren't you happy?" she cried. She was hazy with drink. "The Council, fallen! Fallen at last!"

I winced. The lift was filled with people, too many people, as it plunged into the depths of the ship. They sang and chanted, pumping their fists, but I couldn't hear their words. Instead I heard an echo—Captain Wolff's voice coming back to me, just before she made that last, strangled sound.

They won't follow you. Not after they've discovered that you killed your own mother.

Aleksandra had answered easily: *Good thing they won't find out.* But I knew, I knew—and worst of all? Aleksandra had caught me listening. On her belt she carried a knife, still hot with her mother's blood, sharp as a straight razor and twice as quick.

But I had somewhere to go. Zehava. The purple forests writhed and shifted in the corners of my memory. And I had someone waiting for me too. The boy—*my* boy—the one who'd haunted my dreams for months. He'd keep me safe from Aleksandra, and from the bodies that jostled me in their drunken fervor as they spilled from the lift. He'd be my home. My haven. My sanctuary.

He just didn't know it yet.

I stumbled from the lift into the crowded shuttle bay.

Once, the bay had been closed to all but necessary personnel—shuttle pilots and their crews, the captain, the Council. But someone had cracked the lift's control panel open. It trailed wires like a jumble of guts. When we arrived, the doors opened easily. Already the room was packed with people who elbowed one another, shouting. Most carried handcrafted weapons, table legs broken off or knives filched from their galley drawers. Someone had a shepherd's crook they'd broken down into a splintered spear. I had to duck under it as I scrambled toward the air lock entrance.

At first I just stood there staring, my bare feet flat against the rusted floor. The air lock was open. Inside waited row upon row of shuttles, gleaming beneath the dim track lighting. We'd prepared for years for disembarking. In school Rebbe Davison had taken us through the necessary drills: meeting with our muster groups, filing in one group at a time. Of course, it had only ever been for practice. I'd only ever seen snatches of the air lock before—with its precarious walkway and its long tunnels that reached out into the universe beyond—just before the air lock shut.

I heard a familiar *ding*. When I glanced back, I saw the lift doors open again. Still more people spilled out. I was frozen, my dress in my hands. But then I saw a face in the crowd in the lift. Aleksandra, her pale features drawn, stood among the new group. I wondered if they knew that she was their leader. I hadn't—it had been a secret, well kept. But now it seemed the news was spreading as quickly as a winter cold. Field-workers bowed their heads to whisper to specialists. Merchants lifted their eyes, squared their shoulders, and pressed two fingers to their hearts. They rushed toward her, flanking her on all sides. It give me time, but not much. I had to hurry as the people raised their weapons in salute. I pressed forward through the crowd, nearing the air lock door.

I'd almost reached it when I heard a familiar voice, touched with awe.

"Is that her, Deck? Is it true?"

I whipped my head up. There stood Laurel Selberlicht, her honey-brown eyes as bright as beacons. Deklan Levitt was beside her, one burly arm thrown over her shoulders. I'd known the pair my whole life; they'd been my classmates first, flirting during recess, passing notes to each other when Rebbe Davison's back was turned. Later I'd grown used to seeing them in the shadowed library, to pressing my fingers to my heart in salute when we passed each other in the dome. He was a plowman; in one season his work had transformed him from a narrow reed of a boy into a well-muscled man. But Laurel was slight, willowy. Her shoulder still bore the rank cords she'd been given by the High Council. A silver twist of thread—a special color, reserved for shuttle pilots like her.

I didn't even stop to think about it. I reached out and took her slender, cool hand in mine.

"Laurel," I said. When she lifted her eyes, they went hazy. I could smell the wine on her breath. "Laurel, come with me. I need your help."

"Sure, Terra," she said, and though there was a note of confusion in her voice, she let me pull her through the crowd. But a gruff tenor called out to us. Deklan, his unruly eyebrows low.

"Hey, where are you taking her?"

We were almost at the air lock door when I looked back. He was following us, but he wasn't alone. Two other rebels flanked him, one on either side, their expressions mirroring his concern. One, familiar—Rebbe Davison, Mordecai, our teacher, his lush black curls threaded gray. The other, a stranger, small in stature, whose shoulder bore the blue knot of a specialist.

"It's okay!" I called through the clamor, but I don't think they heard me. The trio followed us, as close as magnets, as I pulled Laurel down past the air lock entrance and into the long, dim hallway.

"What's going on, Terra?" she asked as we stopped on the narrow walkway. The air was cooler here, quieter. Few citizens had made it into the air lock. Only a pair of dark silhouettes could be seen in the distance, standing beside one of the waiting shuttles.

"You've trained as a pilot," I said, narrowing my gaze on her. "You can get us to Zehava."

"But we're not supposed to leave until we receive word back from the shuttle crew."

By now Deklan and his companions had reached us. He grabbed her to him, holding on tight—as if I were going to snatch her away. To be fair, I had already snatched her away once. If I wanted Laurel's help, it seemed I'd need to convince Deklan, too.

"She's trained all year for this, Deklan. She's a strong, capable pilot. Don't you want to see her fulfill her dreams?"

His expression shadowed with guilt. He looked down at Laurel, and I saw then the love that tethered them together. He was proud of her vocation, of all she'd done with her life, no matter how much he hid that behind gruffness and bluster.

"Of course I do," he said softly. Tucked beneath his arm, Laurel glowed. But she didn't answer me, not yet. I glanced toward the figures behind them.

Rebbe Davison lurked there, his face clouded with concern. On a night when most of the ship's population was alive with exuberant energy, he suddenly looked much older. I saw the wrinkles at the corners of his eyes, the deep frown circling his mouth.

"Rebbe Davison," I said. "You taught us our muster drills, all the procedures for disembarking when we were young. Who gave you those orders?"

He paused—behind him the sound of the crowd swelled.

"The Council," he said. "The curriculum always came from the Council."

"And what was all this for," I demanded, gesturing back toward the shuttle bay, packed with bodies, "if we're going to stay under their thumbs? They'd want us to wait, I'm sure. But that planet is our inheritance. Not this ship!"

"She's right," Laurel said. I blinked back my surprise; I hadn't expected agreement to come so quickly. Deklan held her tightly, but she squirmed away. "No, Deck. This is what I've been training for. I can *do this*. The planet is ours. Isn't it?"

Without waiting for an answer, she turned and walked away from him. There was a panel built into the wall. Her hands moved breezily over it. As she worked, I glanced back over my shoulder. The crowd was pressing closer now, threatening to spill over the precipice of the air lock. I saw a cutting figure among them, her wool-wrapped shoulders square. Aleksandra, knife in her hand, parting the crowd like they were sheep to be herded. Coming close.

But then the air lock door began to slide back into place. Her eyes widened. She shouted something, but the words were lost beneath the shouts and songs of the rebels who surrounded her. They didn't matter. *She* didn't. The door sealed shut, and we were left alone in the darkness.

Laurel turned on the heel of her leather-soled shoe to make her way briskly through the air lock. At first I hesitated beside Rebbe Davison and his friend, watching as Deklan scrambled after her.

"You're not going alone!" he cried, fixing a hand on her shoulder. She spun around, tossing her curls as she faced him.

"Then come with us."

His eyes met mine, murky with confusion, as if he couldn't believe what the rebellion had wrought: his love was ready to leap off the ship and into the void of space without him. Then he looked to the specialist and to Rebbe Davison.

"Are you going?"

At first our teacher looked wary, uncertain. But then he let his eyes slide shut. Behind us the sound of the rioting crowd could still be heard, a dozen muffled hands pounding on the air lock door again and again. When Rebbe Davison opened his eyes, they were filled with a new, razor-sharp certainty.

"Liberty on Zehava," he said, softly at first, but then again, louder. "Liberty on Zehava! Terra's right. The planet. The planet is *ours*."

There was something strange, garbled about his words. In class this kindhearted man had always spoken with confidence. Even when someone misbehaved, he'd laughed it off easily, taking every disaster in stride. Now he seemed hazy.

Drunk. They were all drunk, I realized. I'd swallowed down a full skein of wine that evening myself, but now that I was driven by a single goal, the night had taken on an uncanny clarity. I could see the rust on the grating beneath us, every rivet on every shuttle, and the cobwebs that would soon be blasted away when the ship's outer port opened. Anyone left behind in the air lock would be lost to the vacuum of space—and I wasn't about to open up the door to the shuttle bay again. So even though I heard the slur in my teacher's words, I nodded. I needed them to come with me, and fast.

"Good. Let's board, then," I said.

Rebbe Davison looked at the specialist, who considered for a moment, mouth open. But soon he nodded too. We all turned toward the shuttles and made our way toward one at the back.

"I only have access to this one," Laurel said as we neared shuttle number twenty-eight. But the door was blocked by a pair of figures. An old man with a fringe of white hair and a bulbous nose—and a dark-haired girl, no older than ten. The man was my neighbor, Mar Schneider. He'd been a part of our clandestine library meetings too, and when he saw us, he lifted two fingers to his heart.

"She wanted to see the shuttles," he said, almost apologetically, holding the girl's hand tight. I recognized her as his granddaughter, who sat on his stoop with him sometimes to watch the traffic of the afternoon, but in that moment I couldn't remember her name. As Laurel shouldered them aside to punch in her access code, Rebbe Davison set a hand on the old man's shoulder. He spoke just a few decibels louder than necessary.

"Abraham, we're going to the planet! Would you like to join us?"

Mar Schneider lifted a hand to touch his scratchy white beard. He smacked his lips, considering. But his granddaughter didn't need time to consider. She jumped up and down on the balls of her feet.

"Yes! Yes! *Zayde*, please?"

As if it were nothing more than a request for a box of candy, he sighed. My heart was pounding. Behind me the door to the shuttle bay was pounding too—a low, steady thunder.

"Oh, I suppose."

One by one we climbed inside. The shuttle was small, meant to carry only a dozen people. That night we were half that. But our meager crew would have to do. As we boarded, Laurel turned toward a storage space in back.

"The flight suits are in there. Everybody suit up. And be sure to buckle up." She pulled the heavy door closed behind us. I couldn't be sure, but I thought I saw a shadow of doubt in her pale eyes. I ignored it. I needed her if I was going to reach Zehava—if I was going to find my boy, waiting for me. She added, "It might be a bumpy ride."